Reading Bodies in Victorian Fiction

Edinburgh Critical Studies in Victorian Culture

Recent books in the series:
Rereading Orphanhood: Texts, Inheritance, Kin
Diane Warren and Laura Peters

Plotting the News in the Victorian Novel
Jessica R. Valdez

Reading Ideas in Victorian Literature: Literary Content as Artistic Experience
Patrick Fessenbecker

Home and Identity in Nineteenth-Century Literary London
Lisa C. Robertson

Writing the Sphinx: Literature, Culture and Egyptology
Eleanor Dobson

Oscar Wilde and the Radical Politics of the Fin de Siècle
Deaglán Ó Donghaile

The Sculptural Body in Victorian Literature: Encrypted Sexualities
Patricia Pulham

New Media and the Rise of the Popular Woman Writer, 1832–1860
Alexis Easley

Elizabeth Robins Pennell: Critical Essays
Dave Buchanan and Kimberly Morse-Jones

Reading Bodies in Victorian Fiction: Associationism, Empathy and Literary Authority
Peter Katz

For a complete list of titles published visit the Edinburgh Critical Studies in Victorian Culture web page at www.edinburghuniversitypress.com/series/ECVC

Also Available:
Victoriographies – A Journal of Nineteenth-Century Writing, 1790–1914, edited by Diane Piccitto and Patricia Pulham
ISSN: 2044-2416
www.eupjournals.com/vic

Reading Bodies in Victorian Fiction

Associationism, Empathy and Literary Authority

Peter J. Katz

EDINBURGH
University Press

Edinburgh University Press is one of the leading university presses in the UK. We publish academic books and journals in our selected subject areas across the humanities and social sciences, combining cutting-edge scholarship with high editorial and production values to produce academic works of lasting importance. For more information visit our website: edinburghuniversitypress.com

© Peter Katz, 2022, 2024

Edinburgh University Press Ltd
The Tun – Holyrood Road
12(2f) Jackson's Entry
Edinburgh EH8 8PJ

First published in hardback by Edinburgh University Press 2022

Typeset in 11/13 Adobe Sabon by
IDSUK (DataConnection) Ltd
Croydon, CR0 4YY

A CIP record for this book is available from the British Library

ISBN 978 1 4744 7620 1 (hardback)
ISBN 978 1 4744 7621 8 (paperback)
ISBN 978 1 4744 7622 5 (webready PDF)
ISBN 978 1 4744 7623 2 (epub)

The right of Peter Katz to be identified as the author of this work has been asserted in accordance with the Copyright, Designs and Patents Act 1988, and the Copyright and Related Rights Regulations 2003 (SI No. 2498).

Contents

Acknowledgements   vi

Introduction: Associationism, Affect and Literary Authority   1

1. Feeling Bodies: Associationism and the Anti-Metaphorics of Materiality   27

2. Symbolic Bodies: The Storyteller, Memory and Suffering in Boz's 'The Hospital Patient'   54

3. Metaphoric Bodies: The Professional Author, Sensation and Serialisation in *Great Expectations*   85

4. Plastic Bodies: The Scientist, Vital Mechanics and Ethical Habits of Character in Wilkie Collins's *The Moonstone*   117

5. Represented Bodies: The Lawyer, Conclusions and Circumstantial Evidence in *Lady Audley's Secret*   160

6. Caring Bodies: The Reformer, Sartorial Exchange and the Work of the Novel in Walter Besant's *Children of Gibeon*   190

Coda: In Defence of Victorian Optimism   219

Bibliography   222
Index   242

Acknowledgements

To the people who shaped me as I grew into me: Dianne and Bruce Katz, Carel and David Mountain, Scott and Lisa Halsey, Dee and Sandi Golles, Kris and Debbie Widmer, and Kris and Sherry Hart. I suppose if anything is outside of language, it's the depth of my debt to you.

To the team at Edinburgh University Press: the anonymous readers who gave initial feedback, copyeditors, designers and other staff, and most especially Susannah Butler and Michelle Houston.

To Ludger Viefhues-Bailey for adopting a young student and teaching him to become a scholar. To Trev Broughton at *JVC* for beating my writing into submission and helping me to learn to articulate my arguments.

To my wonderful, uplifting, mind-bogglingly brilliant PUC students who dealt with an eternity of bodies, bodies, bodies, and a side of feeling (also bodies): all of you, but especially HNRS 380 Society, Sentiment, Science (Spring '16), HNRS 380 Science of Feeling (Spring '18), and HNRS 380 London Streets (Summer '19). You are all my inspiration. Especially to a few of you: Glo Besana for being the only other person in the history of the world to be that excited about Spinoza; Sabrina Mostoufi and Jefferson Richards for reminding me that I really am not a biologist in all the best ways, and for being brave enough to dive into literary and philosophical arguments with me; Dominique Townsend for teaching me about the margins and reminding me what my body cannot know.

To my dearest friends: Staci Stutsman for your wisdom and understanding, and Leah Dopp for grounding me in my most ridiculous moments with your sardonic wit and invaluable friendship.

To my former professors and colleagues at Pacific Union College for their instruction and guidance, emotional support, professional support, friendship and love: Asher Raboy, Aimee Wyrick, Steve Waters, Roy Benton and Greg Schneider. To Georgina Hill for teaching me to teach writing and to write. To Cynthia Westerbeck for teaching me style and grace on the page and in life.

Acknowledgements

To my dearest sister Amanda Katz for being the trolliest and the best all at once. No, there are no pictures. They're expensive. To Kimmy and Jonathan Golles for being my sister and brother, for countless hours of conversation about this and everything else, for carrying me when I couldn't walk (occasionally literally (snow camping sucks, sorry not sorry)).

To Sara Kakazu for teaching me to be a better person and scholar. I wrote a book about empathy and the ethics of care, but you live it.

To Kevin Morrison for your unflinching commitment to making me the best scholar I can be. From publishing opportunities, to networking connections, to honest critique, I owe this book and my scholarly career to you.

To Sarah Tanner for your intellectual and emotional support, for reading literally every word in this entire thing, for pushing me to work through when it was hard, and pushing me not to work when I needed it.

To Sierra McMillan, for countless hours in coffee shops, conversations about publishing minutiae only you and I could care about, believing in the value of me and my work when it felt like nobody else did (especially me), and for your invaluable friendship.

To the gentlest and most poignant critic of power, the most empathetic and embodied scholar, the kindest and best mentor, Donovan Schaefer, for literally making me possible. You are the spatula that pries me off the wall of theoretical complacency.

To Ariane Katz, for sitting beside my hospital bed, beside me for my coursework, quals and dissertation, and beside me through my early years as a professor. You read early drafts, endured endless conversations, and helped me to grow as a scholar and a person. Your wisdom and empathy inspire me. I can't claim to know exactly what to say here, but there is so very much to acknowledge and be grateful for.

And finally, to the most dedicated proponents of my work. You have sat with me through almost every word. Sorry, on me. I mean, on my keyboard: Jabberwocky Algernon Katz and Bandersnatch Elizabeth Katz.

My most emphatic, embodied, unspeakably profound thanks.

Introduction: Associationism, Affect and Literary Authority

Feeling Authoritative

In 1802, William Wordsworth added a passage to his 'Preface' to *Lyrical Ballads*. Here, he articulated a new objective for literature: to 'aid the transfiguration' of science into 'a form of flesh and blood' (Wordsworth and Coleridge 1802: xxxix). A commingling of the two not only seems possible to Wordsworth, but may even be the end goal of each. While he celebrates poetry as the 'first and last of all knowledge', he also seems to suggest that a true science of feeling might well be indistinguishable from poetry:

> If the labours of men of Science should ever create any material revolution, direct or indirect, in our condition, and in the impressions which we habitually receive, the Poet will ... be ready to follow the steps of the man of Science ... he will be at his side, carrying sensation into the midst of the objects of the Science itself ... The remotest discoveries of the Chemist, the Botanist, or Mineralogist, will be as proper objects of the Poet's art as any upon which it can be employed ... and the relations of which they are contemplated by the followers of these respective Sciences shall be manifestly and palpably material to us as enjoying and suffering beings. (xxxviii)

Materiality matters most, here. Ideal science – and ideal poetry – should revolutionise 'the impressions which we habitually receive', to make the world around us 'manifestly and palpably material' in both pleasure and pain. Literature and science can share the same space if they each address both materiality and feeling.

By contrast, in 1924, as he sought to distinguish literary studies as an academic pursuit, I. A. Richards opposed scientific and emotive language in an argument that separates literature from material, lived experience. 'Science is autonomous,' he declares, free from 'distorted references or, more plainly, *fictions*' (Richards 1924: 266). While science gathers its references to determine 'truth' or empirical accuracy, the 'obviousness of [literature's] falsity' makes it 'the supreme form of *emotive* language' (272–3). And in 1949, William Wimsatt and Monroe Beardsley wrote that to consider the emotional effects literature has on its readers 'is a confusion between the poem and its *results* (what it *is* and what it *does*)' (Wimsatt and Beardsley 1949: 31). Feeling has its role, but that role is distinct from empirical concerns.

This book dwells in the time between Wordsworth, who saw the potential for a materialist science and poetry to walk hand-in-hand, and the New Critics, who understood literature as its own domain of knowledge separate from the scientific. I explore a Victorian philosophy of fiction in which literary value depends on a text's capacity to cultivate empathy through feeling. The mid-century emergence of academic literary studies manifested as a contest between scholars and critics on the one hand, and popular readers and authors on the other. The academy and professional critics argued that to understand the truth of texts requires special techniques acquired through labour and attention. Against professional readers, writers of popular fiction argued for emotion. They turned to Associationism – an eighteenth- and nineteenth-century science that understood mental phenomena through physiology – to argue that language is a physiological process that draws bodies together through feeling. At the centre of this debate is literary authority, or who can decide which books are valuable, how readers should derive that value, and which kinds of readers are permitted to make those decisions.

In these authors' texts and philosophies of reading, because language is so fundamentally embodied, to empathise with characters leads to empathy for living bodies. Fiction offers a space to practise for lived experience, but only if it creates material effects. Mid-century novels inundate readers with self-referential, self-justifying representations of reading and writing.[1] In these models of how to read, their methodology is specifically anti-interpretive. Readers must encounter characters as if they are fully embodied – not symbols, metaphors or representations. Ethical feeling arises from reading novels only when readers do not interpret – but rather, when they engage materially.

This is a history of disciplinary knowledge: the way literary studies has decided what questions it should ask, and what kind of knowledge can answer those questions. Along with recent turns to

Jacques Rancière's philosophies of aesthetics and knowledge, this book attends to the way literature

> carv[es] up space and time, the visible and the invisible, speech and noise ... objects that form a common world, the subjects that people that world and the powers they have to see it, name it and act upon it. (Rancière 2011: 4, 7)

In other words, this is an exploration of how readers and authors think about what it feels like to read, and what those feelings can do – and the way that those possibilities recursively define and are defined by what it means 'to know'. It joins the twenty-first-century call for greater attention to the embodied elements of emotion and language, and to place what counts as 'literary' within the historical emergence of literary studies. Associationism offers a culturally contextualised methodology to understand how Victorians imagined what happened in their bodies as they read – and also enables us in the present to think about the move away from linguistic decoding and toward surfaces as an ethical practice.

The Associationist scientists of the mid-nineteenth century and the novelists whose work reflects their thinking would be startled that affect ever became a fallacy – especially one opposed to science. When literacy exploded in the nineteenth century and became something worth fighting over between popular authors and academic thinkers, it was already cocooned in two hundred years of thinking about literature and material science through the same epistemology. The ensuing contest shifted how we think about what matters in literature and who has the authority to decide what matters, and delineated between the domains of materialist science and humanist feeling. In this book, I trace the history of that line and argue that the twenty-first-century re-emergence of surface reading offers an opportunity both to better comprehend how the Victorians understood reading, and to reunite the emotional concerns of the humanities with the materialism of empirical science – to see reading with feeling as an ethical, embodied experience.

Associationism and Affect as Reparative Critique

The antithesis of this argument, again from the New Critics, comes when I. A. Richards writes that 'impressions' – a term taken from Associationism to describe the bodily response to external stimuli – 'are commonly signs' (Richards 1924: 90). This has been the dominant model of interpretation since the New Critics: words are signs, symbols for greater human questions (structuralism), more complex psychological issues (psychoanalytic criticism), the self-referentiality of signs (poststructuralism), or historical context (historicisms).

Affect theory, empathy/sympathy studies, and the overall emphasis on embodiment should initiate a crisis for literary studies in a way it may not for other humanities precisely because the affective turn is, as Donovan Schaefer contends, a shift away from the textual turn (Schaefer 2015: 4–8). And while the textual turn certainly changed what we study in literary studies – as in New Historicism, and our newfound ability to read any object as text – it was not a shift in our core mission, our core methodology. Literary studies has always been about text, always been about language, in a way that other disciplines were not. But herein lies the rub, for if affect studies enables other disciplines to move around or beyond the textual turn, literary studies by definition (it would seem) cannot move away from texts. For us, language matters – but other disciplines' affective turns recognise that language is not matter.

Each of these has a different object of attention, but the same locus: language. Literary studies examines linguistic representations of material objects, because, of course, tea in *Persuasion* is not tea; it is the fictional representation of tea. We explore linguistic representations of readers' encounters with texts, because, of course, we only know how people read based on their records of reading in nonfiction essays or journals. And we study linguistic representations of affect; even when we move away from simply naming an affect and finding its instantiation in a text, one might well argue that it still exists only through language on the page. Language in the textual turn writes itself on bodies; materiality bears the inscriptions of discourse, so that language shapes materiality.

Associationism offers a reconfiguration of language and its roles in the relationships between bodies. It removes the crisis of causality by approaching language and embodiment as part of the same network, rather than a line. In most twentieth- (and some twenty-first-) century criticism, language retains its classical privilege. But the Associationists consider language not as a force that shapes matter discursively, nor as a byproduct of material forces, but rather as part of a biological process in an embodied, social species. Materialism offers a way to think about language not as an external medium, not as a byproduct, but as a part of bodies, wrapped up in bodies.

The affective and material turns call on us to preserve the physicality of bodies and objects. Those who build on the work of Deleuze and Guattari see affect as fundamentally impossible to reduce to words or biological measurements. These thinkers prefer to disaggregate preconscious affects and their conscious, social expressions in emotion and action. Their work emphasises the instability of the subject, and so champions a mode of affect that escapes language and the individual.

On the other hand, Silvan Tomkins and those who use his writings – predominantly through Eve Kosofsky Sedgwick – understand affects as basic motivators of biological bodies. Sedgwick's work has helped to forge what Donovan Schaefer calls 'intimate sets of links between affect, emotion, and cognition' that emerges in the work of these theorists (Schaefer 2019: 5). Their work is often phenomenological in nature, and asks what bodies do and feel like as they interact.

I align emphatically with this school of affect theory. The turn to surface is not a turn away from language, or from the social. Rather, it is a direct commitment to what Ahmed calls 'the lived experiences of being and having a body' within a network of other living bodies (Ahmed 2010: 39, n. 4). Most importantly, I want to consider the lived, embodied experience of Victorian novel readers and how they would have understood those experiences.[2]

Materialism is something of a problem for literary studies, however, since our primary mode of inquiry has been to close-read fiction and its ephemera. In short, the bodies we encounter are often fictional; they are words, not physical bodies. But these do not need to be opposed. Benjamin Morgan argues that 'Victorian aesthetic thought effected an *outward turn*: an exteriorization of mind, consciousness, and the self into networks of matter, sensations, and objects' (Morgan 2017: 6). Through Associationism and the history of literary authority, we can imagine what it would be like if literary studies understood language as many Victorians understood it: as a physical, physiological process meant to draw bodies together through emotions.

Surface proves the best way to understand this mentality. Stephen Best and Sharon Marcus's introduction to 'Surface Reading' in the 2009 special issue of *Representations* articulates a theory of the surface in opposition to 'symptomatic reading', which 'took meaning to be hidden, repressed, deep, and in need of detection and disclosure by an interpreter' (Best and Marcus 2009: 1). They are 'drawn to modes of reading that attend to the surfaces of texts rather than plumb their depths' (1–2). This looks different in each context, of course. Thing theory, object-oriented ontology and their relatives are interested in the physical objects embedded in novels, as in Elaine Freegood's *Ideas in Things* (2006). History of the Book, for example, attends to the material production and reception of texts in their historical context, such as Robert Patten's work on Charles Dickens or Leah Price's *How to Do Things with Books in Victorian Britain* (2013). Affect and cognitive theories explore the psychological and physical responses to reading, sometimes transhistorically as in Lisa Zunshine's *Why We Read Fiction* (2006), Blakey Vermeule's *Why Do We Care about Literary Characters?* (2011), or Norman Holland's *Literature and the Brain* (2009), and sometimes historically as in Nicholas Dames's *Physiology of the Novel* (2007). While these scholars work on different texts, with diverse and even opposing arguments, in each case, attention begins and ends on surfaces, rather than an implicit reading extracted through specialised interpretive techniques. Affect theory, for example, attends to the surfaces of the body, to the feelings at the surface of a reader's experience; the history of the book considers the material surfaces of the page and its circulation rather than latent content. All of these methodologies are implied in Best and Marcus's observation as modes of reading that might well eschew 'symptomatic' reading for hidden meanings or ideologies.

When I say that these methodologies reject hidden meaning, I do not at all mean to imply that they are against critique in a broad sense. In some ways, my work here resonates with the anti-theory calls like Rita Felski's *Limits of Critique*. Felski uses Paul Ricouer's 'hermeneutics of suspicion' to resist the need 'to expose hidden truths and draw out unflattering and counterintuitive meanings that others fail to see' (Felski 2015: 1). Deleuze and Guattari's mandate to ask how rather than why, surface reading, Sedgwick's 'reparative' readings – all of these resist the urge to run a text through a predetermined algorithm that cracks the code and prints out the secret meaning.

But I would rather illuminate how reading surfaces is vital to unpack and understand the effects of power on everyday life; it is perhaps the best way to do so. This is the most important distinction I would make between Felski and myself: I see power as a central part of humanities scholarship. But our approach to power does not need to be an interrogation, a detective case, a historical 'gotcha' in which we trap the text or its context in a social lie. Surfaces replace the conspiratorial paranoia that sees power as a bogeyman pulling puppet strings with an empiricism that understands 'power' through the effects bodies and groups of bodies have on one another. And these effects and affects can be positive as well as negative. They can bring to life the bodies of characters and readers with all their beauty and complexity, to think about what bodies can be rather than simply what controls them.

In other words, surfaces enable explorations of power capable of both critique and celebration – and in celebration, bodies take on materiality much closer to the phenomenological experience of everyday feeling.[3] Rather than approach bodies as weighed down by the social, I want to see them as producers of their environments – in dialogue with the creation of their affective habits, rather than the victims of them.

Literary Authority and Empathy

In an oft-quoted editorial, Wilkie Collins writes of those educated readers whose tastes incline toward the unbound quarto and the penny broadside, a vast readership of some 'three million' whose preferences do not at all intersect with the tastes of the literary elite. 'An immense public has been discovered,' he writes, and once they have been discovered, 'the next thing to be done is, in a literary sense, to teach that public how to read' (Collins 1858: 222). Much discussion has been had about the 'common reader', which I take to mean someone who reads for pleasure, and perhaps self-edification, but who nevertheless would probably not self-identify as a scholar.[4] Altick and other thinkers who have done work in this lineage have repeatedly emphasised the complex reading life of those readers who were not thought of as scholarly.[5] Victorians most certainly understood that common readers possessed their own literary interests and tastes.

Mid-Victorian novelists and literary critics at least implicitly understood the debate over literary authority as a fundamentally political argument: the academy as specialised authority on the one hand, and the literary public as democratic authority on the other. But while the readers that I explore in this book – at least, the readers that the novelists imagine – are common readers, they have their own complex scholarly life outside the academy. Scholars of English literature fought red in tooth and claw for their legitimacy in the face of the much more established Classicists like Matthew Arnold, who were not eager to see English literature with a place in the academy. Because of reticence from Oxbridge, the academic study of English literature was first the domain of the London Colleges – the scholastic pursuit of the common readers. As such, when literary scholarship sought academic legitimacy, it had to do so in conversation with the commons – whether that meant alliance or opposition.

Mudie's Circulating Library offers a microcosm of the confrontation that consumed literary scholarship in the 1850s and 1860s: between those who advocated a culture defined by specialists, and populists who felt the reading public should define its own taste. Mudie found himself in the centre of this argument over literary authority because of his vast influence over popular readership. Most importantly for literary studies, Mudie owed his cultural success to his process of selection. Mudie promised his customers a high bar for literary value, especially important in a market so glutted with new books that, as John Sutherland puts it, 'for every producer above the literary threshold there were ten beneath it' (Sutherland 2013: 5). The great debate over Mudie's library in 1860 centred around which qualities constituted the 'literary threshold' – and, most importantly, who had the authority to define that threshold.

With such a wide selection from which to choose, Mudie felt obligated to curate a collection that represented the best cultural standards of acceptability. A sizeable advertisement in the 17 August 1850 issue of *The Athenaeum* claims that 'preference is given to Works of History, Biography, Travel, Philosophy, Science, and Religion', secondarily accompanied by 'the best Works of Fiction' ('Advertisement' 1850: 859). An advertisement appearing in the 17 February 1855 issue of the *Literary Gazette* italicises the qualifier *best*, emphasising selection as the cultural value of Mudie's library ('Advertisement' 1855: 97). 'Best' as a single, unqualified descriptor epitomises Mudie's role in shaping the new literary authority: a common-sense, shared concept that brought together otherwise disparate categories of value – aesthetic, moral, entertainment – under a common scale of measurement.[6]

Mudie's detractors, on the other hand, insisted that the public had valid literary knowledge of their own, and that Mudie should return control to the public by limiting the degree to which his personal taste interfered with the market.[7] Mudie was lambasted in the debate for 'killing' a book, Arthur Robins's 1860 *Miriam May*, a romance and would-be social problem novel.[8] According to the narrative put forth by Robins, by Mudie, and by a few peripheral participants in the novel's publication and reception, when Mudie read *Miriam May*, he elected not to purchase it in significant quantity. While Mudie maintains that the novel has little literary merit,

Robins counters that the novel was rejected because it lambasts a character who is a hypocritical Dissenter – and Mudie himself was a Dissenter of sorts. This, Robins and his supporters feel, is tantamount to suppression.

The notion that Mudie can use his economic power to limit the breadth of the literary landscape appalled his opponents, who would rather that Mudie sell all the books that came to him. Most importantly, they rejected Mudie as an authority because they believed everyone should be their own authority. A writer under the alias 'Z' writes, 'I do not care what qualifications he may have, but I deny most emphatically that any man has the qualifications for this post of judging for me what books I ought or ought not to read' (Z 1860: 285). The discourse of populism unites free trade with freedom of thought in a framework that invests the right of economic and literary selection in the hands of a new political mass: a nebulous, newly defined public.

Within the Mudie debate, an editorial in the *Saturday Review* portrays the public as intellectuals in their own right. The editorial recognises and supports 'an entirely new class of readers – which twenty years ago seems to have done without books, or to have been satisfied with old ones', who now 'depen[d] entirely for intellectual gratification on Mr Mudie's library' ('Mudie's Library' 1860: 550). Common scholars are no mere consumers, but a cross-class, intellectual culture unto themselves. The *Saturday Review* objects to Mudie's selection because it 'subjects a large section – and in some sense the most important section – of the educated class to a virtual censorship'. To name the common, disparate public the 'most important section . . . of the educated class' radically redefines literary scholarship. No longer is literary value the province of the ivory tower and classical texts; instead, the public possesses both the ability and the right to determine its own values.

And so, in the autumn and winter of 1860, rising tensions around the faultline of literary authority ruptured, with their epicentre in Mudie's Circulating Library. The populists on the one side rallied around the validity of common thinking, common sentiment, common readers. Mudie and his allies on the other raised the banner of the shepherding literary class, the intellectual elite, the need for curators and scholars.

This is more complex than a mere binary. The contest for literary authority took place over two core concepts: professionalisation and embodiment. Any reader or writer had to validate their own authority within literary society: in which circles of professional writing and reading does one circulate? What counts as professional in those circles? And how well regarded is that profession outside of itself? A Classicist, an English professor, a critic and a journalist are all professional writers, but each of them enacts that professionalism in a very different way. On the other hand, novelists (sometimes) and novel readers were seen as decidedly unprofessional, undertrained readers and writers. The professionals claimed to have the heuristic tools for writing and analysis: techniques for rational, hermeneutic decoding. Novelists and novel readers lacked this professional training and only had recourse to sentiment and sensationalism.

And so, this distinction between common readers and academic readers destabilised as English Literature began to carve out a place in the London Colleges. As with any genealogy, the history of professionalisation of English as an academic discipline has nebulous beginnings, and the barrier between itself and other forms of scholarship – and between itself and common reading – was less than solid.[9] One might begin such a genealogy in 1759, for example, when Hugh Blair took the first chair of Rhetoric and Belles Lettres at the University of Edinburgh, or in 1828, when Thomas Dale was appointed Professor of English Language and Literature at University College. As the difference in these men's titles suggests, the ambiguity of these beginnings stems in part from the project of defining 'English' as an academic discipline. I place 'English' in quotation marks here because the title itself was an entanglement, a collision of domains that crossed religion, philology, Classics, literacy, composition, taste and history.

To demarcate the domain of English literary studies – and what kinds of claims it could make, with which evidence, supplied by which tools – took a great deal of time, in no small part because it spoke to both the academy and the commons alike. When King's College advertised in 1830 for a professor to teach both English literature and 'Modern History', they 'initiated a movement that, as the century progressed, aligned literary study even more closely with the representational value of literature' tied to history (Court 1992: 87). English also had to find its relationship with philology, which scholars sought to separate from the 'positivistic study of derivations and give an epistemological basis more conducive to speculation and interpretation' (97–8). To situate themselves alongside but also apart from Classics, the academy grappled with the relationship between the classics of English – Chaucer, Shakespeare, Milton – and popular, contemporary literature. Ultimately, the domain of knowledge that began to form in the 1850s came to define the professionalisation of literary study and its relationship to the literary public.

In the face of this populist literacy, the academy faced a new conundrum: how academic literary studies should interact with the general populace of readers. The 1860s saw the rise of modern literary criticism in the work of scholars like Matthew Arnold and Mark Pattison, both of whom saw literary analysis as inextricably enmeshed in the domain of literary knowledge that emerged in the 1860s, and who felt strongly that the academy should be the guiding hand that brought common readers to good taste. In his 1877 article 'Books and Critics', Mark Pattison begins with the declaration that 'literature is a commodity, and as such it is subject to economic law' – an assumption that was contested and decided in part by the understanding that Mudie's circulation was a business enmeshed with culture (Pattison 1877: 659). In a concession to the success of circulating libraries, Pattison admits that as a result of these economic laws, 'the character of general literature is determined by the taste of the reading public', because while 'any man may write what he likes . . . if he cannot get the public to buy it, his book can hardly be said to be published' (662). This is a sort of inversion of the *Miriam May* controversy, for here, Pattison fears that public taste may well 'kill' an otherwise deserving text.

But he divides readers 'into two classes – the general public and the professional literary man' (667). This distinction is at once familiar and different, for where Mudie's supporters called for *someone* to regulate selection as public censor, they did not have the language of professionality. Now, however, at the height of the debate over the professionalisation of English literary study, Pattison can demarcate a boundary between the literary public and the literary professional. For the general public, reading is 'a solace of . . . leisure hours', and because these hours may be few, they must have some method to choose from the mélange of new books (663). Readers must, therefore, 'read by selection'. But, he tells them, 'for your selection you will be guided – you are so in fact – by the opinion of . . . critics' (667). The professional literary man differs from Mudie in that Mudie makes a profession of selling books, but Pattison's 'literary man' makes a profession of *reading* books. His article exhorts readers to reject the voices of 'the ignorant, the indolent, and the vulgar who now create that demand which the publisher [he names Smith and Mudie] has to meet', to abandon 'universal suffrage in the choice of books' and instead heed the selection of the 'aristocracy of intellect' (673). Arnold best summarises the distinction between these kinds of readers in 'The Function of Criticism at the Present Time': criticism, he says, 'can never be popular' (Arnold 1864a: 248).

In 1869, Arnold would rearticulate this definition of the public not as a tradition in its own right, but as a safe and viable rebuttal to the democratic upheavals of 1866. Arnold addresses the new, liberal definition of the public through a refutation of Roebuck's simplistic claim that 'the English ideal is that every one should be free to do and to look just as he likes' (quoted in Arnold 1869: 17). This is the mark of a 'new and more democratic force', different and perhaps even more dangerous to Arnold's ideals than even the 'vulgarity of middle-class liberalism' (38). The antidote to Roebuck, of course, is culture.

Importantly, Arnold condemns the new liberalism on literary grounds; he invites his reader to 'observe the literature they [these new democrats] read', and to consider the values their literature promulgates. Literary value figures prominently in Arnold's work – particularly the threat that liberalism and common readers pose to the moral integrity of the country.[10] Arnold argues that 'in literature the absence of any authoritative centre, like an Academy', leads to the dissolution of the public's moral centre (Arnold 1869: 112–13). In a contemporaneous article, he maintained that his era was one devoid of 'the true life of literature', and that the era of the Classics was 'promised land . . . not ours to enter' (Arnold 1864a: 251). This was because, as he argues in 'The Literary Influence of Academies', the lack of an academy without a 'centre of correct information, correct judgement, correct taste' would produce a populist taste he called 'provinciality' (Arnold 1864b: 163). Provinciality stands in direct opposition to the 'classical', which is 'the only work [that], in the long run, can stand' (163). Without this morality, the public cannot operate with 'a scale of value for judgements' of literary and moral value, and instead flounders in relativism (Arnold 1869: 37–8, 112–13). Common literature struggled to claim the moral high ground when it was, in essence, a commodity. Arnold bemoans the 'multitudes of a common sort of readers' who desire 'masses of a common sort of literature' that 'is becoming a vast and profitable industry' (Arnold 1880: xlvii). Most importantly, Arnold patrols the boundary between the literary and cultural expert and the mere consumer – the cultural guardian and the public.

In Arnold and Pattison's writing, the domain of literary criticism emerges more fully formed than it appeared in 1860 but dressed in the same rhetorical trappings. It grapples with the relationship between economics and taste: who buys books, how those books should be chosen, and the effects of those purchases on the quality of the national literature. Most importantly, it also interrogates the relationship between taste and politics: universal suffrage in matters of taste leads to vulgarity, while the literary aristocracy offer the grounds for a stronger national culture.

From the opposite end, though, the historical and cultural circumstances around English literary studies made possible the cultivation of a readership who were not part of the academy, but who had some academic inclinations. In the debate over whether English literature should be an academic subject, it was taken almost for granted that it was the literature of common readers. Oxford and Cambridge were reticent to adopt English as an academic discipline (1894 and 1919, respectively), so disciplinary definition of the field embraced the commons, and made their home in the London Colleges.

As the new, public face of academic literary studies, mid-century professors of English faced the task of justifying vernacular literature as an intellectual pursuit. Alexander John Scott's 1848 inaugural lecture as professor of English at University College, London, 'On the Academical Study of a Vernacular Literature', justifies English literature as viably academic because popular literature invigorates language and connects it to lived experience. He suggests English literature as an antidote to other 'mental occupations, which, as comparatively abstract, and remote, might have formalised the whole intellect, or separated it from the life around us . . . given us words and sentences indeed, but not a living language, the utterance of our own actual being' (Scott 1849: 24). For Scott, the classics are separate from lived experience, while English literature is the literature of the everyday. In 1851, just before he took Scott's place at University College, David Masson proposed an affinity between 'literary men' and 'the working classes', thereby suggesting that common readers can also be literary – that is, they can be scholars (Masson 1851a: 385–6).

Scott, Masson and the rest were, I would argue, ultimately successful. In 1856–7, for example, A. J. Scott's English Literature course was the most popular subject of all the night classes for labourers at Owens College (Palmer 1965: 57). Scholars cultivated in these city colleges began to make space for themselves in the academic discourse on literature. Popular literature could be popular, but also worthy of academic reading. Common readers might be common, but they, too, were capable of academic thinking.

But exactly how public readers might go about thinking academically remained a problem. Outside the academy, the common reader enjoyed sentiment; within the academy, literary scholarship held higher moral aspirations. On the one hand, emotion and embodiment; on the other, hermeneutics and distance. Mid-century novelists, I suggest, picked up on this conflict, and through their representations of scholarship and readers offered a new claim: emotion was the best way to achieve higher moral goals. At its core, this debate was about professional authority – but it was also about bodies. Professionals accused common readers of being too emotional and too embodied. But novelists and thinkers at the forefront of popular literature argued that emotion and embodiment are in fact the keys to good literature and good reading. As these novelists saw it, the ethical reader of their texts would read first and foremost to better themselves, so that they could better the world around them.

The Return to Empathy

The superlative measure of a Victorian ethical theory was its ability to cultivate embodied, emotional resonance with others – whether they called it fellow-feeling, sympathy, universal brotherhood/sisterhood, or some similar variation. Because these sentiments (which I will call 'empathy' for now, and further unpack in later chapters) are in part psychological phenomena, *how* one thought became just as important as what one thought or did. This cultivation of right thinking, which Elaine Hadley calls 'practices of moralized cognition', traces a genealogy through Utilitarians like John and James Mill and Jeremy Bentham, back to 'their enlightenment ancestors, such as those associative mental operations so prized by John Locke or the refined thoughts of David Hume' (Hadley 2010: 9). Associationism walks hand-in-hand with liberalism – both the moral and political philosophies.

Many of these political thinkers – the Mills in particular – also contributed to the Victorian reimagining of earlier theories of Associationism. But because of their strict materialism, they understood the etiology of these psychological phenomena as inextricably physiological. This intersection meant that ethicists not only sought to articulate modes of moralised thinking, but also understood the science of cognition as an ethical practice in itself. The logic would be something like: if I can learn to think better, I am in fact cultivating and changing my body; if I can change my physiological response to stimuli, then I can change how I receive and respond to others' bodies. I can, in short, feel my way into more ethical living.

This is a heavy ethical mandate, to be sure. It is important to acknowledge Suzanne Keen's warning that 'A society that insists on receiving immediate ethical and political yields from the recreational reading of its citizens puts too great a burden on both empathy and the novel' (Keen 2007: 168). But in the contest over literary studies in the nineteenth century – over what literature was and could become – authors and critics *did* place precisely that burden on novels. The demand would perhaps be too great if, as Keen contends, 'the very fictionality of novels predisposes readers to empathize with characters' in textual 'safe zones' that do not produce 'a resultant demand on real-world action' (4). But Associationism eliminates that safe zone. It challenges readers to improve themselves in a manner so common to the cultural zeitgeist of the time, what Andrew Miller calls 'moral perfectionism' – not a genre or philosophy, but a 'noumenal cominatoire' that stretches across literature, politics and science (A. Miller 2008: 19). Associationist scientists and the novelists whom I explore alongside them hitch their ploughs somewhere in the affective field of perfectionism, but their materialist scepticism somewhat ameliorates the 'burden' Keen and Miller identify. There is an ethical command, yes, but scientific thinking in part alleviates the weight, or at least shifts it (more on *to whom* below).

In fact, I argue, the intersection between Associationist science and the ethics of care is crucial to understanding the Victorian theory of the novel at the very least. Key works on science and the theory of the novel have taught us the value of inhabiting historical scientific paradigms. Nicholas Dames sets out an invaluable framework for how literary critics can use historical science in his *Physiology of the Novel*. His overall project, to recapture a theory of the novel before the linguistic turn, incorporating Victorian schemata and thinkers, confronts us with the risk of presentism and the need to immerse ourselves in an archive. And when he suggests that 'physiology was the metalanguage of nineteenth-century novel theory', Dames illuminates the need to inhabit alternative paradigms of sense-making in order to understand literary artefacts (Dames 2007: 39). More recently, David Sweeney Coombs's *Reading with the Senses* 'resituat[es] literary studies' interpretive practices in relation to the perceptual process involved in reading' with acute attention to how exactly Victorians understood those perceptual processes (Coombs 2019: 20). Through studies of Thomas Reid, Hermann von Helmholtz and others, Coombs shows that 'Since the end of the eighteenth century, scientific accounts of perception have taken for granted that a great deal of interpretive work goes into our everyday perceptual experiences of the world' – and that if we are to understand the relationship between perception and interpretation, we must thoroughly explore the model of perception that created any interpretive, theoretical apparatus (13). Both studies are foundational to any work on the Victorian theory of the novel and its intersection with coeval science.

At the same time, I draw attention to the inextricable ties between science, novelistic interpretation, and the ethics of empathy that mid-century authors strove to cultivate through sensation and feeling. This reads both authors and scientists against the grain of a common perception that the Victorian 'ethos of self-abnegation . . . aimed to "repress the aspiring, desiring, emotion-ridden self and everything merely personal, contingent, historical, material that might get in the way of acquiring knowledge"' (Coombs 2019: 16; citing G. Levine 2002: 2). Rather, I suggest that these authors set up sensational, uncritical, materially bound reactions to stimuli as the primary path to empathetic self-abnegation.

Perhaps the clearest articulation of this unity between Associative sensation and the ethics of care comes from James Martineau's 1885 *Types of Ethical Theory*. Martineau is a strange ally for scientific ethics, since he is decidedly hostile to the concept. But his desire to define which kinds of questions and knowledge can speak about ethics led him to a surprising alliance with Associationism. His work in the 1860s, particularly his critique of Alexander Bain, is deeply committed to separating domains of knowledge: what one branch of science may or may not speak to, which kinds of knowledge are unattainable by scientific means. He attacks Bain for wanting 'to paint his Madonna with the skin off' – to reduce humanity and consciousness to mere mechanisms (Martineau 1866: 254). To protect from mechanism, he insists that there should be a 'dualistic grouping of the Sciences . . . prescribed by the fundamental conditions of Intelligence itself', that separates psychological sciences that look at consciousness from material sciences that look at physical matter (250). The two are so different, he argues, 'that whilst neither can question, not either may borrow, the language and methods of the other' (250). Not only would he divide psychology from physical sciences, but he would also separate the humanities from the sciences, for

> if I am to know humanity, human I must be; and all its memorials . . . are but the extension of my self-conscious being. In this distinction we have the true dividing-line between the departments of Science and Literature, and the principle of their profound difference of operation on the minds exclusively occupied with either. (251)

To rescue humanity from mechanistic reduction, Martineau seeks distinct categories of knowledge. His work in the mid-century, in short, demands that psychologists stay in their lane – and defines their work as neither a physical science nor a philosophy of aesthetics.

And yet, by 1885, Martineau allows for interplay between psychology, science and ethics. In *Types of Ethical Theory*, he attempts to defend religious ethics in a world after Darwin, in which the foundations for altruism and empathy appear (to him) shaken.[11] In the preface, Martineau indicates a shift from his 1860s mode of thinking: he acknowledges that moral philosophy requires connection to physical experience. If a moral philosopher in the nineteenth century wants to make claims about something like volition, then they must contend with the burgeoning nexus between physiology and psychology. However begrudgingly, he admits that 'to indicate what ought to be is . . . impossible without a large study of what is; so that Ethics are dependent upon scientific conditions' (Martineau 1885a: vi). This concession creates the slim space for Associationism to occupy in Martineau's philosophy and mid-century Victorian moral thinking writ large, even moralists opposed to what they perceived as mechanism or biological reductionism.

In an odd, quite short section that follows a vitriolic takedown of Benthamite Utilitarianism, and preceding a longer, more ambivalent discussion of J. S. Mill (whom Martineau personally liked and respected), Martineau grants the validity of what he calls 'psychological hedonism'. He allows as a 'more than probable hypothesis' that attachment to family, country, fellow humans and so on results from 'the chemistry of association operating on data of pleasurable consciousness' (Martineau 1885b: 301). That being the case, this subset of scientists who subscribe to Associationism

> has distinctly traced, step by step, a transition from self-regard, not exactly into self-forgetfulness, but into self-identification with the well-being of others; and has shown that, under healthy conditions, the nature crown of a course commencing in motive pleasure is a real disinterestedness. (301)

This book traces the history of this ethical system: the transition from self-regard into what we might call empathy through a biological, physiological process – and how mid-century novelists claimed authority for popular literature as an ideal site to cultivate that growth.

Nineteenth-century models of reading as an exercise in empathy have made a grand return to the academy in the last decade or so (if ever they truly disappeared). In literary studies, social science and neuroscience alike, the return to feeling has engaged novels via the core question: can reading make one a better, more moral, more ethical person?

Often and especially in public iterations of this conversation, the answer to this question has been resoundingly affirmative. According to much of the conversation, novels inherently produce empathy, and this empathy is inherently a prerequisite for civil society.[12] In the preface to *The Age of Empathy* (2009), Frans de Waal writes, 'Empathy is the grand theme of our time' (Waal 2009: ix). On the civic role of empathy, Barack Obama says, 'the most important stuff I've learned [about citizenship] I think I've learned from novels. It has to do with empathy' (Robinson and Obama 2015). He makes the connection between reading, empathy and civic duty in a single gesture that treats the intersection as though it were obvious.

But, in popular, twenty-first-century thinking, to develop and instil empathetic habits requires a high-quality text, a truly *literary* text, not just any old thing. Annie Murphy Paul argues that empathy-building is not 'likely to happen when we're scrolling through TMZ', in part because the kind of reading one does online is 'information driven' (Paul 2013). These sorts of popular, less worthy texts lack the capacity to 'vigorously' exercise the 'reading circuits' of the human brain. Instead, Paul calls for what she terms 'deep reading' that is 'slow, immersive, rich in sensory detail and emotional and moral complexity'. Only deep reading has the capacity to 'prope[l] us inside the heads of fictional characters' and can 'increas[e] our real-life capacity for empathy'. But really, the only element of 'deep reading' that has to do with the phenomenon of *reading* is its speed (slow); the rest describes the qualities of the text, and what makes that text worthy of deep reading.

Arguments that only certain kinds of literature (that is, high-quality) can cultivate empathy trace their ancestry back to the emergence of English literary studies in the mid-nineteenth century. Studies of literature and empathy have tended to employ the language and evidence of science – particularly neuroscience – to justify reading literature as a socially productive act. Benjamin Morgan rightly argues:

> Issues of materiality and embodiment, as they were framed in the nineteenth century, lie at the heart of many recent critical developments because as literary and cultural studies have reopened themselves to scientific concepts and methods, they have been thrown back into the midst of problems that preceded the professionalization of interpretive humanities disciplines. (Morgan 2017: 15)

The inverse is also true: as the humanities disciplines face increasing pressure to justify their role in production-driven economies, we find ourselves revisiting the same issues that literary studies used to justify itself in its inception.

No wonder, then, that these scientists find themselves pointing to a particular kind of reading of a particular kind of text as morally preferable. Social psychologists David Comer Kidd and Emanuele Castano make this delineation most explicit: 'not any kind of fiction' develops empathy, but instead, 'it is literary fiction that forces the reader to engage in [Theory of Mind] processes' that cultivate an awareness of others' feelings (Kidd and Castano 2013: 377). All these models require a reader who does not read 'pragmatically and instrumentally', but instead engages with the text with an emotional respect for the literariness of fiction. This *je ne sais quoi* of good literature – whatever it is that manages to appropriately exercise our reading circuits – apparently does not appear in bad literature or non-literary reading, for reasons that are more or less unexplained. What we read and how we read depends on if we cultivate empathy; if we read good books, greater moral effects will follow. The great irony, of course, is that the texts that Paul, Kidd and Castano, and others call 'literary' are those that were explicitly *not* literary in the mid-century: novels brimming with sentiment and sensation, like the work of Charles Dickens, which is now considered 'great literature' but which in the nineteenth century was popular in all senses of the word.

The history of science and emotion explains how we arrived at this paradox. The perhaps unlikely pairing of cognitive studies with emotional reading has its roots in Associationism and the mid-century novelists. Associationist science understood language as inherently emotive and embodied. To differentiate between academic readers who employed hermeneutics and uneducated readers who used feeling, literary studies rejected emotion as grounds for proper reading. By the time of the New Critics, science, the uneducated reader and emotion had become antonyms of literary reading. As scholars return to an emphasis on reading and its capacity to generate empathy, it is unsurprising that they find themselves examining Dickens and other mid-Victorians, since those novels were written with precisely that project in mind.

This book recovers that mid-century discourse when the domain of literary authority teetered between the hermeneutics of the academy and ethical feeling. It inhabits the space of the Associationist, materialist authors whose texts self-reflexively address what it means to read well: to read ethically, to read empathetically, to read with feeling. The first chapter, 'Feeling Bodies: Associationism and the Anti-Metaphorics of Materiality', offers a genealogy and lexicon of Associationism, particularly its theory of language and materiality. Associationism insists on a physical stimulus as instigator of any physical or psychological response. And yet, it also offered a philosophical and scientific basis for Victorian novelists and advocates of popular reading to contend that the real work of reading is emotional rather than hermeneutic. Through the core concept 'impressions', Associationism conceives of words as their own motive force, capable of transmitting not simply feeling, but also the impulse of objects as if that matter were empirically present. After reaching briefly back to John Locke, this chapter considers eighteenth- and nineteenth-century Associationists – David Hume, Joseph Priestley, Dugald Stewart and Alexander Bain – to propose that the Associationists understood language as part of the material and physical response to stimuli – and so, embodied reading could become a basis for ethics.

The most obvious critique of embodied literary studies and the relationship between readers' and characters' bodies is that fictional characters are not, in fact, physical. The second chapter, 'Symbolic Bodies: Memory, the Storyteller and Suffering in Boz's "The Hospital Patient"', addresses this problem through Associationist science on memory and imagination – particularly James Mill, Dugald Stewart and David Hartley – alongside Charles Dickens's 'The Hospital Patient', a short story from his 1836 *Sketches by Boz*. Obscure though it may be, this short story is a reading manual: a how-to guide for materialist reading through Associationism. In this sketch, science must attend to the specific and particular, rather than the general. It must consider material, physical individuals instead of what I call *symbolic bodies* that stand in for all other bodies. Only through attention to material detail and sensation can fictional bodies impact reading bodies, Boz suggests – and then, the physical responses of the readers make fictional stimuli real through memory and imagination as Associationism understands them. Here, with Smith, Hume and contemporary theorists of empathy, I unpack the nuances of how Associationism understood this complex feeling-for-others that goes by so many names: empathy, sympathy, fellow-feeling.

But how does the author ensure that readers really *feel* for characters rather than simply pluck out a moral lesson? Chapter 3, 'Metaphoric Bodies: The Professional Author, Sensation and Serialisation in *Great Expectations*', considers the publication history of *Great Expectations* and its representations of reading. This novel suggests that while serialisation appealed to the common reader's desire for sensation, it used that sensation to connect straight to their bodies. Mid-century novelists – who often published in serial – celebrated embodied, self-less reading as ethical, but faced a quandary: the very language and ideas they used to condemn those who abstracted bodies to perform the work of academic reading was the language those critics used to condemn serial publication. Common literature struggled to claim the moral high ground when it was, in essence, a commodity. The novel turns critiques of serial – that it is too fast, and too sensational – into positive attributes. Because seriality is fast and sensational, it is also fundamentally associative, and therefore best suited to cultivate ethical, empathetic embodiment.

To accomplish this argument, *Great Expectations* rejects bodies as metaphors, and metaphors for bodies – where an external object or a part of a body stands in for the whole. Serial simultaneously enables readers to slide associatively from one instalment to the next, and tempts them to speculate on what will come next. This speculation is a kind of literary work on the formal level, one duplicated on the semantic level through metaphor. Within the novel, Pip Pirrip tends to metaphorise bodies: both to read bodies through objects, and to read bodies as metaphors for abstract concepts. His repeated misreadings of others' intentions teach readers not to jump to conclusions, and not to read for codes and linearity, but instead to embrace embodied reading. And this admonition is bound up in the serial form, for the novel uses its form to reinforce this practice emotionally; it draws readers in, baits them into guessing and metaphorising, and then punishes them alongside Pip.

The only way that literature and science can be ethical, these mid-century authors suggest, is through unwavering commitment to materiality. Chapter 4, 'Plastic Bodies: The Scientist, Vital Mechanics and Ethical Habits of Character in Wilkie Collins's *The Moonstone*', explores the Associationist ethics of selflessness through contributions to the mid-century mechanist/vitalist debate – most prominently William Benjamin Carpenter and Thomas Huxley – and their appearance in Wilkie Collins's *The Moonstone*. The scientific conversation centres around two competing understandings of character: the mechanists, who hold that mind is a phenomenon reducible to its physical components; and the vitalists, who argued that human character is external to purely material causes. Carpenter's work from the 1850s through to the 1870s shifts toward a synthesis between these two built around the idea that character, mind and brains are subject to the psychological inertia of 'habit', but nevertheless malleable.

Collins sets up *The Moonstone* as a novelistic exploration of 'the influence of character on circumstances' – in other words, the capacity for apparently subjective psychology to produce material effects. The novel explores how mechanism or vitalism might shape 'character', most explicitly through direct citation of Carpenter's work. This is the culmination of the intersection of Associationist science and ethical reading: only through materialist science can one read surfaces – texts, bodies, feelings – empathetically, and only empathy can ameliorate others' suffering.

But Collins's empathy has a dark side: self-suspension is in fact self-annihilation. Miller's study ends with a chapter on sacrifice, and notes that often 'Within the domestic world' of the Victorians, 'it seems we deny our passion by sacrificing others' (A. Miller 2008: 217). I argue that this sacrifice takes place most commonly to teach a male character to read more ethically. Ostensibly successful readers in *The Moonstone* read at the expense of bodies sacrificed in the margins of the text. Most of these bodies never find a voice: the Indians, Penelope Betteredge, Rosanna Spearman. And the only one who does find a voice, Ezra Jennings, is silenced as his body falls apart. But rather than condone this sacrifice of others to improve the self, these novels push back against the entire formula; sacrificing someone else does not contest self-regard, and to sacrifice someone else in the pursuit of knowledge is fundamentally unethical.

Mary Elizabeth Braddon's *Lady Audley's Secret* exposes the unethical practice of fetishised self-renunciation for the self-annihilation machine it really is. Chapter 5, 'Represented Bodies: The Lawyer, Conclusions and Circumstantial Evidence in *Lady Audley's Secret*', challenges the epistemology of knowledge writ large. While Jennings is the hero of *The Moonstone* because he can suspend himself, the compulsion to self-suspend transforms the ethical person – especially the ethical woman – into an interpretive framework rather than a body. The publication history of *Lady Audley's Secret* suggests that Mary Elizabeth Braddon felt profoundly ambivalent about the work of her novel. On the one hand, she enjoyed sensation; on the other, she felt shame for writing merely popular literature. When the initial serialisation of the novel fell through due to the collapse of the publication where it appeared, Braddon wrote that she never intended to finish the novel. 'Unfinished' becomes the mantra of the chapter, which explores what it means to attend to surfaces as surfaces, rather than for the interpretive conclusion beneath. Like Braddon's own ambivalence, *Lady Audley's Secret* wants to cultivate an ethics of acknowledgement over knowledge, but it refuses to do so through a naïve materialism merely draped in the trappings of materiality.

Robert Audley's continued failure to read texts – reading letters, paintings, newspapers and novels – mirrors his failure to read the bodies of the women around him. However, he insists on his patriarchal and legal prerogative to *representations*, or external models of bodies that illuminate inner motives and psyches. This culminates in his legal recourse to circumstantial evidence in terms that appear to draw on Associationism, but which in fact flatten the complexity of material experience. Through readings of Alexander Bain and legal writings on circumstantial evidence, I argue that the novel calls into question literary and scientific conclusions drawn from interpretive hermeneutics. Where the New Critics celebrate literature's proclivity for representation, *Lady Audley's Secret* insists that both science and literature should refrain from interpreting bodies' interiors altogether, because to read a body is to sacrifice its vitality. The novel condemns a flattened science that produces knowledge through legible bodies. As an alternative to knowledge, the novel embraces surface as critique: pure pain instead of representation, affect instead of tidy conclusions.

By way of conclusion, Chapter 6 follows the political results of the mid-century contest over literary authority and affect as it appears in 1880s liberalism through Walter Besant's *Children of Gibeon*. The move to Besant may seem a strange turn for a book on affect, embodiment and science. Thanks in part to Deleuze's work, it is common to look to Thomas Hardy and the 1890s for examples of 'collectives of intensive sensations' (Deleuze and Parnet 2007: 39–40). Hugh Epstein makes a compelling case for Hardy as a kind of literary impressionist who works in scientific empiricism, in terms that dwell happily alongside the Associationists in this book (Epstein 2020). William Cohen looks to Hardy and Gerard Manley Hopkins for his exploration of embodiment and affect, though I will have more to say on his metaphorics later (Cohen 2009). And Elisha Cohn looks to Hardy in a brilliant study of the rejection of 'any straightforward prospect of literary instrumentality', the mandate for novels to improve readers (Cohn 2016: 150). Benjamin Morgan's work traces the direct line through the mid-century 'outward turn' to aestheticism, a convincing trajectory that provides a more complete image of how the empirical sciences and the arts intertwined toward the end of the century. These are all perfectly valid and valuable contributions, and not at odds with what I am doing here.

But this book lies somewhere between, say, Miller and Morgan: I look to Associationist science as a domain from which several lines of flight emerge. One trajectory produces Hardy, Hopkins and impressionism. Another produces the aesthetic thinkers like John Ruskin, or the aesthetics of politics like William Morris. The line I trace intersects with the trajectories of political liberalism, philosophical and moral perfectionism, and the continued attempt to define what reading a novel can *do* (ethically speaking). Liberalism's concern for material conditions of late-century workers opens space to think about language and reading as a bodily process intimately bound up with an ethics of care. This challenges the argument that to read about or to imagine a suffering body does not, in fact, necessitate action, but it also challenges the idea that the action that must take place needs to be a form of benevolence or self-sacrifice. It offers a materialist ethics that does not necessarily need to produce or know or even act so much as acknowledge. Valentine's journey in *Children of Gibeon* is a journey through modes of representation – from symbols to representations – that culminates in intimate, physical care for her sisters. This materialism that begins in the abstract and moves to the concrete offers a defence of Victorian optimism, and suggests that reading bodies with attention to the surface encourages attention to the material pain of living bodies.

A champion of optimistic empathy, Walter Besant suggests a way to integrate materialism, language and empathy in a mode that does not require the self-annihilation of marginalised bodies. Through his novels, Besant sets out the ethics of a social programme that rests on materialist, embodied empathy. In these texts, he opposes the hermeneutics of academics (political economists) and the abstract rationality of the socialists to the embodied care of liberal reformers. The heroines of these novels are a political economist and socialist, fully capable of hermeneutics, but they both learn that materialism better answers the problems of the working class. Rather than interpret bodies, they instead encounter them through materiality and empathy. This offers a new model of empathy: one that does not seek to hand people solutions for their suffering from on high, but rather seeks to sit with them in their pain.

Notes

1. Elaine Scarry argues that these texts 'giv[e] us a set of instructions for how to construct or imagine' the physical bodies they represent (Scarry 1999: 5). This is part of the meta-construction of knowledge – how these texts offer schemata by which we are meant to understand them – but rather than address Realism/mimesis (as Scarry does), I am more interested in the ways these texts' ethics resist their own representational and interpretive paradigms.

2. My studies focus on professional critics and scholars. I hope to lay the groundwork to delve into the archive of readers' journals and ephemera, to better understand how readers would have felt about their reading in their own terms.
3. This distinction distinguishes this version of affect theory from, say, Raymond Williams's 'structures of feeling'. Williams describes structures of feeling as 'social experiences *in solution*, as distinct from other social semantic formations which have been precipitated and are more evidently and more immediately available (Williams 1978: 133–4). As a good Marxist, Williams emphasises the social. But emphasis on the social produces an affect of suspicion, one that depends on the conflicts and oppositions that form the scaffolding around which Williams builds his structures of feeling. As a result, the scaffolding occludes the phenomenological, biological experience of feeling. Mitchum Huehls writes that 'if you can identify a nexus of social relations and experiences as a structure of feeling, you are either observing a historical configuration that has lost its indeterminate dynamism, or your observation will be imprecise and provisional because structures of feeling actually precede articulation' (Huehls 2010: 419). And he is correct – insofar as Williams's model necessitates that scepticism, and that sense that bodies are forever and always outside of language. But language does not have to be an opposition to feeling, and feeling does not have to ossify to be experienced, spoken of, or explored. The same rings true of Pierre Bourdieu's 'habitus'. Bourdieu's work is crucial to this book, especially in its analysis of capital and exchange. But the density of Bourdieu's network wrapped around the body at the centre of the habitus ultimately pushes one toward abstraction, hermeneutics and a sense of suspicion. Like Williams's structures of feeling, one must unwrap the linens that mummify the phenomenological experience of feeling if ever one hopes to feel or see a moving body.
4. Influential works on the formation of the identity of common readers and the reading public include Richard Altick's *The English Common Reader* (1957), Beth Palmer and Adelene Buckland's *A Return to the Common Reader* (2011), and Jonathan Rose's 'Rereading the English Common Reader: A Preface to a History of Audiences' (1992) and *The Intellectual Life of the British Working Classes* (2010).
5. Jesse Cordes Selbin offers valuable insight into the literary training of the common reader in his recent article '"Read with Attention"' (2016), where he explores John Cassell's 'RULES FOR READING', which, alongside some other contemporary essays, 'anticipate certain New Critical modes of close reading' for a wide, common audience.
6. As Lewis Roberts puts it in his study of Mudie's moral and pecuniary economics, 'selection ultimately depends on the inherent, and obvious, quality of books themselves. The economic (commercial) and the literary (or moral) are seemingly harmonised through Mudie's commonsensical

argument' that because he cannot house all books, he must therefore house the best (Roberts 2006: 11).
7. See my article 'Redefining the Republic of Letters' (2017) for more on how Mudie and his detractors alike amalgamated the discourses of economics, aesthetics and politics into one domain of literary authority.
8. Outside of my own brief reading of this book, the most contact a twenty-first-century Victorianist is likely to have with *Miriam May* is as a passing mention in the *Quarterly Review*'s 'Sensation Novels', where the novel appears in a list of 'specimens of the theological novel, which emplo[y] the nerves as a vehicle for preaching in the literary sense of the term' (Mansel 1863: 504).
9. For more thorough histories of English in the Victorian era, see the foundational Gerald Graff, *Professing Literature* (1989); the Marxist cultural analysis of Brian Doyle, *English and Englishness* (1989); John Sutherland, 'Journalism, Scholarship, and the University College London English Department' (1998); Amanda Anderson and Joseph Valente (eds), *Disciplinarity at the Fin de Siècle* (2002); and H. S. Jones, *Intellect and Character in Victorian England* (2007). While not specifically Victorian, Ian Reid, *Wordsworth and the Formation of English Studies* is also a valuable resource for this subject (2004).
10. In terms of cultural history, Arnold has been variously championed and rejected as the grandfather of modern literary studies. While he valued literary study as a broad category, Matthew Arnold was himself a Classicist at heart and was sceptical of studying English literature qua English literature; in fact, he 'objected . . . to the establishment of English Literature as an entirely independent subject within the university' (Collini 1991: 362–3). See James Walter Caufield's *Overcoming Matthew Arnold* (2012) for a defence of Arnold's role in the formation of English studies.
11. Martineau is in fact convinced that 'the uneasiness so often manifested lest the theory of Evolution should eat away the basis of human duty has no justification, except in the prevalence of the very confusion of thought which it exemplifies', and that 'the whole group of natural sciences is left absolutely free to legitimate development, without the possibility of collision with Ethics' (Martineau 1885a: xv, xiv).
12. This is the case in Martin Hoffman's *Empathy and Moral Development* (2001), Heidi Maibom's anthology *Empathy and Morality* (2014), and the majority of Amy Coplan and Peter Goldie's anthology *Empathy: Philosophical and Psychological Perspectives* (2014).

Chapter 1

Feeling Bodies: Associationism and the Anti-Metaphorics of Materiality

When he writes that 'for scientific language a difference in the references [of words] is failure', I. A. Richards concisely articulates a crisis that plagues scientific discourse: modern science is the paradoxical struggle to describe things as they are within a language that overflows with metaphor, that describes things very much not as they are (Richards 1924: 268). Quarks may be strange, but they are not charming; electrons are not pessimists; genes do not want anything.

The science of feeling in particular seems to demand metaphor. You walk into a silent room and know that the conversation was tense moments before – maybe we call it 'temperature', though the cold-shoulder is hardly an endothermic reaction. A look in your friend's eyes makes your stomach tighten – you know something is wrong 'in your gut', though your digestive tract lacks cognitive capacity.

Throughout the seventeenth and eighteenth centuries, Associationist science and its predecessors sought to describe things precisely as they were. And the scientists who serve as interlocutors for this book belonged to a particularly stringent line of thinking that brooked no abstraction in cause, effect or explanation. The 1693 epistolary exchange between Isaac Newton and the grandfather of philology and English literary criticism, Richard Bentley, presents a neatly packaged summary of this demand. Bentley had recently been nominated as the first Boyle Lecturer, an (ongoing) endowed lecture on science and Christianity, and had opted to use Newton's exciting theories of gravity to accomplish the title of his lectures, 'A Confutation of Atheism'. The enormity of space – the space between objects at an astronomical level, and the space between atoms at the microscopic level – suggested to Bentley some sort of agent behind the initial gravitational attraction that brought matter together.

Given the vastness of space, how could any atom have ever of its own accord drawn other atoms to it? (This was, of course, long before a cosmological model that proposed an origin of extreme density and rapid expansion.) He calculated the size of the universe, estimated the amount of matter in it, spread those atoms equidistant from one another, and determined: they simply would not affect one another. With an imminent press deadline on his lectures, Bentley hurriedly wrote to Newton to ask his opinion on his calculations and conclusions.

The materialism of Bentley's claim is of utmost importance to Newton: any physically traceable effect must have an equally traceable physical cause. Newton praised in particular an axiom of Bentley's that offers a proper framework for understanding materialism. Bentley rejects the idea of innate gravity, which understood gravity as an attribute of matter – something like colour, or shape. Gravity cannot be an attribute of matter, because it would violate materialist principles. 'Tis unconceivable', Bentley writes, 'that inanimate brute matter should (without a divine impression) operate upon & affect other matter without mutual contact: as it must, if gravitation be essential and inherent in it' (Bentley 1693: 3). In other words, the atoms did not bring themselves together as an attribute of their substance. In Bentley's mind, only God could have brought the atoms together.

Newton celebrates the empirical elements of Bentley's claim. He diplomatically elides the question of gravity as proof of God with the equivocation: 'Gravity must be caused by an agent [acting] consta[ntly] according to certain laws, but whether this agent be material or immaterial is a question I have left to the consideration of my readers' (Newton 1959: 7r–7v). But he wholeheartedly agrees, almost word for word, with Bentley that 'Tis unconceivable that inanimate brute matter should (without the mediation of something else which is not material) operate upon & affect other matter without mutual contact' (7r). Matter only acts on matter through physically measurable means. There is no need for abstraction to fill the space between objects; gravity bridges the gap.

This chapter argues that Associationism's empirical epistemology understands language and embodiment as part of the same surface. Gravity is the perfect metaphor for an Associationist understanding of language. Newton insists that there can be no way that matter can affect other matter without an outside intercessor – because he understood that gravity is in fact a mediator, a physical force. Newton's materialism continues through English philosophical tradition, through proto-Associationists like John Locke and David Hume to the Associationists proper. Associationists gradually overturned the idea that memories, imaginations and living bodies cannot elicit physical change in other bodies, because they understood that language is in fact a mediator, a physical force that, like gravity between atoms, bridges the gap between bodies.

And yet, I have just committed the very sin Newton, Dugald Stewart and other hard-line materialists decried: I have turned to metaphor. Metaphor is accepted or even expected in the humanities, of course, but waxing poetic about feeling and bodies is an ethical misstep, according to the Associationists and the mid-Victorian novelists who make use of them. Dugald Stewart might have objected to being classified as a materialist, but if anything, his accusation was that materialism was not material enough. In his takedown of David Hartley, an eighteenth-century Associationist, Stewart writes that 'instead . . . of objecting to the scheme of materialism, that its conclusions are false, it would be more accurate to say, that its aim is unphilosophical' (D. Stewart 1802: 4–5).[1] We cannot conceive of the essence of something like mind or matter, Stewart argues; we only know them by their effects. So, 'when we attempt to explain the nature of that principle which feels and thinks and wills, by saying that it is a *material* substance . . . we impose on ourselves by words' (5). In other words, we metaphorise.[2]

Stewart argues that if we metaphorise bodies, we reduce them to symbols, metaphors or representations of ourselves and our own ideas. We silence their ability to feel and move and exist on their own terms. For this reason, he laments, the philosophy of mind, 'a science so interesting in its nature, and so important in its applications, that it could scarcely have failed, in these inquisitive and enlightened times, to have excited a very general attention', was dismissed as mere academic speculation to die in obscurity alongside the other 'vain and unprofitable disquisitions of the schoolmen' (2). Scholarly metaphorisation transforms material bodies into intellectual riddles irrelevant to lived experience.

To metaphorise bodies is an ethical problem, I argue, because it divorces them from lived experience. The scholarly metaphorisation of bodies aims to apprehend and crack the mystery of the exterior in order to access the interior. If one can know a body – that is, to apply knowledge, to read, to unpack, to determine – one can unlock the puzzle of their personhood. Encounters with bodies become opportunities to reflect on oneself and one's own knowledge and scholastic accomplishments. This is the key to my emphasis on surfaces in literature: they are planes of contact and engagement that we miss if we hurry to interpretation.[3] Disembodied, hermeneutic reading dives straight into the abstract realm of decoding without touching, feeling, connecting to the surface. Scholastic reading is so intent on making sense that it forgets to sense.[4] Rather than the intellectual knowledge by which one 'makes sense of' a body, Associationism would have literary scholarship turn to emotional acknowledgement that senses and connects with bodies. My language here draws extensively on the work of Stanley Cavell, who offers the opposition between knowledge and acknowledgement.[5] Rather than deploy knowledge about a situation, what a person means, or what a body means, Cavell argues that we should let the body speak for itself and acknowledge people's bodies and voices on their own terms. Scholarly thinking seeks to derive interpretation, metaphor, hermeneutic unpacking – in a word, knowledge. In opposition, the scientists, novelists and ethicists of Associationism utilise sensation, connection and opening up space for other bodies to feel and express themselves – in a word, acknowledgement. Where knowing merely interprets with hermeneutics, the Associationists would have scholars acknowledge and use language as a tool of embodied feeling.

Disembodied Scholars, Disembodied Metaphors

Mid-Victorian authors accuse scholastic methods of reading as over-determined attempts to prioritise the scholar's knowledge over others' lived reality. To find the Key to All Mythologies is to claim the ability to read all social relationships, all bodies, so that all human history is subsumed within the scholar's knowledge. In short, their scholarship reads everything through themselves, or what Martineau called 'self-regard'.

Literary scholarship has treated texts as puzzles since at least as far back as the Protestant Reformation. To distinguish between popular texts and the academic profession, early literary scholars grounded their interpretive methodologies in the idea that texts had a determined meaning. Marcus Walsh understands the now ubiquitous tool of close reading through the framework of biblical hermeneutics, specifically Anglican hermeneutics, which seeks to find the middle ground between 'the Romanist insistence that scriptural interpretation can rest securely only on the authority of the Church of Rome, and the Puritan reference of interpretation to private reason or the individual spirit' (Walsh 1997: 31). In other words, these scholars believed that texts 'contained a true sense' that a scholar could determine (31). Interpretation was made possible through 'rational and mostly, though not exclusively, intrinsic criteria' (31).

Texts themselves offered the keys to their own interpretation, if supplemented with historical knowledge (40). Veneration for pillars of English literature like Chaucer, Shakespeare and Milton led scholars to 's[eek] to recover what their authors intended to write and what their authors intended to mean', an endeavour accomplished in part through 'close examination of the text' (2). This method of classical literary scholarship creates a domain of knowledge ripe for the methods of scholars like Edward Casaubon of *Middlemarch* or Roger Wendover of *Robert Elsmere*. Texts provide their own keys to interpretation, and because of their interdependence with historical knowledge, they also offer the key to unlocking history as text.

Both Casaubon and Wendover seek to interpret history through story and language, mythology and philology. Both ultimately fail in their projects, and most importantly, their projects are literally the death of them. These novels object to theories that reduce language to mere hermeneutics – that is, to a determinable, singular interpretation. Such theories place language outside of embodiment, as a medium that communicates information that can be reduced to simple formulae. In these novels, compulsory embodiment belies this model of language; while both characters are often described as 'disembodied', they are in fact profoundly and fatally reminded of their own bodies.

When failed scholars read, they prioritise abstraction and ideas rather than the embodied people around them – a methodology that resonates with the historical development of literary studies. Some professors of the new study of English literature operated with a similar model of language, one that encouraged disembodied thinking. In his essay 'The Teaching of English', J. W. Hales decries the imposition of Latin grammatical schemata on English, a language with its own character – but only because he believes that English study would benefit from tighter, more deliberately applied schemata. He argues that 'the ordinary knowledge of English is altogether one of facts, not of principles; [it] is thoroughly superficial, not fundamental' (Hales 1867: 294). This search for fundamental principles was both the preoccupation and the occupation of the scholar. David Masson writes in his review of Mayhew's *London Labour and the London Poor*:

> Of all men in the world, a literary man is expected to sit loose to sordid worldly considerations; seeing that the business he is constantly engaged in is the handling, not of material realities, such as cash or manufactured goods, but of those untangible and aerial shapes and substances called notions, imaginations, propositions, general truth. The Literary Man is the aspirant after the general, the devotee of the unseen. (Masson 1851a: 383)

As the 'devotee of the unseen' who rises above 'material realities', the literary man must search out not the merely 'empirical', as Hales puts it (Hales 1867: 294). Instead, the scholar should study the abstract, the general. To put it simply, this model of literary study is as far from a materialist modality of language as one can be.

While Masson's characterisation of the literary man unites a disembodied affect with a pursuit of general principles, the tragedies of Eliot and Ward's scholars challenge the ethical veracity of his paradigm. Both Casaubon and Squire Wendover carry the pursuit of general principles to its greatest extreme. Wendover's monograph of higher criticism and Casaubon's *Key to All Mythologies* offer just that: a key to all religious and anthropological knowledge. A. D. Nuttall (2003) provides a plethora of possible sources as the key to Eliot's idea of the key, many of them derived from John Clark Pratt and Victor A. Neufeldt's introduction to the *Middlemarch* notebooks (1979). These scholars suggest multiple possible sources of inspiration: John Mayor, Jacob Bryant, Henry James Summer Maine and George Grote, among others.[6] Each of these scholars attempts to create a grand unified theory of human society, to find a key that explains all religious and social phenomena across history and geography. Crucially, their treatises endeavour to unravel and demystify embodiment, to provide an intellectual means to explain and ultimately transcend the lesser, mundane experience of the material world.

The litany of possible inspirations for Casaubon includes Max Müller, whose work makes sense as a forerunner of Casaubon and Wendover but, more interestingly, exposes their disembodied scholarship as a mere masquerade. In fact, Müller's work is deeply embodied. That Müller had grand designs appropriate to his era is undeniable. He emphasised in his *Lectures on the Science of Language* that 'the key that is to open one [language] must open all; otherwise it cannot be the right key' (Müller 1877: 448). But Müller's model of language is strikingly conversant with Associationists' material interests. He writes that 'all words expressive of immaterial conceptions are derived by metaphor from words expressive of sensible ideas' – that behind all abstract and general ideas lies a physical experience (372). His linguistic maxim is reminiscent of the Associationists of his era: 'All roots, i.e. all the material elements of language, are expressive of sensuous impressions, and of sensuous impressions only' (372). Müller takes this perhaps one step further, to argue that physical sensation is in fact the key to all languages, if such a key exists. He offers this example:

the Greek *thymós*, the soul, comes from *theýin*, to rush, to move violently, the Sanskrit *dhû*, to shake. From *dhû* we have in Sanskrit *dhûli*, dust, which comes from the same root, and *dhûma*, smoke, the Latin *fummus*. In Greek, the same root supplied, *thýella* storm-wind, and *thymós*, the soul, as the seat of the passions . . . Plato guesses correctly when he says (Crat. P. 419) that *thymós*, soul, is so called ἀπὸ τῆςθύσεως καὶ ζέσεως τῆς ψυχῆς [from the raging and boiling of life]. (375)

The signifier for the abstract idea 'soul' is a doubly physical marker. First, it is an attempt to describe the physical sensation of soul, an unseen, ethereal, animating movement. Then, language localises this invisible motivator in an empirical equivalent: smoke, dust, wind. The accuracy of Müller's claims is less relevant than that he finds the key to all mythologies in material experience. Casaubon and Wendover's disembodied performance of scholarship, then, is a misnomer. Disembodied interpretation of symbolism is not scholarship; it is merely performing scholarship.

Scholarly disembodiment is an affect in both the common and theoretical sense of the word: fictional scholars perform literariness, and this charade manifests through their physical bodies. They draw boundaries around their own bodies, as if the pursuit of knowledge demands that they abandon materiality.[7] One might well imagine that Müller chastises scholars like Wendover when he writes in words strikingly resonant with Dugald Stewart's critique: 'The mischief begins when language forgets itself, and when we mistake the Word for the Thing, the Quality for the Substance, the *Nomen* [name] for the *Numen* [spirit]' (Müller 1877: 633).[8]

But Wendover does supplant the thing with his words. Most importantly, Wendover's inversion of Müller's maxim plays out on his body. Ostensibly disembodied scholars nevertheless bear the physical strain of their intellectual labour. Casaubon has a 'want of muscular curve' and has 'been using up [his] eyesight on old characters' (Eliot 1871: 97). So, too, Wendover's 'lower-half had a thin and shrunken look, but the shoulders, which had the scholar's stoop, and the head were massively and squarely outlined' (Ward 1888: 228). While we might think about these bodies as lacking something – eyesight, musculature – I would rather not think of bodies in terms of repression and impotence. It is more valuable to think about what bodies generate. If we must be metaphorical, Wendover's lower half indicates that scholastic thinking reproduces intellectually; it propagates through ideas rather than intimacy. The celebration of ideas over intimacy drives Wendover's political philosophy and demarcates the distance between himself and other bodies. His 'scholar's stoop' metaphorises the weight of his mind, the heaviness of his ideas.

But both readings are incomplete. After all, if we aim to rescue bodies from metaphorisation, we would be better off paying attention to Wendover's actual embodiment. His lower half shrinks from time spent sitting in his study; his stoop comes from hours hunched over his manuscript and other books. (I like to imagine that you, Dear Reader, just sat up a bit straighter as I do every time I read this section.) These are not metaphors; rather, they are physical formations of the scholar's body. The scholar transforms anatomical structures into signs that create the problematically disembodied affect of literary authority. The problem is that he deliberately performs this kind of disembodiment as though it is a symbol: he holds intellect over intimacy, believes infertility of body is a product of fertility of mind, and thinks that a stoop which makes one look down is a metaphor for not looking at the people around him. This is something of a paradox, for the novel imposes meaning-making on to a body, and then tells the reader not to supplant bodies with meaning-making. The texts themselves encode Casaubon and Elsmere's bodies with hermeneutic meaning, and thereby set up a paradox that implodes on its own scholarly weight.

Ironically, the scholar is always drawn back to his body – often terminally. Casaubon, Wendover and Elsmere all die. Sickness and sickliness, one must remember, are profoundly embodying experiences.[9] These bodies are physically incarnate. Disembodiment is an affect within a body that attempts to reject itself. Scholarly intellect is not the opposite of a body; it is just another arrangement of the body.

And here is the crux of how Wendover, Casaubon and disembodied scholars appear in mid-century literature: the literary scholar is not necessarily all that literary, but he performs as though he is. He strives to be read as literary, but disembodiment is an affect preoccupied with the self. For the mid-century novelists, this mode of scholarship lacks literary and ethical authority. First and foremost, it commits the mistake of self-regard, the antithesis of empathy and care for others; I will address this ethical element further in later chapters. This chapter is interested in how disembodied linguistic scholarship commits a categorical mistake when it sees language as something outside of biological connections between bodies. As this chapter will demonstrate, Associationism understands language as a material, even bodily process; an ethical model of language rejects metaphor and returns always to material bodies.

Locke, Hume and the Gravity of Language

John Locke's work in the *Essay Concerning Human Understanding* (1689) builds the foundation of this materialist theory of language. For Locke, language is communicative and social – and, most importantly, sensory. Language is not pure rationality, nor is it even intellectual; it communicates embodiment.

In Locke's *Essay*, all language comes from sensory experience. Analysis of any language, he argues, will demonstrate 'how great a dependence our words have on common sensible ideas' (Locke 1849: 289). And not merely words that have clear physical connotations; even 'those which are made use of to stand for actions and notions quite removed from sense, have their rise from thence, and from obvious sensible ideas are transferred to more abstruse significations' (289). In a sequence clearly influential on Max Müller, he argues that 'spirit' comes from 'breath', and 'angel' from 'messenger'. Ideas, which seem like the product of the mind, in fact 'depen[d] wholly upon our senses' (53). Behind even the most abstract of words, he argues, lies a physical experience.

The material origins of language mean language exists to communicate affective states between bodies. To make language more than mere sounds, humans need 'to use these sounds as signs of internal conceptions, and to make them stand as marks for the ideas within [their] own mind; whereby they might be made known to others, and the thoughts of men's minds be conveyed from one to another' (288). Of course, Locke emphasises the communication of a mind to another mind; he is, after all, a philosopher of rationality. But bodies are embedded within his language. Communication is flesh made word, 'external sensible signs, whereby those invisible ideas which his thoughts are made up of might be made known to others' (290). And those abstract ideas, he has previously informed us, are derived from and articulated through sensory experience.

Language's sensory origins allow it to mediate between physical experience and consciousness – in both directions. It is possible to communicate one's internal state to someone else because language transmits material impressions. Locke writes that 'there comes, by constant use, to be such a connexion between certain sounds and the ideas they stand for, that the names heard almost as readily excite certain ideas, as if the objects themselves which are apt to produce them did actually affect the senses' (292). This quote is one of the most important in the genealogy of Associationism: language is the interlocutor that makes sense of sensory experience, and that transmits that experience between bodies by phenomenologically conjuring up the original stimuli.

But this sense-making comes late to the process. Though he is a staunch rationalist, Locke must admit that the noise of bodily sensation cannot be shut off: 'As the bodies that surround us do diversely affect our organs, the mind is forced to receive the impressions, and cannot avoid the perception of those ideas that are annexed to them' (63). The mind cannot avoid the body or the senses; one cannot simply ignore the transmissions. David Hume pushes this idea to a startling philosophical extreme: body and feeling come first, and rationality lags in a desperate attempt to impose sense.

For Hume, the gap between psychological phenomena and material reality comes not from a privileging of spirit, but rather from a foregrounding of the physical. Rationality is merely an attempt to make sense of sensation. A physical object creates an impression, which then produces ideas: 'two objects are connected by the relation of cause and effect when the one produces a motion or any action in the other . . . [or] when it has the power of producing it' (Hume 1739: 12).[10] However, his emphasis on materiality leads Hume to argue that cause and effect is essentially a story that we tell ourselves to make sense of our sensations.

If scientists truly embrace materialism, Hume argues, they can really only observe and measure the physical effects that we call 'feelings', not the psychological causes behind them. We can only know causes through inference. He writes that one can establish the existence of a cause only 'by an immediate perception of our memory or sense, or by an inference from other causes; which causes again we must ascertain in the same manner, either by a present impression, or by an inference from *their* causes, and so on, till we arrive at some object, which we see or remember' (82–3). In other words, consciousness enters in only after a physical stimulus, perception of the object, and response to the object have already completed. Reason merely projects causality in reverse on to chains of events. Because feelings are always feelings about physical objects, only objects can be causes. Arguments about cause and effect, Hume concludes, are simply connections we infer between our feelings and the objects around us (84). All memories, all senses of cause and effect, all conscious thoughts, begin first as materiality.

I will come back to Hume many times over the course of this book. But for this section of this chapter, what matters most is this idea that bodies perceive and act first, and then consciousness creates a reason after the fact. We should remember, of course, that Hume is talking about phenomenology here: what it feels like to be a perceiving body, what consciousness feels like. He is absolutely not talking about the nature of reality; in fact, elsewhere, he argues vociferously for the necessity that a cause temporally precedes its effects.[11] As a 'keen advocate of empirical science', Hume 'takes causal laws seriously' by necessity, for eighteenth-century science is nothing without empirically measurable correlations between cause and effect (Millican 2010: 614). Hume maintains that no 'rational' and 'modest' scientist would 'ever pretend to assign the ultimate cause of any natural operation, or to know distinctly the action of that power which produces any single effect in the universe' (Hume 1777: 26). Both the *Treatise* and the *Enquiry* challenge abstraction and the presumption of absolute knowledge.

But he is also what Stephen Buckle calls a 'sceptical materialist': material, objective reality exists, but reason lacks the capacity to accurately apprehend that reality. In more complex terms, reason 'responds to the exigencies of everyday circumstances, rather than to some overall *telos* of human life – to efficient rather than final causes' (Buckle 2007: 571–2). When combined, Hume's emphasis on materiality and his scepticism about rationality lead him to one of his most famous claims, that

> All the perceptions of the human mind resolve themselves into two distinct kinds ... IMPRESSIONS and IDEAS. The difference betwixt these consists in the degrees of force and liveliness with which they strike upon the mind, and make their way into our thought or consciousness. (Hume 1739: 1)

And between these two, impressions are the more forceful, the more lively. In fact, he argues in the *Enquiry* that simple ideas derive always from an impression; they are 'feeble perceptions' that merely 'cop[y] ... more lively' impressions (Hume 1777: 19). Materiality extends, bodies respond, and any gestures toward abstract Idealism are fantastic afterthought.[12]

Hume understands the causal relationship between materiality and the mind as a fiction that consciousness tells itself to make sense of a body it cannot comprehend. At the beginning of the nineteenth century, however, the science of sensation shifted to embrace the fictionality of this story. Where science previously understood language as an unbridgeable gorge between material and mind, the nineteenth-century Associationists asserted that language *is* the bridge.

Hartley, Stewart and the Poetics of Feeling

At the end of the eighteenth century, impressions and language agglomerate together as biological phenomena. In fact, the language of Associationist science became so standard for discussing both feeling and the way words affect bodies that, as this section will demonstrate, Wordsworth is a synecdoche for a moment where the science of feeling and poetics merge into a common discourse. There is a long-standing scholarly debate over the extent to which David Hartley influenced Wordsworth's criticism: from 1922, when Arthur Beatty argued that Hartley was the primary influence on Wordsworth, to 2001, when Alan Richardson argued that Wordsworth may not ever have read Hartley, to 2013, when Benjamin Kim once again took up the issue (see also Hayden 1984). I have no investment in either side. In fact, the very existence of the debate is the best evidence for my approach, for Associationism was so ubiquitous in the psychological theories of the eighteenth and nineteenth centuries that it is nigh on impossible to tell if Wordsworth read one particular book, or simply absorbed its terminology through popular discourse.

In 1749, David Hartley's *Observations on Man* turned Hume's philosophical ideas into a science of feeling. He argues that impressions manifest as 'vibrations', which travel through 'the Brain [the *medulla oblongata*, he later specifies] and spinal Marrow, along the Nerves' (Hartley 1749: 7). These vibrations emanate from objects, move the nerves, and move the brain. Hartley locates impressions in the body through the physical traces of object-driven perceptions, memories, feelings, sensations. Impressions make it possible to think about feeling as the internal, material manifestation of external stimuli, not an independent psychological phenomenon.

How scientists should talk about this physical manifestation of psychological phenomena is the core of Dugald Stewart's 1792 *Philosophy of the Human Mind*. Stewart is adjacent to, but not exactly in line with, the Associationist lineage from Hume to the Victorians. In fact, Stewart is in many ways the hinge on which this lineage turns. He emphasises materiality much like his Associationist counterparts: 'when an object is placed in a certain situation with respect to a particular organ of the body, a perception arises in the mind: when the object is removed, the perception ceases' (D. Stewart 1792: 80). But he breaks with Associationism proper precisely because of its tendencies to use analogical language to describe psychological phenomena. Importantly, he moves away from the animism that ascribes consciousness to objects *moving* the mind. Stewart berates those scientists (especially Hartley) who ascribe 'power, force, energy, and causation' to inanimate matter (74). In fact, he argues, these attributes seem reasonable only because scientists regularly use metaphors of causation to cover up gaps in their empirical knowledge.

But these scientists are not wholly at fault, he continues, for language itself reinforces these tendencies: particularly regarding scientific explanations for causes behind physical phenomena, 'language is merely analogical' (74). Even scientific language, which purports a degree of objectivity, creates meaning through metaphor. In Hartley, perception is social and caused by language, while sensation is personal and outside language (Ablow 2014: 682). Stewart objects to this bifurcation. Language, he concludes, 'has no essential connection with that process of the mind, which is properly called reasoning', because it describes the mind's attempt to make sense of its own processes (D. Stewart 1792: 178). Language is merely a mechanism to describe sensation and cognition to the mind sensing and cogitating. Science errs when it mistakes the analogy of language as evidence for anything other than a story the mind tells itself.

Stewart critiques Hartley's philosophy of mind because it ignores 'the ambiguity of words' and the limitations of language. Stewart summarises this perhaps ambiguous phrase most concisely in a footnote, where he writes that words 'signif[y] two things, a sensation in the mind, and the unknown quality which fits it to excite that sensation' (560). In other words, when one uses a word like 'happy', one really only describes the sensation of 'happiness' and the accompanying, unknown, material stimulus about which one feels 'happy'.

This theory extends beyond emotive words. To explain his theory of language, Stewart borrows an example from Thomas Reid's interpretation of Descartes: the smell of a rose. The word 'smell', Stewart argues, describes the rose's effect on the observer's mind – that is, when an observer sniffs a rose, conscious thought assigns 'smell' to the body's response. The conflation of cause and effect leads observers to attribute a certain smell to the rose, when in fact, the word describes a change in the observer and not a given quality of the rose.

And yet, he concludes, where the ambiguity of language challenges the science of mind, the power of literature depends entirely on its extra-linguistic effects. Poetry affords Stewart a particularly apt example, for in poetry, 'even when strung together in sentences which convey no meaning, [words] produce some effect on the mind of a reader of sensibility' (374). Literature proves language's inaccuracy precisely because semantically null language nevertheless causes bodily effects. If meaningless language produces physical effects, then sensation is both the origin of meaning and the only ascertainable meaning:

> the mind is so formed, that certain impressions produced on our organs of sense by external objects, are followed by correspondent sensations; and that these sensations, (which have no more resemblance to the qualities of matter, than the words of a language have to the things they denote,) are followed by a perception of the existence and qualities of the bodies by which the impressions are made; [and] that all the steps of this process are equally incomprehensible. (92)

Again, sensations do not provide knowledge about the material object that inspires them, but instead only impart a kind of 'incomprehensible' information about the mind's reaction to those objects.

Enter the Romantic poets. It is at this point that literature picks up the scientific question of feelings and seeks to make use of that knowledge (see especially Rauch 2001). William Wordsworth's 'Preface' to *Lyrical Ballads* is a literary criticism steeped in the materialist physiology of its day, one that synthesises Hartley's empiricism with Stewart's linguistics. When he claims that the 'principal object' of the poems is to 'trac[e] in them . . . the primary laws of our nature: chiefly as far as regards the manner in which we associate ideas in a state of excitement', the very least one can say is that he employs the language of the association of ideas (Wordsworth and Coleridge 1800: x). But his literary criticism offers more than verbal overlap, for association, emotion and language connect 'elementary feelings' through ordinary language (xi). When we arrive at the most quoted moment of the 'Preface' – 'poetry is the spontaneous overflow of powerful feelings' – we might consider what follows the proverb as something more invested in Associationist thought (xxxiii). He writes that 'our continued influxes of feeling are modified and directed by our thoughts, which are indeed the representatives of all our past feelings'. This passage feels particularly Hartleyan as it considers the relationship between material perception, impressions and their transmission. Through these representations, poets build up 'habits of mind' so acutely receptive to our natural impulses that they 'blindly and mechanically' (as in, the body's mechanics) can link 'objects' and 'sentiments' – with such power that they affect others (xxxiii–xxxiv). This sequence offers an Associationist dictionary, an index of critical concepts and terms that will occupy the rest of this book: the causal relationship between feeling and thought; representation; memory; habits of mind; mechanism; materiality and its ties to sensation. Whether Wordsworth is a Hartleyan or simply steeped in popular psychology, his analysis of poetry and its function is inarguably an engagement with the science of feeling.

Wordsworth's most interesting literary science lies in his fear that powerful words might inspire excessive emotion, for here, language becomes an actor rather than a mediator, capable of affecting bodies directly. Because poetry invokes objects and the sensation the poet derived from those objects, poetry evokes sensations in the reader. And 'if the words by which this excitement is produced are in themselves powerful ... there is a danger that the excitement may be carried beyond its proper bounds' (xxx). My primary interest here is not Wordsworth's prudishness, but rather, the notion that the words themselves can elicit feelings. As a materialist science, Associationism demands physical objects to inspire feeling; here, words become their own motive force, capable of transmitting not simply feeling but also the empirical impulse of objects and contexts. The poet is an Eolian Harp across which words play because Associationism (particularly Hartleyan Associationism) understands bodies as matter that is affected in a Spinozistic sense: that is, as matter that responds to the motive force of other objects. Wordsworth transforms language into a material stimulus with poets as the masters best attuned to their vibrations, and best able to transmit those bodily responses. Literary authority depends on affect.

Wordsworth's boundaries around excess emotion expanded in the mid-century to a split in literary culture. While both sides advocated reading as an ethical pedagogy, a way to improve oneself and one's interactions with others, literary scholarship diverged in how it understood that training. The advocates of the common scholar preserved a Wordsworthian sense of reading, wherein readers honed their ethics through memory. For Wordsworth, the 'powerful feelings' of poetry originate 'from emotion recollected in tranquillity'; through deliberate 'contemplation', these recollections become 'an emotion, similar to that which was before the subject of contemplation' (xxxiii–xxxiv). Most importantly, these emotions 'actually exist in the mind' – which is to say, ideas give way to feeling, which in turn produces a bodily change. Of course, this initially describes the author who is so central to Wordsworth's criticism, but the good poet 'communicate[s] to his Reader' those feelings he has conjured (xxxiv). Through memory, words evoke feelings, which then transmit bodily changes to the reader.

On the other hand, in response to the new, mass readership, academic literary scholarship sought to redefine reading – true reading – as a kind of specialised work. For Matthew Arnold, that work required readers to temper their emotions through the fires of the classics. Good intentions are insufficient for Arnold. It is not enough that one feel; one must feel correctly, and that proper feeling comes only through training. Crucially, Arnold pulls back from the material, so that good literature (in this case, poetry) 'attaches its emotion to the idea; the idea *is* the fact' (Arnold 1880: xvii). The labour of literary reading deals in ideas rather than sensations, and in universal human truths rather than materiality. While emotion remains the core of the best literature, to feel those emotions, one must be steeped in 'truth [philosophoteron] and seriousness [spoudaioteron]' – that is, in classical philosophy and scholarly earnestness.

The labour of reading directly opposes actual labour; it sets the literary, educated class apart from the merely literate working class. Arnold would probably have agreed with Wordsworth's articulation of the causal relationship between 'the encreasing accumulation of men in cities, where the uniformity of their occupations produces a craving for extraordinary incident which the rapid communication of intelligence hourly gratifies' on the one hand, and the rise of 'frantic novels, sickly and stupid German Tragedies, and deluges of idle and extravagant stories in [sentimental] verse' (Wordsworth and Coleridge 1800: xix). That is to say, urbanisation leads to sensation (read, poor) literature. This is quite ironic, since the Associationism that permeates his writing became the rallying standard for the advocates of popular literature. But, when the 'Preface' articulates the oft-repeated and hardly original denigration of the common reader, it signals a historical shift that only becomes more dramatic throughout the nineteenth century: the rise of popular literacy. David Mitch estimates that between 1700 and 1800, literacy rates were approximately 40 per cent for men and 25 per cent for women; by 1800, when Wordsworth published the 'Preface', those numbers had risen to 65 per cent for men and 45 per cent for women (Mitch 2004: 344). Those numbers would both reach over 90 per cent by the end of the nineteenth century. In short, an increasingly literate populace put new pressure on the specialness of ostensibly 'high' literature; where once the academy hardly needed to defend its boundaries, the ivory tower found itself beleaguered by abundant readers.

Looking back, the correlation between reading, emotion and science is unsurprising: in 1802, Wordsworth's theory of language is deeply invested in science. Despite his footnote that opposes science and poetry – a distinction others made more prominent through repeated emphasis in their readings of Wordsworth, like that of

J. S. Mill's 'Notes on Poetry' – Wordsworth sees space for coexistence. 'Poetry', he writes in a new section added in the 1802 Preface, 'is the impassioned expression which is in the countenance of all Science' (Wordsworth and Coleridge 1802: xxxvii).

We *should* be surprised, then, when in 1938 Cleanth Brooks and Robert Penn Warren claim in the preface to *Understanding Poetry* that 'scientific precision can be brought to bear only on certain kinds of material', for 'certain kinds of communication are not possible to scientific statement' – or in other words, that science has its boundaries, and those boundaries do not overlap with literature (Brooks and Warren 1938: xxxvii). Literature addresses 'such elusive matters as feelings and attitudes', while science deals only in 'absolute precision' (2). Between Wordsworth and the New Critics, something in the understanding of language shifted.

Alexander Bain's Material Language

That faultline lies between the Associationists and novelists who used their science to argue for feeling on the one hand, and academic hermeneutics on the other. For the Victorian Associationists, sensation becomes the *only* intelligible, ethical way of knowing.

Stewart's assault on Hartley had far-reaching effects on Associationism's theory of language, but perhaps in the opposite direction than he intended. Rather than shy away from ascribing causality to language, Victorian Associationists embraced the deconstruction of language's semantic power in favour of its sensational effects. In his 1889 *Logic*, Alexander Bain, the Victorian scientist who brought Associationism up to date in the mid-nineteenth century, articulates a theory of language indebted to Stewart:

> The two-sidedness of the phenomena [of mind] appears in language. The terms of mind had all an objective origin; and, while some of them have now an almost exclusively subjective meaning ... others have also an objective reference ... In these last, the language is ambiguous; we cannot always tell whether the physical or the mental is aimed at. (Bain 1889: 507)

Language, Bain goes on to argue, bridges the gap between the physical and the mental precisely through its ambiguity; because mental processes are indescribable, language accretes connotations and sensations around an experience, so that words might best approximate the feelings of mental experience. Associationism, in short, entangles language with sensation.

It is not quite accurate to say that, for Bain, language translates or conveys sensation to the mind. Rather, language is part of sensation. The physical object impresses the physical body through sensations, the conscious mind develops ideas about sensations – and language is the mechanism through which the mind understands sensation. Much like the eye is the organ of sight, language is the organ of impressions. Bain writes that

> recollections, thoughts, conceptions and imaginings are an inextricable mixture of language and ideas of things. The notions that we acquire through oral instruction, or from books, are made up in part by the subject matter purely, and in part by the phraseology that conveyed it . . . So in many sciences, there is a combination of visible or tangible notions with language. (Bain 1855: 552)

Combination is key, here, for sensation is rarely perception of a single order alone. Sight unites with touch, with internal states, and so on. The list at the beginning of Bain's argument is a list of ideas as opposed to sensations: recollections, thoughts, conceptions and imaginings. But because of Bain's materialism, each of these ideas both has a root in a past or present sensation and has the capacity to evoke new sensations. Rather than separating language from feeling, Bain understands it as 'the medium for indicating the things that are to be brought together' in the formation of complex sensations (590). The complexity of the sensorium requires links between perceptive organs, and between those perceptive organs and consciousness. To explain these associations, Bain's model of language functions as a kind of supersensory organ, 'not being confined to the articulate organs, but extending over the senses of hearing and sight' – and reciprocally, is 'influenced by the emotions' (465). Bain understands language as a kind of connective tissue, a mechanism that brings the senses together and unites them with consciousness.

Bain leaves open the possibility that all ideas are in fact physical. This is the most interesting and most important element of Bain's philosophy: that sensation also moves in the other direction to create physical perception from mere ideas. Language connects perceptions with one another, and then translates those perceptions into consciousness – in short, to link ideas with the physical. In the first edition of *Senses and Intellect*, published in 1855, Bain posits that

> The emotions and passions distinct from, but often accompanying sensations, are likewise similarly manifested in the reality and in the idea. Anger takes exactly the same course in the system whether it be at a person present or at some one remembered or imagined. (336)

Bain's attention to emotions' physical traces enables him to correlate a perceived body, a remembered body and an imagined body, because in all cases, the emotional effect plays out in the body perceiving, remembering or imagining. Coupled with his argument that language enables one to conceive original objects, this could well explain the force behind the emotions readers feel for imagined characters. Through this material linguistics,

> language that might otherwise be deemed figurative becomes literal. The imagination of visible objects is a process of seeing; the musician's imagination is hearing; the phantasies of the cook and the gourmand tickle the palate; the fear of a whipping actually makes the skin to tingle. (339)

One might well add, 'the suffering of the novelist's character plucks the strings of sympathy'. Language is a two-way, reciprocal loop: here, ideas become perceptions, which in turn create new ideas, which presumably create new perceptions, *ad infinitum*.

In the first edition of his work, Bain's theory of imagination explains how the mutually constitutive arrangement of perception and consciousness unfolds in fiction. But over the course of the second and third editions of his text, his argument narrows from a general principle to an ethical theory – a theory of altruism, of how one's concern for others can supersede self-interest. In the first edition, Bain opens the latter excerpt with an argument about 'the general doctrine now contended for' – the reciprocal relationship between mind and body, and the physical effects of imagination and memory. This doctrine 'helps us in some measure to localise *these processes*', a phrase which in the 1855 edition denotes the perception of imagined sensation. But the second edition, published in 1864, replaces the 'general doctrine' with a more specific reading of sympathy's effects on the relationship between the mind and the body. The 'general doctrine' becomes instead the claim that 'thoughts persist by a law that is not subject to the will', or in other words, that rationality is not the foundational law for social relations. Instead, 'the mere operation of will . . . is strictly within the limits of self-conservation' (Bain 1864: 350–1). Social relations built on rationality alone produce (one might say require) self-interested individuals. Sympathetic feelings, though, can 'interfere with the course of our actions and the pursuit of our interests' even and especially outside of self-conservation (350–1). Imagination's power over the will explains how 'an idea [can] act itself out' on the body – and ultimately, for Bain, 'explain[s] the great fact of our nature, denominated sympathy, fellow-feeling, pity, compassion, disinterestedness' (350). Sympathy exists in that nexus between imagined ideas and the physical perceptions they create – perceptions that can persist against and even override self-interest. And in this suspension of self-interest, the imagined entity becomes a training ground for sympathy.

This connection is most important for Victorian fiction because it suggests one can physically encounter an imaginary body. Bain argues that language is the 'greatest of all' mechanisms to 'conceive an object differing from any that we have ever known' (590). In *The Senses and the Intellect*, he first uses this claim to explore representation and its links to consciousness and memory. But the possibility that language might enable one literally to sense a body one has never encountered is particularly seductive for Victorian popular science and novelists – because if one can feel imagined bodies, one might be able to use literature to practise and hone sympathy.

David Masson, Charles Dickens and the Ontology of Feeling

In his description of how imagination might inspire direct physical sensation, Bain articulates a theory of fiction that makes literature into a possible training ground for sympathy. He argues that language has such power that 'our recollections of what we have gone through do not occur as pure ideas of the actions and scenes themselves, but as ideas mixed up with verbal descriptions, which last are constantly disposed to intrude themselves into our recollections' (Bain 1855: 447). Through this model of language, Associationism-inspired authors resist the mere representation of bodies, and instead emphasise language's capacity to cultivate empathy as the basis of literary value. Ideas (manifested through sense) here operate like a drive or motive force. Language generates sensations, and sparks physical action in response, so that words are the connective tissue that binds bodies to each other across time and space. He writes:

> We become possessed with the mere idea of pain, there being no reality corresponding; but yet this idea will induce us to act as if it represented

a reality of our own experience. To see another person hungry and cold is to take on the idea of those miseries, and we are induced by the power of the idea to relieve the pain that occasioned it. (Bain 1864: 350)

Language provides the medium for the mere idea of pain to persist and create actualities. And, *pace* twenty-first-century scepticism, when confronted with pain, the body cannot help but act. For

> the intellect, which can form ideas of the mental condition of other sensitive beings, urges us to make those ideas actualities, or to induce the conduct that they would suggest, if the pains or pleasures were personal to ourselves. This is sympathy and disinterested conduct, which is an undoubted fact of our nature. (350)

Victorian novelists, through this understanding of language, imagined self-reflexive readers for whom language is a sense, an embodied process, and in whom fiction inspired biological responses. Fiction uses readers' embodied experience of language to connect to their sensorium. According to this logic, novels matter because of the embodied feelings their characters' bodies evoke.[13]

With the professionalisation of literary studies and the increasing prominence of Associationism, the grounds for literary value shifted. While Realism or alignment with reason or artistry once bestowed value on a book, the mid-century turned toward valuing the intensity of feeling a text inspired, and the actions those feelings might inspire. To unpack this transformation, I turn to a figure who also served as a bridge between academic and professional literary criticism, David Masson. Masson's 1851 review of *David Copperfield* and Thackeray's *Pendennis* offers an ethics of fiction that sees language and sensation as intimately connected. Masson was, as Jack Downs has recently argued, a scholar trained in Scottish *belles lettres*.[14] As such, he should align with Thackeray's artistry and disparage Dickens's pedantry. As expected, all of Masson's evidence points toward Thackeray as the author more purely aligned with standards of literary value. And yet, in the end, he finds Dickens equally praiseworthy because of his text's tendency to evoke strong feeling. That his theory pre-dates the sensation novel calls attention to the longer history of British literary criticism's preoccupation with sensation.

Initially, Masson seems prepared to condemn Dickens for the common critique of writing unrealistic characters in contrived plots. Masson bases his reading on character-analysis, because 'it is by the originality and interest of its characters that a novel is chiefly judged'

(Masson 1851b: 76). He argues that Thackeray deserves praise because 'in almost all his . . . characters his study seems to be to give the good and the bad together, in very nearly the same proportions that the cunning apothecary, Nature herself, uses' (75). Thackeray's characters are more artistic because they appear analogous to people in the lived world. Dickens, on the other hand, creates characters who 'are real only thus far, that they are transcendental renderings of certain hints furnished by nature' (75). Masson here critiques Dickens on the traditional grounds of probability: it is improbable that people are as 'thoroughly and ideally detestable' as Fagin or Bill Sikes, or as 'thoroughly and purely perfect' as Oliver or Nancy. Dickens's 'habit of representing objects in an ideal light' rather than representing them as they are likely to exist in the lived world produces characters who embody philosophical abstractions rather than 'imitate Nature' (80). So, according to Masson, while Thackeray's writing is 'within the limits, and rigidly true to the features, of real existence', he argues that 'it is nonsense to say of [Dickens's] characters . . . that they are life-like' (74). According to Masson's traditional epistemology of literary value, Dickens is in every way the inferior author. Thackeray's characters are probable; one is likely to encounter an Arthur Pendennis or a Miss Amory in one's daily life. Dickens's characters are improbable; it is unlikely that there exists a preponderance of incorruptible, secretly wealthy orphans whose accents and moral fortitude resist the tarnish of the street.

And yet, Masson's conclusion turns sharply away from the expected judgement and validates sentiment as its own grounds for literary value. Masson writes that Dickens's work in the 1840s, from *The Old Curiosity Shop* to *David Copperfield*, 'aspir[es] after sentimental perfection' (80). With the notion of 'sentimental perfection' Masson introduces a new mode of evidence with which to measure the success of a novel. This aspiration epitomises what Masson calls 'the Ideal' style, which 'take[s] the mind out of itself into a region of higher possibilities, wherein objects shall be more glorious, and modes of action more transcendent, than any we see, *and yet all shall seem in nature*' (69–70, emphasis added). Here, the seeds of a new theory of literary value emerge. While Dickens's writing may not be probable, the feelings that his characters evoke are indeed natural.

Contrary to what Bain would write a decade later, Masson believes that nature is in fact the purview of the novelist, for the ethics of feeling is natural. Dickens's 'sentimental perfection' gives rise to what Masson calls a 'speculative ethics' that aims not to describe the world, but to describe the potential of human interactions through a series of feelings and relationships (81). To consider sensation as ethical – especially sensation from a novel – posits a new way of understanding popular literature and its value.

The 1851 review indicates a new trajectory in professional literary studies toward accepting sensation as a valid function of literature. This is part of a larger movement that simultaneously broadened which texts could count as literary, and which readers counted as literary readers. To read a Dickens novel, Masson suggests, is to explore the possibilities of emotion. Masson later writes that Dickens composes novels in which competing ideals come together to ask:

> What can be made out of this [novel]; with what human conclusions, ends, and aspirations can it be imaginatively interwoven, so that the whole, though attached to nature by its origin, shall transcend or overlie nature on the side of the possibly existent – the might, could, or should be . . .? (Masson 1859: 251)

It is not at all surprising to read a Victorian thinker who claims that novel reading and writing are moral or ethical issues, but it is important to recognise the frequency with which the ethics of novel reading and writing is bound up in the discourse of Associationism.[15] Masson says that a good author

> lays the foundation of his work in the region of the familiar and the real, [so that novels'] highest pinnacles reach into a brighter and purer region . . . whence those who ascend may look down with a strengthened vision upon the extended prospect of the familiar and the real. (214)

The truth of fiction here lies in its ability to illuminate the physical. Dickens himself offers a similar philosophy in his preface to the second edition of *Oliver Twist*: 'It is useless to discuss whether the conduct and character of [Nancy] seems natural or unnatural, probable or improbable . . . IT IS TRUE' (Dickens 1840: xi). This truth lies not in the closeness of Nancy to probability, but instead, in the impressions Nancy transmits. The value of a text lies in the reader's own sensations.[16]

These ethical theories of sensation emerged hand-in-hand with scientific ethics of feeling. Because of their investment in both philosophy and empirical science, the rhetoric of Associationist scientists readily slides from scientific description to ethical exhortation. They begin with a subject who encounters a physical object through a drive for physical pleasure or the avoidance of physical pain. But these base sentiments quickly accrete previous experiences, objects and relationships, so that the observer can understand the initial encounter through a broader if not universal framework. Crucially, this 'understanding' is an embodied, intuitive, emotional understanding, rather than a mere rationalisation. The embodied scientist builds relationships between objects and people, and empathises with the feelings of others without the taint of his own ignoble desires.

This ethical prioritisation of feeling is not simply resonant with the language of Associationism; it is built on Associationism, particularly theories of impressions. Ultimately, impressions matter more than any explicit articulation of a philosophy, Masson argues, for

> The moral effect of a novel or poem . . . lies not so much in any specific proposition that can be extracted out of it as its essence, and appended to it in the shape of an ethical summary, as in the whole power of the work in all its parts to stir and instruct the mind, in the entire worth of the thoughts which it suggests, and in the number and intensity of the impressions which it leaves. (Masson 1859: 118)[17]

In this framework, the novel is a series of impressions designed to evoke feelings and thoughts that lead to ethical improvement – and that improvement is the source of literary authority. The Associationists and the Victorian authors who make use of their science reject metaphor as poor science and poor literature. In both fields, bodies must not be symbolic, metaphoric, representational; they must be bodies.

The rest of this book takes up that exhortation as a challenge: can we, as literary scholars, think about bodies without resorting to metaphor? For example, William Cohen writes that 'Giving palpable form to affects by representing them in terms of bodily sensation addresses a basic problem of representation . . . namely, how to convey and evoke states of being in the metaphorical terms of feeling' (Cohen 2009: 6).[18] But as this chapter has shown, the Associationists strive to explore feeling in decisively *non*-metaphoric terms.[19] And so, rather than explore what metaphors (or representations or symbols) a body conjures, this book aims to look at the body itself. To utter a shrill yell is not a metaphor for speaking the subject into existence or failing to do so; nor is it a representation of fear. A bodily expression of a feeling is neither metaphor nor sign; it is the feeling itself.

Notes

1. This wording is from the 1802 second edition. The language of the first edition is not quite as precise in its critique of metaphor.

2. For a recent study of the sweeping influence of metaphor in natural philosophy, see Ian Duncan's discussion of Kant and Herder's debate over analogy and metaphor in *Human Forms* (Duncan 2019: 34, 49–50).
3. In his 2017 article 'Does Grandcourt Exist?', David Sweeney Coombs argues for the importance of John Grote's 1865 *Exploratio Philosophica* in the conversation about how we know bodies and fictional characters. Grote makes a distinction between 'the sensory/pictorial "knowledge by acquaintance"' and 'the logical/verbal "knowledge about"' (Coombs 2017: 391). Later thinkers like G. H. Lewes picked up this distinction to develop their theories of language.
4. Sense-making comes from the work of Giovanna Colombetti's *The Feeling Body*, in which she contends that bodies 'inhabit a world that is significant for them', and that 'even the simplest living systems have a capacity to be sensitive to what matters to them' (Colombetti 2014: 2). This constitutes 'primordial affectivity', a baseline embodiment deeper than cognition and emotion (82). Colombetti's book paradigmatically shifted my work in ways that are difficult to cite parenthetically.
5. This opposition is central to the chapter 'Knowing and Acknowledging' from *Must We Mean What We Say?* (Cavell 2002: 257). For Cavell's extensive relationship with literature, see his *Disowning Knowledge* (2003), Colin Davis's chapter on Cavell in *Critical Excess* (2010), and David Rudrum's *Stanley Cavell and the Claim of Literature* (2013), as well as Andrew Miller's work with Cavell in *The Burdens of Perfection* (2008).
6. John Mayor's opening to his article on 'Latin-English Lexicography' promises that the science of language will place a key in the hands of its practitioners, a key 'which will open ways long barred up by hopeless difficulties and seeming contradictions', and that the key of language 'fits so many locks', those who wield it should 'believe that it is a master-key' (Mayor 1855: 273; see Pratt and Neufeldt 1979: xlvi). Nuttall also suggests Jacob Bryant's *New System* (1774–6), along with several other books written after 1832, including Henry James Summer Maine's *Ancient Law* (1861) and George Grote's *History of Greece* (1846–56). Mark Pattison, who wrote a biography of the sixteenth-century scholar Isaac Casaubon, has also been posited as an inspiration for Casaubon.
7. Tertius Lydgate of *Middlemarch* replicates this mode of embodiment. Alan Mintz writes that 'independence, as Lydgate understands it, means aloofness and disdain – even exploitation – of others who would tamper with the solitary generativity of the self' (Mintz 1978: 91). Charles Dickens's Silas Wegg (*Our Mutual Friend*) and Pickwick (*The Pickwick Papers*) fall handily into this trope as well.
8. Ian Duncan argues that Robert William Mackay's 1850 *Progress of the Intellect* 'marks a midpoint in the Victorian uncoupling of mythology from doctrinal allegory' (Duncan 2019: 179). Mackay would have agreed with Müller, for he writes that when 'symbols ... usurp an

independent character as truths and persons', people 'mistake a sign for the thing signified, [and fall] into a ridiculous superstition' (cited in Duncan 2019: 180).
9. George Levine writes that Thomas Carlyle's struggle with undiagnosed stomach pain led him to reject materialism in an attempt to escape his body (G. Levine 2002: 82). I would counter with the emotionally if not theoretically compelling evidence of personal experience that one cannot reject or escape a chronically sick body, a body that rebels. Materiality interjects and interrupts intellectual attempts to reason oneself out of embodiment. As I hope this book demonstrates, the hospital bed is an ill-suited site to develop a disembodied philosophy.
10. I take most of my citations intentionally from the *Treatise*. Usually, a more materialist, sceptical position turns to the *Enquiry* as a more mature version of Hume's philosophy. I have tried to stick with the *Treatise* as much as possible to suggest that Hume's materialism and scepticism of rationality persist through his early work.
11. Fierce debate rages over whether Hume is an idealist, a causal realist, a determinist or a materialist (or if indeed those conflict, as Peter Millican argues regarding the last three of these categories in 'Hume's Determinism' (2010)), and how deep his scepticism goes. See Michael Costa's 'Hume's Argument for the Temporal Priority of Cause over Effect' (1986) for a foundational 'Old Hume' style reading. See also John P. Wright's 'Hume's Causal Realism: Recovering a Traditional Interpretation' and Edward Craig's 'Hume on Causality: Projectivist *and* Realist?' in *The New Hume Debate* (2000).
12. Catherine Wilson (2016) calls this 'vital materialism', a term that resonates with the project of the late-nineteenth-century scientists who occupy much of Chapter 4. The paradox between objective reality (materialism) and subjective perception (vitality) is an obsession of Franklin Blake in Wilkie Collins's *The Moonstone*, as well as of his contemporaneous scientists like Thomas Huxley and William Benjamin Carpenter.
13. This book is not particularly invested in a theory of Realism, but it is adjacent to these conversations. As an emergent genre alongside an emergent field of scholarship, Realist novels offer a primer on how to read characters in Realist novels. Theorists of language as text recognise this self-reflection as a kind of control – a control not entirely benevolent, as John R. Reed argues, for Dickens 'wanted both to assist his readers in interpreting [novels] correctly and to retain control of the mode of that interpretation' (Reed 2006: 15). Fiction affirms this paradox: the language of realism can only ever represent, but it must disavow that representation to perform the moral work of describing reality as it truly is. In her 2016 *The Victorian Novel Dreams of the Real*, Audrey Jaffe explores how Victorian novels' desperately self-validating epistemology pervades even the theoretical apparatuses we use to analyse those novels. She argues that Realist novels, as a Victorian

genre, 'represent not the real but the desire for it, and in doing so render it desirable for readers as well' (Jaffe 2016: 5). In other words, Realism is not about mimesis or an accurate representation of reality; rather, it seeks to produce a desire for 'accurate' representations of reality – for itself. See Greiner 2012, Coombs 2019 and Duncan 2019 for more recent work on the subject.

14. See Jack Downs's 'David Masson, *Belles Lettres*, and a Victorian Theory of the Novel' for more on Masson's impact on Victorian literary theories and the influence of Hugh Blair's *belles lettres* theories from his *Lectures* on Masson's work. While I agree with Downs when he argues that Masson would adhere to Blair's belief that 'artistry should never be sacrificed to the message' (Downs 2015: 8), his reading of this particular review (a single paragraph) forces Masson's work on Dickens and Thackeray to adhere to a formulaic structure (propriety, taste and sublimity) without confronting this review's surprising resolution of the latent tension between *belles lettres* and sentiment.

15. See Alan Rauch's *Useful Knowledge*, where he uses a history of science to offer historically innovative readings of knowledge production as 'a morally responsible activity' (Rauch 2001: 2).

16. Patrick Brantlinger argues that 'the sensation novels of Collins, Braddon, Wood, Reade, and others all start from the assumption that empiricism and its corollary, fictional realism, are inevitable, hegemonic, the only sensible, accurate way to understand and portray the world' (Brantlinger 1998: 146). As I have shown, however, the basis for empiricism and Reality depends not on objective reality, but on an ontology of sensation. 'Novels are not science', George Levine notes, 'but both incorporate the fundamental notions of the real that dominate the culture' (G. Levine 1992: 13) – and the fundamental notions of the real that dominated mid-Victorian literary culture were Associationist.

17. Jonathan Farina's 'On David Masson's *British Novelists and their Styles* (1859) and the Establishment of Novels as an Object of Academic Study' links Masson's claim here to Walter Pater's conclusion in *The Renaissance*, which gives the ethical charge 'to be for ever curiously testing new opinions and courting new impressions' (Pater 1888: 250).

18. I want to acknowledge the depths of my debt to Cohen and *Embodied*. Even though this book ultimately moved in a different direction, Cohen's work was central in early drafts.

19. Ian Duncan's *Human Forms* (2019) provides an impressive array of primary sources (eighteenth- and nineteenth-century) in the debate over whether metaphor is a fundamental element of human cognition (as Herder argues) or an error (as Kant and Darwin argue).

Chapter 2

Symbolic Bodies: The Storyteller, Memory and Suffering in Boz's 'The Hospital Patient'

In the Introduction, I aligned the Associationists and the twenty-first-century turn to surface reading. But I also argued that we cannot separate Associationism's linguistics, science or ethical mandate from one another. Surface reading and the loose collection of scholars engaged in that exploration, on the other hand, often find empathy is no longer a sufficient motivator, and reading no longer a promise of social improvement. Best and Marcus write:

> Where it had become common for literary scholars to equate their work with political activism, the disasters and triumphs of the last decade have shown that literary criticism alone is not sufficient to effect change. (Best and Marcus 2009: 2)

Regardless of where one stands on this particular question, the rejection of empathy or social change as the purpose of reading is a crucial departure from the Victorian schema. Surface reading eschews the authority of the scholarly interpreter, but it also often rejects the ethical project of the populist Victorian novelists. This is because its scholars have become sceptical of the paranoid reading that sees political ghosts beneath the surface.

The authors that I examine, however, would not see politics as a hermeneutic domain; rather, they would see it as feeling, as surface. The Associationist understanding of affect and literary authority had explicitly political implications for the Victorians. Because language is a physical process, characters' bodies and emotions can effect changes in readers' bodies. The point of literature according to these writers was to create embodied connection on a personal level, and thereby to cultivate the feelings required for social reform.

For this to be true, readers needed to connect to characters emotionally and physically so that they might hone their compassion for bodies in the lived world. To fulfil this project, these authors understood language as fundamentally embodied, and condemned hermeneutic reading because it reduced fictional bodies to mere representations or metaphors. Because scholarly reading understood language as a merely logical system, these authors suggest, it evacuates fictional bodies of their emotive power.

The scholars of the last chapter performed disembodiment and assumed it granted them a kind of academic disinterest. Victorian liberalism, Amanda Anderson's foundational argument informs us, saw disinterestedness as a crucial step in cultivating one's own morality and ultimately in improving the world around oneself (Anderson 2001). In an incisive intervention into the discourse of the hardworking Victorian liberal, Elisha Cohn's brilliant *Still Life* (2016) looks particularly at moments in novels where characters leave off – leave off labour, or politics, or attention. She recovers 'states of passivity, stillness, and inaction as quiet avowals of art's non-transformative fascinations', as rejections of perfection as an end (Cohn 2016: 6). Instead, Cohn sees 'Victorian liberalism [as] an aesthetic framework insofar as it values process – the renewable effort of engagement, deliberation, and responsiveness – over achieved perfection' (8). Reverie raises the spectre of ambivalence and rejects the need for constant improvement.

Associationism adds to Cohn's argument the possibility that reverie gives up perfection in the hopes of giving up self-interest – and instead giving space to attend to others. If we understand language and affect as wholly embodied, then moments of distraction and inattention – moments of self-suspension – are crucial to cultivate a politics of empathy. Reading bodies can eliminate their inclinations to interpret, to know and solve, and instead attend to the feelings of others. Rational disinterestedness, emotional investment and neutral stillness move together toward embodied connection that eliminates barriers between self and others.

Fictions

In February of 1836, Victorian publisher John Macrone released a collection of short stories by the mysterious 'Boz'. Boz had been popular since his stories began in 1833 – though his name had not appeared until 1834 – but it was also well known that he was a pseudonym, a fictional character overlayed on top of an unknown, physical body.

Fictional though he may be, Boz was 'a close and acute observer of character and manners' as they actually were (Hogarth, quoted in Schlicke 1999: 546). A reviewer in *The Examiner* wrote that Boz 'shows his strength in bringing out the meaning and interest of objects which would altogether escape the observation of ordinary minds' ('Sketches' 1836: 132). Boz's attention to material detail allowed him to fulfil his mission: to present pictures of life as it was.

The book was a success. So successful, in fact, 'Boz' was able to sell his name and copyright to another publisher, the *Carlton Chronicle and National Conservative Journal* (Patten 2012: 32). A fictional narrator, made real by his observation, fictionalised again as intellectual property – and then again suddenly made flesh. One week before his first short story appeared in the *Carlton Chronicle*, an advertisement for the second edition of the *Sketches* revealed Charles Dickens as the author behind 'Boz'. This chapter will use that oscillation between physicality and fictionality to collapse that distinction altogether.

As far as we know, the *Carlton Chronicle* only published two of Dickens's 'Boz' stories. This chapter is dedicated to the first of these, 'The Hospital Patient', which appeared on 6 August 1836. The history of Boz mirrors one of the sketch's primary concerns: the relationship between living bodies like Dickens and fictional bodies like Boz.

Specifically, Boz uses Associationism's materialist understanding of language and affect to explore what it means to feel for fictional characters. In a mere 1,500 or so words, Boz asks philosophical questions about sympathy/empathy (more on that distinction later), and then answers these questions through his own practice of memory and storytelling. He begins on the streets, where the reflection of light in a window reminds him of candlelight in hospital windows. These windows then bring him to the streets around the hospital, where he considers the mass of poor and sick bodies as they suffer around him. These initial experiences remind him of a court case in which he follows the magistrates to the bedside of the titular Hospital Patient. She is the victim of domestic abuse, and the magistrates (with Boz in tow) bring her abuser to the hospital for a deposition. Boz watches their brief exchange, and then the Hospital Patient dies. The flurry of memories, imaginings and generalisations is, in a word, associative: from streetlights to windows, from windows to hospitals, from hospitals to the street, from the street to the court, from the court back to the hospital. Association enables Boz to bridge the gap between different kinds of materiality: between imagined bodies, fictional bodies, remembered bodies and living bodies.

Throughout 'The Hospital Patient', Boz confronts the question: can readers feel empathy for fictional characters, and what can readers do with that empathy?[1] Or, as Boz puts it:

> Who can tell the anguish of those weary hours, when the only sound the sick man hears, is the disjointed wanderings of some feverish slumberer near him, the low moan of pain, or perhaps the muttered, long-forgotten prayer of a dying man? (Dickens 1837: 134)

This question is more than coincidentally resonant with Adam Smith's own inquiry: 'what are the pangs of a mother when she hears the moanings of her infant that during the agony of disease cannot express what it feels?' (Smith 1759: 10). The problem is the same: can we really know the pain of others? How can a person feel the suffering of the bodies around them? Even outside the usual philosophical quandaries of sympathy – how does one know what another body feels? – an increasingly urban London builds further barriers between bodies. Dense populations turn neighbours into strangers; government oversight of medicine quarantines the sick from the well; the physical walls of the hospital loom up between Boz and the bodies with whom he wants to sympathise. If he can connect fictional and living bodies, Boz can use narrative to cultivate an ethics of care.

Boz strives desperately to connect with suffering bodies. But rather than answer his first question, he offers a follow-up question. This second move simultaneously insists on the barriers between the reader and the occupants of the hospital, and suggests a means of permeating those boundaries. Who can tell the anguish?

> Who, but those who have felt it, can imagine the sense of loneliness and isolation which must be the portion of those who in the hour of dangerous illness are left to be tended by strangers; for what hands, be they ever so gentle, can wipe the clammy brow, or smooth the restless bed, like those of mother, wife, or child? (Dickens 1837: 134)

The most important part of this sentence is the opening phrase: 'Who but those who have felt it can imagine'. In one vein, it suggests that bodily resonance comes only from experience, that only those who have previously known this kind of pain can understand how the hospital patients feel.

Alternatively, the phrase suggests that sensations can, in fact, translate from one body to another. Perhaps one has not felt the pain of the hospital patient, but one has felt pain. And if one reads about similar pain, one can follow the impressions to the material origin – provided that the bodies in the text are material. Characters must be bodies overflowing with material specificity, rather than fictional tropes intended to stand in for a general class of bodies like 'the London poor' or what I will call 'symbolic bodies'. According to the genealogy of Associationism I will trace here, the ethical reader and writer must reject symbolism and generalities. Fleshed-out characters transform reading about suffering into practice for material encounters. Associationism's materialism turns fictional suffering bodies not into memories, symbols or abstractions, but into bodies.

Boz's narrative poses an ethical challenge, and this challenge is particularly interested in reading: when you read, can you imagine the pain? Can you, reader, tell the anguish? To address this question of literary authority, Boz turns to bodies imagined and remembered. And therein lies the Associationist intervention into fiction: while imaginations and memories are not obviously physical, they nevertheless inspire physical sensations. So, too, does fiction – and by the same mechanism that narrows from general impressions to specific memories and, finally, to particular bodies.

According to Boz, to 'tell' – both to narrate and to understand – the anguish of those who suffer, one must read with the scientific and literary attention that turns stories into material experience. Boz appears as storyteller and Associationist scientist, but both positions require him to act on feeling. The story itself becomes a model for readers, to teach them to read empathetically – because he believes feeling is the source of literary authority. Early Victorian fiction understands itself as a mediator between readers, fictional bodies and other bodies in the lived world. Empathy makes this mediation ethical. To read is to feel; to feel is to empathise; and empathy is an ethical act that can produce social change.

Optics

Of course, none of the bodies Boz encounters or remembers are living bodies, because Boz is not a living body. But as the publication history of 'The Hospital Patient' reminds us, Boz's body is tied to a living body, and has a kind of materiality that differs from fictional characters who are only characters and not also storytellers. Boz sits somewhere between reality and fiction, between materiality and immateriality.

Abstract as Boz's *who can tell?* challenge may be, he precedes it with an example of this strange, dialectical im/materiality: the light in the window of the hospital. The hospital presents the problem. Boz's ethical answer begins with windows, reflections and the impressions they make possible. The sketch begins:

> In our rambles through the streets of London after evening has set in, we have often paused beneath the windows of some public hospital, and pictured to ourself the gloomy and mournful scenes that were passing within. The sudden moving of a taper as its feeble ray shot from window after window, until its light gradually disappeared, as if it were carried further back into the room to the bedside of some suffering patient, has been enough to awaken a whole crowd of reflections. (Dickens 1837: 133)

The trajectory of the sentence itself moves from the material to the symbolic: he moves from the streets, to the light in windows, to an imagined, generalised 'suffering patient'. These imaginations begin Boz's journey back to the material.

But the relationship between materiality and imagined ideas is not a simple equivalence. The light that instigates this sentence emphasises the paradoxical materiality and immateriality of imagined impressions. Its 'sudden movement' as it 'sho[ots] from window after window' imbues it with the energy of association that moves from one material object to the next – but the light is not exactly material. Light itself is empirically observable, but is not as tactile as a hospital wall. It is likely that, by 1836, Dickens and his readers would have subscribed to a wave theory of light; while in the mid-1820s the particle/wave debate leaned heavily toward particles, the work of D. F. J. Fresnel in France – and in England by John Herschel – was so pervasive that by 'the 1830s, optical theory became very nearly synonymous with ether dynamics' and its associated wave theory (Buchwald 1989: 308). Light offers the first of Boz's paradoxically material and immaterial objects: it is an empirical, physical phenomenon, but one that carries more affinity with energy than matter. Moreover, it is observable primarily through its effects on the ether, rather than for its own properties. Victorian theories of optics offer a productive analogy to consider fiction as a kind of materiality, physical but elusive, easier to track through its effects rather than its own properties.

Optics helps us to get at a core question of reading and empathy: can one empathise with a body that is not on the same level of materiality as oneself? Can a reader really empathise with a character, whose body is (hypothetically) a different kind of material? And can empathy for characters be translated back to living bodies? Light, like Boz's dialectical existence as fiction and living body, is a small-scale example of these larger Associationist questions. Psychological phenomena like memory, for example, have material origins in the brain and body, but do not literally summon the objects remembered. More importantly, the novelists in conversation with Associationism interrogate the equivalence between knowing about bodies' exteriors – their physical, material substances – on the one hand, and knowing bodies' interior feelings and thoughts more essentially.

This amounts to an interrogation of how much one can know another person's body. To choose exactly which word best communicates the idea of these connections is a semantic game that is now part of the genre of studies in empathy.[2] I have opted to refer to these connections as 'empathy', distinct from the options 'sympathy' or 'fellow-feeling'. The word 'empathy' is an anachronistic term, for it was not until 1909 that Edward Titchener introduced the word as a translation for the German *Einfühlung*, a word which was first used in Robert Vischer's 1873 *On the Optical Sense of Form*. But the distinction I want to draw between these two is that where 'sympathy' connotes a rational process by which one imagines what the other might feel by mentally placing oneself in a similar, hypothetical situation, empathy is a preconscious response to others' feelings that occurs on and within bodies at the level of affect.

Admittedly, the connections that appear in 'The Hospital Patient' begin with something like Smithean sympathy. Smith sets up sympathy as an effect of sensory limitation, for because our senses 'never did and never can carry us beyond our own persons', we therefore 'have no immediate experience of what other men feel' (Smith 1759: 2). This hard line distinguishes Smithean sympathy from the kinds of empathy that concern materialists. For Smith, any resonance between bodies must of necessity begin with observation and speculation. Faced with this limitation, Smith then offers a most compelling claim: through imagination, 'we enter as it were into his body and become in some measure him, and thence form some idea of his sensations, and even feel something which, though weaker in degree, is not altogether unlike them' (2–3). Imagination here is a sort of pseudo-sense, but it is always bound to sight.[3] This is why Smith's sympathiser is first and foremost a 'spectator' (6). Observation allows one to then imagine what one would feel in the other's situation (2, 10). This kind of sympathy is 'a highly abstract operation [ultimately meant] for producing fellow-feeling', as Rae Greiner puts it (Greiner 2012: 16). The spectator observes a passion, then considers 'the situation which excites it', and finally imagines how that situation and passion would make the spectator feel (Smith 1759: 9). The sensory limitation – that we cannot feel what the other feels – is somewhat ameliorated by sight and self-reflection.

Smithean sympathy is not Boz's ultimate goal, however, for while he begins with symbols and decoding, he wants to end with a more material connection – specifically, with a body he cannot see. Greiner defines sympathy as an 'operation of mind, fundamentally a cognitive process' which one uses to 'imagine and (sometimes) produce feelings' (Greiner 2012: 16). In short, sympathy is mental – a mechanism of knowledge. Even as Smith insists that sympathy is always embodied, it ultimately '"does away" with bodies in order to produce representations', Audrey Jaffe argues (Jaffe 2000: 11). Subsuming living bodies into mere representations is the worst possible outcome in fiction, according to Dickens and his contemporaries. An incredibly unfavourable review of the *Sketches* begins:

> Writers who attempt this style of representation, however much they may desire to abide by reality, ever find, that unless they call in the aid of imagination, both to dispose of facts and real scenes in a picturesque order, and to colour these with strikingly contrasted tints, they fail in producing anything that is at all equal with the effect experienced by their own sensibilities when eye-witnesses of such realities. ('Review' 1836: 350)

In other words, the paradox of real-life sketch writing is that while Boz desires to depict life as it is, to transmit the feeling of being immersed in a real situation requires fanciful exaggeration. To replace bodies with general symbols is the modus operandi of the common sketch writer and the Smithean spectator. To make readers feel the suffering of the bodies around them, according to both Jaffe and the *Monthly Review* writer, the author 'replac[es] persons with mental pictures, generalised images of ease and suffering' (Jaffe 2000: 11). 'The Hospital Patient' attempts to work in the opposite direction: to move from the general to the particular, to move away from sight and into something more immediately corporeal.

This is why I find 'empathy' a more accurate term to describe the connection between bodies that the Associationists advocate: its origin, the German neologism *Einfühlung*, is literally to feel-into.[4] This connection owes much to one of Hume's understandings of sympathy, which is more directly embodied.[5] Hume's use of the word 'sympathy' is slippery and multifaceted, but at times he refers to something like emotional contagion.[6] He writes that 'the minds of men are mirrors to one another, not only because they reflect each other's emotions, but also because those rays of passions, sentiments and opinions may be often reverberated, and may decay away by insensible degrees' (Hume 1739: 365). The most crucial part of this passage is that the relationship here is non-linear, for each body affects the other, and the effects that they exchange also impact their bodies.

Here is where Hume's deconstruction of causality intersects with affect theory – and with the ethics of reading. In contradistinction to Smith's solipsistic model that insists that observers feel and understand their own passions, and then apply them to others, Hume suggests that 'we are only sensible of [passions'] causes or effects' rather than their essence (576). Rather than coming from knowledge of the feeling in ourselves, empathy derives from the relationship between these causes and effects; the resonance between bodily effects 'forms such a lively idea of the passions, as is presently converted into the passion itself' (576). Ultimately, because passions are material rather than abstractly essential, 'all the affections pass from one person to another' through a kind of bodily resonance (576).[7] In short, this sympathy is a recursive network of affect. This is why he can argue that 'the passions are . . . contagious' (603), for unlike Smith's model of sympathy in which the feeling arises from the mind of the observer alone, this kind of sympathy is ultimately epigenetic; that is, it emanates from the relationship between two bodies, rather than from a single source or immediately traceable etiology.[8] And most importantly, it is traceable only in its effects. Whether the body that begins the feelings is fictional, imagined or remembered, its effects are physiologically similar. Phenomenologically, the affective response to these bodies renders irrelevant the question of if readers really can empathise, because readers do.

'The Hospital Patient' seeks to answer the problem of Smithean sympathy – that we cannot, in fact, feel what the other feels – through an Associationist model of memory and imagination. Humean sympathy suggests the solution to this problem is to move beyond seeing bodies as symbols and instead to feel them as matter.[9] This project is ultimately ethical, for, to borrow James Martineau's language, 'The Hospital Patient' explores, step by step, the transition from self-regard to self-identification with others.

Walls

Imagine a hospital.

Specifically, imagine your hospital, the one you would go to if the need arose. Picture the building, the way that it shapes the geography around it.

The hospital, as both a geographic location and an institution, exerts what I think of as an intense 'affective gravity': an effect that warps and pulls and realigns affects around it. Much like extreme astronomical density bends space-time, the institutional density of a hospital moulds the affective fabric of the populace around it. 'Take me to the hospital' is an affect qualitatively different from calling a healer to your home or addressing an ailment by yourself or within your household. It absorbs bodies in a way particular to the hospital; it treats those bodies in a manner particular to the hospital. The hospital draws all injury-related affects toward itself with its gravity, and shapes the bodies of both the suffering and those who would sympathise with them.

This is why, after his philosophical preamble, Boz begins his narrative with barriers: 'In our rambles through the streets of London after evening has set in, we have often paused beneath the windows of some public hospital, and pictured to ourself the gloomy and mournful scenes that were passing within' (Dickens 1837: 133). The descriptor 'some public hospital' universalises the experience at a basic level, perhaps. But universality does not yield relatability in this case, for the gloomy and mournful scenes within are doubly removed: once because they are within the hospital, and twice because they are not even within a particular hospital. This kind of attention to the hospital as a discursive and physical wall between the public and suffering bodies initiates a motif in which Boz encounters something that prevents bodies from being fully material, and must confront the barriers' permeability and impermeability.

The hospital impedes Boz's desire to identify with the well-being of others, for it closes off those whose suffering is perhaps most evident. As much as it is a site of suffering, 'some public hospital' also firmly ensconced that suffering within discursive and legal control that reached a new zenith in the 1830s. Increasing state standardisation of medicine in the 1830s discursively cordoned off the suffering bodies within the hospital as solidly as physical architecture bars them from Boz's view. The report from the Select Committee on Medical Education, published in the *London and Westminster*

Review in 1836, demonstrates rising state control over both medical standards and medical knowledge as a discourse. The Legislature's memo acknowledges that 'it is in the interest of every individual in the community that every medical practitioner should be in possession of [the] minimum of knowledge' required to practise medicine (T. Smith 1836: 59). To ensure this minimum of knowledge, medicine must fall under the purview of the state, for the Legislature also declares the common citizen 'incapable of detecting ignorance and imposture' and thus 'in need of the protection of the Legislature' (59). To protect the public from its own ignorance, the Legislature declares that the state '*can* regulate, with the utmost ease and completeness, everything relating to medical education' (59, emphasis original). Because the public lacks the capacity to detect medical practitioners' ignorance, the state must intervene. Regulation complicates the struggle to know the suffering of the bodies within the hospital beyond the mere philosophical inaccessibility of the other, for 'to know' requires a specialised school of state-authorised knowledge.[10]

The hospital's barriers are physical as well as discursive, for the hospital is not a mere metaphor; it is a material presence. Even as growing governmental attention to the medical profession minimised access to medical knowledge, the hospital as a physical building expanded in both size and prominence in the public conception of the geography of London. The Charing Cross Hospital, reborn in 1834 from the former Royal West London Infirmary, sat in what the Edwardian historian J. Holden Macmichael charmingly called 'a series of the most awful slums, swarming with the wrack of Modern Babylon' (Macmichael 1906: 139). The Charing Cross site expanded its patient capacity to serve triple the patients it had seen at its previous site. In 1821, at its site in Villiers Street, Charing Cross saw some 10,000 patients (Minney 1967: 21); in 1834, after its expansion, the hospital saw some 30,000 'poor sick persons', and saw 'sometimes as many as eight' accidents every day (Macmichael 1906: 139). Charing Cross's expansion was part of a broader trend of medical expansion – geographically, legislatively and discursively – in the early nineteenth century. As part of this increased presence in the geographic imagination of the public, the edifice of 'some' public hospital in Boz's sketch redefines the physical space of the street and the bodies around it. The material presence of hospitals manifested legislative walls that further occluded 'poor sick persons' from the common reader. Medicine emerged as a field of knowledge simultaneously present in the public geographic space but distinctly separate from public reach.

The desire to feel the suffering of others, and to surmount the material and metaphysical barriers that prevent empathy, lies at the heart of 'The Hospital Patient'. Imagination offers one of the means to circumvent those barriers. In fact, the disjointed and ambling structure of the narrative suggests that the primary narrative is not about the Hospital Patient but is in fact about Boz and his relationship to the various hospital patients he imagines and encounters. The sketch follows him as he fulfils his desire to connect with his imagined, suffering bodies in the hospital by increasing proximity to more material suffering bodies. The plot itself, if such a thing exists, is a circle that begins and ends with the hospital and the patients who lie behind its walls.

The hospital bars Boz both from medical knowledge and from the physical bodies medicine treats. The walls of the hospital prevent him from seeing and touching the sufferers; the walls of legislation bar him epistemologically from the knowledge of medicine, the knowledge to alleviate suffering. Boz's ethical quandary – who can tell the anguish? – is also therefore a question of space and knowledge: one need not struggle with the unknowability of the suffering other if one cannot even physically access the other, or if one is told that one cannot adequately understand suffering. More specifically, these questions emphasise the need to move beyond abstracted bodies. One might well know of a symbolic body, but that knowledge does not enable one to empathise.

In response to this twofold problem of knowledge and materiality, Boz provides a twofold answer. To know suffering bodies, Boz turns to narrative and knowledge born of sensation: if he can feel empathy for imagined, suffering characters in narrative, it might be possible to redirect and focus that empathy toward specific individuals he encounters in his lived experience. Storytelling might increase his sense of how he resembles those bodies, and improve his imagination's capacity to transfer the idea of a feeling into its actual impression. Literary authority is about and derives from feeling.

Here, Boz turns to Associationism, and uses the imagined bodies within the hospital to invoke the idea of impressions, which might ultimately become the impressions themselves. For Smith, we see others' feelings, imagine ourselves in their position, and then 'infe[r] how we would feel in those circumstances' (Hearn 2016: 216); for Hume, we resonate with others' feelings, so that our minds generate an 'idea' of the feeling, which imagination then 'inliven[s] as to become the very sentiment or passion' (Hume 1739: 319). Resemblance facilitates our capacity to resonate, and imagination transforms the idea of feelings with which one resonates into those feelings in and of themselves. Imagination, in short, helps surpass the barrier between readers and representations of other bodies. Through imagination, Boz transforms the physical walls of the hospital and the windows into symbolic sites that circumvent themselves.

Windows

In the opening gesture of the sketch, the light's movement initiates a series of associated memories, or a 'crowd of reflections' – but their origin is not empirical; rather, they come from Boz's imagination. To understand Dickens's conception of how imagination might be enough to inspire memories, I turn first to the key material mechanism in Boz's recollections: the windows. Akin to the transient materiality/immateriality of light waves, windows offer empirical observation even as they deter it. Translucent glass suggests penetration of the hospital wall between the narrator and the suffering patient.

And yet, Boz does not look *through* them. While Boz sees the initial flickering of the taper in the windows, the light becomes metaphor and conjecture. As the light 'gradually disappear[s]', Boz can only observe through his own imagination. The light moves '*as if* it were carried further back into the room' (Dickens 1837: 133). The light is removed from materiality on multiple levels: it fades; it moves only *as if*, for Boz does not know its actual trajectory. Even if he watches it move back into the room, that room is within the hospital, physically and discursively obscured from Boz's vision. He can mark the 'mere glimmering of the low-burning lamps, which . . . denote the chamber' housing the patients, but the patients exist only through inference (133). Somehow, however, these imagined possibilities 'have been enough' to inspire a series of memories. Boz must turn to language because he faces a truly material conundrum: the window does not simply open up the hospital to his gaze, for it reflects and interferes even as it allows him access. To better empathise, he takes on the hybrid role of literary scholar and scientist, to take in signs and interpret the materiality they imply.

As a material surface, the glass insists on its presence even when it enables connection between the inside and outside. In fact, the 'low-burning lamps' that shine out at him from the inside further illuminate the materiality of the glass pane, for the light becomes visible only because it refracts within the glass itself. Isobel Armstrong argues in *Victorian Glassworlds* that 'in the nineteenth century ['windows'] became a third or middle term: [they] interposed an almost invisible layer of matter between the seer and the seen' (I. Armstrong 2008: 3). Acting as 'both medium and barrier', glass makes its presence known even as it effaces itself. It comes 'alive with images and traces of images' so that 'the observer is accompanied continuously by a secondary world of figment' (8). Boz mobilises this secondary world and makes figment a means to real affects. Even as the windows reiterate the hospital's barriers, they also offer a medium on which Boz can write descriptions of suffering bodies.

Rather than open the barrier, then, the windows become a meeting point for two sets of impressions. The light from the tapers shoots from window to window, and draws Boz from the outside on the street into the hospital; from within the hospital, glimmers of lamps 'denote' (Boz's word) the presence of unseen bodies to those on the streets outside. Reflections turn the glass into both a barrier and a site of access. Through the dialectic between materiality and immateriality, windows promise to make legible the bodies behind the glass, even as one can only read those bodies through their interposed surfaces.

Though physical and discursive barriers bar Boz from the lights and the bodies they suggest, his sensory experience of the windows evokes impressions and memories. 'Feeble' though the light may be, its effect is 'sudden' and strong enough to 'awaken a whole crowd of reflections' (Dickens 1837: 133). The window's mediating presence bars the bodies within from pure sight, and so these reflections instead come through sound:

> Who can tell the anguish of those weary hours, when the only sound the sick man hears, is the disjointed wanderings of some feverish slumberer near him, the low moan of pain, or perhaps the muttered, long-forgotten prayer of a dying man? (134)

Elaborate description expands 'the only sound the sick man hears' into the 'disjointed wanderings of some feverish slumberer', 'the low moan of pain', and the 'muttered, long-forgotten prayer of a dying man'. Boz hears these sounds through the ears of the sick man; he positions the feverish slumberer 'near him', the listener. Associative impressions momentarily circumvent the visual barrier of the window and make present the bodies behind it. This is in fact a more complicated chain of mediations: light reflects off the windows; these reflections inspire imaginations; the imaginations inspire memories; the memories begin a series of philosophical questions; and then Boz answers these questions with imagined bodies. A similar rhetorical manoeuvre conjures a mother's embodied 'hands . . . [that] wipe the clammy brow, or smooth the restless bed' inside the hospital (134). Rooted in material (if imagined) observers, these sensations articulate the sounds and tactile experiences within the hospital as if – but only *as if* – Boz empirically observes them.

According to Associationism, consciousness is first and foremost consciousness of physical sensation. The material and the immaterial create reality out of feeling. Rather than consider suffering through heady abstraction, Boz imagines bodies to keep his ethical musings materially grounded. In keeping with the Associationist maxims of Locke, Hume, Stewart and beyond: 'sensations, ideas of sensation, and association, generate and account for the principal complications of our mental nature' (Mill 1869: xi). When presented with boundaries that separate him from the bodies in pain behind the physical and discursive walls of the hospital, Boz turns to the window as a surface that can translate and transmit sensations. The sound the sick man hears provides a physical stimulus and evokes a set of impressions that move Boz much closer to the connection he seeks with suffering bodies. Imagined bodies materialise as physical experience.

Storytelling

Empathy for textual characters requires that readers feel both the need to empathise with characters, and that such empathy is even possible.[11] While the Associationists made every effort to ground their arguments in empirical fact, narratives of sensation take over where the narratives of science fail. Dugald Stewart's initial discourse on association in his *Elements* holds striking resonance with Boz's logic of materiality and its relationship with memory in the opening to 'The Hospital Patient':[12]

> In passing along a road we have formerly travelled in the company of a friend, the particulars of the conversation in which we were then engaged, are frequently suggested to us by the object we meet with. In such a scene, we recollect that a particular subject was started; and, in passing the different houses, and plantations, and rivers, the arguments we were discussing when we last saw them, recur spontaneously to the memory. (D. Stewart 1792: 279)

Physical objects evoke memories and transport the observer's mind and sensations to different times and places. The subject of conversation, the scenery, the houses – all of these become a single sense unit. These memories, imaginations and sensations are inextricable from the language that manifests them. Objects translate emotional states across space and time in both Boz's encounter with the hospital and Stewart's narrative journey in his opening: the road is an actor and can 'sugges[t]', for 'the sight of an external object recalls former occurrences, and revives former feelings' (278). Stewart places special emphasis on the 'influence of perceptible objects' in the process of recalling feelings. And yet, these perceptible objects here derive their force through narrative rather than observable data; Stewart begins his discourse on Associationism not with philosophy or physiology, but with the story of walking down the road.

In the nineteenth century, Stewart's trend toward a materialist understanding of language becomes even more prominent in the work of James Mill. For Mill, language functions as a translator of sensation much like Locke proposed. Language makes sense legible to the bodies that feel them and conveys sensations to other bodies. However, where Stewart emphasises a single body's interpretation, Mill is interested in the social communication of sensation. In Mill's theory of language from *Analysis*, written words are 'SENSIBLE OBJECTS' that function 'as SIGNS of our inward feelings' (Mill 1869: 84–5). Rather than something like signifiers, signs point to 'cluster[s] of sensations' (91). This 'cluster', or 'compound' as he later calls it, is an important development on Stewart's model. For Stewart, sensation and perception connect through 'incomprehensible' processes; for Mill, the process itself is not as important. Rather, the cluster of sensations and perceptions becomes its own node of feeling.

To explain language as the medium for experiencing clusters of sensations, he expands on the 'rose' thought-experiment: 'the name rose, is the mark of a sensation of colour, a sensation of shape, a sensation of touch, a sensation of smell, all in conjunction . . . regarded not separately, but as a compound' (92). This dialectic between materiality and immateriality culminates in questions of narrative, for while the rose itself is a physical object, it consists of a cluster of sensations which one conveys through words. Language relates the totality of those sensations. The word 'rose' connotes a similar set of sensations from one body to the next, albeit with difference. This repetition with difference makes language the ideal site for Associationism to explore the transmission of sensations across different kinds of materiality, for if the repetition of sensations is held common enough between bodies, it might be possible to feel for living bodies what one felt for characters.

Both Associationism and this theory of ethical reading depend on this equivalence between fiction and feeling. The sensations one feels about a textual body equate to the sensations one could feel about a living body. Sensations, sympathy and empathy foremost among them, make this equivalence possible. As Rae Greiner suggests, authors 'fashioned realism to equip the mind to comprehend a reality that was itself sympathetic, a reality whose realism found sanction in the imaginative fellowship we have with others' (Greiner 2012: 4). The sympathetic relationships that these texts evoke constitute the 'reality' toward which realism gestures; these texts seem real because of the real-feeling sensations they elicit. After he confronts the reader with the complexity of the window and the impressions that it can trigger, Boz moves from one impression to a similar impression – and though the source of that impression is a different object entirely, because he feels the same affect (empathy for pain), these stories are equivalent. Narrative moves from impression to impression, rather than from hermeneutic interpretation. Literary authority, then, depends on the ability to resonate with those impressions – whether to create them as an author, or to feel them as a reader.

Empathy for pain, even and especially when that pain exists only through readers' imaginations, tautologically validates reading fiction. According to Boz, fiction as the realm of sensation best teaches readers about ethical feeling. This is because narrative enables one to move from generalisations to specifics, or from an abstraction to materiality. After he deploys the window to consider the ethical charge 'who can tell the anguish?', the narrator's impressions of the bodies within the hospital turn to the suffering bodies outside the hospital: 'Impressed with these thoughts, we have turned away, through the nearly deserted streets; and the sight of the few miserable creatures still hovering about them, has not tended to lessen the pain which such meditations awaken' (Dickens 1837: 134–5). To encounter the 'few miserable creatures' outside the hospital evokes impressions that resonate with the 'pain which such meditations [on the hospital patients] awaken'. This turn to the street signals a shift in the objects that inspire Boz's thoughts and sensations, but not a change in the impressions themselves. In fact, he ensures this continuity when he bemoans the persistence of suffering, and that watching the people around the hospital 'has not tended to lessen the pain' he feels for the hospital patients (135). Crucially, the bodies within the hospital and the bodies on the street are materially different: the hospital bodies are imagined, part of Boz's narrative, while these miserable creatures are of the same kind of materiality as Boz himself. The persistence of suffering and empathy, however, ameliorates these differences.

The hospital walls place Boz between two sets of bodies in pain: those within that he cannot see, and those without that he can. This is a key moment in the sketch for the link between Associationism, literary authority and empathy, for, having imagined the pain of the hospital patients behind the window, Boz finds himself better equipped to confront the miserable creatures around him. He recognises them as outcasts who 'but for such institutions [as the hospital] must die in the streets and door-ways' (135). He understands that 'the hospital is a refuge and resting-place for hundreds' of people similar to the miserable creatures (135). This understanding evokes similar questions to those the window poses: 'what can be the feelings of outcasts like these', Boz wonders, 'when they are stretched on the bed of sickness with scarcely a hope of recovery?' (135). One set of impressions gives way to a similar set of impressions, or, as Hume puts it, 'our imagination runs easily from one idea to any other that *resembles* it' (Hume 1739: 11). Boz's impressions of suffering bodies can therefore begin behind the window and run into the street.

On the street, Boz can begin to use storytelling to fulfil his desire to tell the anguish of suffering bodies. As Boz turns to the street, he replaces the vague 'forms . . . writhing with pain, or wasting with disease' who began the story in the window reflection with a 'wretched woman who lingers about the pavement' and a 'miserable shadow of a man – the ghastly remnant that want and drunkenness have left' (Dickens 1837: 135). Tortured adjectives (wretched, miserable, ghastly) and emaciated nouns and verbs (lingers, shadow, remnant, want) make these bodies feel tangible.

Here, Boz begins to hone his scientific abilities of observation. A shift from inference to observation moves toward an answer to his question 'who can feel?'. Impressions provide bodily understanding of others' feelings, so that the problem of '*knowing* others [as] the centre around which . . . social and ethical theory is organised' is also a problem of *feeling* the sensations and impressions others inspire (Pinch 2010: 39, emphasis added). Boz wants to feel sympathy for the bodies behind the window, but struggles to connect to their materiality. In response, he shifts the epistemological grounds by which he understands bodies, so that sensation can bridge gaps in knowledge. He may not be able to see or know the bodies behind the windows, but narrative can link empathy for the miserable creatures' observable bodies with empathy for the unobserved hospital patients. He can observe the bodies around him like a scientist, and tell stories about them as an author. And most importantly, as a representation of a popular reader, he can feel them.

Boz suggests that symbolic bodies allow insight into suffering even as they do not depict real suffering. And yet, when he encounters this barrier, he nevertheless demands that one still feel the anguish of the bodies behind it. Like the windows on which Boz fixates, narrative becomes a barrier that at once reflects and separates the viewer from the viewed, but also enables one to see through and observe the suffering on the other side. Language as a material medium of sensation connects living and fictional bodies. These connections make reading an ethical act, for it trains readers to draw on memories and fiction to sense others' suffering – not merely to think about suffering, but to sense it, to feel it in their own bodies.

Memory

And yet, as he wanders among the miserable creatures and tells their stories, Boz's narrative grapples with the ever-receding goal of knowing others' sensations. His narratively inspired impressions allow him to permeate the boundaries between himself and the other bodies around him, but the stories he tells draw attention to narrative as a mediator. While these people resonate more tangibly than the imagined hospital patients, the wretched woman and miserable man still exist somewhere between material bodies and imagined fictions. Boz has moved from reflected symbols in the window, but he still feels for generalisations rather than individuals.

These miserable creatures' bodies challenge the materiality of Boz's florid description, and his claims slide from the physical to the general: for all the adjectives, the miserable creatures remain simply 'a' man and woman (Gallagher 1994: 61). Even their alliterative names, 'wretched woman' and 'miserable man', point to their own construction. Boz offers a means to know bodies, but simultaneously challenges the validity of that 'knowledge' through its self-referentiality. These bodies are symbols, generalised gestures toward physicality with no specific referent.

As with the other liminal objects that appear at once material and immaterial – windows, light, memory, imagination – this tension becomes productive, a way to inspire impressions that can move between these different kinds of materiality and feel the sensations of others. Associationism offers an answer to the social and ethical problematics of telling other people's stories, for a scientific approach to narrative can translate symbols into materiality.

Memory is the key to this translation. In my treatment of imagination, I read the 'crowd of reflections' as literal reflections to better understand the materiality of imagined bodies. Now, I read the 'crowd of reflections' as a crowd of remembrances – that is, reflections on the past. The dual meaning is almost certainly embedded in the sketch itself, and this second reading feels more proper to the contextual semantics of the sentence. But for the Associationists, both memory and imagination are deeply bound up in materiality. As with imagination, the validity of these memories depends on the sensations that they can inspire. Mediating windows provide a material framework through which Boz begins to think about imagination, and imagination enables him to consider memory: if the flicker of dissipated light in obscuring windows can call up imagined impressions, then perhaps the memories of bodies can do the same. And here, Boz begins to answer his question 'who can tell the anguish?'. If one can correctly imagine symbols, those symbols might trigger the correct memories, and those memories can separate the self from observation – and thereby make those observations more material.

According to the Associationists, imagination works alongside memory in the dialectic between materiality and the immaterial. In his *Analysis*, James Mill posits memory as the interlocutor between pure sensation and pure knowledge or ideas. If consciousness were only sensation, Mill argues, 'we could never have any knowledge, excepting that of the present instant', for as soon as a sensation passed, it would be forever lost (Mill 1869: 231). On the other hand, 'if we only had ideas in addition to sensations . . . the idea, after the sensation, would give no more information, than one sensation after another' (232). Ideas would function independently of one another, and would constitute little more than consciousness of sensation. Memory unites sensations and ideas in succession, and thereby makes consciousness possible, he concludes (233). Memory is a metaphysical component of consciousness, but it is also tangible in that it recalls sensations that mark the remembering body. In other words, memory embodies ideas.

It might be readily objected that the memory of a feeling is not in fact the same as that feeling in the present. But for Associationists like James Mill and Dugald Stewart, memories affect the body independently from their temporality; when one remembers a sensation, one's body feels that sensation in the present. In his *Elements*, Stewart suggests that at the onset of a memory, the body cannot distinguish between remembered sensations and responses to present stimuli. When memory concerns 'things and their relations', Stewart argues that similar relations between things 'may recur to us, without suggesting the idea of the past, or any modification of time whatever' (D. Stewart 1792: 398). Memories of objects, their relationships, and the bodily sensations that accompany them can contain no marked temporal difference from present experience.

Stewart suggests that memories of events can in fact be of a similar kind to memories of objects – that they, too, initially bear no temporal distinction from the present. In the recollection of an event, memory operates in two stages: 'the mind first forms a conception of the event, and then judges from circumstances, of the period of time to which it is to be referred' (399). Sensations and ideas surrounding the event occur first, independently of context, and *then* the mind makes the distinction between past and present. This means, Stewart continues, that when 'we are occupied with the conception of any particular object connected with the event, we believe the present existence of the object' (400). Memory as Stewart frames it resonates with light-wave motion, or with the Victorian window: a dialectic both abstract and material.

The merging of past and present enables Boz to answer his central ethical question: who can tell the anguish? Throughout the sketch, Boz tries to make sense of the suffering of multiple groups of people: the patients he imagines behind the windows, the miserable creatures, and, ultimately, the Hospital Patient herself. Memory enables Boz to deploy the different kinds of bodies to rethink and re-feel the others. In the chapter's introduction, I alluded to the publication history of the sketch: Dickens wrote this sketch for a different publisher than the usual *Boz* sketches. He sold the Boz name a second time – and only a week after he was revealed as Boz. At the time 'The Hospital Patient' was published, then, Boz himself is a light wave, a glass window: he is both real and unreal, a fiction separate from Dickens, but with tangible monetary and social effects.

Dickens wrestles with what this dialectic means for literary authority – what constitutes good reading, and good writing – throughout the sketch. And so, Boz takes a strange narratological position as simultaneous narrative, reader and character. As he considers the narratology of Boz's storytelling, Julian Breslow makes the relatively obvious but integrally important observation that in the 'Scenes' section of the *Sketches*, 'the reader is usually made aware that he is on a one-guide tour, and that he is seeing the world exclusively through the narrator's eyes' (Breslow 1997: 136). Rather than disguise the narrator, Dickens insists on Boz's physical presence in the story. The opening sentence of 'The Hospital Patient' emphasises that the narrative comes from a body which walks through the London streets:

'In our rambles through the streets of London after evening has set in, we have often paused beneath the windows.' The plurality of the opening 'our', while a typical narrative gesture, also makes Boz both character and narrator. The story is the narrator's story, for he speaks from the present about his past. Boz's status as both character (a body in the narrative) and narrator (a body which tells the narrative) gives him two temporal perspectives on the reflections of the windows: they occur in the present for Boz the character, but in the past for Boz the narrator. But because memories of sensations occur in the present, when Boz-narrator in the present recounts Boz-character's past feelings, he can feel those sensations again – and use the insight he has gained from later experiences to unpack those past feelings.

The simultaneity of these multiple Bozes destabilises the idea of a single self – a breakdown of barriers necessary for empathy. His recursivity destabilises the self by suggesting what Hume had earlier made more explicit: that self is merely an entanglement of effects. What psychology calls the mind, Hume argues, is in fact a series of interrelated encounters with physical objects (causes) and the impressions (effects) they evoke. One becomes a 'chain of causes and effects, which constitute our self or person' (Hume 1739: 261–2). Narrative is sense-making for sensible organisms. Boz's multiple temporal and narrative positions allow him to shift constantly away from his own subjectivity – to at once imagine the suffering hospital patients, and observe himself imagining. The Boz of the streets around the hospital is not the Boz who tells the story, and is not the same Boz who later goes to visit the Hospital Patient herself at the end of the sketch.[13] For Dickens to explore his questions about reading and writing, Boz must occupy these multiple positions; in other words, Boz needs to be both past and present, to both present the events as an authority and experience them for the first time.

Boz can occupy these multiple positions because the sketch is so preoccupied with memory. For the Associationists, memory dissolves the idea of self, and makes sense-experience relational rather than individual. In his *Analysis*, Mill offers a narrative of memory: he narrates his own 'lively recollection of Polyphemus's cave' from a second reading of *The Odyssey*:

> In this recollection there is, first of all, the ideas, or simple conceptions of the objects and acts; and along with these ideas, and so closely combined as not to be separable, the idea of my having formerly had those same ideas. And this idea of my having formerly had those ideas, is a very complicated idea; including the idea of myself of the present moment

remembering, and that of myself of the past moment conceiving; and the whole series of the states of consciousness, which intervened between myself remembering, and myself conceiving. (Mill 1869: 331)

Mill's ludic relation of the elements of memory accurately – albeit, not at all clearly – describes the phenomenological experiences of reading. When he rereads about Odysseus blinding Polyphemus, for example, Mill feels the impressions of the story and its objects: sheep's wool, blindness, fear, and so on. At the same time, he remembers having read this before. He therefore at once reads the account of Odysseus, and the account of Mill reading Homer in the past. In *Analysis*, he now tells and reads the narrative of Mill reading Mill reading Homer (*ad infinitum*). And so, the moment one first remembers an impression, 'the mind runs back from that moment to the moment of perception' (331). That is, the mind 'runs over the intervening states of consciousness' until it arrives at the sensations it experienced at the moment of the original event remembered. This infinite recollection is consistent with the Associationist philosophy that memory emerges first in consciousness as a series of sensations without temporal markers, for when one remembers one feels both past and present; one remembers and observes oneself remembering.

To use past encounters with suffering in the future requires a convoluted enfolding of past, present and future. Boz tells readers that his experience with the Hospital Patient took place some 'twelvemonth ago' – that is, a year before his initial musings on the flickers of light in the window. At the time Boz entered the hospital a year prior, Boz tells readers, he felt 'an irrepressible curiosity to witness this interview [between the Hospital Patient and her abuser, Jack]', but notes that 'it is hard to tell why at this instant [when he reflects on the light in the windows], for we knew [the experience] must be a painful one' (Dickens 1837: 137). The Boz of the present relays the story of twelvemonth ago, and simultaneously jumps back to the present to admit that he 'at this instant' does not understand his year-ago impulse. The doubling underlines the complexity of reading time: the pain of the interview exists in a vague past for Boz, twelvemonth ago; even so, he feels it again as the storytelling narrator in the present and wonders at his past motivation (see S. Winter 2011: 15). Some of the language suggests that the event took place in the past, but because the text unfolds in the present, the pain takes place now. On yet another temporal line, the Hospital Patient's pain does not take place for readers until the interview. From the perspective of the initial ethical challenge (who can tell the anguish?), the Hospital Patient's pain occurs in the future. No matter at what point the narrative claims to take place, sensations reach across temporality as well as materiality to condition readers for the future.

This sequence of selves paves a path to something like self-forgetfulness, or at the very least, an ability to see beyond self-regard. In an earlier iteration of this definition of memory, Hume argues that memory undoes individual identity, for one cannot necessarily remember one's 'thoughts and actions of the first of January 1715', and so 'the present self is not the same person with the self of that time' (Hume 1739: 261). The self does not exist as a persistent entity through time. The idea of a persistent identity is an illusion derived from one's ability to 'extend the same chain of causes, and consequently the identity of our persons beyond our memory' (262). In fact, 'identity depends on the relations of ideas; and these relations produce identity', so that narrative once again mediates between abstraction (self) and physical experience (262). Because the reader is always a reader remembering past readings, and simultaneously imagining textual bodies, the self one might regard is lost in a sea of fluid bodies.

Diffusion of self leads to literary authority – both as author and as reader. By empathising outside of himself, Boz finds the necessary detachment to both feel the impressions first-hand, and to analyse the process of association from the outside. 'Detachment', according to Amanda Anderson's *The Powers of Distance*, does not correspond to 'absolute objectivity', but instead an *'aspiration* to a distanced view', one from which the Victorian subject can analyse and understand phenomena without the interference of overinvestment (Anderson 2001: 6). Here, Boz is an amateur Associationist who endeavours to understand sensations through material observation rather than abstraction. Associationism's commitment to self-identification with the suffering of others is in this sense a kind of detachment. Associationism is a framework that shapes what one feels and knows, and how one comports one's body. At the same time as he is a scientist, Boz is a reader – one who faces the quandary that scientific knowledge requires detachment, but knowledge of others comes from sensations that require closeness. Boz in part ameliorates this complication when he acknowledges and maintains the duality of knowledge (detached/close) through his multiple bodies in the sketch. And, again, Boz operates within the dialectic of abstraction and materiality: he is a detached scientist, but a close reader.

Surfaces

Throughout the opening half of the sketch, Boz works to understand suffering bodies through a series of surfaces. To read suffering bodies, he refracts off the surfaces of objects around them and imagines other suffering bodies: hospital walls, windows, imagined hospital patients, miserable creatures and their imagined stories. But throughout, he combats the inclination to turn bodies into symbols. The imagined patients, the miserable man and the wretched woman were mere symbols of suffering – but Boz uses those symbols to leave behind abstraction for materiality. He must imagine to remember, and remember to tell the story. Finally, once he arrives at the bar, bodies in pain acquire their own materiality. Only by attending to what is on the surface can he let go of anxiety about being an authority – and therein, he finds an empathetic ethics that makes him a literary authority.

Boz's language itself offers an early and crucial indication of this change. As he cultivates detachment, poetic musing gives way to journalistic observation. Excepting the initial description of the 'powerful, ill-looking young fellow' later called Jack, Boz's depiction modulates from the adjective-choked narrative of the hospital window and the outcasts in the surrounding streets, to something like a report:

> Several witnesses bore testimony to acts of the grossest brutality; and a certificate was read from the house-surgeon of a neighbouring hospital, describing the nature of the injuries the woman had received, and intimating that her recovery was extremely doubtful. Some question appeared to have been raised about the identity of the prisoner; for when it was agreed that the two magistrates should visit the hospital at eight o'clock that evening, to take her deposition, it was settled that the man should be taken there also. (Dickens 1837: 136–7)

Where the previous crowds of reflections consist of stories and sensational narratives, this selection reads as a list of events observed from afar. Boz even adds subjunctive distance when he says that 'some question *appeared* to have been raised' (137). From this point, Boz leaves behind speculation on the internal consciousness of his subjects in favour of attention to empirical, physical details. Upon hearing that he will accompany the magistrates, Jack 'turn[s] deadly pale', and Boz observes that the young man 'clench[es] the bar very hard, when the order was given' (137). When he arrives at the hospital, Boz reports that 'it was easy to see ... by the livid whiteness of his countenance, and the constant twitching of the muscles of his face, that [Jack] dreaded what was to come' (137). Before, vague contact with 'a' man outside the hospital inspired a life's story; now, Boz backs up his claims about others' sensations with physical evidence – the 'whiteness of his countenance' and 'twitching . . . muscles'. Jack's body becomes its own window, its own surface that reflects the inside (Jack's feelings) and the outside (Boz's observations). (We will interrogate this reflection of interiority in Chapter 5.)

Detached, journalistic observation makes productive the complexity of the multiple oscillations between materiality/immateriality that occurred earlier in the sketch (windows, light, narrative, memory). Boz speaks both to the scientific problem of knowing other bodies' suffering, and the literary authority's capacity to provide that knowledge. Narrative helps Boz understand emotion, while at the same time, detached, physical observation frees him from subjective influence as best as possible. This creates a kind of distance that nevertheless makes one close to the thing observed, a condition necessary for the Associationist reader who demands simultaneous scientific objectivity and an attunement to sensation.

Boz's entry into the 'casualty ward' provides a more concrete example of this dialectic between intimate proximity and distance. The narrative retains its preference for physical detail over metaphysical speculation, but returns to the affectively pungent, sentimental tone exercised in the initial description of the imagined hospital patients. I quote at length for the totality of the impression:

> In one bed lay a child enveloped in bandages, with its body half consumed by fire; in another, a female, rendered hideous by some dreadful accident, was wildly beating her clenched fists on the coverlet, in an agony of pain; on a third, there lay stretched a young girl, apparently in that heavy stupor which is sometimes the immediate precursor of death: her face was stained with blood, and her breast and arms were bound up in folds of linen. (138–9)

Where Boz's initial attempts at empathy strained against physical and textual barriers, these descriptions more readily acquire tangible corporeality. Attention to specific physical details resurrects the highly wrought adjectives of the first half of the sketch (ghastly appearance, hapless creatures, rendered hideous, dreadful accident) – but this time, rather than attaching to abstracted reflections on the internal state of the individual in question, Boz describes physical attributes. Only after this litany of broken bodies does Boz finally note that 'on every *face was stamped the expression* of anguish and suffering' (139, emphasis added). The narrator need not question what feelings lie within the interior consciousness of these patients, because their emotions present themselves on surfaces.

When Boz arrives at the bedside of the young woman who suffered abuse at Jack's hand, he uses his scientific detachment to readdress the boundaries between observation of a body and knowledge of that body. Empathy motivates the Associationists' observations of other bodies, but scientific distance creates space between the sensations of the observers and the observed. The Associationist reader therefore seeks to inhabit completely the sensations of other bodies, as if the observing body becomes one with the observed. The young woman, though nameless, receives the full descriptive treatment: Boz notes that she is 'about two or three and twenty'; he observes that her 'long black hair had been hastily cut from about the wounds on her head'; 'her face bore frightful marks of the ill-usage she had received' (139). He provides purely physical evidence rather than psychological speculation on her trauma. At this point, Boz separates his capacity to encounter a body from his capacity to *know* that body: 'her hand was pressed upon her side, *as if* her chief pain were there' (140, emphasis added). The 'as if' in this sentence suggests that Boz's confidence in his knowledge and linguistic alacrity fail when confronted with the reality of a specific, individual body. In order to enhance his sympathy with the young woman, Boz must move beyond imagination, but here, he begins to move beyond observation as well. The inescapable alterity of the young woman's body forces Boz to recognise the limits of detachment: that is, if one remains detached, one must acknowledge that one's own detachment prevents closeness.

Herein lies the critical turn of Boz's empathy: his Associationism eliminates interpretation of depths in favour of impressions on the surface. This new relationship depends heavily on what Boz does *not* say, for the narrative turns simply to dialogue. After this point, Boz distances himself so completely as to absorb his imaginative and interpretive capacities wholly into Jack's and the woman's bodies. The girl speaks, the first major dialogue of the story (the exception being the simple order, 'Take off his hat', the magistrate utters a few paragraphs previous):

> 'Oh, no, gentlemen,' said the girl, raising herself once more, and folding her hands together; 'no, no, gentlemen! I did it myself – it was nobody's fault – it was an accident. He didn't hurt me; he wouldn't for the world. Jack, dear Jack, you know you wouldn't.' (141)

The stumbling, repetitive utterances strike a marked contrast to Boz's ornate narration. The young woman's ineloquence emphasises her unknowability, her irreducible difference from Boz's narratively inflected perspective. Precisely because of this linguistic gap, Boz steps further back from his self and his interpretative faculties. The narrative focuses purely on the words the young woman speaks, the bodily exchange between her and Jack. Her sight fails; her hand 'grope[s] over the bed-clothes in search of his'; he 'turn[s] his face from the bed, and sob[s] aloud' (141). The scene is sentimental, yes – but it is also physical, rooted in observation and the suffering of other bodies. These bodies exceed mere symbolism and generate their own impressions without need for translation through another medium such as a window. As Boz grows closer to the physicality of the bodies he encounters, his simultaneous distance and closeness collapse into empathy for suffering. Because he has acknowledged that he cannot completely render the sensations of the other at the risk of mischaracterising both the other and himself, Boz's language shifts away from speculation and toward the embodied. He eliminates the self of the self-other equation, so only the bodies of Jack and the young woman remain.

Most importantly, Jack and the young woman are not symbols. Where the miserable man and wretched woman were mere generalities, symbolic of more specific suffering bodies, these two bodies are physical. Boz's incorporation of science with storytelling makes his characters concrete. He observes rather than interprets. Where the law (the magistrates) comes to interrogate interiors, Boz's Associationism attends to surfaces. When the Hospital Patient protects her abuser, her body rebels; knowledge of the depths of the mind gives way to acknowledgement of the body's surface.

From the Text to the Street

To think about empathy with suffering bodies, 'The Hospital Patient' investigates the development of empathy with textual bodies. The sketch poses the question 'who can tell the anguish?', and answers that those who learn to read bodies – to read about textual bodies, and thereby to understand living bodies – can tell. Fiction, the sketch suggests, offers an understanding of emotion unconcerned with the order of knowledge derived from symbols and interpretation. Instead, Associationism's scientific observation enables readers to observe from outside themselves, and to find ethical reading and writing through attention to others' sensations.

A crucial aside that will become increasingly relevant as this book moves later into the nineteenth century: assimilation of the self into the other covers up – to say 'resolves' would embrace the mystification that actually occurs – a critical tension in Associationist understandings of sympathy. On the one hand, Dickens is deeply invested in forming empathetic relationships with other individuals, including and sometimes especially the poor. On the other hand, however, Dickens and his contemporaries harbour deep fears about the permeability of the self, and worst of all, the possibility of contamination. Contagion seems an apt term for the fear that, while in the process of empathising with suffering bodies, one might accidentally become *too* close (Greiner 2012: 87). Boz's sympathy tries to have both worlds: intimate closeness that preserves boundaries between bodies. But as we will see, more often than not the self that is asked to be abandoned is an already marginalised self. It is easy for the male, upper-middle-class Dickens to enter into a working-class woman's feelings and then return to himself. It is not so easy for someone with less power to abandon what little agency they have.

Narrative offers an important site for Associationists interested in empathy because it is an *intentionally* dualistic mode: it is aware of its own fictionality, but simultaneously claims to mirror lived experience. This is true both of narrative as a category, and of fiction's formal qualities. The form of the short story lends itself particularly well to association because of its truncated, abrupt termination. Readers encounter the young hospital patient and Jack, Boz guides readers to feel the sensations of suffering bodies, and then the truncated form of the sketch cuts it all off. The suddenness of the missing conclusion compels the reader to seek out the continuation of empathy beyond the bounds of form. Here arises the now-familiar humanist claim that reading makes one a more empathetic person, a better citizen. But there is a particularly nineteenth-century twist: reading makes one a better person in that fiction prepares readers to move beyond symbolism and into materiality. Association makes this possible, for the imaginations, memories and different perceptive selves commingle with material experience.

To tell a story is insufficient, for the story must be about bodies, not symbols. Boz constructs narratives for multiple sets of bodies: for the imagined hospital patients, the miserable creatures, the pickpocket, and finally for Jack and the Hospital Patient. The narrative is in part about Boz's initial encounters with these bodies, but ultimately, the stories endeavour to make the bodies around Boz more concrete. The sketch invites readers to follow the 'intervening states of consciousness' that brought Boz from the windows of a hospital at the opening of the narrative to empathy for the Hospital Patient at the conclusion to explicitly trace the movement from symbol to physicality. Reading supplements experience, so that to read and feel empathy becomes a way to revise past memories and prepare for later ethical engagement – but only if the characters one reads are physical. Who, then, can tell the anguish? Readers who read bodies not as symbols, and not as interiors, but as material surfaces.

Notes

1. Throughout this chapter, I will refer to 'Boz' when the person in question is the narrator of or the character within the sketch, and 'Dickens' when I refer to the historical author.
2. I do not mean to diminish the importance of choosing the word. It does, however, seem possible to choose interchangeably depending on one's intellectual project. David Marshall makes a convincing argument in his *Surprising Effects of Sympathy* for exactly the opposite of what I argue here (Marshall 1988: 3).
3. Examples of the prominence of sight abound early in Smith's description of sympathy: 'we *see* a stroke aimed and just ready to fall upon the leg or arm of another person' (Smith 1759: 3); the mob '*gaz[es]* at a dancer on the slack rope' (4); 'persons of delicate fibres . . . complain that in *looking* on the sores and ulcers' of beggars in the streets (4); 'men of the most robust make, observe that in *looking* upon sore eyes they often feel a very sensible soreness in their own' (4); 'sympathy may seem to arise merely from the *view* of a certain emotion in another person' (6).
4. For a thorough history of the word and its use, see Karsten Stueber's *Rediscovering Empathy* (2010).
5. Greiner notes that 'if a model of sympathy prevails in Dickens, it appears to be David Hume's, not Smith's. Humean emotional contagion, vibrating unstoppably from one body to the next, seems to animate the typical Dickensian text' (Greiner 2012: 87).
6. The library of studies on Hume and empathy is a large one. Most important to my work are Adela Pinch's *Strange Fits of Passion* (1996) and Jacqueline Taylor's *Reflecting Subjects* (2015). It is also important to note that, as Jonathan Hearn (2016) explains in 'Once More with Feeling', this model of sympathy as musical, poetic resonance differs drastically from Hume's original, far more mechanistic understanding of sympathy in his earlier work.
7. I would not suggest that this experience of others' feelings is universal. Rather, it is probably more accurate to imagine a spectrum between

purely rational derivation of others' feelings and this kind of immersive experience of others' bodies. I would also stress that I do not posit an ethical evaluation of this spectrum that suggests one is 'better' than the other as a starting point; again, the effects are the only relevant inquiry.
8. While difference does not foreclose on the possibility of empathy, 'resemblance' of 'manners, or character, or country, or language ... facilitates the sympathy' that one might feel for others (Hume 1739: 318). It would be unfair to Hume (and Smith) to pretend that Hume did not have tendencies toward the same solipsism that mars Smith's sympathy, for Hume writes that 'when we sympathise with the passions and sentiments of others, these movements appear first in *our* minds as mere ideas, and are conceiv'd to belong to another person' (319). This is why Hume's use of the word 'sympathy' is so very slippery, for this definition seems contradictory to the version I claimed above for contagious feeling or for empathy.
9. For more on the many similarities and particular differences between Smith's and Hume's ideas of sympathy, see Geoffrey Sayre-McCord's 'Hume and Smith on Sympathy, Approbation, and Moral Judgement' (2013).
10. For more on the regulation of bodies in the nineteenth century – particularly the intersection of medicine, democratisation and state power – see Pamela Gilbert's *The Citizen's Body* (2007).
11. A condensed survey of some of the key texts on novels as pedagogies of knowledge about feeling include: Terry Lovell's *Consuming Fiction* (1987), Ann Cvetkovich's *Mixed Feelings* (1992), Garrett Stewart's *Dear Reader* (1996), Patrick Brantlinger's *The Reading Lesson* (1998), Alan Rauch's *Useful Knowledge* (2001), George Levine's *Dying to Know* (2002), Peter Garratt's *Victorian Empiricism* (2010), Rebecca Mitchell's *Victorian Lessons in Empathy and Difference* (2011), and Rae Greiner's *Sympathetic Realism* (2012).
12. Thanks to Michael S. Kearns (1986), we know that Dickens owned a copy of the 1792 edition of the *Elements*.
13. Dana Brand calls attention to the relationship between memory and Boz's push beyond typical literary representations of *flânerie*. He writes: 'In the *Sketches by Boz*, Dickens strains against the limitations of the flaneur's sketch', particularly in the way that it addresses 'the experience of time' (Brand 1991: 58). Boz's multiple narrative and temporal positions enable this deconstruction of *flânerie*.

Chapter 3

Metaphoric Bodies: The Professional Author, Sensation and Serialisation in *Great Expectations*

Great Expectations is not likely to top a list of famous sensation fiction. We typically define the sensation novel by its plot: secret identities, murder mysteries and graphic (for the Victorians) bodily horrors. While these elements arguably comprise portions of *Great Expectations*, more importantly, these are not necessarily the defining characteristics by which Victorian literary critics understood the genre.[1] Instead, the Victorians understood sensation fiction primarily through the impressions it created and the physiological avenues it used to create them.[2] The project of the novelist who wants to claim that one can read sensation fiction ethically, then, is to teach readers to connect to bodies through heightened impressions.

As the focal character of a text which is part sensation fiction, part mystery novel, part *Bildungsroman*, Pip Pirrip must learn to read impressions, to read clues and secrets, and to read himself. Like Boz, as the narrator of his own story, Pip has the capacity to look back and comment on his reading responses. At the same time, one would do well to suspect that Pip did not properly learn his reading lessons, for there is a disjuncture between the form of the novel and Pip's reading. Throughout his narrative, Pip struggles to navigate material language that connects him to others; instead, he has a proclivity to hold his knowledge and assumptions about others' feelings in higher regard than their actual lived experience.

In his early reading experiences, though, Pip's model of language is profoundly material; words are a sense organ that produce bodily relationships. As he endeavours to articulate his own identity, Pip reads the inscriptions on his parents' gravestones. From the 'shape of the letters' on his father's tombstone, Pip reads 'a square, stout, dark man, with curly black hair' (Dickens 1860a: 169). His mother's inscription reads 'Also Georgiana Wife of the Above'. These six words conjure an entire body: he decides that his mother 'was freckled and sickly' (169). But Pip does not derive this meaning from the words themselves; instead, he reads the 'character and turn of the inscription' (169). Through language's materiality, Pip can similarly read the five stones of his siblings' graves, which inspire a 'religiou[s]' belief in five boys 'born on their backs with their hands in their trousers-pockets, [who] had never taken them out in this state of existence' (169). For the young Pip, language and letters move beyond representation to physical bodies that the words connote.

Readers first meet Pip while he reads. But he does not simply read: he reads his own identity. But he does not simply read his own identity: he reads his own identity through the (imagined) bodies of others. Even as he uses representation to fashion a sense of self, he overturns the representational formula that redirects language back to knowledge and assumption. If Pip can read it, he can imagine it; if he can imagine it, he can feel it. Most importantly, if he can feel it, then these bodies have the potential to evoke other feelings, to take on a life of their own. These graveside readings epitomise the novel's central concern with embodied reading: can one read and know bodies, but not reduce them to mere mirrors? The ethical charge of Pip's early reading lessons is to read bodies not as texts with linear, metaphoric meanings, but as potentials.

It is perhaps also a mischaracterisation to refer to *Great Expectations* as a *Bildungsroman*, for while Pip technically comes of age, he fails to grow as a person. In fact, the opening moment in the graveyard and the subsequent instalment of the novel may constitute the zenith of Pip's reading practices. Throughout the narrative of young-Pip's graveside readings, the 'I' that is narrator-Pip objects to young-Pip's readings. His 'first fancies' of his family, the narrator claims, are 'unreasonably derived': his depiction of his father is 'an odd idea'; his understanding of his mother is a 'childish conclusion'; the 'religio[sity]' of his belief in his brothers' perpetually pocketed hands mocks itself in its ridiculousness (169). Narrator-Pip finds his childhood reading practices reprehensible, or at least laughable.

And yet, invalidation of child-Pip's gravestone conjurations requires more than simply taking the word of the older narrator-Pip's reflections on his past. Martine Hennard Dutheil, in 'La Leçon de Lecture de *Great Expectations*', argues that the young Pip's reading practices surpass those of the later Pip. While the narrator mocks young-Pip for his blind faith in the tangibility of language and his ability to read bodies, Dutheil suggests that this same faith resurfaces ironically in a reader who, although complicit with the narrator in that she or he shares the amused view [of the narrator] regarding the naïve reading practices of the young child, lets themself be caught up in the game of referential illusion and, like the young Pip, supplies imagination for the words on the page. (Dutheil 1993: 112, my translation)[3]

If the reader agrees with the narrator's critique of Pip's fervent, bodily belief in the materiality of language then, paradoxically, they have replicated Pip's mode of reading. To laugh at young-Pip acknowledges that he has an existence worth mocking. And of course, the most important sensation the reader might feel here is sympathy. It seems safe to say that a terrified child crying over his dead family in a graveyard should conjure at least a slight degree of sympathy – and if a reader finds Pip at all emotionally sympathetic, then the bodies of his family should be worthy of the same quality of reality. When bodies in the opening pages of *Great Expectations* inspire sensations in the reader, Pip's sensations from graveyard epitaphs became equally valid. A paradox ensues: narrator-Pip accuses young-Pip of naïveté, but if the reader agrees with his castigation of young-Pip, the reader deserves the same chastisement.

The ontology of feeling explains the reader's paradox. Fictional narrative can evoke physical changes in a living reader because sensation is always real – material, tangible, embodied – no matter its temporality or origin. Alexander Bain's theory of language in his 1855 *The Senses and the Intellect* can shed some light on this bizarre enfolding of time. Bain's ontology of feeling locates the impetus for reality in the sensations one feels, not their source, so that 'the imagination of visible objects is a process of seeing' equivalent to seeing an object in the lived world (Bain 1855: 339). He seeks to reduce the degree to which Associationism relies on metaphor, and to instead ground its theories of cognition in empirical anatomy and physiology. So, even as the imagined body affects the physical body, the etiology of feeling must remain material.

To this end, Bain emphasises the physical location of formerly abstract concepts like memory. Rather than refer to memory as an idea, he argues that 'renewed feeling[s]' – which includes memory and imagination together – 'occup[y] the very same parts [of the brain] and in the same manner as the original feeling, and no other parts, nor in any other manner than can be assigned' (333). There exists no 'memory centre' in the brain. Instead, a memory merely activates the same neural pattern of sensation as the first stimulation. The most important implication of this claim is that memory and imagination are not merely conceptually tied – they are physically bound up together across the brain. If one can imagine a sensation, then, this imagination is conceptually, sensually and physically correlative with the *memory* of a sensation.

Most importantly for young Pip, language is one of the most influential mechanisms to connect imagination and memory with a sensing body. When he turns specifically to written language, Bain emphasises the mind's capacity to derive sensation from words: 'The more alive we are to the influence of words, the larger is the share of reviving efficacy that belongs to them' (478). In other words, the more one believes in the power of language to evoke sensations, the more powerful language becomes, for 'an eye very much arrested and impressed with language is to that degree prone to such revivals [of sensation]' (480). Bain shifts into a first-person narrative to convey the power of language:

> I am uttering a connected series of words, and among these, one, two, or three, have by chance the echo of one of the falls of an old utterance; instantly I feel myself plunged in the entire current of the past. (477)

To trace the epitaphs with a body receptive and 'alive' to the potential impressions behind the words utilises the 'reviving efficacy' of language. Pip's attention to the minutiae of the words that make up his mother's epitaph suggest that he is 'very much arrested and impressed with language', and so can link the written word to imaginations – imaginations that carry the sensational force of memory. His imaginations, in short, allow him to remember his parents even though he never met them.

Memory is crucial to Dickens's project, because according to Associationism, the memory or imagination of a body and its associated impressions is of the same mode as a physical body. Bain draws a parallel – not a metaphor – between 'the organic feelings of Muscle, and the states produced by exercise in its various forms, [which] can be sustained for some time after the physical cause has ceased' and 'the Sensations of the senses, [which] can be sustained in like manner' (332). Memory is something like a gymnasium for the senses. Where similar exercise will evoke similar physical states, the 'associating forces' that once inspired an impression can revive that impression once more (332).[4] The difference between the physical sensation of a cannon firing and the memory of that cannon firing is a difference of 'intensity' only, and otherwise, from a physiological perspective, 'the mode of existence of a sensation enduring after the fact is essentially the same as its mode of existence during the fact' (333). While the quantity of sensation may vary, the quality or kind of sensation does not vary because 'the renewed feeling occupies the very same parts and in the same manner as the original feeling' (333). When faced with a similar stimulus, even if the impression is 'reproduced by mental causes alone', the 'train of feeling is re-instated on the same parts as first vibrated to the original stimulus, and that recollection is merely a repetition which does not usually go quite the same length' (334). Imagined sensations, with 'frequent usage', can 'supersede' similarity so that what was once imagined instead becomes 'efforts of mere adhesive recollection' – or in other words, a kind of memory.

Serialisation – the regular, piecemeal publication of a text over time, and the most common mode of publication for sensation fiction – enables Dickens to plug into this practice of embodied memory. Serialised sensation repeats ethical, intuitive acknowledgement of other bodies until those imaginations become memories. Sense-making occurs not only in a conscious mind, but also in a remembering body. To continue to make sense of a text is to repeatedly recall past states of embodiment as if they were present states of embodiment, and to connect them to one another across time. Rather than imagine serial as a sequence of reading time punctuated by periods of waiting, Associationism suggests a continuity of sensations and complex identities that contain not simply a past self reading, but the effects of that past self on the present self remembering.

Earlier, I characterised surfaces as planes of contact that invite embodied connection, and which scholars dive past too hurriedly. Here, I want to complicate the temporality of that gloss. Surfaces occur both fast and slow, for affect distorts linear time. The gravity of intense affects like the starts and shocks of a sensation novel create a spike, a surface that strikes immediately and suddenly. But the shockwave also spreads as the initial affective density dissipates and spreads. A surface is both immediate and immense. These distortions do not require digging into, or unpacking; they afford different affective modes that bend and redouble. A serialised sensation novel produces a dense knot of affect in its initial reading, and that folding pulls the affects that follow in the intervening days or weeks between instalments. An escaped criminal in the beginning of *Great Expectations*, for example, creates a sudden start in the initial reading experience but may also diffuse into the time between issues of *All the Year Round*: a policeman, an execution, a jail may both conjure up the fictional criminal, and also be distorted by the fictional criminal.

This chapter explores the intersection between speed, the economics and form of serial publication, and embodiment. To unpack this network, I turn to Charles Dickens's *Great Expectations*. The novel is directly concerned with sensation fiction's production and consumption, and as with the other works I explore, *Great Expectations* offers a theory of language concerned with reading and ethics. The main character, Pip Pirrip, finds himself divided between the performance of scholarship and more material, sensational readings. In *Great Expectations*, language's materiality offers the promise of self-identification with the well-being of others. But Pip's reliance on his own knowledge and speculations means that language could at any moment transition back to self-regard. Defenders of sensation argued that common readers differ from scholars because of their proclivity for embodiment, and so must cling to embodiment lest they fall into the false performance of disembodiment that turns other bodies around them into mere conduits for capital. This manifests in the serial form of *Great Expectations*, for the novel suggests that serialisation does not commodify literature, but instead cultivates ethical embodiment in the literary public: embodiment that feels and cares, rather than interprets through knowledge.

Serialisation and Speed

On 28 December 1861, an anonymous *Spectator* author warned his readers with an ominous declaration: 'We are threatened with a new variety of the sensation novel' ('The Enigma Novel' 1861: 1428). This article initiated a new Victorian foray into generic definition. To combat the threat of the sensation novel, the Victorians needed to classify and understand its origin. And its origin, they determined, was a new mode of embodiment that demanded shocking, intense feelings.

Critics insisted that 'sensation' was both a foreign word and a foreign feeling, but that in the mid-century, British physiology was changing. Worse still, British physiology was metamorphosing into the worst possible mode of embodiment: American. Fast, seeking out fits and starts, the American body was invading the homeland through their sensational fiction. A poem in an 1864 issue of the *Dublin University Magazine* derides sensation as a particularly American invention. While 'some would have it an age of Sensation', the poet insists that 'the word's not *Old* England's creation, / but New England's, over the sea' ('SENSATION!' 1864: ll. 1, 3–4). The

United States provide an environment primed for sensation because they are a 'land of fast life and fast laws' where 'all's in the high-pressure way' (ll. 9, 5). People who live at high speed more readily accept – or demand, even – that the 'able Editors' of their journals and newspapers should 'lump' all events 'under one standing head of "sensation"' (ll. 23–4). According to the poet, this kind of speed is foreign to England, and better suited to the rapidity across the pond. This is a statement about physiology as much as it is a statement of literary critique, for it implies the British constitution should be slower and less excitable.[5]

Victorian critics purported that the accelerated pace of life alters bodies so that they require more intense sensation. Sensation fiction prefers plots that occur contemporaneously with their readers, or so these critics argue, for temporal proximity provides fiction with a sensation of immediacy better suited to faster, modern life. Alfred Austin wrote a series in *Temple Bar* entitled 'Our Novels', in which he created taxonomies for contemporary novel genres. For the 'Sensational School', Austin crafted a genealogy through Greek *erotikoi*, Shakespeare, Walpole, Radcliffe, Lewis, and the highwayman novels featuring Turpin, Duval and Sheppard. But, he revealed in a sensational twist, it is all a ruse. The sensation novel departs from these previous forms because its subject matter is always as present as possible: the Romance takes place in old castles and monasteries that hearken back to the medieval, and the Criminal Romance specifically brings to life criminals of the eighteenth century (Austin 1870b: 412). In contradistinction to the vague historicity of previous genres, Austin wryly notes the sensation novel's proclivity for specific dates: 'if the novel is printed about 1860, care is taken to inform us, early in its pages, that "three days after this, the 14th of June, 1856", such an event occurred to the heroine'. Demarcated dates inevitably lead to the present, so 'the reader may thus well hope to reach 1860 before the end of the third volume' (412). This kind of temporal proximity brings the events of the novel 'almost to [the reader's] own door' – a temporal immediacy that makes all events irrefutably present and thereby irrefutably shocking.

Immediate, sensationalised reading was coded as immoral reading – and all the more so because it was decidedly a common (and not scholarly) genre. Sensation fiction inspires quick, ephemeral reading in place of deeper and ostensibly more meaningful reading practices. The *Dublin University Magazine* poet helps to unpack the intersection between speed, bodies and morality. The poem satirically inflates common discursive tropes of anti-sensation critics who suggest that the shift in British readers' physiology could produce a less moral society. According to the printed marginalia that the poet affixes to the poem, the first lines 'mourneth over the good old Tory times':

> Ah! once the stream of English life would flow
> So humdrum, solemn, decent, and so slow!
> Such were the days of all our moral sires,
> The ancient race of heavy, honest squires. ('SENSATION' 1864: ll. 1–4)

But, the poem continues:

> Now for this ancient type we look in vain,
> The sound old ale is turned to thin champagne.
> See how bursts forth the smoke, the flame, the crash!
> SENSATION Comes! the spasm and the flash! (ll. 9–12)

The simplistic binary presents a 'slow' and 'humdrum' past with 'moral' roots in opposition to a patently orgasmic present speed. Where 'SENSATION!' mocks the simplicity of both sensation fiction's readers and its critics, its hyperbole exposes the rhetoric common to anti-sensation arguments. The opposition between slow romances of the past and the rapid sensations of the present are fundamentally embodied, to the extent that many critics turned to food metaphors. The 'diet' of older literature no longer satisfies, for 'Sensation finds Cayenne to spice the dish' (ll. 25–6).[6] The 'fierce ingredients' of sensation's 'nightmare dishes, mixed with goblin yeast' appeal to the hedonistic pleasures of a crass audience whose literal tastes have changed, and who now crave spice of sensation (ll. 41, 46). Sensation here responds to a change not only in the internal rhythms of bodies, but also in the ways in which bodies apprehend the world around them. The faster life produces new (literal) tastes, because the rhythm of bodies has accelerated.

According to mid-century critics, the unscholarly public had undergone a physiological change that made them desire florid sensation and extreme embodiment over useful knowledge. They also accused sensation novelists of obliging these desires simply because it would be profitable to do so. As mass-produced commodities, sensation novels' characters were flat, unrealistic and devoid of complexity. In short, sensation authors reduced the moral and intellectual value of literature merely to make money.

These accusations were in some part founded in observable market patterns. Technology, particularly transportation technology, was the harbinger of this faster life that brought about new sensations.

As Austin's article indicates, the sensation novel offered a material site for the Victorians to theorise the ways that a faster life changed readers' physical and emotional perceptions. Changes like the railroad pragmatically speed up the time and place of reading. Wolfgang Schivelbusch's *The Railway Journey* offers a foundational iteration of this argument: advances like the locomotive, factory production and photography brought about 'the annihilation of time and space', a compression of spatial distance and temporal progression (Schivelbusch 1986).[7] And indeed, when Austin claims that the sensation novel's present temporality transports the text 'almost to [the reader's] own door', he conflates time and space in precisely this way. This conflation takes place on a broad spectrum: faster reading habits change the temporal relationship between an individual reader and an individual book, and faster consumption changes the relationship between readers as a whole and book publication as a whole.

The frequency with which readers purchased new books, the time they took to read them, and the location of reading intimately commingled with speed. An article in *Fraser's* summarises this shift when the author observes that 'no boy or girl undertakes an hour's journey by railroad without investing a preliminary shilling at the book-stall' (M. M. 1860: 210). The purchase and consumption of books has accelerated as well, for rather than rely on a library, one can buy a novel at a bookstall and read on the trip. These changes also reflect a collapse of time and space in broader terms: in the first section of his series on 'Our Novels', Austin declares that 'the proclamation of the Empire was the proclamation of the reign of fast things and fast people' (Austin 1870a: 180). According to Victorian theorists, as the world from the colonies to the hearth accelerated, so too did reading and writing.[8] As reading time accelerates, so does the physiology of the reader – and so must the pace of novels.

These physical changes were in part the result of the dramatic changes in the demographics of popular readership.[9] A virtually stagnant growth of male literacy between 1800 and 1840 (60 per cent in 1800 to 67 per cent in 1840) and a diminishing literacy for women (45 per cent to 40 per cent) exploded to 81 per cent of men and 73 per cent of women by 1871.[10] This literacy was particularly popular rather than academic, since the growth takes place before the Forster Act 1870, which vastly expanded public education. The rise of the self-educated masses changed the critical stakes for fiction. An article in *The Spectator* compares the sensation novel's stage counterpart, sensation drama, and emphasises a shift in readership. The author argues that 'the writer of the sensation-drama appeals to quite a new class of play-goers' than the previously dominant melodrama ('The New Sensation Drama' 1861: 16). Though members of the novel's audience 'are too much worked in the daytime to want fresh thought in the evening', they are no mere uneducated working class. These new playgoers are 'people who, though educated, want to be amused without the trouble of too much thought'. While critics understood sensation theatre as an innocuous form of entertainment, probably because it was originally addressed to the working class, they held the newly defined sensation novel to a higher standard – again, probably because of its association with the middle class. Where melodrama connoted working-class, uneducated playgoers, when used as a modifier for 'fiction', sensation signalled a new readership: an educated, middle-class audience.

For the Victorians, the proliferation of sensation novels both came from and affirmed the aggregation of temporal and spatial acceleration; the rapid material production of books accompanied a change in the speed of the narratives and the ways readers consumed those narratives.[11] A confluence of changes in material print practices came together with the advent of the sensation novel: the 1858 invention of the horizontal rotary press made possible rapid production of cheap serial instalments, and the 1860 end of a long paper shortage primed the market for a flood of book production.[12] The increasing speed with which physical books could be printed, shipped and sold, and the wider circulation of novels through sources like Mudie's Circulating Library, led to the production of more books.[13] The mass production of books encouraged accelerated reading, and according to the critics of the sensation novel, the faster readers read, the more immoral were their readings.

To diagnose the public's predilection for sensation fiction, the *Medical Critic and Psychological Journal* suggests that readers' interest lies 'in the crimes absolutely, not in their counterfeit presentments in the pages of a novel, and it attaches itself in a far greater degree, therefore, to the actual than to the fictitious' ('Sensation Novels' 1863: 514). The market drives sensation, for 'writers have not been slow to perceive that the columns of the daily papers were becoming formidable rivals to quiet novels' (514). The *Medical Critic*'s argument juxtaposes the speed of 'daily papers' to the pace of 'quiet novels', and changing physiology that preferred the shocks and starts of journalism to moralising fiction. Aspiring novelists were to take advantage of 'the admirable organisation of the literary market', which is the primary reason 'that a supply of acceptable fiction has so closely followed, or has even in some degree anticipated and created the demand' for, sensational journalism (514).

Discourses of pathology unite with the language of temporality and the market to reflect an overall trend in Victorian criticism of sensation: gone are 'quiet novels', replaced by a 'light literature' that has 'becom[e] "fast"' (514).[14] While the *Medical Critic* does not abhor the shift – acceleration of daily life, the author writes, 'is only commensurate with the immense increase and wonderful diffusion of wealth and superficial knowledge' accompanying an age of general prosperity (514) – the article is nevertheless deeply entrenched in the critical discourse around sensation. Even Best and Marcus, in their discussion of surface reading, resonate far more with Arnold than with Dickens, for they argue that hermeneutic readers may 'find themselves unable to sustain the slow pace, receptiveness, and fixed attention it requires' to read surfaces (Best and Marcus 2009: 18). These terms are distinctly Victorian, but they are the terms of the Victorian scholar, rather than the literary public. Technological and social changes have sped up readers' bodies and evoked in them a desire for literature more akin to sensation journalism than to the quiet novels of old. With a faster sensorium came a new market for literature to fulfil those desires.

Critics of sensation fiction focused on the rapidity of its publication as a sign of its immorality and lack of literary quality. Margaret Oliphant correlates sensation reading with drug addiction, and claims that 'the violent stimulant of serial publication – of *weekly* publication, with its necessity for frequent and rapid recurrence of piquant situation and startling incident' – will cultivate in readers the 'germ' of immorality, and 'bring it to fuller and darker bearing' (Oliphant 1862: 568). The market-enforced temporality of weekly serial, according to Oliphant, compels novelists into mere sensationalism. Her description emphasises the temporal ties between literary production and the reading experience: as a result of weekly publication, reading becomes 'frequent' and 'rapid', a string of 'startling' and disjointed 'incident[s]' that undermines morality and sacrifices literary quality for sales. Oliphant traces a progression from an absent morality lost through a particular form of embodiment contingent on acceleration and speed.

Where Oliphant makes the connection between rapid incident and hedonism through an implicit logic, Henry Longueville Mansel turns that logic into a quantifiable calculation. Mansel makes even more explicit the tie between serialised temporality and market forces:

> A periodical, from its very nature, must contain many articles of an ephemeral interest, and of the character of goods made to order. The material part of it is a fixed quantity, determined by rigid boundaries

of space and time; and on this Procrustean bed the spiritual part must needs be stretched to fit. A given number sheets of print, containing so many lines per sheet, must be produced weekly or monthly, and the diviner element must accommodate itself to these conditions. (Mansel 1863: 483–4)

Serialised production's 'rigid boundaries of space and time' transform novels into 'goods made to order' – mere commodities. Any moral boon or 'diviner element' surrenders to economic motive. The 'fixed quantity' of material serial production inflicts its speed on reading, down to the level of the quantified sentence that fulfils part of the demand for 'so many lines per sheet'. 'Interest' and reading become 'ephemeral' because serialised writing is ephemeral. For both Oliphant and Mansel, the great crime here is that literature abandons its higher moral calling in favour of making an extra shilling.[15]

Associative Chains

In direct opposition to this claim, Dickens suggests that serialisation offers an ideal method to teach ethical reading. Like readers of sensation fiction, Pip has a proclivity for intense affect. But, also like these readers, the young Pip is on a trajectory to confuse his feelings for facts, and ultimately to value his own knowledge and interpretations over lived experience.

Serialisation becomes a mechanism to teach the reader to suspend knowledge, and instead to acknowledge the complexity of others' affects. Pip tends to foreclose on affective possibilities, and to insist on direct representational knowledge of others' interiority, so that their feelings are immediately legible. To know others' feelings, Pip turns their bodies into metaphors. Both to resist the commodification of his novels and to validate narrative as an emotional and humanising force, Dickens uses serial form in *Great Expectations* to condemn Pip's reading practices – and to teach the reader to acknowledge others' sensations rather than impose their own knowledge.

Pip is well aware of materiality, but he treats bodies as metaphors rather than matter. As he hides from a storm at the opening of the novel, Pip encounters the escaped convict, Abel Magwitch. Pip meets Magwitch first and foremost through an enumeration of physical traits and conditions: he 'had been soaked in water, and smothered in mud, and lamed by stones, and cut by flints, and stung by nettles, and torn by briars' (Dickens 1860a: 169). Magwitch's body *acts*: he 'limp[s], and shiver[s], and glare[s] and growl[s]' (169). Pip's attention to embodiment enables Magwitch to connect their bodies. Magwitch 'seize[s Pip] by the chin', and thereby shackles their bodies together (169). Magwitch's grasping hand resonates with the singularly identifying material marker of his body that Pip observes in his initial description: the 'great iron on his leg' (169). But all these profoundly embodied details collapse into mere metaphors for criminality.

As the aspiring scholars of *Middlemarch* and *Robert Elsmere* turn to metaphor because it seems academic, here, metaphoric reading of bodies leads Pip to far more consternation than reality merits. Pip obsesses over the shackles as a metaphor embodied in Magwitch's great iron, his grasping hand, and a set of cuffs at the end of the second instalment. On the one hand, Pip self-identifies with Magwitch's suffering, but he also sees it as a sign to be interpreted – a sign which points back to himself. As a pedagogical tool, the initial instalments of *Great Expectations* seek to forge those metaphoric associations, but to then separate them with the finality of a file, to teach readers that metaphoric knowledge leads ultimately back to problematic self-obsession.

The connection Pip forges between his body and Magwitch's body is part of an associative chain.[16] This concept is central to Associationism's understanding of cognition; in its simplest form, an associative chain is best summed up by Alexander Bain's 'Law of Contiguity':

> Actions, Sensations, and States of Feeling, occurring together or in close succession, tend to grow together or cohere, in such a way that, when any one of them is afterwards presented to the mind, the others are apt to be brought up in idea. (Bain 1855: 318)

If, for example, as a man walks through the London streets beside a hospital, he notices flickering candlelight in the windows and suffering bodies on the street, he may come to associate reflected candles with those bodies suffering, so that the sight of a candle calls up feelings of empathy or longing. This Law is accompanied by the Law of Similarity:

> *Present* Actions, Sensations, Thoughts, or Emotions tend to revive their *like* among *previous* Impressions. (451)

So that if that same man feels a longing to empathise with the suffering bodies around him, that impression may call to mind a past experience with a particular suffering body in which he felt the same desire for empathy. Impressions connect objects to one another even if those objects appear to have little other correlation (candles and suffering bodies), and can connect across time as well. For Pip, the grasping hand and the shackles link him to Magwitch. When he sends him home for food, Magwitch threatens Pip with the spectre of a 'young man' who accompanies him, and who is even more dangerous than he. The metaphoric shackles turn the young man into a metaphor as well – a metaphor for Pip himself.

Pip's experiences throughout the first and second instalment cohere so that the objects around him all seem to indict him as a criminal. When Pip's sister, Mrs. Joe, serves Pip and his brother-in-law Joe their bread-and-butter, Pip transforms it into a marker of criminality – a shackle. He opts to hold it 'in reserve' for Magwitch and 'his ally the still more dreadful young man', and secrets it away 'down the leg of [his] trousers' (Dickens 1860a: 172).[17] This act feels criminal to Pip: it requires an 'effort of resolution' that he finds 'awful'. When Joe notices that Pip has appeared to finish his bread, he declares that Pip will 'do [himself] a mischief' – a minor offence, but an offence nonetheless. The bread becomes a constant reminder not only of Magwitch's crime, but of Pip's as well: he describes it as a 'load upon my leg' and notes that it tends to impede his movement by sliding down to his ankle – a bread-and-butter shackle (173). Though an indeterminate amount of time passes between when Pip finally deposits the bread in his room and the next passage, the narrative flows straight from Pip's bedroom to 'great guns' firing as a signal that a convict has escaped. Obviously, the guns refer to Magwitch, but in this instance, it is Pip who has just escaped his shackle. When he then silently 'put [his] mouth into the forms of saying to Joe, "What's a convict?"', of Joe's silent response, Pip 'could make out nothing of it but the single word "Pip"' (173). His naïve associations transform his world into a chain of metaphoric accusations: 'every board' and 'every crack in every board' of the stairs calls 'Stop thief!' (173); a 'hare hanging up by the heels' like a pirate from a gibbet 'wink[s]' at him (174). Even the cows accuse Pip of being a thief (Dickens 1860b: 193). Pip becomes a metaphor for criminality, enmeshed in a metaphoric world where all matter is synecdoche.

Ultimately, Pip's tendency to read himself as the referent of all signs leads him to rewrite his own body as a criminal body. Pip's 'fat cheeks' and his 'heart and liver', which Magwitch says he wants to eat, become embodied in a pork pie Pip steals from his aunt. He must feed himself to the criminals whether he steals or not (Dickens 1860a: 169, 170, 174). This cannibalism further binds their bodies together – and perhaps ultimately binds them, for it is difficult to think of a materially closer relationship between two bodies than one literally inside the other.

As his material world demonstrates in its propensity toward criminal chains, Pip lacks the capacity to separate himself from Magwitch's criminality – and so he convicts himself. Pip confesses:

> I was in mortal terror of the young man who wanted my heart and liver; I was in mortal terror of my interlocutor with the ironed leg; *I was in mortal terror of myself*, from whom an awful promise had been extracted. (Dickens 1860a: 173)

The story of the young man, the ambiguity of Magwitch's shackled body, and Pip's own fluctuating self intertwine into one metaphoric relationship. Magwitch does not state that Pip is a criminal; he simply sets in motion the impressions of criminality and guilt and allows the physical connections between objects and bodies to forge the links. Pip himself offers a sketch of these material sources and their final symbolic link: 'the fugitive out on the marshes with the ironed leg, the mysterious young man, the file, the food', all chained to 'the dreadful pledge I was under to commit a larceny on those sheltering premises' (Dickens 1860a: 171). Magwitch's fiction is ambiguous: he neither specifies the identity of the young man, nor indicts Pip for his larceny. Rather, Pip inserts himself into the narrative through metaphor.

Economic Speculation and Seriality

Serial publication is, in a word, associative. Pip's tendency to put himself into the narrative reflects the inevitable temporality of serial narrative: in the gap from one instalment to the next, readers find themselves literally between the narrative. Linda Hughes and Michael Lund observe that 'because the reading time [of a serial] was so long, interpretation of the literature went on during the expansive middle of serial works' (Hughes and Lund 1991: 8). Narrative evokes a series of impressions that link otherwise disparate objects together across time. These feelings recur and redouble over time; the lived world and the textual world collide.[18] Rather than impede reading, serialised fiction like *Great Expectations* suggests, the gaps and leaps of serial fiction replicate the embodied experience of reading, so that fictional characters persist in the sensations they evoke. But it is also, in another word, speculative.[19]

Serialisation is particularly prone to this critique because it is a mode of production based on the promise of work. When readers experience the beginning instalment of *Great Expectations*, for example, the rest of the novel exists only in potential rather than as a purchasable commodity, and so readers make an investment (temporal, emotional and economic) in the initial instalment based on the author's promise of more to follow. Advertisement for the novel began as far back as 27 October 1860, a full five weeks before the 1 December first instalment ('Advertisement' 1860). The advertisement announces a 'new serial story' by Charles Dickens along with the initial instalment date and the issue in which it will appear, and announces that the story will 'be continued from week to week until completed in about EIGHT MONTHS'. Outside of the more familiar trappings of novel advertisements, I draw attention to the combination of the start date and the estimation of 'about eight months'. Through this information, the advertisement offers readers the chance to calculate approximately how much they will spend to read the novel, and when they will have to spend it. And, indeed, Dickens concluded *Great Expectations* exactly eight months of instalments after he began.

Seriality is the literary equivalent of speculative investment.[20] Dickens, who serially published sensation fiction in his magazines but also abhorred speculation, was deeply concerned with the argument that sensation and serialisation turn literature into a mere commodity. He spent some of his childhood beside his father, who was in Marshalsea Prison for debt – but his objections ran deeper than biography. Claudia Klaver argues in 'Natural Values and Unnatural Agents' that 'Dickens place[s] the ultimate blame for [Britain's systemic] instabilities on the speculative economic relations at the basis of the capitalist commercial system' (Klaver 1999: 14).[21] To confront this paradox, Dickens used serialised sensations as lessons in morality. He staunchly 'defend[ed] the relevance of a moral vocabulary to transactions in the economic domain', according to Mary Poovey, and held that 'the ethically neutral language of classical political economy was no more appropriate to the shenanigans of unscrupulous investors than it was to the sufferings of the downtrodden factory hand' (Poovey 2008: 156). Political economy fails to account for interiority and treats individuals as mere scientific data; the commodified text does the same, in that it treats characters' interiors as a means to profit.

In the face of speculative capitalism's flattening massification, to read and acknowledge a character's interiority values the complexity of affect. Deidre Lynch, in her foundational *Economy of Character*, argues that the persistence of interiority in the face of capitalism supplies readers with a reservoir of 'imaginative resources' they can mobilise to 'make themselves into individuals, to expand their own interior resources of sensibility' (Lynch 1998: 126). But rather than use economic language, Dickens turns to Associationism for a moral language to consider both literary exchange and interaction with literary characters. To humanise economics, he must humanise characters – and so he turns to serial temporality capacity to address bodies directly.

A coterie of mid-Victorian novel critics – including some members of the Associationist school following Alexander Bain – understood accelerated reading as 'a training ground for industrialised consciousness' (Dames 2007: 7).[22] These scholars who studied 'the physiology of the novel' felt that rapid consumption, flighty and ephemeral attention, and frequent and rapid incident arose inexorably from any attempt to read in an industrialised society. If the novel were to survive, they concluded, it 'could cohere only if it stopped resisting distraction and started instead to allow for, even encourage, mental drift' (83). Because distraction was inevitable, authors must accommodate it, and even make use of it to slow down readers' impulses to consume quickly.

Though they work with similar models, these thinkers came to a conclusion directly opposite those novelists who worked within the earlier paradigm of Associationism I have been tracing. They feared that 'the more diffusive currents of emotional waves which are known primarily through visceral or central nervous networks' prevented readers from ethical edification (97). The remedy, they suggested, was to 'becom[e] disembodied' (97). Contrary to this line of thought, Dickens's model of reading dives directly into the 'diffusive currents' in order to trigger the viscera and nerves. The sensation novel embraced modern reading, on the assumption that serialised sensation is a direct line to embodiment. In Dickens's work, this synchronisation is not only a market strategy; it is also a pedagogical strategy, a way to teach ethics through novel reading. Through embedded sensations of suspense and surprise within the abortive structure of serialisation, Dickens struggles to transform a mode of production accused of superficiality and commodification into a tool specifically against both – a humanising empathy derived from fast reading.

Associationism enables authors to recode speed, ephemerality and sensationalism as positive avenues to ethical growth. In the associative space between instalments of serial fiction, readers can better develop bodily impulses toward empathy – precisely because of its speed of publication, of reading, and of plot. Intuitive sense-making supersedes the hermeneutics of making sense because of the speed at which sensation moves in the body: impressions arise at first without temporal distinction between past and present, and without distinction between fiction and reality. Dickens's seriality intentionally activates these sensations to train readers' new, faster, sensation-prone bodies to accelerate past thought and interpretation, and thereby to acknowledge bodies and feelings.

Formal Snares and the Reading Lesson of Serial

Dickens writes to teach the common reader to use the toolkit of Associationism – impressions, chains, sensations – to read ethically. He celebrates embodiment and warns against reading bodies through metaphor. And ultimately, he must redeem sensation from the self-regard of capitalism. For this reason, he turns to the medium of serial to provide a reading lesson – to prove that serial and sensation deepen the morality of reading.

The narrative's suspense and its later mysteries create what Caroline Levine calls 'plotted snares' (C. Levine 2003: 8). 'Narrative fiction emerges . . . as a particularly effective way to introduce readers to the activity of hypothesising and testing in order to come to knowledge,' Levine argues, as the novel withholds information that it will only later relate. She goes on to argue that mystery texts such as *Great Expectations*, which depends in large part upon the great expectations of its core questions (i.e. who gave Pip his money?), cultivate a detachment that resonates with 'scientific experimentation, radical politics, and suspenseful storytelling' in that they 'all rely on the act of imagining a future – a future that, despite our best guesses, may or may not come to pass' (C. Levine 2003: 8, 9). These two aspects of Levine's argument come into conversation in the serialisation of *Great Expectations*, where hypothesising and testing almost always, despite anyone's best guesses, turn out incorrect whether the guesses come from characters in the narrative or the reader in the lived world.

While Levine looks for moments in the plot that act as snares, I am particularly interested in formal snares: moments where the snare lies not exclusively in the narrative, but also in the form and materiality of the text. Formal snares mark the moments at which Dickens uses serialisation as a pedagogical tool. Serialised breaks offer some of the novel's most sensational moments: at the conclusion of the twenty-seventh instalment, Pip receives a mysterious note containing only the message 'DON'T GO HOME' (Dickens 1861d: 221) – and there ends the instalment. This sensational suspense exemplifies the affective trend of *Great Expectations*, for after the foreboding message comes little more than a light dinner with a friend and his family; Pip *may* be in danger from another escaped criminal, but the danger is slight, and offset by his friend's ever-ridiculous domestic life. For all its sensational form, the novel's content is rarely sensational.

These moments indicate that impressions can do more than merely entertain: they can provide an intuitive knowledge about emotion that avoids reliance on speculative knowledge. The first and second instalments of *Great Expectations* that I explored above both offer an exemplary formal snare, and link the serial form to the complexity of Pip's lifelong reading lesson. Over the course of these two instalments, Pip struggles with the nuances of reading other bodies metaphorically, so that the only matter that matters is Pip; everything else is a sign for Pip. Here, serialised form initiates an association between criminality, Pip and readers intended to teach readers the same lesson Pip learns: bodies are matter, not metaphors.

Sensational manipulation of readers' expectations sets up the pedagogical lesson of these first instalments. Even as the novel will ultimately condemn Pip for his speculations, its plot and selective withholding of information makes Pip the centre of it all: the narrative focalises through Pip the character, and Pip the narrator tells the story. If one reads with the grain of the text, all signs point to Pip. The first instalment builds up the associative chains, and they intensify through the second instalment – but here end with a material lesson on the proper way to read. After Pip delivers the file to Magwitch, the file's sound follows him home from the third chapter to the fourth, so that he 'fully expected to find a Constable in the kitchen, waiting to take me up' (Dickens 1860b: 195) – an observation that primes the reader for the conclusion of the chapter. At home, he remains under the tyranny of the 'terrible young man' as he ponders whether the Church might protect him if he were to confess his 'wicked secret' (195). Pulled through the chapters' frenetic pace, bombarded with feelings and states of bodies that point toward the criminal, readers' only insight into the text comes through Pip's association of his body with the criminal. If the reader accepts Pip's criminal associations, then the conclusion of the fourth chapter and second instalment seems to confirm Pip's transformation:

> I have never been absolutely certain whether I uttered a shrill yell of terror, merely in spirit, or in the bodily hearing of the company. I felt that I could bear no more, and that I must run away. I released the leg of the table, and ran for my life.
>
> But, I ran no further than the house door, for there I ran head foremost into a party of soldiers with their muskets: one of whom held out a pair of handcuffs to me, saying, 'Here you are, look sharp, come on!' (198)

There ends the instalment – and begins the reading lesson.

'Pip' as a character cannot be simply an abstract fiction, for he seems capable of evoking impressions; at the same time, he must be constructed and writable if the reader is to read his body. As narrator and character, Pip forges associative chains that convince readers of Pip's transformation into a criminal. Themes of criminality and discipline from the first instalment merge with the confessional themes of the second instalment, from the cow with the 'clerical air' (193), to the possibility of confession (195), to Wopsle's sermons (196–7). If the narrative successfully snares readers, the arrival of the soldiers strengthens the criminal chains. The form of the text baits readers into drawing themselves into the associations that link Pip to criminality, into reading bodies through metaphor.

If in fact readers embrace Pip's criminal associations and read the text through these lenses, then they have fallen for Pip's incorrect interpretation of his body and his environment. The soldiers have no interest in arresting Pip. They simply need Joe to 'throw [his] eye' over a pair of handcuffs and do 'a little job' repairing them (Dickens 1860c: 217). The week-long break between the second and third instalments, during which Pip hangs in limbo, the soldiers about to arrest him, perhaps provides a good laugh for the reader (and for Dickens), but also suggests an important element of learning to empathise with textual bodies: the need to suspend interpretation, the need not to speculate. This is not simply a question of mental detachment, for it is not simply a matter of different thinking. Empathy requires a suspension of the interpretive self, a refusal to reduce all signs to referents that point toward the reader. Because of his metaphoric reading of both Magwitch's body and his own, Pip misinterprets the soldier's 'look sharp' and so condemns himself to criminality.

Where Associationism's ideal reader eliminates the judgemental self in order to feel others' impressions, Pip struggles to step out of himself. He cannot help but interpret his body, to apply an interpretive lens (criminality) to every element of his embodiment, so that Magwitch's grasping hand writes shackles and their association with criminality on to his body. Where in these early instalments Pip's representations lead him to read his body incorrectly in a humorous misunderstanding, in later instalments metaphor leads him to far more costly errors like his misreading of Joe, Biddy and Estella. The handcuff gag in the instalment transition entertains, but more importantly it instructs: when readers fall into the trap of believing unconditionally in Pip's criminality, they affirm Pip's proclivity to treat bodies as metaphors that can be known. The serialisation scolds the reader, and offers a corrective: bodies are not metaphors, they are bodies.

Epistemological Speculation and Embodiment

Pip's greatest struggle is his tendency to read everything as metaphor, with himself as the referent of all. This is because he has all the potentially bad habits of the disembodied scholar. He is embodied, but insists on interpretation; his minimal education inclines him to believe his own knowledge over acknowledging others' experiences. As Max Byrd puts it, 'at the beginning of his story Pip cannot read, but his efforts to improvise lead him to create fictions, largely about his own forlorn identity, which he foolishly believes' (Byrd 1976: 259). As a result, 'he falls continually into mistakes of interpretation, so that he launches himself too hastily into a world he has scanned but not yet understood' (259). Pip's journey through capital operates under a similar formula, for his great expectations appear to generate themselves, and his climb up the social ladder arrives *ex nihilo* from Miss Havisham's invitation. While the narrative eventually unveils his assumptions as falsehoods, Pip speculates on his possible relationships with both Biddy and Estella: he imagines their bodies as possible investments that in turn would increase his monetary and social standing. Nowhere does this become more apparent than in his later readings when Joe comes to stay at his apartment – a missed opportunity to throw off the shackles of metaphor and treat a body as a body, and reading as reading.

At the risk of reading too metaphorically, the scene parallels the opening instalments. Having lost his fortune, lost Magwitch, and fallen ill, Pip finds himself reduced to his original state as an adopted ward of Joe Gargery. Pip begins with conjuration similar to his younger readings of his family's gravestones as he 'confound[s] impossible existences with [his] own identity' (Dickens 1861f: 409). His delirium inverts the formulation by which objects become bodies: while gravestones became parents, Pip becomes 'a brick in the house-wall', a 'steel beam of a vast engine' (409). Where he failed to struggle against Magwitch when he was a child, he now 'struggle[s] with real people, in the belief that they [a]re murderers' (409). Where bodies become soldiers and criminals in the opening, these ethereal conjurations 'settle down into the likeness of Joe' (409). Finally, as Magwitch's chokehold physically connected his body to young-Pip's and formed the organic shackle between them, the older Pip exclaims, 'Joe had actually laid his head down on the pillow at my side and *put his arm round my neck*' (410, emphasis added). The opening instalments relate a story of condemnation and failure; now, reduced to a childlike state, bereft of his fortune, Pip lies poised to begin his writing lessons again with a potentially clean slate. The ideally domestic Joe replaces Magwitch's criminality, violence and cunning replaced with Joe's innocent earnestness.[23]

But, as with his failed readings as a child, Pip once again reduces associative relationships to his own benefit, and rejects the potential to associatively connect with Joe through writing. This time, it is not Pip who writes 'J-O, Joe', but rather Joe who has acquired the ability to write. Pip's desperation to affirm his own superiority makes this moment a powerful synecdoche for his misguided reading practices: he reads Joe as a metaphor and forecloses on any possibility other than his belief that Joe is beneath him.

When confronted with Joe's newfound literary abilities, Pip describes Joe's writing in a manner that puts Joe back into the place of ignorant blacksmith and thereby maintains Pip's elevated sense of self. In fact, Pip's description begins by circling back to himself: 'As I lay in bed looking at him, it made me, in my weak state, cry again with pleasure to see the pride with which [Joe] set about his letter' (410). Twice, Pip acknowledges his vulnerability, 'lay[ing] in bed' in a 'weak state', and seeks immediately to defuse his impotence by associating the feeling of Joe's writing with his own pleasure. He links pleasure to the space of writing, the 'writing-table', and moves quickly to lay claim to that object with the appellation 'my own writing-table' (410). Pip condescendingly deems Joe's letter 'his great work' – a rejection that operates through mechanisms of sarcasm and superiority similar to those with which the narrator dismissed his own childhood reading practices. Writing provides the opportunity for an associative chain of emotional connection: the writing desk leads to writing, evokes the pleasure of narrative, links Pip to Joe. Instead, Pip circumvents these openings with commerce and ownership: the writing desk is Pip's, the pleasure is Pip's, and so Pip becomes the arbiter of all meaning.

As the judge of meaning, Pip transforms Joe's writing into manual labour and cements it as an act beneath the man Pip has become. He describes how Joe 'choos[es] a pen from the pen-tray as if it were a chest of large tools, and tuck[s] up his sleeves as if he were going to wield a crowbar or sledge-hammer' (410). The material objects of writing become mere tools, which Joe fails to wield properly. His pen 'sputter[s] extensively', and he 'had a curious idea that the inkstand was on the side of him where it was not, and constantly dipped his pen into space, and seemed quite satisfied with the result' (410). According to Pip, Joe's body is incommensurate with writing. Pip portrays Joe as clownish, unable to control his own body: 'It was necessary for Joe to hold on heavily to the table with this left elbow, and to get his right leg well out behind him, before he could begin' (410). The associative chain here rewrites writing's physical objects so that they either belong to Pip (the writing desk), or become tools foreign to a comical worker's body – an association that portrays Joe as a buffoon, barred from writing. In both instances, Pip uses writing to aggrandise his sense of self: he has an education, and his literary abilities make him superior to Joe.

The depiction of Joe's writing practices as out of place and comical demarcates Pip as a reader of bodies and texts, who is by virtue of his capacity to read and decode above Joe's writing body and the text he writes. Pip, of course, never relates the contents of the letter, because he preoccupies himself with reading his own interpretation of Joe's body. As he once did in the graveyard, here, a few words (unseen, in this instance) conjure an entire body: Joe's body, out of place. Disempowered through illness, Pip must disempower Joe; he must read Joe as a buffoon, a laughable comic-relief rather than a successful rival.

While the narrator for a time invites the reader to validate this denigration, the events of the narrative interrogate Pip's unilateral interpretation. Critical self-reflection begins when, as Pip begins to heal, Joe first calls him 'sir' (412). Pip notes that Joe's shift 'grate[s] on [him]' and decides that the best way to acknowledge the equality he seems to ambivalently desire between the two of them is to 'preten[d] to be weaker than [he is]' (412). This performance essentially fails, and the failure suggests to Pip that he should 'go to Biddy, [and] show her how humbled and repentant' he has become, and thereby win her heart (413). To say this declaration of love also fails is an understatement, since Pip not only fails to win Biddy's love, but discovers that she has married Joe. And through this particular failure, the culmination of an associative chain begun by Pip's misreading of Joe's writing, Pip stumbles upon the idea that the 'old idea of his [friend Herbert's] inaptitude' – Herbert's tendency to confound intention with execution – 'perhaps . . . had never been in him at all, but had been in me' (Dickens 1861g: 436; see also Dickens 1861c: 481). Here, at the end, Pip finally learns his reading lesson: that he cannot assume his own assumptions and hermeneutics wholly encompass the affects of bodies around him. This is precisely the problem that plagues Pip.

Importantly, Pip's inaptitude lies in his propensity to cover up the material bodies around him with his own, preferred, metaphoric readings. He misreads Joe's writing to Biddy as a clownish performance, rather than a lover writing to his partner. He conjures an imaginary Biddy who will fall in love with him and marry him. In short, he fails to recognise that the other characters in the novel have their own feelings, their own bodies, their own lives. This misreading culminates with the sudden realisation that all the ineptitudes Pip has thus far identified in his young reading practices, in Joe, in Estella and in Magwitch perhaps reflect his own adult shortcomings. Pip's unfit reading practices ignore observation in favour of his own psychological phantasms that lead his relationships to ruin.

But these mistakes are not mere misinterpretations, for in fact, *any* interpretation is a misinterpretation. This sets up a complicated duality: a text that seems to valorise the young Pip's capacity to associate and imagine potentials punishes the later Pip for what appear to be similar practices. The problem lies in the Associationists' definition of what constitutes knowledge and how one acquires that knowledge. In Pip's failed associations, he believes reality to be whatever he thinks it should be. He believes that if he can imagine a body, then he knows that body. This creates a kind of warped ontology of sensation, wherein metaphoric imaginations of others' feelings constitute reality. Like the disembodied scholar, his inclination to know rather than to acknowledge overrides his common intuition and leads him to self-regard.

Associative Ethics, Self-Suspension and Sympathy

The serialisation of *Great Expectations* teases readers, for temporal gaps entice readers to speculate even as the form of the novel implicitly scolds them for doing so. Dickens's formal snares call attention to the epistemology that confounds intention with execution, and confuses assumption for truth (Dickens 1861c: 481). The acquisition of knowledge in the narrative cannot come simply from guess-check-and-revise scientific hypotheses; whenever Pip makes such an attempt, he fails. But importantly, his failures as an observer stem from his failures as a reader. In short, his observations arise only from his own interpretations, so that he understands bodies only as signs that point back to the self. These formal snares undercut the generic conventions of the autobiographical *Bildungsroman* to teach readers that even fictional bodies are not mere metaphors. Because readers feel physical sensations when they imagine or remember bodies, they should treat characters with the depth that they should also extend to others.

Empathic depth requires one to acknowledge rather than know. Autobiographical narratives, in which the narrator tells his own story in hindsight, create the illusion that the text offers full access to the character's interiority, or that a character's description of her feelings reveals completely the depth of those feelings. Contrary to that illusion, serial gaps like Pip's aborted relation between Issue 92 and Issue 93 of *All the Year Round* reveal and revel in the fundamental unknowability of the fictional character. In Issue 92, Pip anguishes over the fate of his relationship with Joe and Biddy, and muses, 'If my time had run out, it would have left me still at the height of my perplexities, I dare say. It never did run out, however, but was brought to a premature end, as I proceed to relate' – except that the instalment ends there. He resumes his narrative a week later, in Issue 93 (Dickens 1861a: 390). Even as he refers to his own life, Pip's conjecture resonates with the reading experience of serialisation: at the height of Pip's perplexities on his changing class position, the reader's time runs out for a week, brought to a premature end at the material whim of part-publication. Serialisation acts as a shackle through the market that binds readers and characters through association even when they separate between instalments. And yet, formal snares call attention to the irrevocable reality of fiction's mediation, that the novel is a novel, a separate, immaterial world conveyed through a narrator and a material text. The formal snare's self-referentiality draws attention to the illegibility of characters – and to the illegibility of others' sensations. If the text is a training ground for ethical encounters with other bodies, serialisation offers a training ground for readers to accept that other bodies can never be fully read.

Because these bodies are fictional, along with the complex ethics of materiality, Dickens also offers a material theory of written language. Mrs. Joe is attacked by Orlick and struck in the back of the head. The blow renders her speech 'unintelligible', and so she is forced to communicate through writing alone (386). She 'trace[s] upon the slate, a character that looked like a curious T', and eagerly draws attention to the glyph 'as something she particularly wanted' (386). He assumes that the character is a 'T', and brings everything 'from tar to toast and tub' (386). In each of these readings, Pip forecloses on the possibilities of language, and insists that words must signify directly. Eventually, he determines that 'the sign look[s] like a hammer', and so brings in all of Joe's hammers (386). When that fails, he tries a crutch, which his sister rejects. Pip, like the bumbling policemen on the case of the assault, 'tries to fit the circumstances to the ideas, instead of trying to extract ideas from the circumstances' (386). Even when he allows for the possibility that the 'T' is not a 'T', he still reads linearly, through what he assumes and feels rather than what his sister feels.

Biddy, on the other hand, understands immediately that the T *is* a hammer, but that the hammer in turn signifies Orlick. Like Locke and Müller, she recognises the material origin of language. Caroline Levine calls Biddy the 'epistemological ideal' of *Great Expectations* because she operates under the assumption that 'in order to know the world we must learn to suspend ourselves' (C. Levine 2003: 85). Biddy reads like an Associationist: through an intuitive chain of references, from one body to another – and without the imposition of her own interpretations.

Dickens sets up the practice of reading for impressions in contrast to Jaggers's market-driven declaration 'I'll have no feelings here' (Dickens 1861e: 316). The lawyer demands attention to 'the exact words' and interacts with others only because he is paid. The text juxtaposes his unfeeling interactions, motivated by profit, with the intensity of Joe's feeling. When Jaggers comes to take Pip away, he demands utmost precision of language; he objects to Pip's use of the word 'recommendation', saying, 'no, no, no; it's very well done, but it won't do; you are too young to fix me with it. Recommendation is not the word' (Dickens 1861b: 412). When he presses Joe with the same linear exactitude, on the other hand, Joe utters this articulate soliloquy:

'Which I meantersay ... that if you come to my place bull-baiting and badgering me, come out! Which I meantersay as sech if you're a man, come on! Which I meantersay that what I say, I meantersay and stand or fall by!' (412)

The narrative affirms Joe's sentimental loyalty over Jaggers's economic precision. While Jaggers may be more articulate, his language connects people only because he is paid for it. While Joe's language may lack semantic content, he communicates through sensation. Literary authority comes from earnest, emotional investment. Dickens turns the form of serialisation on its head: where space between instalments encourages readers to fill in the gaps, he invites them to pause – to feel rather than to know.

The ethical language of Associationism comes from its scientific understanding of memory: people are aggregates of their memories, and while chains may link memories, sensations forge meaningful connections between those chains. It is improper – even unethical – to fill in the gaps in someone else's connections with one's own knowledge. This is why Martineau can claim that Associationism enables 'a transition from self-regard, not exactly into self-forgetfulness, but into self-identification with the well-being of others' (Martineau 1885b: 301), or why J. S. Mill can demand the ethical observer become a 'benevolent spectator' (J. S. Mill 1874: 129). Literary authority does not come from knowledge, but rather, the gradual surrender of knowledge. This appears in the reduction of Boz's narrative interjections in 'The Hospital Patient', in Joe's incorporation with Pip's body on Pip's sick-bed, and with Biddy's connection with Mrs. Joe and her mysterious 'T'. In each of these moments, Dickens aims to humanise by locating literary authority in sensation and self-suspension. Associationism enables the reader to throw off the shackles of the market, and to acknowledge others' feelings and bodies rather than claim the profit of knowledge.

And yet, as we will begin to see in the next chapter, something sinister lurks behind this mandate to surrender oneself. It is all well and good for a Victorian gentleman to suspend himself for a brief ramble through the East End, because he knows he will have a self to return to once his escapade concludes. But for the women on the margins – Biddy among them – the call to suspend can be a call to annihilation.

Notes

1. For a more general history of the sensation novel, of which there are many excellent examples, see the foundational work in D. A. Miller's *The Novel and the Police* (1988); Patrick Brantlinger's 'What Is "Sensational" about the "Sensation Novel"?' (1982) and his chapter 'Novel Sensations' in *The Reading Lesson* (1998), and Ann Cvetkovich's

Mixed Feelings (1992). Anna Maria Jones's *Problem Novels* (2007) provides new criticism on sensation fiction and metacriticism on Foucauldian and post-Foucault studies of sensation fiction. See also Caroline Levine's *The Serious Pleasures of Suspense* (2003); Andrew Mangham's *Violent Women and Sensation Fiction* (2007); Lyn Pykett's *The Nineteenth-Century Sensation Novel* (2011); Andrew Maunder and Grace Moore's *Victorian Crime, Madness and Sensation* (2016); and of course the plethora of essays in Pamela Gilbert's *A Companion to Sensation Fiction* (2011).
2. See Tara MacDonald's chapter 'Bodily Sympathy, Affect, and Victorian Sensation Fiction' in *Affect Theory and Literary Critical Practice* (2019) for a similar claim about affect and genre.
3. <<La confiance aveugle dont fait prevue le jeune Pip dans son rapport au langage reproduit ironiquement celle du lecteur qui, bien que complice du narrateur dont il partage le regard amusé sur la lecture naïve que l'enfant fait des signes, se laisse cependant prendre au jeu de l'illusion référentielle et, comme lui, suppléée par l'imagination aux mots sur la page>> (Dutheil 1993: 112). Dutheil published this article in English in the September 1996 *Dickens Quarterly*, but her arguments lose some of their verve in the translation.
4. It could be useful to think of this as part of Bourdieu's 'habitus', though I often find that term too broad to provide much focus to this sort of conversation (see Bourdieu 1977). Monique Scheer's 'Are Emotions a Kind of Practice?' (2012) cogently uses Bourdieu to think about the cultivation of emotional practices as well. In both cases, though, the phenomenologically embodied feeling of emotions seems secondary at best, unlike the Associationist's emphasis on embodiment.
5. In an 1862 article in *Blackwood's*, Margaret Oliphant turns to the American Civil War as both a metaphor to describe sensation and historical evidence for the American inclination toward the genre. She paints the Americans as 'a race *blasée* and lost in universal *ennui*', who live in a society that 'has bethought itself of the grandest expedient for procuring a new sensation': the war (Oliphant 1862: 564). The root of the British craving, she suggests, may come from their English-speaking counterparts in America. The excitement of the war makes dull 'the safe life we lead at home' in Britain, and though 'we follow at a humble distance, we begin to feel the need of a supply of new shocks and wonders' (564). Because the mid-century is 'an age which has turned to be one of events', and particularly of war, Oliphant argues that it is 'only natural that art and literature should . . . attempt a kindred depth of effect and shock of incident' (565).
6. Representations of novels as food were common in Victorian literary criticism. Trollope compared the reading public to those who 'eat pastry after dinner – not without some inward conviction that the taste is vain if not vicious' (quoted in Olmsted 2016: 126). An anonymous

Spectator contributor in 1888 writes of Walter Scott that he 'find[s] the materials of a wholesome interest in that which forms the background of a particular tale of adventure', so that his 'novels supply nourishment as well as stimulus, while the ordinary novel supplies stimulus alone' ('Literary Dram-Drinking' 1888: 13). A lover of mere 'stories', on the other hand, 'wants always to be feeling a thrill of excitement running through his nerves', tantamount to a medical condition. He concludes: 'The habit of dram-drinking, it is said, leads to fatty degeneration of the heart, – i.e., excessive fattening round the heart, and weak action of the heart in consequence. So, too, the habit of exciting novel-reading leads to fatty degeneration of the literary mind, – i.e., to an unhealthy and spasmodic action of the imagination, and a general weakening of the power of entering thoroughly into the solid interests of real life' (13).

7. See also Rebecca Solnit's 'The Annihilation of Time and Space' (2003) on photography.
8. Austin's argument about Empire is worth further exploration. Looking back on the decade in 1870, he argues that the sensationalisation of the domestic space lies in the cultural insularity of the British (and particularly English) citizens of the Empire, especially after its declaration in 1858 (Austin 1870b: 422). The sheer geographic and cultural scope of the Empire, Austin claims, makes cosmopolitan interests all too daunting. Instead, the Empire's citizens are 'deeply curious to the affairs of [their] immediate neighbours, whilst profoundly indifferent to those of people who stand to it in a more remote relationship' (423).
9. Literacy as an element of popular culture stems in part, Fraser and Green suggest, from 'the [1840s] reaction to Chartism and the Chartist press[, which] reveals to what extent national literacy was no longer an upper-class monopoly' (Fraser and Green 2003: 77–8). The sensation novel became, in Winifred Hughes's words, 'an undisputed example of "democratic art", not only being read by all classes of society but having its origins in the less-than-respectable quarters of lower-class literature' (Hughes 2014: 6). See also Walter C. Phillips's *Dickens, Reade, and Collins: Sensation Novelists* (W. C. Phillips 1919: 108), from which Hughes takes her term 'democratic art'.
10. See Kate Flint's *The Woman Reader* (1993) for the origin of these statistics and further analysis.
11. N. N. Feltes argues that the 1852 disbanding of the Booksellers Association transformed novels from expensive, material objects that interpellate their readers as upper class, to commodities produced for a bourgeois audience and produced in a purely capitalist mode (Feltes 1986: 1).
12. The paper shortage was caused by a decrease in materials for paper production like rags, cotton and hemp. According to an 1854 letter from MP Samuel Gregson to MP Charles Wood, who was President of

the Board of Control for the Affairs of India, the general shortage of material had reached a head due to the Crimean War, with the deficit of imported hemp from Russia numbering around 106,000 tons (Gregson 1854: 8). Shortages had reached the point where *The Times* released an advertisement, which Gregson sent to Wood along with his letter, offering a £1,000 reward for the 'inventi[on] or discover[y] of using a cheap substitute' for paper materials. The paper crisis abated suddenly with the 1860 introduction of esparto, a North African grass, as the long-desired substitute. So effective was the replacement that it assisted in the 1861 repeal of the Paper Duty, which had been in place since 1843.

13. For more on mass production and mass readership in the eighteenth and early nineteenth centuries, see also Joseph Heidler, *The History of English Criticism of Prose Fiction* (1928); J. M. S. Tompkins, *The Popular Novel in England* (1976); Michael McKeon, *The Origins of the English Novel* (1987).

14. For more on Victorian uses of the words 'fast' and 'slow' to describe sensation, see Erica Haugtvedt's 'Sympathy of Suspense' (2016), in which she argues that Braddon mobilises the speed of serial to help readers develop deeper sympathy with her characters.

15. Mansel's ironic physical measurements also affirm Benjamin Morgan's argument that Mansel objects to the 'return to a philosophical conception of the human as machine that had guided mechanistic strands of Enlightenment psychology' (Morgan 2017: 142). Mansel decries the reduction of something so fundamentally human as literature to something so basely material – which he sees as opposed to the human.

16. The concept is variously referred to as a 'chain' or a 'train', sometimes by the same theorist.

17. William Cohen observes that the limp Pip acquires from the secreted bread is a 'corporeal metonymy' that further binds his body to Magwitch's bound body (Cohen 1993: 220). Cohen formulates Pip in 'Manual Conduct' as he would later describe the Dickensian subject in *Embodied*, a body 'actively engaged in palpable, reciprocal exchange with the world, including other embodied subjects', and 'at once bounded in the body's material substance and open to being changed and reshaped' (Cohen 2009: 64).

18. Erica Haugtvedt makes a case for this persistence as a cognitive phenomenon related to object permanence. She suggests that 'serial narratives exploit the possibilities of something like object permanence by using the capacities of the human mind to recognise and infer that fictional, humanlike entities go on existing even when we aren't paying attention. Serial character, then, depends upon the condition of temporal persistence – and seems realistic in this regard, even when serial character may not always share other traits of realist characterisation' (Haugtvedt 2017: 413). See Deborah Wynne's *The Sensation Novel and the Victorian Family Magazine* (2001) for more on the relationship between these novels and the audience of their serialisation.

19. Speculation was not a new practice in the 1850s and 1860s, but its increased prominence throughout these decades brought more intense debates about the ethics of capitalist economic practices. Earlier legislation in speculation included the Joint Stock Companies Act 1844, which enabled the incorporation of companies 'without explicit, deliberate, and specific State permission' (Harris 2000: 284). Instead, incorporation became possible through registration with the Registry Office of the Committee of Privy Council for Trade (283). Ease of incorporation made investment and speculation more likely because companies formed more readily, but as limited liability was not a part of the Act, any shareholder of the company might be held monetarily responsible for company failure. The passage of the Limited Liability Act 1855 eliminated this risk for companies larger than twenty-five members with transferable shares and offices in England or Ireland (Haddan 1855: 3). It decreed that shareholders would be responsible only 'to the extent of the portions of their shares respectively in the capital of the company not then paid up', but no greater than that sum (57–60). In other words, a shareholder would no longer lose his or her entire net wealth if a company in which he or she had invested went under; instead, he or she would be responsible only for the amount of capital invested. This was followed by the Joint Stock Company Act 1856, which further freed companies to speculate. 'Instead ... of a "Limited Liability" measure', one contemporary economist suggested, 'it might ... be more properly termed a "No Liability Act"' (C. Wordsworth 1859: v).
20. This mode of production suggested that profit mattered more than narrative. The serialised text reinforces its own commodification: at the conclusion of *All the Year Round* 5.117, which came out on 20 July 1861, there is an advertisement for the Chapman and Hall three-volume edition of *Great Expectations* – though the novel's serialisation would not finish for another two weeks on 3 August 1861 ('Advertisement' 1861). In this sense, the sensation novel epitomises the 'commodity-text', for the form of literary production generated surplus value rather than 'wages, royalties, or profits, as might be the case in a petty-commodity mode of production' (Feltes 1986: 8). Not unlike a railway company or other speculative venture, Dickens provides a sketch or outline of a potential commodity, and asks that readers invest their time and money in his project. Tamara Wagner claims that 'the growing fascination with speculative ventures entered the novel genre at the level of plot structure and as figurative language' (Wagner 2010: 6). Speculation and credit provided novels with a 'figurative language' both to comment on representations of life, and to comment on the practice of representation. These metarepresentations often do not explicitly address capital, but they do address the cultural milieu capital creates. Patrick Brantlinger also argues in *Fictions of State* that mid-nineteenth-century Realist novels turn from critiques of industrialism and begin to address cultural and social issues (Brantlinger 1996: 143).

21. Other scholars have charted an attitude toward speculation more ambivalent than aggressively against. As Wilfred Dvorak puts it, 'the main argument in *All the Year Round* in the 1860s is that something new is happening to the way in which Englishmen accumulate wealth' (Dvorak 1984: 90). Paul Jarvie argues for a similar ambivalence in *Nicholas Nickleby*, although he allows for the possibility of 'Dickens's own art working against the ideological project of the novel' (Jarvie 2005: 47).
22. Nicholas Daly makes a similar argument in *Literature, Technology, and Modernity* when he argues that, through an emphasis on speed, 'the sensation novel provides a species of temporal training' in which 'its deployment of suspense and nervousness . . . synchronises its readers with industrial modernity' (Daly 2004: 37).
23. While they differ in these critical ways, Joe and Magwitch are both social outcasts. Joe is completely out of his element in Miss Havisham's social world. However, where Magwitch's existence outside the social makes him dangerous, the text celebrates Joe's inability to navigate the manipulative complexity of Miss Havisham's world and the credit economy. Joe's emotional earnestness and simplicity makes his connection with Pip a positive association, rather than Magwitch's manipulative association.

Chapter 4

Plastic Bodies: The Scientist, Vital Mechanics and Ethical Habits of Character in Wilkie Collins's *The Moonstone*

In the September 1898 issue of *The Nineteenth Century*, John Haldane's essay 'Vitalism' chronicles that 'about the middle of the present century a great change occurred in the general trend of investigation . . . in animal physiology' away from a model that understood 'life as something essentially different from the phenomena met with in the inorganic world' (Haldane 1898: 400). Instead of this model that held life apart from inorganic phenomena, or *vitalism*, science had moved toward a model called *mechanism*, which held that everything 'must ultimately be susceptible of analysis into a series of physical and chemical processes' (400).[1] As we have seen throughout this book, the materialism of the Associationists places them firmly in this latter camp, as they sought physical explanations for mental phenomena.

Curiously, *The Nineteenth Century* makes an exception for the mind, one motivated by the *fin de siècle* desire to preserve within mechanism a space for vitalist psychology. *The Nineteenth Century* actually says that everything 'apart from consciousness, which of course stands by itself', must submit to mechanical analysis. This gesture is distinctly late-1890s, as the end of the decade saw a resurgence of new vitalist thought. These thinkers found philosophical grounds in the 1840s work of Hermann Lotze, who denounced vitalism, but nevertheless maintained the importance of something he called 'vital force'. On the one hand, Lotze maintained that 'vital force is not to be understood as any distinct force, but rather as the sum of the effect of numerous partial forces acting under given conditions' – a decidedly mechanistic approach to the abstract (Mivart 1887: 696,

Mivart's translation). Nevertheless, he also argued that these various forces and conditions did not 'attach themselves to a lifeless inner nature of things, but must arise out of them, and nothing can take place *between* the individual elements until something has taken place *within* them' (699, Mivart's translation). Lotze offered a strong basis for the late-nineteenth-century return to vitalist understandings of consciousness even while they maintained mechanistic approaches to physics and chemistry.

This Lotze-inspired vitalism bookends the nineteenth century. Vitalism dominated before the 1830s publications of Marshall Hall and Thomas Laycock on reflex actions of the brain, and returned in the 1880s and 90s.[2] But, while early- and late-nineteenth-century scholars made space for consciousness outside of mechanism, mid-century Associationism held firmly to its materialism. George Henry Lewes writes in his *Physical Basis of Mind* that 'mental phenomena when observed in others, although interpretable by our consciousness of what is passing in ourselves, can only be objective phenomena of the vital organism' (Lewes 1877: 3). In other words, while we feel to some degree that we know others' internal states, in fact we only observe the effects of physiological changes. Against vitalism, 'which fills up with a guess the gap' between mental phenomena and material etiology, Lewes levies the charge of being metaphysical, or allowing imaginary abstracts to replace physical reality (22). As a reviewer of Lewes's book puts it: 'Mind and soul are abstractions by which the "logic of signs" groups certain nervous phenomena or refers to them as a fictitious cause' ('Lewes's *Physical Basis of Mind*' 1877: 707). Lewes and other radical materialists of the mid-century refused to make special accommodations for consciousness in their mechanistic models.

It is crucial for literary studies to understand the distinct space carved out for consciousness in our own, post-1890s epistemologies. If we are to understand mid-century representations of bodies and characters, we must avoid the temptation to imbue them with vitalist causality, for the debate about mechanism reached readily from science into literary criticism. In the same language as that with which he condemns abstraction in science, Lewes cautions literary authors against the 'great source of error' that 'much of our thinking is carried on by signs instead of images'; 'vigorous and effective minds', he extols, 'habitually deal with concrete images' (Lewes 1891: 33). This becomes especially important when we consider something like character, where symbolism and interiority are particularly seductive. In *Out of Character: Modernism, Vitalism, Psychic Life*, Omri Moses advocates vitalism as an alternative ethical model to a purportedly static, nineteenth-century mechanism. For, in opposition to 'prescribed rules or principles, vitalists tend to promote a capacity to improvise and adapt to a world that is mutable' (Moses 2014: 2). This particular reading opposes 'affective responses' to the more mechanical (and Associationist) ideas like 'will, habit, and intuition', to ultimately argue that while early-twentieth-century authors provide an ethics for the instability of the actual world, nineteenth-century 'characters enjoy solidity' that works only in their mechanistic (read, unrealistic) world (4, 7). But in fact, as this chapter will demonstrate, while Victorian characters enjoy their materiality, they are hardly 'solid' in the sense of unchanging. If anything, they enjoy their plasticity: a physical, mechanistic consistency that makes complex changes and adaptations in response to external stimuli.

Nowhere in literary studies is this more important than in the consideration of textual bodies. Mid-century novelists reject the metaphorisation of bodies. Here, through a physiological analysis of character and its representation in Wilkie Collins's *The Moonstone*, we will explore a model for studying bodies as bodies. Alfred Austin once accused sensation novels of 'substituting characteristics for character, and palming off the one for the other' (Austin 1870b: 419). But, while Collins admits that this may have been true of his previous novels, in *The Moonstone* he attempts 'to trace the influence of character on circumstances' (Collins 1868o: vii). This arcane statement makes more sense through the lens of Associationist materialism: through a sense of character as material phenomenon based in physiology and not a metaphysical (vitalist) notion of self, Collins endeavours to make sense of how certain physical arrangements impact the material conditions around them. 'Character' has two valences here: both the character in a text, and the notion of someone's character as in the essential constitution of their personality. The former is, in the Associationist novelist's understanding, material; the latter is, according to the Associationist's mechanism, a mere fiction of the logic of signs. Allegedly psychological phenomena like character must have physiological explanations. To think about the effect of character on circumstances, then, Collins's characters must be embodied, and their matter must interact through mechanistic systems.

The core physiological mechanism of *The Moonstone* is the Associationist concept of *habits*: the idea that certain patterns of preconscious cognition and feeling can be exercised and strengthened through intentional conditioning. These are not character traits or personality; instead, these habits appear on the physical body, and shape the material experience of those bodies. If bodies and literary scholarship are at all intertwined – and the Associationist relationship between the imagination, memory and living body suggests that they are – then an ethical reader must cultivate ethical reading habits. In the previous chapters, we have seen that to treat bodies as metaphors produces unethical scholarship; here, in *The Moonstone*, we find a Victorian model for ethical reading which understands that bodies are singularly and irreducibly material. Literary authority comes not only from feeling, but from how one's readings impact others' feelings as well.

From one angle, *The Moonstone* tells the story of its characters learning to become more embodied, to acknowledge rather than to know, to read ethically and materially. But there is a dark side to this celebration: the bodies that are allowed to be bodies procure materiality at the expense of other bodies. White, male characters vampirically transfuse vitality from the female, queer and non-white bodies around them. As men learn to engage with materiality, the more immediately sensational, embodied people around them must give up their bodies to help men preserve their vitality. Biddy's vaunted giving-up of self becomes a suicide-machine, a self-annihilation that produces vitally material men.

Vital Elasticity and William Benjamin Carpenter's Acquired Habitudes of Thought

The core of this paradoxical demand lies in the seemingly irreconcilable rift between Associationism's materialist ethics and the superficial implications of mechanism. It is difficult to reconcile a mechanist system with a model for ethical development. How does one improve oneself if, for example, bodies will consistently respond to a given stimulus like a diseased East End labourer with an affect of disgust, and that reaction is mechanical rather than intentional? This is the sort of question Associationists would like to answer even as they also maintain the non-conscious, associative influence of physiological mechanisms. Through 1870s and 1880s conversations about mechanism, we will see that *habits* offer a mechanistic model with the space for conscious ethical cultivation. Habit-building is in fact a clever way to reconcile mechanism and ethics, and *The Moonstone* provides some positive modes of this unification.

At its root, the scientific debate of the 1870s and 80s is about the nature of *volition*, or the relationship between conscious, psychological intentionality and the ability to create changes in one's environment. As the late Victorians understood it, *mechanism*, as opposed to *vitalism*, rejects the idea that 'there is something in a living organism which controls and directs into suitable channels for the maintenance of the body the available blind physical and chemical forces' referred to as 'vital force' (Haldane 1898: 407–8). Instead, mechanism believes that physiology and physics can account completely for any given psychological phenomenon. Descartes had already put forth this idea regarding non-human animals in his *Passions*, but in the nineteenth century, mechanists like Thomas Huxley extended the claim to human psychology as well:

> all states of consciousness in us, as in [non-human animals], are immediately caused by molecular changes of the brain substance. It seems to me that in men, as in brutes, there is no proof that any state of consciousness is the cause of change in the motion of the matter of the organism. (Huxley 1874: 577)

Huxley claims in his November 1874 article that experiments on animals suggest that their actions are not the result of volition. Rather, motion is the cause, and consciousness is the response by which a mind makes sense of its motion. This leads him to conclude that a 'mental conditio[n] . . . is not the cause of a voluntary act, but the symbol of that state of the brain which is the immediate cause of that act' (577). Consciousness is simply the way bodies make sense of non-volitional changes in their composition.

Huxley's pure mechanism made Associationists like William Benjamin Carpenter uncomfortable, however, because of their attempts to integrate science with ethical philosophy.[3] To work within the materialist framework and yet provide grounds for ethical improvement, Carpenter turns to an organic explanation of the phenomenological sense that we *do* in fact have voluntary control – specifically, through the cerebrum. In December 1874, in direct response to Huxley's article, Carpenter argues that 'the doctrine of pure automatism, based entirely on the physical, is in direct opposition to the physical' because it overlooks the complexity of the nervous system (Carpenter 1874: 413). He derives this model from his earlier (1871) separation of the body into the cranio-spinal axis (analogous to the peripheral nervous system), which is primarily automatic, and the cerebrum (analogous to the central nervous system), which is volitional, but has no direct communication with muscles. The two are connected by 'nerves of the internal sense' (Carpenter 1871: 198). Through these nerves, the cerebrum 'puts the body in movement . . . by its power of making the automatic apparatus' or non-conscious, mechanical system of the body 'perform anything that lies within its capacity' (Carpenter 1874: 413). In other words, to account for choice while still locating a physiological cause for any psychological phenomenon, Carpenter suggests that volition operates on and through unconscious, bodily mechanisms under the direction of the cerebrum (414). This model remains mechanistic, or is perhaps even more mechanistic, for it envisions the body as a series of systems that drive one another: 'even in the most purely volitional movements . . . the Will does not directly produce the result, but plays, as it were, upon the Automatic apparatus, by which the requisite nervo-muscular combination is brought into action' (Carpenter 1871: 196). And yet, at the same time, it ultimately allows for a degree of conscious choice, for the cerebrum can to a certain degree elect which of the machines should activate.

All the equivocation of the previous sentence is a product of Carpenter's own cautious model for volition. Separated from direct communication with autonomic systems, the cerebrum is hardly a musician electing which notes to play; rather, it is an instrument itself. But this appeals to other Associationists: it maintains the non-conscious mechanisms for association, and yet allows for minute modification. Carpenter allows that 'we cannot help . . . the recurrence of ideas called up by local or personal associations; nor can we help the feelings of pain or pleasure, of aversion or desire, which are inseparably connected in our minds with these ideas' (Carpenter 1874: 415). These are products of automatic systems which appear volitional only in a phenomenological sense, but which are in fact outside of conscious direction. Frederic Rogers, another contributor to the conversation on Huxley's thesis, points out the ways in which common rhetoric admits associations' automatism with examples like 'I do not know what it was in his face that put me on my guard against him' and similar instances where one's feelings seem to be causes of unknown effects (Rogers 1875: 629). These sorts of moments indicate that 'the practical connection between sensation and volition is more rapid than that of specific recognition of motives, and therefore may, and often does, precede and even dispense with it [consciousness]' (629). But, Carpenter and Rogers both suggest, the lines of thought that associations follow are the products of *habit*. The rapidity of the connection between sensation and volition – or an external cause and the thoughts and feelings which are its effects – 'pass[es] in proportion as the act is habitual' (630). In other words, while the cerebrum may be the seat of conscious thought, because it is a mechanical organ, even its conscious thoughts tend to become mechanistic themselves.

The mechanical cerebrum is ultimately driven by habit, so that most of its apparent volition is rather the effect of previously cultivated responses. Carpenter constructs a mechanistic brain and body that modify one another through a reciprocal exchange between volitional habit-forming and the involuntary influence of those habits. Following up on his initial response to Huxley, Carpenter lays out the foundations for his theory of habits in his fourth preface to his *Principles of Mental Physiology*. He writes that 'an automatic action may take place in the cerebrum, which, without any intervention of consciousness, may evolve products usually accounted mental, yet in all such cases *the action takes place on the lines previously laid down by volitional direction*' (Carpenter 1876: xxix). In other words, the cerebrum will often follow particular associative chains and elicit the associated sensations and feelings completely unbound to volition – and yet, the path of those chains and the response to those sensations and feelings will tend toward the responses of previous iterations.

The example he provides comes from David Hartley's 'acquired automatism' from his much earlier (1749) *Observations on Man*. From Hartley, Carpenter gives the example of a child walking: an intensely volitional action which nevertheless 'is generated by proper combinations and associations of the automatic motions' (Hartley 1749: 162).[4] When the child has grown up, however, walking is a 'secondarily automatic' action, as most adults do not need to think about the motions required to walk from one point to another (163). These physical habits explain directly what appear to be psychological habits, for 'we may pass from one of these categories to the other by a series of steps so gradational, that it is impossible to draw a distinct line of separation between them' (Carpenter 1872: 296). And so, he arrives at a model of cognition that is mechanistic but avoids the extreme determinism of Huxley's mechanism. Here, volition remains largely a symbol or effect of mechanistic causes; and yet, at the same time, one can modify those mechanistic systems through the volitional cultivation of habits.

Carpenter's theories of habit culminate in *acquired habitudes of thought*: autonomic schemata of non-conscious stimulus response, which one can condition (albeit slowly). Between vitalism and mechanism, Carpenter argues for a third way, for the existence of 'a set of acquired habits of thought, which, no less than those dependent upon original constitution, determine the consequences of any particular impression upon the "ideational consciousness"' (Carpenter 1876: 770). These *acquired habitudes of thought* are on the one hand volitional, for they are *acquired*. They are also mechanistic, for once they are acquired, they '*determine* the consequences' or responses of a body to an external object. One can consciously learn and shape acquired habitudes, but can also unconsciously learn and shape them, so that both their causes and effects are organic and material. A mechanical body, therefore, can become more ethical through the intentional cultivation of habits of empathy. And as Dickens, Collins and the other proponents of popular literary authority would have it, there is no better way to cultivate these habits than the sensations of novel reading.

The Science of Character

The search for exactly how one cultivates these habits intersects with the conversations of popular Associationism from the decades previous. To be as concise as possible: fiction hones the body's ethical habits. The novel provides a training ground of sorts, where readers' bodies can engage with the bodies in the text. But as we will see in *The Moonstone*, this only works when the bodies in the text are bodies, and when the reader recognises them as such.

While this idea plays a central role in the plot of *The Moonstone*, I want to emphasise here the role it plays in the reading experience of *The Moonstone*. In his introduction to *The Moonstone*, Collins articulates Carpenter's theory of habits as the primary paradigm for the novel's theory of character. As I quoted in the introduction to this chapter, according to his self-declared goal, in *The Moonstone* Collins attempts 'to trace the influence of character on circumstances' (Collins 1868o: vii). With Carpenter's Associationist definition of character, the novel considers the unconscious, non-volitional effects of bodies' cultivated responses. This is true in the plot: the novel explores how the bodily habits of Gabriel Betteredge, Sergeant Cuff, Franklin Blake and Ezra Jennings change the circumstances around them. But readers are also meant to pay particular attention to the habits they have cultivated through reading the novel. 'Our feelings towards persons and objects may undergo most important changes', Carpenter observes, 'without our being in the least degree aware, until we have our attention directed to our own mental state, of the alteration which has taken place in them' – and the novel seeks to draw attention to those alterations (Carpenter 1853: 819). In particular, the novel asks readers to think of novel reading as an exercise to cultivate proper feeling.

In Collins's introduction, he announces that in *The Moonstone*, he intends to explore the effect of character on circumstances. But his version of character, I suggest, is far less stable than the psychological phenomenon usually called 'character'. Rather than refer to a core identity, Collins here means the set of acquired habitudes of thought that define the preconscious, embodied reactions one has to other bodies. A science of mind necessarily must posit a degree of uniformity in both physical mechanics and their psychological manifestations. Even as it accounts for individual variation, the mechanisms must be held in common across subjects for them to operate as mechanisms. Alexander Bain gives a concise summary of this conundrum in his *Study of Character*:

> The SCIENCE OF MIND, properly so called, unfolds the mechanism of our common mental constitutions. Adverting but slightly in the first instance to the differences between one man and another, it endeavours to give a full account of the internal mechanism that we all possess alike – of the sensations and emotions, intellectual faculties and volitions, of which we are every one of us conscious. (Bain 1861: 29)

The definition here emphasises the universality of Associationism's claims. Mental formations are held in 'common', we 'possess alike' the internal mechanisms of the mind, and 'we are every one of us conscious' of the phenomenological experience of these physical commonalities.

This would seem to provide a rigid model for character. But in fact, Bain's book on character endeavours to distinguish between phrenology as a science of character inadequate to describe the mind, and Associationism as the science that can make up for phrenology's shortcomings. The most significant error of phrenology according to Bain is that it does not account for 'the particular mode of retentiveness where different impressions concurring in the mind, adhere and make up a whole, of which one part shall afterwards read and recal[l] the rest' (266). By this point, the formulation should be familiar: phrenology does not account for association. Phrenology's naïve materialism is as insufficient as abstraction, for they both overlook the phenomenological fluidity of embodiment. Phrenology cannot account for the acquisition of new impressions and new ideas, and so offers an ossified model of character. Like Carpenter's critique of Huxley, Bain here critiques phrenology for missing the material because its definition of materiality is too limited. When phrenology interprets psychological phenomena through the measurement of the cranium, it overlooks the complex mechanical system that is the plastic mind.

Associationism's emphasis on the plastic mind as a more accurate, more material understanding of the embodied condition provides Carpenter – and ultimately Collins – with a model of character that replaces abstraction or reduction with complex mechanism. Carpenter distances himself further from the short-sighted reductionism of phrenology than even Bain does; in fact, he finds suspect models like Bain's which emphasise physical commonality. Carpenter rejects those theories that demand 'certain *uniformities of mental action* for each individual, which constitute what is termed his "character"' (Carpenter 1853: 794). Here Carpenter rejects the phrenological determinism that insists all bodies be similarly legible representations of their interiors. Instead, he writes:

> as the external conditions in which every individual is placed, differ to a certain extent from those which affect each one of his fellows, so does it happen that, as the development of every kind of capacity for mental action is augmented (like the nutrition of muscle and nerve) by its habitual exercise, the strength of that capacity, and its tendency to exert an active influence on the course of thought, will partly depend upon the degree in which circumstances call it into play. (794)

I want to draw attention here to the notion that one can exercise mental paths like a muscle. For Carpenter, one can develop and shape acquired habitudes of thought through intentional use. While the systems that determine associations may be mechanical, and the body's reaction to those associations may be equally mechanical, one can strengthen particular associations and responses through volition. These acquired habits of association and response, Carpenter concludes, 'form part of the "character" of each individual, at any one period of his existence' (794). He owes this model of character to John Stuart Mill, whose autobiography he references in his preface to *Principles of Mental Physiology* (Carpenter 1876: xliv). Mill writes that while

> character is formed by circumstances, our own desire can do much to shape those circumstances; and that what is really inspiriting and ennobling in the doctrine of free-will, is the conviction that *we have real power over the formation of our own character*; that our will, by influencing some of our circumstances, can modify our future habits and capacities of willing. (J. S. Mill 1874: 169)

Character, in short, is not an innate condition or a measurable psychological phenomenon, but rather, the product of reinforced habits.

The strengthening of habit here is not an abstract psychology, but a concrete, material physiology. These mental actions are strengthened like muscles because, like muscles, they are a physical part of the body.

Because these habits are embodied and not the product of intention, even as one can shape one's character through volition, one can also exercise habits even unintentionally. And here, we arrive at *The Moonstone*. The return to vitalism occurs in the 1870s, between six and eight years after the publication of *The Moonstone*. As this chapter will demonstrate, Collins is deeply indebted to Carpenter's earlier, seminal work on plastic mechanism, the *Principles of Human Physiology*.[5] The vitalism/mechanism debate and the related discourses on character have their roots in the conversations of earlier decades – of which *The Moonstone* is a part. Through Carpenter, Collins builds a novel centred on one of the foundational insights of *Human Physiology*: 'unconscious cerebration', or the changes in bodies' habits that occur outside of awareness (Carpenter 1853: 819).[6] 'Unconscious cerebration' describes the whole process by which the cerebrum takes in an impression, catalogues it associatively, continues to process those impressions unconsciously, and later recalls them through association. Because these are mechanistic processes, unconscious cerebration operates through pre-existing mechanisms on other pre-existing mechanisms, so that one can form and strengthen habits through exercise even when one does not intend to do so.

Novel reading is a vital site of this ethical cultivation, for Collins uses the mystery genre like Dickens uses serial: to teach readers to value acknowledgement over knowledge. The nature of the detective novel is such that the reader is invited to speculate on the solution to the mystery as the characters uncover evidence. Reading evidence, in this case, is a practice of reading bodies. And, as we have seen, this is a practice that often understands bodies as or through representation. Here, however, those methods have catastrophic results that result in everything from ruined careers to suicide. Metaphor kills. The only ethical literary authority, the novel ultimately suggests, is to read bodies as bodies. There is no mystical vitalism that drives bodies, no metaphoric or representational secret that unlocks interiority. There are only bodies: material, physical, feeling machines. Any kind of reading that seeks or depends on knowledge erases those bodies' materiality. To read *The Moonstone* is to work out one's acquired habitude of reading – both reading bodies and reading texts.

The Moonstone is a novel about reading. The central plot of the novel is relatively straightforward: Rachel Verinder inherits the Moonstone, a massive diamond, which is then almost immediately stolen. After several failed lines of inquiry, Verinder's cousin, Franklin Blake, learns that he stole the diamond while under the influence of opium administered in secret by the local doctor; when he then collapsed, one of Verinder's other cousins, Godfrey Ablewhite, stole the diamond and tried to escape. Ablewhite is ultimately hunted down and killed by the diamond's original owners, Brahmins in the service of Vishnu. But the written text of the novel takes place around this plot: after the resolution of the above events, Franklin Blake compiles his own and ten other autobiographical narratives of characters' thoughts and actions during the theft and investigation.[7] These narratives often depict people reading texts like novels, religious tracts, letters and scientific treatises. Characters' approaches to reading texts mirror their approaches to reading bodies, so that the insights of literary scholarship appear to explain social interaction.

And yet, *The Moonstone* is a particularly fruitful site to think about the relationship between reading literature and bodies because so few of its readers successfully read bodies. Everyone reads texts, and everyone reads bodies, but only Ezra Jennings solves the mystery of the Moonstone. Misreadings have grave consequences, from the death of relationships to literal death – and each of these misreadings begins with someone treating bodies as something other than bodies. Gabriel Betteredge and Drusilla Clack fetishise the material text as an intercessor or supplement for bodies, and read for the social capital attributed to scholarship. They bestow upon books a kind of mystical vitalism, something that propels book-objects outside the physical and confers spiritual power. Despite their claims to scholarship, Betteredge and Clack are buffoons, and the reader is clearly meant to disregard them. They are, however, a useful springboard to think about the more serious protagonists of the text, Franklin Blake and Sergeant Cuff, who take on the role of detective. Their detection is a scholarship of sorts that treats bodies as text: that is, as codes meant to be unpacked and understood, and which the scholar can ultimately read with as much ease as one might unpack a literary text. We might well think of this reading as the kind of mechanism that overlooks the mechanical, à la Huxley and phrenology. Their science is a disembodied science, one that neglects the complexity of material bodies. While Betteredge and Clack's misreadings are largely harmless, Blake and Cuff's scholarship results in the suicide of the falsely accused Rosanna Spearman. And finally, I will come to Ezra Jennings, who can read texts and bodies to bring others together. Only Ezra Jennings, with his training in Associationism and his intensely embodied self, can accurately read bodies as bodies – and thereby resolve the mystery.

Margins: The Brahmins

Of all the readers in *The Moonstone*, the Indian Brahmins read best – or at least, most effectively – but their reading practices remain perpetually inaccessible for the British characters of the novel. In their search for the Moonstone diamond, the Brahmins recruit a young boy off the streets of London. Penelope, Gabriel Betteredge's daughter, relates the following narrative of the Indians' interaction with the boy:

> The [head] Indian took a bottle from his bosom, and poured out of it some black stuff, like ink, into the palm of the boy's hand. The Indian – first touching the boy's head, and making signs over it in the air – then said, 'Look.' The boy became quite stiff, and stood like a statue, looking into the ink in the hollow of his hand. (Collins 1868a: 79)

The ink seems to activate the boy's power of clairvoyance, and he answers a series of questions regarding Franklin Blake, the 'English gentleman from foreign parts': 'Is it on the road to this house, and on no other, that the English gentleman will travel to-day?'; 'Has the English gentleman got It about him?' (79). While Penelope does not assign the power's origin to either the boy or the ink, she does note that the Indian, 'after making more signs on the boy's head, blew on his forehead, and so woke him up with a start' (79). Such control over the boy's body suggests that the Indian wields the power and the boy acts simply as a receptacle. In this sense, Penelope witnesses the most effective reading of a mystery in a text filled with blundering readings of mysteries. The Brahmin needs an answer to a question; he roots his reading in the physical materiality of writing (the ink), and so reads and writes his answer through the boy's body. To initiate and to end his reading, the Brahmin connects physically to the boy's body, first with a touch and then by blowing on his forehead. A physical body becomes a legible body, and a legible body becomes a text written in ink.

The Brahmins repeat their successful reading at the conclusion of the novel, when they recover the Moonstone – a feat none of the British detectives could manage. But throughout, the British characters refuse to acknowledge the power of the Brahmins' readings. The bumbling Mr Bruff denies the possibility of Indian mysticism, and instead he claims 'that any explanation based on the theory of clairvoyance was an explanation which would carry no conviction whatever with it, to [his] mind' (Collins 1868g: 554). Mr Murthwaite affirms this sentiment with a paternalistic reading of clairvoyance as 'a development of the romantic side of the Indian character', and an illusion that 'no doubt reflected what was already in the mind of the person mesmerising [the boy]' (554–5). This pseudo-scientific rejection, built upon a framework of what Murthwaite clearly conceives of as solid British common sense, creates a tear in the imperial flag the British characters plant in the soil of reading. One must either read through a superior yet foreign romantic mysticism, or a simple and solipsistic façade of logic.

Unable to feel or rationalise the power of Indian reading, British claims to superior, rational reading practices collapse. Indian reading skills so completely surpass Betteredge's comprehension that he can describe them only as 'juggling' and 'hocus pocus' (Collins 1868a: 79). One can say of Indian reading in *The Moonstone* what Ian Duncan claims about the novel's deployment of India in general: 'Stylised, spectral, confected from the tropes of Gothic romance, India[n reading] represents an alternative symbolic economy that defies scientific detection and sympathetic reciprocity alike' (Duncan 1994: 304). The British cannot read Indian reading, cannot make sense of its negotiation of bodies and their representations.[8] Contrary to the British representation of their reading, however, the Brahmins' reading is not merely mystical; it is intuitive, rooted in a physicality foreign to the British observers.

The Moonstone's contemporaries certainly recognised the 'positive alterity of India' and its potential to override British authority (301). An anonymous reviewer of the novel in *Lippincott's Magazine*, refuting the critique of *The Moonstone*'s failure to provide verisimilitude, reminds his or her readers that 'when we remember the force and extent of Hindoo superstition, we can scarcely venture to pronounce it [the story] improbable' ('The Moonstone', *Lippincott's*, 1868: 679). In an otherwise less-than-favourable review of *The Moonstone* in *The Athenaeum*, Victorian critic Geraldine Jewsbury acknowledges:

> The 'epilogue' of *The Moonstone* is beautiful. It redeems the somewhat sordid detective element, by a strain of solemn and pathetic human interest. Few will read of the final destiny of *The Moonstone* without feeling the tears rise in their eyes as they catch the last glimpse of the three men, who have sacrificed their caste in the service of their God, when the vast crowd of worshippers opens for them, as they embrace each other and separate to begin their lonely and never-ending pilgrimage of expiation. The deepest emotion is certainly reserved to the last. (Jewsbury 1868: 106)

For Jewsbury, the emotional connection with the Brahmins 'redeems the somewhat sordid detective element' of the rest of the novel. She rejects the British characters' investigations as too sensational, too immoral. The Brahmins are the most tangible characters in a novel of circumstances. Though denied voice themselves, the Brahmins' readings tear a gaping hole in any monological narrative of *The Moonstone* or its representation of imperial power.[9]

Drusilla Clack, Gabriel Betteredge and the Vitalism of the Book

To explore acquired habitudes, the novel offers up an example of popular readers who subscribe to a kind of vitalism of the book: a sense that the book-object itself has a mystical power. These readers supplant bodies with books, and use books to mediate or even replace human relations. Most importantly, they essentially do not read bodies at all; they read bodies through books.

Armed with evangelical tracts from 'A Word With You On Your Cap-Ribbons' to *The Serpent at Home*, Rachel Verinder's cousin Drusilla Clack fills the world with her book-objects at the expense of any human connection. Clack's obsession with her tracts plays out around the deathbed of Lady Verinder, Rachel Verinder's mother. Lady Verinder, with the knowledge that she will die soon, speaks to Clack of her will: 'I hope you won't think yourself neglected, Drusilla ... I mean to give you your little legacy, my dear, with my own hand' (Collins 1868f: 437). Clack does indeed consider herself rather neglected, and Lady Verinder's gesture here is meant as a sort of peace offering intended to restore their relationship or at least move toward reconciliation. Drusilla, however, does not engage Lady Verinder as a suffering body; instead, she immediately responds with *The Serpent at Home*, pointedly opening it to the section 'Satan among the Sofa Cushions'. Clack's tracts offer a usefully concise example of how the vitalist book can supplant relationships with living bodies: Lady Verinder is dying and makes a gesture of conciliation and concern toward her niece, who responds with an out-of-context book.

Beneath the events of the narrative here lies a curious distortion of the relationship between materiality and reading. Under doctor's orders, Lady Verinder explains, she cannot read Clack's book, and if she reads at all, she can only 'read the lightest and the most amusing books' (438). The comparative weight of these books – the heavy tract opposed to the 'light' novel – draws attention to the materiality of these texts, even as it inverts the physical difference between a much shorter tract and a sizeable nineteenth-century novel. Sickened and weak, Lady Verinder's body cannot physically sustain a reading of a 'heavy' text.

Clack understands reading as a material action but refutes it through a kind of literary vitalism that fetishises book-objects. She rejects the domain of 'the infidel profession of Medicine', as Clack refers to it, because it operates under a 'blinded materialism' (437). To counter materialism, she turns to something that looks like materialism, but which in fact is a kind of vitalism:

> I slipped it [the book] under the sofa cushions, half in, and half out, close by her handkerchief, and her smelling-bottle. Every time her hand searched for either of these, it would touch the book; and, sooner or later (who knows) the book might touch *her*. (438)

Clack describes with impressive clarity Associationism's philosophy of materiality and emotion: physical objects transmit a chain of impressions and affect the bodies that encounter them. Considered without attention to the specific details of a reading experience, she seems to understand Associationism more scientifically than most. But she forgets the crucial necessity of material bodies for empathy, and instead, assumes that the book will empathise for her.

Clack's reading vitalises the book-object so that it becomes an agent on its own rather than a medium for empathy between two people. For Clack, the possibility that 'the book might touch [Lady Verinder]' constitutes its own end. She races about the dying woman's house and hides tracts in flowerpots, among birdseed, atop the piano, on the chimneypiece, in the bedroom, and in the bathroom. The possibility that Lady Verinder might encounter these tracts gives Clack 'pleasure' as she 'reflect[s] on the *true* riches which [she] had scattered with such a lavish hand, from top to bottom of the house' (438). Clack does not seem particularly invested in the effects of Lady Verinder's reading, let alone her health – only that she finds the tracts. Ostensibly, 'true riches' indicate something like spiritual conversion, but Clack's blindness to how her philosophy of reading replaces bodies with a fetishised book unveils a crucial disjuncture between tract reading and ethical reading. In her formulation, materialism seeks to 'rob [her] of the only right of property that [her] poverty could claim – [her] right of spiritual property in [her] perishing aunt' (438). Even if one ignores Lady Verinder's desire to give Clack actual property through her will, the concept of 'spiritual property' takes primacy not only over wealth, but also over Lady Verinder's physical well-being. To read a tract provides its own reward: namely, that one has read a tract. Tract reading produces 'spiritual property' of its own accord, as if the book-object supersedes human physicality. Vitalism produces a fetish *par excellence*, a commodity that takes on the power of social relations, and that reduces other bodies to commodities and sources of further (in this case, spiritual) wealth.

Clack replaces the ethical relationships between people with a fetishised relationship between the book and its reader. She does not need to use books to connect with others because she believes the book will accomplish positive change in a body all on its own if they simply touch the book. Clack's veneration elevates books to the level of religious artefacts that supplant materiality with a vitalist force unique only to books. In short, she substitutes objects for ethical subjects.

This process is even more pronounced, and more complex, in the reading habits of Gabriel Betteredge, the steward of the Verinder manor. Betteredge occupies himself primarily with reading, though he restricts his reading exclusively to a single text: *Robinson Crusoe*. Throughout the novel, Betteredge consults *Robinson Crusoe* like a religious tome: when faced with a dilemma, he opens the novel to a random passage, and then reads that passage as a guide to his problem. From the initial moment the reader meets Betteredge – the first line of *The Moonstone*'s main body, in fact – Betteredge explains his narrative with a citation of *Crusoe* by chapter and verse:

> In the first part of *Robinson Crusoe*, at page one hundred and twenty-nine, you will find it thus written: 'Now I saw, though too late, the Folly of beginning a Work before we count the Cost, and before we judge rightly of our own Strength to go through with it.' (Collins 1868a: 75)

Betteredge's absurd consultation of Defoe's novel depends on a religious practice akin to Crusoe's own reading methods. When trapped on his island, Crusoe decides to read his Bible daily to 'exercise [himself] with new Thoughts'. He opens the Bible randomly, and allows the text to choose the most apt verse for him to read:

> One Morning being very sad, I open'd the Bible upon these Words, *I will never, never leave thee, nor forsake thee;* immediately it occur'd, That these Words were to me, Why else should they be directed in such a Manner, just at the Moment when I was mourning over my Condition, as one forsaken of God and Man? (Defoe 1719: 114)

To open the Bible with the belief that the words will address the reader and his current situation directly is a kind of 'biblical lottery' or *sortes*

Biblicae, in which the reader entrusts 'providence to choose a relevant passage' (Hunter 1966: 159).[10] Within this mode of reading, the physical book-object has a direct, tangible relationship with Crusoe and responds to his sensations and thoughts with a vital life of its own. Crusoe decides to 'exercise' his thoughts with this kind of reading after an earlier, accidental *sortes Biblicae* offered 'Words [which] were very apt to [his] Case' (Defoe 1719: 110). In this accidental reading, Crusoe notes that 'the Word had no Sound' at the time, for 'the Thing was . . . remote . . . impossible in my Apprehension of Things'. This is an observation about both the spiritual and physical elements of reading: he means to say that he was unprepared to accept the divinations of the text, but his empirical language is telling. He was removed from the materiality of the text, the Thing itself, and yet 'the Words made a great Impression upon [him]', so that their effects increased over time. The text's vitality supersedes its content, for the object itself selects the passage, and its impressions extend beyond the words to exercise the body of the reader.

The *sortes* of *sortes Biblicae* is not a Christian practice; it comes from an earlier practice in which readers would 'randomly ope[n] a copy of Homer's *Iliad* or Virgil's *Aeneid* and interpre[t] as prophetic the first line upon which the eye settled' (Metzger 2004: 473). But, of course, Betteredge insists that his veneration of Robinson Crusoe has nothing to do with pagan ignorance. 'I am not superstitious,' he assures the reader, for 'I have read a heap of books in my time' (Collins 1868a: 76). In fact, he continues, 'I am a scholar in my own way'. He studies *Crusoe* for its insight into the feelings and actions of others. Locating religious reading practices in Betteredge's methods has been, as Marty Gould puts it, 'commonplace' (Gould 2012: 39).[11] A materialist approach to religious reading practices, however, offers a new angle on this commonplace reading. To read Betteredge's *Crusoe* as a physical object uncovers the ethical and social complexity of Collins's critique of this kind of reading. Rather than critique Betteredge for his theology, a materialist reading emphasises Betteredge's true sin: his vitalist understanding of text, and subsequent substitution of books for living bodies.[12]

To parse the vitalism at the heart of Betteredge's reading depends paradoxically on his obsession with the materiality of his reading practice. I return to Betteredge's first citation, in which he tells the reader that, 'In the first part of *Robinson Crusoe*, at page one hundred and twenty-nine, you will find it thus written' (Collins 1868a: 75). The quote itself has less import than the larger trajectory of Betteredge's reading practice. While Betteredge emphasises the excerpts he draws from the text, the words only carry such weight because they derive from *Robinson Crusoe*; the novel as a whole gives credence to the parts. Along with the page citation that opens his narrative, Betteredge gives another three citations by page number.

He also gives a publication history of his own reading: 'I have worn out six stout *Robinson Crusoe*s with hard work in my service. On my lady's last birthday she gave me a seventh . . . Price four shillings and sixpence, bound in blue, with a picture into the bargain' (76). Betteredge provides such detailed bibliographic information that it seems he refers to an actual, physical edition of the text. Granted, Betteredge is not a 'real' person and therefore does not read a 'real' edition, but Betteredge provides such detailed bibliographic information about his *Crusoe* that it seems as though these details were not mere fictions of Collins's mind, but that instead, they referred to a fictional version of a physical text. As Katie Lanning posits, he is almost certainly reading J. W. Clark's 1866 edition published by Macmillan and Company (Lanning 2012: 4). In his bibliography, Betteredge says that his latest edition cost 'four shillings and sixpence' (13); according to a review in *The Spectator*, Clark's 1866 edition also cost 'a neat four-and-sixpenny' ('Robinson Crusoe' 1866). His edition is 'bound in blue', as was Clark's. He also happily notes that the purchase of the book came with 'a picture into the bargain'. It is unclear if Betteredge refers to the engraving on the cover, or to the image on the title page, but either suffices. This *Crusoe* is a physical object, and Betteredge cares deeply – perhaps too deeply – about its physicality.

This bibliography is important in large part because Betteredge seems so insistent that his readers take the time to read his description. That Betteredge reads an actual edition of *Robinson Crusoe* ties Defoe's novel, Betteredge's contribution to *The Moonstone*, and Collins's novel to the consumption experiences of *The Moonstone*'s readers, Katie Lanning argues, because Clark's 'edition was a real, buyable commodity for Collins's readers' (Lanning 2012: 5). But the notion that Collins's readers would have this most recent, particularly scholarly edition overlooks the saturation and permutations of *Crusoe* by the mid-century. According to Richard Phillips, at least 200 new editions of *Crusoe* saw publication by the end of the nineteenth century for an average of more than two new editions each year during the Victorian period (R. Phillips 1997: 23). Unlike Betteredge's copy with '*a* picture', these 'modern editions' were filled with illustrations, from Bell and Daldy's 'seventy characteristic wood engravings' and 'twelve engravings on steel' (1865) to the Henry Lea edition (1850), which has a decorative border around every page and an illustration on nearly every other page. These heavily illustrated editions reflected the tendency to read *Crusoe* as children's literature. Indeed, many editions of *Crusoe* were children's literature, from *Robinson Crusoe, Jr: A Story for Little Folks* (1863) to *Robinson Crusoe in Words of One Syllable* (1869). The text also saw myriad permutations, such as the mystifying *Robinson Crusoe's Farmyard* (1849, reprinted in 1866), which offers stories and facts about the animals Crusoe encountered, but not a single mention of Crusoe himself other than in the title. Betteredge's text is a material commodity, yes – but it is a commodity drowning in a sea of other mass-produced replicas of itself.

More importantly, Betteredge's edition of *Crusoe* is not particularly attractive to the non-scholarly reader. This is one reason why Betteredge gives so much detail about his text: his scholarly edition calls attention to his scholarly reading, provided that we use 'scholarly' to indicate disembodied performance of hermeneutics. Clark's lack of illustrations is part of his editorial project to 'reproduce faithfully the original text', to create what we would now refer to as a scholarly edition of a popularised text (Clark 1866). Part of this project seems to separate the novel from children's literature: the *Spectator* review predicts that 'the boys . . . will be dismayed by the look of the book' ('Robinson Crusoe' 1866: 22). Clark's edition is 'calculated to afford quite a new sensation to those who are acquainted only with modern editions', particularly, as the review puts it, 'grown-up readers' (22). Betteredge insists that he is a scholar in his own way, and so it would make some sense that he owns a scholarly edition. But he disregards the content of the text when it does not suit him; the text exists only to serve Betteredge. Clark's edition encodes its grown-up audience in its content as well as its form, for it concurs with Defoe's original preface when he says that 'abridging this Work, [is] as scandalous, as it is knavish and ridiculous' (Clark 1866). And indeed, where many 1840–1860 editions abridge the second part, Clark's *Crusoe* contains some 50,000 words more in 'Part 2' than, for example, Bickers and Bush's 1862 edition. In the Clark, 'Part 2' begins on page 316; Betteredge's last quote is from page 318, and it hardly counts as a citation:

> 'With those Thoughts, I considered my new Engagement, that I had a Wife' – (Observe! so had Mr Franklin!) – 'one Child born' – (Observe again! that might yet be Mr Franklin's case, too!) – 'and my Wife then' – What Robinson Crusoe's wife did, or did not do, 'then', I felt no desire to discover. (Collins 1868n: 198; citing Defoe 1866: 318)

His use of the word *discover* implies that the remainder of the book is as much a mystery as the titular diamond. If Betteredge only ever owned abridged editions, which is likely, and he has yet to 'discover' what happens next, it seems possible that he might not have read the remaining 300 pages of *Crusoe*. To Betteredge, though, these gaps in his knowledge make little or no difference, because his mode of reading *Robinson Crusoe* is not about Robinson Crusoe: it is, first and foremost, about Betteredge.

His readings are patently absurd not only because they take *Crusoe* completely out of context, but because those decontextualised citations speak specifically and exclusively to Betteredge's life. As a self-made scholar, he has the tendency to read through simple metaphor with himself as the primary significance. This is why his readings are associative, but they are not Associationist. He depends on the seemingly arbitrary links between the text and his lived experience, and he knows that 'Persons and Things do turn up so vexatiously in this life, and will in a manner insist on being noticed' (Collins 1868b: 97). Moreover, in this superficially associative reading, he recognises the almost ethical imperative to 'put the Person before the Thing' – although he suggests that to do so constitutes mere 'common politeness' (97). The problem arises, however, when each of these associations begins, flows through, and ends with himself.

Even the temporality of Betteredge's own reading turns everything back to him. The events of *The Moonstone* take place in 1848, and Betteredge writes his narrative in 1850. The Clark edition of *Crusoe* that Betteredge owns is not published until 1866. In short, he could not have owned it. Few – more likely, none – of Collins's readers would have performed this kind of bibliographic work, but that is the point exactly. Betteredge's obsessive attention to the physicality of his text is a kind of veneration, as with a relic: he values the text's physicality only in as much as it is the house for a vital force that gives him insight into the world around him. This is something of a snare itself; Betteredge's attention to the bibliography of his *Crusoe* leads away from the bodies around him, and the text rejects this level of detail even as it offers it.

Betteredge's writing underscores his tendency to read everything through himself. The story of Betteredge from 1848 is subsumed by the story of his writing process in 1850. Franklin Blake commands him to 'take the pen in hand, and start the story' (Collins 1868a: 75). In a bizarre acknowledgement of the discrepancy between narrative time and writing time, Betteredge continues: 'Two hours have passed since Mr Franklin left me. As soon as his back was turned, I went to my writing-desk to start the story. There I have sat helpless (in spite of my abilities) ever since' (76). Much like Robinson Crusoe, who sails out three times before finally coming to the shipwreck that starts the real substance of his story, Betteredge's narrative refuses to start. Self-regard prevents Betteredge from using language to connect himself to other bodies; instead, Betteredge invests his book with the capacity to interact with other people for him. At the close of *The Moonstone*, Betteredge implores Blake to convert to Crusoism, and shows him the last passage I cited above from *Robinson Crusoe*, which he believes prophesises Franklin Blake and Rachel Verinder's baby: 'With those Thoughts, I considered my new Engagement, that I had a Wife, one Child born, and my wife then – ' (Collins 1868n: 198). Even before he encounters Blake, Betteredge's reading of this passage rejects the bodies circulating in it. Crusoe's wife does not matter; instead, Betteredge 'score[s] the bit about the Child with [his] pencil, and put[s] a morsel of paper for a mark to keep the place' (198).[13] And, just as Crusoe's wife does not matter, Blake and Verinder do not matter to Betteredge's Crusoe crusade. Months later, Franklin Blake comes to Betteredge with news of Rachel's pregnancy, and Betteredge turns the opportunity into a moment to bring Blake to the Church of Crusoe. Even his language is evangelical: after he tells Blake of his prophetic reading, he asks, '*Now*, sir, do you believe in *Robinson Crusoe*?' (199). He tells his readers after his meeting with Blake that he 'shook hands with me – and I felt that I had converted him' (199). Whenever Betteredge makes use of *Crusoe* in this manner, he transforms texts from possible connection with others into fetishised objects. His attempts to convince himself and his readers of his literary abilities smother the human connections that reading could otherwise evoke.

Betteredge unites the scientific philosophy of vitalism with the reading habits of the disembodied scholar. By imbuing the text with a special kind of vitality only he seems able to unlock, he recursively validates himself as a literary scholar with access to texts' special knowledge. Much in the same way that vitalism relies on an abstract, almost mystical power that vivifies organic matter, the scholar relies on an abstract, mystical power of the text that reaches beyond the average reader's experience. His acquired habitude, then, is the performance of special, literary knowledge – and most importantly, this performance precludes and prevents empathic engagement with living bodies.

Margins: Penelope

Betteredge's continued attention to the temporality of writing ultimately elevates his own writing process above the content of what he writes. The 1850 narrative pulls him continually back to the same point in the 1848 story of the Moonstone theft. He cannot seem to begin: the first chapter ends, 'We will take a new sheet of paper, if you please, and begin over again' (Collins 1868a: 76); the second ends with 'another false start, and more waste of good writing-paper' (77). Only Penelope – who practises her own writing in her diary, from whence Betteredge takes most of his dates – can step briefly into the role of model reader/writer to pull Betteredge out of his abortive starts. She invokes an Associationist model of memory, suggesting that Betteredge 'should set down what happened, regularly day by day', and that if he were to 'fix [his] memory on a date in this way, it is wonderful what [his] memory will pick up for [him] upon that compulsion' (77). If Betteredge would engage with the temporality of the Moonstone diamond, he might trigger an associative chain that could produce the evidence for which he and Blake search. Penelope puts aside her own writing to propel the narrative out of the self-indulgent rut Betteredge carves. She objects that 'what [Betteredge] has done so far isn't in the least what [he] was wanted to do. [He was] asked to tell the story of the Diamond', but has instead 'been telling the story of [his] own self' (77). Betteredge finds the gravitational force of his self-centredness 'curious, and quite beyond [him] to account for' (77). 'I wonder', he continues, 'whether the gentlemen who make a business and a living out of writing books, ever find their own selves getting in the way of their subjects, like me? If they do, I can feel for them' (77). Betteredge feels for them because he is one of them, a writer who continually subjugates the story to his self.

Sergeant Cuff and the Mechanism of Justice

On the other side of vitalism, *The Moonstone* presents a pair of more formal scholars, Franklin Blake and Sergeant Cuff. As an alternative to Betteredge and Clack's vitalist readings, Blake and Cuff read with what they believe to be objective distance and appropriately disembodied logic. However, their observations and deductions produce spectacular misreadings with grave consequences, including the death of Rosanna Spearman. In this section, I will argue that while Blake and Cuff claim that their superior intellects and detachment make them the adept readers of texts and bodies, the narrative rejects their mode of reading because they mistake disembodiment for logic; they do not account for bodies as bodies. Their materialism, like Huxley's, overlooks actual matter in its obsession with the mechanical. Two acts of reading and writing epitomise these failures: Cuff's reading and writing of Rosanna Spearman's narrative, and the compilation of the Moonstone journals themselves.

Narrative constitutes the whole of Cuff's modus operandi, both his motive and his means to tell the story of the Moonstone theft. Sergeant Cuff is a detective similar to Edgar Allan Poe's C. Auguste Dupin and the later Sherlock Holmes, in that he uses observations of minutiae as clues to solve his cases. In theory, this practice depends upon a kind of association: the detective constructs narratives of the crime based on material objects, and then uses those narratives to form connections between bodies (sometimes living, but not always). Associative readings afford detectives the capacity to read bodies, to uncover their interiors, and to use these readings as evidence with sufficient legal merit.

A mystery depends upon stories yet untold – in this case, the story of the Moonstone's theft, the story of Ablewhite's conspiracy. Cuff realises that to unravel the mystery, the detective must tell those stories. In his initial investigation of the theft, Cuff concocts a story about Rosanna Spearman, and concludes that she has stolen the diamond (Collins 1868e). The detective's tendency to create stories, Ross Murfin posits, makes Cuff something of an author in his own right. He suggests that 'Cuff certainly seems like an author's self-representation when his hypotheses about Rosanna Spearman ... turn out to be correct' – though incorrect about her motives (Murfin 1982: 657). Here, in an apotheosis of Betteredge's desire to make reading into prophecy, Cuff authors reality; what he writes becomes fact. 'When we read the long letter that Rosanna wrote just before killing herself', Murfin goes on to explain, 'we realise that most of Rosanna's written story was imagined by Sergeant Cuff some two hundred pages earlier' (657). Cuff's legal authority gives him the capacity to act both as a character within the narrative and as a narrator of that same narrative. At the same time, he recursively derives legal authority from his ability to piece together material evidence into a coherent narrative. Cuff's storytelling bolsters his detective work because he predicts (or, at least, purports to predict) others' actions and feelings.

Most importantly for this chapter's argument, Cuff builds these narratives on a foundation of observation. He certainly has an eye for material detail, for where Superintendent Seegrave dismisses the need to identify precisely which petticoat smeared the door as 'a mere trifle', Cuff insists he 'ha[s] never met with such a thing as a trifle yet' (Collins 1868d: 221). As D. A. Miller points out in *The Novel and the Police*, Cuff 'turn[s] trifles into "telling" details, telling – what else? – a story' (D. A. Miller 1988: 35). Cuff emphasises the importance of material objects' connections to bodies and memory through narrative. The connective logic that enables him to read bodies, however, is metaphoric and ultimately intended to decode interiors. Material objects like a petticoat connect the detective to a body, and enable him to speculate on that body's motives.

In this theory of reading, Cuff assumes that objects are metaphors for the bodies around them and can thereby tell the narratives of their mysterious interiors. Moreover, the bodies he reads are automata, condemned by the rules of narrative representation to follow a prescribed path. Because he is in the business of reading bodies, Cuff must believe that bodies can be read. The problem mirrors the phrenological demand for uniformity with which Bain engages, and which Carpenter rejects outright. Like the scientist, the detective must consistently make bodies legible, for if the detective cannot read the external signs of bodies as representations of their interior, he cannot uncover their hidden stories.

It is curious, therefore, that perhaps the most critical line of Cuff's in *The Moonstone* deeply complicates the assumption of bodies' legibility and the detective's ability to read them. After he incorrectly suspects Rosanna and Rachel of a conspiracy, he retires in some disgrace from the case and the police force in general. Cuff then receives a letter from Blake that details the events of the year following his retirement. 'Before I went to bed', Cuff says to Blake, 'I read your letter. There's only one thing to be said about the matter, on my side. I completely mistook my case' (Collins 1868m: 172). In the end, Cuff declares, 'It's only in books that the officers of the detective force are superior to the weakness of making a mistake.' In a text as preoccupied with its own textuality as *The Moonstone*, this moment is directly self-referential. 'Only in books' are detectives unerring – but Cuff is in a book highly aware of its own bookishness, and he has erred. According to his theory of fiction, fictional detectives can read bodies because textual bodies are straightforward, so that if one observes them with the proper scholarly disembodiment, one can trace fictional objects and bodies to the end of the mystery. But his failure suggests otherwise: he mistook Spearman for the thief because he misread the emotional motives behind her actions. He understood Rosanna's actions as criminal, when in fact she acted out of her love for Blake. Cuff's trajectory shows that bodies' legibility depends not simply on detached, scholarly observation, for disembodiment makes empathy impossible.

Because he relies on a combination of narrative knowledge and objective observation, Cuff's bodies are not matter: they are determinist machines of the most reductive order. To solve the mystery requires the detective to identify the machinations of the thief, but the body is secondary; to locate and acquire the Moonstone is the primary goal. *The Moonstone*'s plot and emotional investments hardly centre around the identity of who actually stole the Moonstone, so that Cuff's stories, as Murfin points out, 'seem unimportant and anticlimactic' (Murfin 1982: 659). At the close of the novel, when the body of the true thief is discovered, Cuff writes a name – 'Godfrey Ablewhite' – on a piece of paper before he sends Franklin Blake in to identify Ablewhite's body. But at this point in the story, with Spearman and Jennings dead, the diamond irretrievably lost, and Blake acquitted, Cuff's note comes off as a sort of cheap magician's gag. The note is naked self-regard, an attempt to recover from his failure and draw attention to his scholarly prowess. Likewise, the report Cuff files as the sixth narrative details largely irrelevant information with such lack of emotion that it hardly seems to bear on the larger questions circulating around Franklin Blake and Rachel Verinder's relationship, Rosanna Spearman's suicide, and the more human investments of the other characters. While he understands the importance of matter enough to make observations, he does not connect matter with life; his materialism is not tempered by empathy, so that he fetishises objects over bodies and looks to himself as the arbiter of others' interiority.

Franklin Blake and the Failure of Philosophy

Despite Cuff's error, however, bodies' legibility remains crucial to the detective story as a genre. This legibility is also crucial to Associationism, for if scientists cannot read and predict emotions and cognition, they cannot map their anatomy and physiology. And most importantly, it would seem to be important to any kind of literary authority that claimed to read bodies. Instead, as Franklin Blake learns, no matter what philosophical mode he employs, he lacks the ability to read properly unless he suspends his knowledge and reads only through emotional connections with others.

The models of reading we have explored so far are insufficient for Collins's project of understanding character. Betteredge and Clack's vitalism invokes the simultaneously too embodied and self-serving, popular reader; Cuff's determinist representations and automata invoke the performatively disembodied scholar. To navigate between these two models, the novel offers Franklin Blake – a man who is both something of a formal scholar, and something of a common reader, who epitomises this philosophical tension between bodies' emotional complexity and the need to interpret impressions. Blake offers the unique chance to trace a character who learns to read emotion not only through empathy and experience, but also through an explicit science lesson – from an Associationist treatise.

Even before his reading lessons, Blake is no stranger to philosophy and science, and he reads impressions through a deliberately associative logic. He can read others' impressions as they read: as he watches Betteredge read Rosanna Spearman's notes, Blake observes that 'He read the first without appearing to be much interested in it. But the second – the memorandum – produced a strong impression on him' (Collins 1868h: 581). And he is aware of the impressions reading generates in him: after he reads his own name on his nightgown and thus discovers himself as the thief, he admits, 'I have not a word to say about my own sensations. My impression is, that the shock inflicted on me completely suspended my thinking and feeling power' (Collins 1868i: 601). All these readings seize Blake at a nervous level, an unconscious and embodied reaction such that after he discovers himself as the thief, he confesses in words that seem to come straight from Rogers's analysis of associations' preconscious etiology, 'I certainly could not have known what I was about' (601). An embodied reader who understands and invites physical impressions born of texts and bodies, Blake has the basic tools to read through association.

And yet, he still has a lesson to learn, for as with Cuff, Blake becomes too obsessed with his own cleverness, and his 'system' (his word) occludes the bodies with which he interacts. 'There is a curious want of system in the English mind,' Blake admonishes Betteredge (Collins 1868c: 122). In place of such 'slovenly-minded' English thinking, Blake proposes to employ his French and German education to consider the subjective and objective elements of the mystery (122, 124). His French model has something of the vitalist in it: a tendency to turn to the mystical or abstract. The German, on the other hand, has something of the determinist in it: a reduction to inanimate machines. A *Spectator* reviewer calls the section in which he explains his notion of a subjective/objective dialectic 'clums[y]' and 'burdensome', and finds Blake's philosophy 'nonsensical' – and indeed, they are, so I forbear extended close reading of Blake's logic ('The Moonstone', *Spectator*, 1868: 881). But this clumsiness has a purpose: to point out the insufficiency of abstract philosophy to describe human relations. After all his philosophising, Blake fruitlessly concludes, 'From all I can see, one interpretation is just as likely to be right as the other' (Collins 1868c: 124). Oscillation between these national pseudo-logics neither prepares the Verinder household for the arrival of the diamond, nor prevents its theft; the disembodied 'system' Blake proposes cannot answer to the intricacies of social interaction. His system enables him to read bodies, but these readings result in useless stagnation. As he turns his system toward reading and writing, stagnation produces scholarly self-regard: he reads to increase his social standing.

From his 1848 investigation to his 1850 compilation of the Moonstone journals, Blake attempts to establish and maintain his mastery over knowledge. When neither Blake's abstract continental education nor his English pragmatism unravels the mystery of the Moonstone diamond, he enlists the other narrators to write their Moonstone journals. He claims that his motive is consistent with his detached, systematic philosophy: to approach all sides of a problem. Blake comes to Betteredge on 21 May 1850 and tells him that 'the whole story [of the Moonstone] ought, in the interest of truth, to be placed on record in writing' (Collins 1868a: 75). Beginning with personal relations, the story will proceed 'from . . . plain facts . . . as far as our own personal experience extends, and no farther' (75). But, by this point in May 1850, Blake knows nearly everything *The Moonstone* novel will finally tell, for the narratives document events prior to 1850 – except Murthwaite's epilogue, the tale of the diamond in India post-1850. By the date in the diegetic world that Blake conscripts the other narrators, Jennings's experiment and Ablewhite's death have solved the mystery of the theft and exonerated all innocent parties. Blake's scientific endeavour to compile 'plain facts', then, is more properly an attempt to suture any remaining tears in his own reputation and control over knowledge. Knowledge – of the Moonstone's location, of Rachel Verinder's feelings, of the thief, of Rosanna Spearman's motives – eludes Blake whether he takes the subjective, objective or common-sense approach. Motivated by self-regard, Blake can only fail to read others' interiors.

Ezra Jennings, Suffering and Self-Abnegation

Self-regard unsurprisingly emerges as the toxin that corrupts both vitalist and determinist readings of bodies. Betteredge and Clack's vitalism bestows special knowledge on texts so that they can mobilise that special knowledge; Cuff's determinism and Blake's in-between models both ultimately seek to make the academic the arbiter of knowledge. And so, in order to find a model that reads bodies as bodies, and which retains the capacity to empathise with those bodies, Collins seeks an acquired habitude free from self-regard.

Ezra Jennings, the doctor's assistant, literally embodies this habitude. Other characters in *The Moonstone* and Victorian reviewers alike recognise that Jennings's body has a distinctive physicality that other characters lack. Geraldine Jewsbury, in a review in *The Athenaeum*, claims that of all the characters in the novel, Jennings 'is the one personage who makes himself felt by the reader' (Jewsbury 1868: 106). This emphasis on Jennings's capacity to 'mak[e] himself *felt*' carries two important associative valences. First, the sense that Jennings inspires emotional resonance; and second, more important than the first but bound up within it, that his body has a tangible materiality to it. Jewsbury was not alone in her sentiments. While perhaps even less impressed with the novel than Jewsbury, the *Spectator* reviewer still notes that Jennings 'is introduced with [a] flourish of physiognomical trumpets' ('The Moonstone', *Spectator*, 1868: 881). Though the *Spectator* reviewer may not care for the description, and Jewsbury may find herself relatively apathetic overall, they both acknowledge that the reader encounters Jennings through embodiment.

So, too, Jennings impacts the fictional bodies around him within the world of the text – but within the world of the text, the affective gravity of his body attracts others and then augments their attention to their own bodies. Even though Blake finds Jennings's body 'more or less calculated to produce an unfavourable impression of him on a stranger's mind', the doctor's assistant still 'ma[kes] some inscrutable appeal to [Blake's] sympathies which [he] f[inds] impossible to resist' (Collins 1868k: 73). The emotional force of Jennings's body overrides Blake's interpretive faculties: 'This strange face', Blake says, and 'stranger' eyes, 'took your attention captive at their will' (Collins 1868i: 606). While this description is powerful on its own, for Blake, who so heavily emphasises his ability to direct his will toward a problem (the subjective and the objective, for example), to lose his will from Jennings's mere appearance carries even more weight. Jennings has a physical predisposition to evoke impressions in other bodies, and like a window, to both draw them in and reflect them back on themselves.

Jennings's own body draws others' attention, but he more importantly acts as an interlocutor between other bodies. He demonstrates his ability to link other bodies when he takes captive Blake's attention. In his description of Jennings, Blake's syntax slips from his usual first person to a second-person 'you' when he says that Jennings can take 'your' attention captive. Though he acknowledges this shift with the caveat 'in my case, at least', Blake cannot seem to help but address his imagined reader in this moment. This connection between Blake and his imagined reader takes place because Jennings's physiognomy, while striking, also resists reading. His 'figure and his movements' suggest youth, while his 'face, and [a] compar[ison] with Betteredge' suggest age (Collins 1868k: 73). His national origin confuses Blake, for he bears a 'complexion . . . of a gipsy darkness' and his 'nose presented the fine shape and modelling so often found among the ancient people of the East' (Collins 1868i: 606); later, Blake observes 'the mixture of some foreign race in his English blood' (Collins 1868k: 74).[14] Most strikingly, his hair runs both black and white 'in the most startlingly partial and capricious manner' with 'no sort of regularity' (Collins 1868i: 606).[15] Such a litany of physical description leads Blake to declare that Jennings's body 'produce[s] too strong an impression on me to be immediately dismissed from my thoughts' (Collins 1868k: 73). Young and old, Eastern 'gipsy' and European, black and white, Jennings's body is an unresolvable enigma – a body whose codes refuse to be read. Confronted with a body he cannot read, Blake momentarily can only turn outward; even his attempt to read himself turns up only illegibility. He finds his 'curiosity . . . quite impossible to control'. Illegibility becomes a space where Blake loses himself, and briefly connects with both Jennings and the reader on the other side of the journal.

Though his body is initially difficult to read, this is his strength: his indeterminate physicality means he can empathise with others' sensations without interference from his own identity or feelings. Wracked with pain from a mysterious disease (77), neither English nor wholly foreign, devoid of any recorded past, Jennings's exterior pre-codes his identity as a self perpetually slipping away. His body is predisposed to sympathy: treating Dr Candy causes him to 'burst out crying', a wholly embodied sympathy that he explains to Blake through the (problematic) formulation 'Physiology says, and says truly, that some men are born with female constitutions – and I am one of them!' (74). His 'female constitution' is part of his sexual ambiguity. Philippa Levine argues that 'homosexuality was frequently seen as foreign or colonial in origin' (P. Levine 2006: 139), and while Jennings and Blake do not engage in any explicit sexual relationship, Jennings's uncertain nationality and queer sexuality mutually constitute one another.[16] In short, Jennings destabilises normative boundaries around multiple axes of identity: race, gender/sexuality, age, ability. Jennings's constantly eroding, liminal body slides through these categories and eludes stable identification, and primes him to step outside of self-regard.

There is a problem at the root of self-renunciation, one which has been creeping in at the margins in the interludes of this chapter: it is easy to renounce the self when that self is stable. A wealthy, white, married man can easily step outside himself with the knowledge that his body will remain intact while he is gone. But when that body is both figuratively and literally under attack, when that body is female, queer, non-white, self-renunciation becomes compulsory and reiterates hierarchy. And, as Biddy, the Indians, Penelope and Rosanna demonstrate, it is ultimately dangerous. *The Moonstone* – and, as the next chapter will argue, *Lady Audley's Secret* – seek a way to integrate empathy and the ethics of Associationism while also rejecting self-renunciation.[17] For a marginalised body, self-renunciation is in fact self-annihilation.

Jennings is predisposed to annihilation: he is sick and dying from the beginning, and is ejected from the text before the novel finishes. His eroding body enables Jennings to mediate between Franklin Blake and Dr Candy, and between Blake and Blake's body. Devoid of an interpretive self, Jennings understands bodies not as metaphors that need decoding or representations that point to interiors, but as physical, living matter. Jennings's fleshy body brings us back to the question of pain. Rather than fall back on metaphor, *The Moonstone* offers a model of language that connects bodies at a material level, even and especially when at least one of those bodies feels pain.

True pain, the *idée reçue* goes, is outside of language.[18] But this commits the same accidental logocentrism as the argument that affect is always outside of language; it makes language purely rational, always-already separated from the body. Rather, we might well include cries of pain within a model that understands language as sense-making rather than sensible. Compassion for pain, Carpenter argues, is both innate and cultivated. Some of the more primal feelings 'exist in very different intensity in different individuals', but 'are particularly susceptible of development . . . by appropriate culture' (Carpenter 1876: 210). This is particularly the case in 'emotions of sympathy', in which 'the Perception of the pain or distress of another tends to call forth (except in individuals of a peculiarly unsympathetic temperament) a corresponding affection in the percipient Self' (210–11). While the initial impulse to sympathy may be natural, novel reading provides the 'appropriate culture' to cultivate sympathy.

Language is not outside of pain and empathy, but in fact the primary mechanism by which empathy flourishes. More importantly, from an Associationist, mechanist perspective, a cry of pain may not convey the experience of pain itself, but it impacts the listener (except, as Carpenter says, those of peculiarly unsympathetic temperament) with the force of a body in crisis – a force to which a body cannot help but respond.

The expression of pain draws attention to the somatic content of language rather than the semantic content. This is crucial for popular literary authority, for if the question is 'who can tell the anguish?', and everything must be ultimately mechanist, there must exist a link between language and suffering. Outside of this link, fictional depictions of suffering are ethically useless. In *The Moonstone*, Jennings's physical suffering offers a reading lesson in how to read bodies' language as expressions of their physicality. As Blake and Jennings walk down the road, Jennings stops to pick some wildflowers. He bemoans that 'few people in England seem to admire them as they deserve', which prompts Blake to inquire, 'You have not always been in England?' (Collins 1868k: 74). Jennings stutters a response in fits and starts:

> No. I was born, and partly brought up, in one of our colonies. My father was an Englishman: but my mother – We are straying away from our subject, Mr Blake; and it is my fault. The truth is, I have associations with these modest little hedgeside flowers – It doesn't matter. (74)

As far as the words he speaks, Jennings provides very little. And yet, 'connecting the few words about himself which thus reluctantly escaped him, with the melancholy view of life which led him to place the conditions of human happiness in complete oblivion of the past', Blake relates to the reader, 'I felt satisfied that the story which *I had read in his face* was, in two particulars at least, the story that it really told' (74, emphasis added). In this moment, Blake models an exemplary associative reading. He begins not with himself, but instead with the associative chain of impressions the nosegays inspire in Jennings. Through the connection between the nosegay and his reading of Jennings's feelings, Blake encounters Jennings's face as physical matter he can 'read' to find that Jennings 'had suffered as few men suffer' (74). The chain traces a complex network of impressions: nosegays evoke impressions in Jennings; Jennings's impressions, as part of a mechanist system, play out on his body; Blake, as a body, feels the impressions in Jennings's body. Most importantly, Blake's realisation that Jennings 'had suffered as few men suffer' refers to a series of unspoken, past experiences. And yet, they are spoken: Jennings's 'few words about himself' connect his body to Blake precisely because his body suffers.

Language as sense-making mechanism, understood as a part of bodily experience, finds literary authority in sensation. It is through language – not its semantic content, but its use as a mechanism to connect bodies – that bodies collide, that the suffering of one becomes the suffering of both. As Rachel Ablow argues, 'the distinction . . . between physical and psychological suffering means very little' for Associationist theories of pain (Ablow 2014: 679; see also Ablow 2017). It would be vitalism of the highest order to assume that language has something beyond the physical, and only the most reductive mechanism would demand that language articulate precisely the hormones involved in pain rather than the phenomenological experience of being in pain.

As part of sense-making, language expresses and shapes bodies' physicality. Language and fiction enable empathy, then, in that they shape character through acquired habits. By reading about Jennings's body in pain, the reader stands beside Blake and better shapes his or her body's receptivity to the language of suffering. Jennings is the exemplar of embodied language, for he suffers, he has a tendency toward self-renunciation, a material inclination to connect with other bodies. And it is because of this that he serves as a model for how bodies can be read, and how to read. By stepping outside of himself, Jennings solves the mystery of the diamond's theft. Dr Candy falls ill, and in his delirium, utters 'disconnected words, and fragments of sentences' (Collins 1868l: 98–9). Here, two bodies come together and form the basis for associative reading. After Blake confesses that he believes he himself unconsciously took the diamond, Jennings races to his home and takes up the transcription of Dr Candy's ramblings:

> Mr Franklin Blake . . . and agreeable . . . down a peg . . . medicine . . . Confesses . . . slept at night . . . tell him . . . out of order . . . medicine . . . he tells me . . . and groping in the dark mean one and the same thing . . . all the company at the dinner table . . . I say . . . groping after sleep . . . nothing but medicine . . . (99)

And so on. Jennings uses this rambling to solve the mystery; he allows his own constantly eroding body to slide away, and instead embodies Candy's thoughts and feelings to deduce the missing words:

> Mr Franklin Blake is clever and agreeable, but he wants taking down a peg when he talks of medicine. He confesses that he has been suffering from want of sleep at night. I tell him that his nerves are out of order, and that he ought to take medicine. He tells me that taking medicine and

groping in the dark mean one and the same thing. This before all the company at the dinner table. I say to him, you are groping after sleep, and nothing but medicine can help you to find it. (99)

From this transcription, Blake learns that he did indeed take the Moonstone while under the influence of Dr Candy's opium sleep-aid. The notion that Jennings could somehow fill in these exact words from Candy's delirious ramblings borders on the absurd, perhaps, but the event is more instructive than realistic. Because of his embodied habitude for empathy, Jennings can give up his own body, to become Dr Candy, and ultimately, to disappear and simply mediate between Dr Candy and Franklin Blake.

The novel returns repeatedly to suffering in this interaction between Blake, Jennings and Candy, so that suffering becomes the basis of their connection, and language the bridge between their various sufferings. I have already said much of Jennings's suffering; Candy himself suffers from delirium and amnesia after his illness; Blake suffers from want of sleep. The deeper illness, however, is that Candy and Blake do not communicate with one another. It is only through Jennings's self-renunciation that Blake and Candy can finally connect – and it is only through Carpenter's mechanism that the mystery is solved.

The origin of Jennings's habitude and study brings us back to the beginning of this chapter, for Jennings himself is an Associationist scientist whose work emphasises the material origins of psychological phenomena. Through William Benjamin Carpenter, Jennings maps memory and impressions directly on to the anatomy of the cerebrum and bases his reading of the Moonstone diamond's theft on the brain's physical plasticity – its tendency to change physically and cognitively based on repeated practice. Where Betteredge and Cuff based their conclusions on character, Jennings bases his on bodies and mechanisms. Jennings believes that Blake's brain has an anatomical predisposition toward insomnia, as a result of his attempt to give up smoking. When he puts together the pieces of the mystery, Jennings proposes an experiment on Blake's unconscious mind and the physical structures of his brain. To prove the validity of his experiment, Jennings directs Blake's attention to the origin of his philosophy of habit, William Benjamin Carpenter's *Principles of Human Physiology*:

There seems much ground for the belief, that *every* sensory impression which has once been recognised by the perceptive consciousness, is registered (so to speak) in the brain, and may be reproduced at some subsequent time, although there may be no consciousness of its existence in the mind during the whole intermediate period. (Collins 1868l: 100; Carpenter 1853: 807–8)[19]

Therefore, he concludes, if he and Blake can replicate the circumstances that precipitated the Moonstone's theft, they should be able to evoke the same sensory impressions. The direct quotation from Carpenter mirrors Betteredge's quotations from Crusoe, but directly counteracts Betteredge's scholarship: where Betteredge uses texts to stand in for social relations, Jennings uses texts to make connections on a material level. In fact, the direct citation of a physiological treatise might well be read as a paradoxical indictment of fiction. But instead, the emphasis falls on the reader, rather than the text. Jennings reads to better acknowledge bodies, rather than to supplant or know them.

With this third model of scholarship, *The Moonstone* models the ideal reading practice. For Jennings (and Collins, through Carpenter), habit literally shapes bodies; empathy marks the physical structures of thinking and feeling. To continue Carpenter's metaphor, one can exercise and strengthen desirable acquired habitudes of thought like a muscle. Suffering primes Jennings's body for ethical reading, and most importantly, for the ability to teach and transmit ethical reading to other bodies.

Carpenter's Associationism gives readers the authority to understand the material effects of reading on their bodies, and to use those material effects as an ethical pedagogy to train their bodies for encounters in the lived world. When the reader encounters Jennings's body and his capacity to move beyond self-regard, then the reading lesson can begin: the reader can develop this habitude from reading about Jennings. The novel becomes a place to exercise empathy.

Margins: Rosanna

And yet, against the grain, the text does not succeed so smoothly. *The Moonstone* mirrors its own form, for it tells multiple narratives within itself. It tells the subversive story of the power of Indian mysticism and its superiority to British control even as it reifies Orientalist tropes of the East. It spends a great deal of time on methods of reading it will later reject. To distil the ideological bent of *The Moonstone* into a single narrative flattens the complexity of the fight it wages against itself.

Tension between narratives of subversion and narratives of repression within *The Moonstone* provides the best metaphor for the text: the text itself. By virtue of their overlapping roles, Blake and Wilkie Collins slide toward interchangeability: Collins arranges the journals, but writes a narrative in which Blake arranges them. As with the novel, this amalgamation provides a multitude of narratives about reading.

Perhaps we might read Collins and Blake against one another, and frame Collins's novel *The Moonstone* against the compositor of the Moonstone journals. A reading that remains conscious of publication dates and processes – a reading born of Betteredge's anachronistic *Crusoe* and Jennings's impossible reading of Carpenter – suggests that Blake fails to learn his lesson. His 1850 endeavour to compile evidence and save his reputation means that he still views narrative as a means of self-aggrandisement and solidifying knowledge.

More provocative still, Blake's self-recuperative motives might mirror Collins's normativising motives as a sort of unconscious cerebration. Both men desire to give voice to narratives they also find dangerous, and ultimately sequester them on the margins. The novel does not recognise that it might well condemn Blake for assembling the journals in large part because Collins does not recognise his own imposition of control on bodies and feelings.

In a genre meant to inculcate intuitive acknowledgement of others' bodies, novelists like Dickens and Collins grounded literary authority – for authors and readers alike – in proper embodiment. And, as we have explored, this mode of embodiment is one inclined to give up its own knowledge and even its sense of self to allow other bodies to speak for themselves. In *Great Expectations*, for example, Biddy's ability to step outside herself depends on her feminine virtue. She is a body already coded as virtuous: she is 'pleasant and wholesome and sweet tempered', with 'curiously thoughtful and attentive eyes; eyes that were very pretty and very good' (Dickens 1861a: 387). In *The Moonstone*, Jennings's liminal body readily disappears into Candy or Blake. The ability to read bodies depends on one's own mutability.

John Ruskin, in his lecture 'Lilies: Of Queens' Gardens', explicitly links reading with women's cultivation of feelings at the micro- and macrosocial levels of family and nation. Regarding women's education, Ruskin emphasises that men 'first have to mould her physical frame', for it is through her body that she transmits emotional, ethical perfection (Ruskin 1865: 154).[20] Education here first takes the form of a physical shaping – by men, of course. Once her body has been shaped, a woman can 'be taught to extend the limits of her sympathy with respect to that history which is being for ever determined' (157). This sequence emphasises the importance of the female body's physicality in the process of sympathy; the physical structures must come first. To hone sympathy, a woman should read 'to exercise herself in imagining what would be the effects upon her mind and conduct' of 'contemporary calamity' (157). Here, again, we have the idea that reading is a kind of gymnasium, a practice ground for bodies and affect. All this training matters to Ruskin because the woman's body must ultimately be cultivated to serve men. Women must learn to transmit sympathy, for 'men are feeble in sympathy, and contracted in hope; it is only [women] who can feel the depths of pain; and conceive the way of its healing' (186). This final point emphasises the ethical dimension of women's reading as Ruskin forms it: proper reading cultivates proper feeling, which women can then transmit to men in order to alleviate suffering and remedy social ills.

Often, as with Biddy, the female body disappears to become a mediator between men, or men and texts (including other legible women). Ruskin posits 'self-renunciation' as one of the primary objectives behind women's education: women 'must be enduringly, incorruptibly good; instinctively, infallibly wise – wise, not for self-development, but for self-renunciation' (149–50). The term comes from Thomas Carlyle's *Selbst-töbdtung*, which he calls 'the first preliminary moral act', and describes an ethical framework that locates emotional knowledge in the denial of one's own interests, and ultimately in the complete incorporation of one's self into the interests of the other (Carlyle 1831: 128–9). As a form of emotional education, reading is one of the first and most important sites where this discipline takes place. In novels' representations of reading, feminine characters use their gendered, intuitive knowledge to help men know other bodies and texts. Through self-renunciation, Victorian women build the emotional foundations of the domestic, bourgeois family. These novels link domesticity, emotion and the female body's tendency toward both sympathy and legibility to 'establish the woman's authority over a specific domain of knowledge – that of the emotions' (N. Armstrong 1987: 43). Literary representation both resonated with and formed actual social conditions: emotional, self-renouncing women in the novel contributed to the social perception of women as emotional and self-renouncing. In this dominant Victorian theory of gender and knowledge, women's intuitive understanding of emotion makes them ideal translators between narrative and the men who attempt to read texts and other bodies. But, as mediators, these women cannot retain their own bodily sensations. 'Victorian culture', Caroline Levine glosses, 'insistently cast self-suspension as a quintessentially feminine virtue' (C. Levine 2003: 85). In short, the Victorian woman fully realises her subjectivity when she loses her subjectivity.

And so, as the moral and emotional locus of literary authority, female characters' primary function often lies in the erasure of their bodies. By stepping in, connecting with a male body, and then stepping back, these women enable the men around them to read other bodies. These mediating relationships readily fit into Eve Kosofsky Sedgwick's homosocial triangle, in which women operate 'as exchangeable, perhaps symbolic, property for the primary purpose of cementing the bonds of men with men' (Sedgwick 1985: 25–6). When these triangles depend on a woman reading, they become what Catherine Golden calls a 'Dickensian angel'. Golden posits that H. K. Browne's illustrations, in their depictions of women reading, 'establis[h] the book as a prop of gentility' (Golden 2003: 148). 'Prop' conveys the inanimate, objectified way these angels read books, for the illustrations show them holding books unused, unread, on their laps or nearby. The Dickensian angel, a model self-renouncing reader, does not read. Instead, the angel waits for men to interrupt her so that she can offer her domestic or emotional assistance (148). The angel reads to be interrupted because the interruption indicates male dominance over her body; if the man can read her body, and she can read texts, then he therefore can read all bodies through her.

But they do not in fact read her body; if they could read bodies that fluently, they would not need her to mediate. Rather, she turns herself into a legible text that the man can know, and then superimposes her body as a permeable surface that maps knowledge of herself on to other bodies. Often, as in the case of Biddy and Mrs. Joe, the self-renouncing appears voluntary: Biddy willingly uses her body to give Pip knowledge. But with Penelope Betteredge, Ezra Jennings and Rosanna Spearman, appearance of voluntary self-renunciation is only an appearance; it is in fact a coercive dissection, or worse, a mandated self-vivisection. In short, the Victorian woman reader fully realises her embodiment when she loses her body.

In *The Moonstone*, Rosanna Spearman suffers the worst abuse at the hands of these normativising impulses. Even the then-dead Jennings's journals become their own narrative, a rite denied Rosanna. While Rosanna appears prominently in Betteredge's narrative and Blake reprints her letter, she never acquires her own space to write. What appeared to be voluntary connection between bodies instead is mandatory dissection. Like Jennings, her body is undefinable: she 'had been a thief', but 'there was just a dash of something that wasn't like a housemaid, and that *was* like a lady, about her' (Collins 1868b: 97, 98). Cuff and Blake require Rosanna's body to be legible, and her compulsory abjection dissolves her entirely. Self-renunciation becomes abject self-annihilation.

Where Jennings dies on the margins of the text, Rosanna dies on the margins of both the text and the text's geography. Like Jennings, she knows that she is dying – but unlike Jennings, her prophecy has less to do with science and more to do with a sensation, a feeling that her 'grave is waiting for [her] here' in the sands surrounding the manor where most of the novel takes place. At her words, the sands transform into a sensational nightmare, for 'it looks as if it had hundreds of suffocating people under it – all struggling to get to the surface, and all sinking lower and lower in the dreadful deeps!' (Collins 1868i: 603). In the end, these sands swallow her, bind her to the periphery – but her ghost haunts the novel with her letter.

The text mirrors these sands: drawing Rosanna to the margins, seeking to suffocate her voice. Blake reprints her letter in his Moonstone journal, but he envelops it in his own narrative. The entire letter is given in quotation marks, to reinforce that it is not a primary part of the narrative in question. To his credit, Betteredge answers that Blake should 'let her speak for herself' – an important phrase, given that they refuse to read her narrative aloud (Collins 1868j: 4). But even after the anxieties are ameliorated, when Blake collects the journals, he leaves 'the miserable story of Rosanna Spearman . . . to suggest for itself all that is here purposely left unsaid' (4). She remains ostensibly outside of language, barred from the novel, on the margins.

For *The Moonstone*'s pedagogy to succeed, the novel must drown Rosanna. Her illegibility codes her as subversive and dangerous – and as a dangerous woman, she must be controlled or expelled. Her mysterious body is a threat to others, to herself, and most importantly to the social order of the Verinder estate. She refuses to stay in her designated role as a housemaid, and this refusal exposes the self-destructive impetus beneath the self-righteous veneer of self-sacrifice. She takes self-renunciation to its fullest conclusion: she literally annihilates herself for Blake and commits suicide after she protects him from discovery. Where liminality authorises Jennings as an ethical reader, it invalidates Rosanna as a writer. In compiling the narratives, Blake and *The Moonstone* might give voice to marginalised voices and provide the space for ethical connections, but behind these ostensible connections lies a realm of unfettered ambiguity that ostensibly scientific, ethical reading must tame.

Notes

1. For more on the definitions of these terms, see Garland Allen's 'Mechanism, Vitalism and Organicism in Late Nineteenth and Twentieth-Century Biology: The Importance of Historical Context' (2005).
2. See 'On the Reflex Function of the Medulla Oblongata and Medulla Spinalis' in the *Philosophical Transactions of the Royal Society* by Marshall Hall (1833), and Thomas Laycock's 'On the Reflex Function of the Brain' in the *British and Foreign Medical Journal* (1845).
3. For Carpenter's place in the genealogy of Associationism, see Edward S. Reed's *From Soul to Mind* (1998), particularly pages 76–80. Alison Winter's chapter 'The Construction of Orthodoxies and Heterodoxies in the Early Victorian Life Sciences' in *Victorian Science in Context* (1997), particularly pages 35–43, explores Carpenter's rise to prominence and his negotiation of materialism. For a more nuanced investigation of Carpenter's genealogy within thinking about volition and the unconscious, see Jenny Bourne Taylor's article 'Fallacies of Memory in Nineteenth-Century Psychology' (2000).
4. While Carpenter does not discuss him, Dugald Stewart's Associationism also plays a part in the genealogy of habit: Stewart argues that 'by means of habit, a particular associating principle may be strengthened to such a degree, as to give us a command of all the different ideas in our mind, which have a certain relation to each other; so that when any one of the class occurs to us, we have almost a certainty that it will suggest the rest' (D. Stewart 1792: 218).
5. Citations are from the fourth edition (1853) because many of the ideas central to this chapter do not appear in the first (1842) edition.
6. Vanessa Ryan explores Carpenter and 'unconscious cerebration' through many of Collins's novels in *Thinking Without Thinking in the Victorian Novel* (2012), particularly her introduction and first chapter, 'The Reflexive Mind'. In 'The Reflexive Mind', she pays special attention to Collins's extradiegetic relationship with science, and his pairing of physiology with mesmerism in *The Moonstone*. While Ryan highlights the broad range of philosophies that emphasise ideas similar to unconscious cerebration, I am as always interested in tracing the scientific origin and physical elements of unconscious cerebration alongside the broader scientific conversations of Associationism.
7. Where necessary, I will refer to the characters' independent narratives as 'the Moonstone journals' to distinguish them from Collins's 1868 novel *The Moonstone*. This will be important when the characters interact with the written journals, since they do interact with a physical text, but that text is obviously not the Collins novel.
8. Duncan reads the Brahmins' power to subvert the symbolic economy of British readers in opposition to D. A. Miller's Foucauldian/Bakhtinian reading of the novel. For Duncan, Miller's reading operates on the erroneous assumption that 'the mystery novel is supposed to cure a crisis of

representation with a hermeneutic virtuosity that regulates the relation between world and subject' (Duncan 1994: 301). According to Miller's formulation, power in *The Moonstone* 'is thoroughly *monological*', so that 'the securities of perception and language' are 'incontestably truthful' (D. A. Miller 1988: 54). Duncan instead suggests that 'the positive alterity of India, its victory over English police skill', complicates Miller's argument (Duncan 1994: 301). Rather than enabling 'epistemological totalisation and ideological closure in the name of an omniscient detection', the Brahmins' successful reading practices problematise the stability of British logic and reading (301).

9. For a reading of Jennings's hybridity and *The Moonstone* as purporting 'an ideology of inclusion', see Vicki Corkran Willey's 'Wilkie Collins's "Secret Dictate"' in *Victorian Sensations* (2006).
10. This practice comes from Augustine, as Homer O. Brown points out in 'The Displaced Self in the Novels of Daniel Defoe' (1971). See also Katie Lanning's 'Tessellating Texts' (2012).
11. Among these readings, a few stand out as innovative, particularly in their connections to the larger imperial undertones of the text. Patrick Brantlinger perhaps began the connection between Betteredge's religious readings and imperialism when he asserts Betteredge's practice as part of the Victorian trend toward using imperialism as a kind of religion or stand-in for religion (Brantlinger 1988: 228). Jaya Mehta extends Brantlinger's argument when she ties Betteredge's proof-texting readings of *Crusoe* to Crusoe's biblical proof-texting to expose *Crusoe*'s preoccupation with using the European narrative of colonialism like 'a combination Bible and Ouija board' (Mehta 1995: 622). Sabina Falzi further reads Betteredge's reading as a kind of 'hocus pocus' (Betteredge's phrase) akin to the Indian agents' mysticism (Falzi 2012: 159).
12. For similar theoretical approaches, see Leah Price's *How to Do Things with Books in Victorian Britain* (2013) and Daniel Hack's *The Material Interests of the Victorian Novel* (2005).
13. Betteredge's reading practice here – scoring and marking the paper when he comes to an excerpt suited for his purposes – resonates with derogatory depictions of popular readers who fixate on their own literary prowess. In *Vanity Fair*, Thackeray imagines his reader, Jones, 'taking out his pencil and scoring under the words "foolish, twaddling", &c., and adding to them his own remark of "*quite true*"' (Thackeray 1849: 6). George Eliot references Jones in her own consideration of 'moral comments' in 'Silly Novels by Lady Novelists'. In her essay, Eliot invokes 'a class of readers' who 'doubly and trebly scor[e] [such comments] with the pencil', and whose 'delicate hands giv[e] in their determined adhesion to these hardy novelties by a distinct *très vrai* [very true], emphasised by many notes of exclamation' (Eliot 1856: 449). Eliot writes against a particular kind of author, a particularly female kind of author – but in this moment, she gestures with equal disdain toward a kind of reader. Betteredge performs his reading with the same pretension as the imagined readers' '*très*

vrai' and exclamation points, especially when he delivers his readers the injunction 'You are welcome to be as merry as you please over everything else I have written. But when I write of *Robinson Crusoe*, by the Lord it's serious – and I request you to take it accordingly!' (Collins 1868n: 198). Along with the rhetorical absurdity of his over-earnest declaration 'by the Lord it's serious', the events of Betteredge's own narrative fail to authorise his reading.

14. His national origin confuses scholars as well, Sharleen Mondal points out in 'Racing Desire' (2009). Vicki Corkran Willey calls him 'biracial' (Willey 2006: 229), Jaya Mehta calls him 'half caste' and 'Eurasian' (Mehta 1995: 628, 630), and Ronald Thomas designates him 'an Exile from India' and, most colourfully, 'the bastard child of the British Empire' (Thomas 1991: 241, 242).
15. See Vicki Corkran Willey's 'Wilkie Collins's "Secret Dictate"' in *Victorian Sensations* (2006) for a reading of Jennings's hair and hybridity.
16. Mondal (2009) provides a fairly compelling argument for a more explicitly sexual reading of Jennings and Blake.
17. The structure of this book's argument places *Lady Audley* after *The Moonstone* – but it is worth arguing that Jennings's collapsing body is something of a queer version of Lady Audley. Jennings's queerness – his gender, his race, his body – allows Collins to transfer to a male body the self-annihilation that Lady Audley embraces (has thrust upon her?).
18. In *The Body in Pain*, Elaine Scarry writes that 'physical pain does not simply resist language but actively destroys it, bringing about an immediate reversion to *a state anterior to language*, to the sounds and cries a human being makes before language is learned' (Scarry 1985: 4).
19. While Jennings could have read the first edition of Carpenter, he in fact could not have provided this particular quotation because it comes from an edition published after the events of *The Moonstone*. Elaboration on unconscious cerebration and its relationship to the structures of the cerebrum do not appear until Carpenter's fourth English edition, published in 1853. According to Dr Candy's narrative, Jennings dies on 19 September 1849. Simply put, Jennings could not have quoted the fourth edition. Collins also edits the quotation to make it more legible for readers, exchanging 'cerebrum' for 'brain' in the phrase 'is registered (so to speak) in the *brain*'. Unlike Betteredge's *Crusoe* anachronism, however, I do not think this particularly temporal shift serves any intentional or even coincidental purpose. I suspect that Collins was either not aware of the discrepancy, or felt that the content of the quotation justified a useful fiction.
20. Physicality and materiality are critical to Ruskin's ethics of sympathy and feeling. After all, the foundation of women's education depends first and foremost on shaping their bodies. Ruskin rejects the idea that beauty 'is dependent on the association of ideas' in *Modern Painters I* as an 'erring or inconsistent positio[n]' (Ruskin 1888: 30); at the same time, according

to George Landow's study of Ruskin's aesthetics, he also used 'associative reading' to 'exten[d] to art what the associationist psychologists . . . had claimed for literature: its power to engage, embody, and guide the whole mind, including the imagination' (Landow 1971: 199). Ruskin's ethical aesthetics requires wholly embodied engagement with material objects, so that even if he objects to particular Associationist theorisations of beauty, his work converses with Associationism's emphasis on materiality and its ethical implications.

Chapter 5

Represented Bodies: The Lawyer, Conclusions and Circumstantial Evidence in *Lady Audley's Secret*

Reading, according to Associationism, is a material act, for as we have seen, language is a part of the sensorium, and reading bodies undergo physical changes inspired by the imaginations and memories which reading inspires. It is tempting to read this trajectory in the other direction, and thereby to claim that bodies are legible as texts.

The conflation of these two, however, is precisely where things fall apart. While the physiological response to a given stimulus may be within a statistical norm, the expression of that response is not nearly so predictable. This is especially true when probable outcomes depend on the mediation of a third body's adherence to a social role, as in the cases of women as domestic guardians of moral and emotional knowledge. When Rosanna Spearman mediates between Franklin Blake and Sergeant Cuff as the embodiment of the legal institution, she does not in fact inhabit Blake's body. Rather, she replicates probable social roles, for her social role is to enable a male body to interpret another body. Benjamin Morgan draws attention to the 'powerfully normative dimensions of Bain's account of the mind' that produce 'the pleasures of regularity, order, and subordination' (Morgan 2017: 97). In short, predictable physiological response does not yield predictable social response; rather, predictable social response yields predictable social response. But it is easy to read this backwards, so that one believes that probable social interaction presupposes consistent physiological etiology.

Mary Elizabeth Braddon's *Lady Audley's Secret*, I suggest, sees the conflation of the social and physiological as contest over knowledge itself – scientific, legal and emotional. While knowledge often bears the trappings of empiricism, it is only ever naïvely mechanistic, for it believes that bodies can be reduced to apprehensible formulae. Flattened versions of science must bifurcate bodies into external representations that make interiors legible. Here, 'representations' means reproductions of bodies in part or in whole. Sometimes, these representations are obvious reproductions, as in portraiture; in other instances, these representations are more abstract, as in letters composed by the bodies in question, or sweeping data sets. Representations differ from metaphors in that they are not code, but rather, direct glimpses into a body's interior. Robert Audley, the nascent lawyer through whom the novel is focalised, holds that if he can read an exterior representation of a body, he can read that body's interior.

In the end, conclusions matter. 'Conclusions' in multiple valences: Robert's pseudo-scientific conclusions about interiors; his legal conclusions derived from those scientific conclusions; and ultimately, the conclusions of the novel in the third volume of the triple-decker. On a broader theoretical level, this chapter confronts scientific conclusions about sensation and bodily possibilities. Braddon rejects the representation of bodies, particularly female bodies, as a tool to understand bodies' interiors. *Lady Audley's Secret* resists a 'flattened' application of Associationism, which claims that the science of sensation enables one to know sensations in the Cavellian sense, to transform female bodies into representations that knowledgeable men can decode.

Lady Audley's Secret rebels against conclusions and the scholarly methods that derive them, for there is nothing virtuous about self-renunciation if female bodies exist only to be read and discarded to the margins. Flattened science that reads bodies for their use-value offers only self-annihilation, not empathy. While it is tempting to read the novel as pure rejection of patriarchy, as revelling in the redemptive power of small moments of resistance, to do so effaces the violence of self-annihilation. Lady Audley turns the mandate to self-renounce against itself in a kind of *mise en abyme*: an infinite recursion of images that recede into themselves, a technique that gives the illusion of depth while remaining entirely surface. But *mise en abyme* nevertheless still places her into the abyss. She reveals interpretation as the product of flattened science and flattened reading, as a cog in a self-destruction machine.

To achieve these insights into bodies through their representations, Robert Audley depends on the cachet of Associationism's scientificity – that is, the authority that nineteenth-century thinkers grant discourses with the appearance of scientific knowledge, but without recourse to actual science. Through this knowledge, Robert insists that bodies and texts are interchangeable, and that each enables readers to read the other. Morgan argues that Bain and Martineau 'turn the mind "outward," rendering properties that had once been thought of as contained within the self as legible on the surface of the body' (Morgan 2017: 98). *Lady Audley's Secret*, I argue, insists that the exterior is not nearly so legible as they might want it to be. The body is not a text. Chiara Briganti says that 'Robert's confidence in the unproblematic interchangeability of text and body is misplaced and amusing' (Briganti 1991: 204). Misplaced, certainly, in that he believes himself to be an Associationist but is in fact more of a novelist, and a poor one at that. It is far from amusing, however, for Robert's reading practices lead him to assume that he has complete command of texts and bodies – particularly female bodies – in the same way. This kind of reading is commensurate with making objects and bodies useful: books cultivate readers' intuitive knowledge about emotion, and bodies reveal their interiority so that men can read them. He performs literariness and scientificity to gain profit and social standing.

A robust and complex history of feminist readings surround Lady Audley and her moments of violence and resistance. Those critics who read for small moments of resistance tend to find the novel subversive. They often argue that Lady Audley's violence and sexuality undermine the stability of the domestic sphere. With attention to small moments of power, Sandra Gilbert and Susan Gubar argue that, because they are 'denied the freedom to act openly out in the world, [Braddon's] heroines exploit their intuitive understanding of the needs of the male ego in order to provide comfortable places for themselves in society' (Gilbert and Gubar 1979: 473). Reading for these moments ascribes a certain degree of agency to Lady Audley, in that it suggests she consciously manipulates the system that oppresses her. These kinds of arguments account for serialised reading practices. In the weeks between one instalment and the next, before Lady Audley is punished or defeated, readers can take pleasure in her subversiveness. Natalie Schroeder summarises the underlying epistemology of these arguments, claiming that 'the novelists undercut the defeats [of women like Lady Audley] by the energy and daring of their female characters, who emerge as far more interesting than and superior to their male adversaries' (Schroeder 1988: 101). While it is true that the ending does allege resolution, Lady Audley and the other women of the novel remain far more interesting than the conclusions that constrain them.[1]

The model resists literary authority derived from the annihilation of other bodies. It champions acknowledgement, and rejects conclusions drawn from knowledge – of lawyerly scholarship, of physiognomy, of detective work. And most importantly, it rejects the authority of male readers at the expense of women. This challenges the larger negotiation around literary authority by confronting the question itself: whether authority comes from scholarly hermeneutics or popular feeling, if that power comes from or at the expense of another person, it is unethical.

Lady Audley's Secret is sceptical of a version of Associationism that requires legible bodies, that demands women annihilate themselves for men, and that equates representations of bodies and lived bodies. But it is not simply an anti-Association novel. Instead, it is deeply invested in the refutation of simplified science that lacks self-criticism and claims totalising knowledge. The philosophical quandary at the core of the novel challenges Associationist thinkers to consider both their faithfulness to the epistemological foundations of Associationism, and the social implications of a totalising science of feeling that sees bodies through either metaphors or representations.

Unfinished Bodies

Lady Audley's Secret is a book of surfaces: portraits, letters, novels, bodies. While each of these surfaces seems to beg dissection, any character's attempts to uncover the inside fail; the moment interpretation begins, the surface slides out from beneath the scalpel and leaves scholarly surgeons simply to cut themselves. It is difficult to write about interpretation and representation in *Lady Audley's Secret* and also to keep focus on Lady Audley herself. As she constantly evades the investigatory magnifying glasses of other characters, so too I find she evades my own scholarly readings. To make matters worse, Robert Audley does the same: as he constantly tries to make *Lady Audley's Secret* about himself, so too he repeatedly butts into this chapter and attempts to show off his own reading practices. Lady Audley's self-annihilation and Robert's desperate self-regard both point perpetually back to materiality and surface: Lady Audley because she depends on the slipperiness of surface, and Robert because he naïvely insists on his ability to penetrate surface through abstraction. Both of these characters intersect with the idea of bodies as mere representations of interiority.

Robert's insistence that he can read and interpret bodies – and his repeated failure to do so – reveal his ignorance not only of feeling, but also of the external, embodied signs of feelings. Through the second volume of the novel, Robert and Alicia have an off-and-on romantic interest in one another, which Robert attempts to use for his own emotional and moral edification. Most of the 'off' of their romance comes from Robert's proclivity to supplant actual embodiment with his own predetermined knowledge. The narrator says that Alicia

> might have been over head and ears in love with him; and she might have told him so, in some charming, roundabout, womanly fashion, a hundred times in a day for all the three hundred and sixty-five days in the year; but unless she had waited for some privileged 29th of February, and walked straight up to him, saying, 'Robert, please will you marry me'? I very much doubt if he would ever have discovered the state of her feelings. (Braddon 1861b: 145)

In this section, the hypothetical Alicia conveys interiority indirectly through language. Robert is unaware of the complex social valences of language, for he would not understand 'roundabout' phrases – only the direct declaration of love would register. This is particularly useful in conjunction with the paragraph that immediately follows:

> Again, had he been in love with her himself, I fancy that the tender passion would, with him, have been so vague and feeble a sentiment that he might have gone down to his grave with a dim sense of some uneasy sensation which might be love or indigestion, and with, beyond this, no knowledge whatever of his state. (145)

Here, the indications of love are distinctly embodied. The sensation of love is equivalent to indigestion: directly attributable to a bodily sensation, even to a system or particular organs. Of course Robert struggles to read others' feelings, if he is unable to interpret his own body and its expression of his sensations.

Together, these two paragraphs suggest a connection between linguistic and embodied expression of sensation, in which language once again mediates between physical bodies. Robert does not understand the distinction between representations of bodies and physical bodies, and he is unable to interpret either of them in this section. He registers neither Alicia's (embodied) linguistic articulation of her own sensations, nor his own body's expression.

Robert's poor reading of sensation marks him as a profoundly short-sighted, unauthoritative reader, and therefore ill-suited to empathy and the task of uncovering Lady Audley's real identity. As the patterns I have traced should lead us to expect, Robert's myopathy comes from his belief that he *knows* other people's feelings. He tends to treat physical expression as foregone conclusions to which he already knows the answer.

This is because he acquaints himself with bodies through their representations. I am using the word 'representations' here in a different sense than 'metaphoric' from the chapter previous. For Pip, the chain was a reference to Magwitch's criminal body, in the same way that the pie was a reference to his own criminal body. The signifying relationship between objects and metaphoric bodies encodes those bodies with a sort of indexing marker: Pip is a criminal; Joe is a buffoon. In representation, the signifying relationship enables representations like images or writing to stand in for bodies: Lady Audley's portrait *is* Lady Audley; her letter *is* her.

An early example of this mechanism at work in *Lady Audley's Secret* comes when Robert examines a letter from Lady Audley. He remarks that, while he has 'never believed in those fellows who ask you for thirteen postage stamps, and offer to tell you what you have never been able to find out yourself', something about Lady Audley's writing conveys her body (Braddon 1861b: 146). He dismisses postage-stamp readers as charlatans, but insists that 'I think if I had never seen your aunt [more on this in a moment], I should know what she was like by this slip of paper' (146). Lady Audley's handwriting alone conveys her physical body to Robert, for he sees in her writing 'the feathery, gold-shot, flaxen curls, the pencilled eyebrows, the tiny straight nose, the winning childish smile' (146). Robert's mode of reading appears praiseworthy, for like Pip, he conjures physical bodies from mere writing. He is alive to the physical properties of language and understands that textual bodies can evoke sensations as powerfully as if they were immediately present. But it is much more sinister than that.

This early example of reading reveals Robert's tendency to conflate physical bodies, interiors and textuality. While speaking to his cousin, Alicia – he even calls her by name in this section of dialogue – Robert says that he could see 'your aunt' in her handwriting, for Lady Audley is Alicia's stepmother and *his* aunt. Maybe this is a copyediting error, but the shift in person here persists beyond the original serialisation and into later revised editions. We might therefore make this strange slip into something productive: a moment where Robert conveys that when he reads representations of bodies, his readings always return to himself.

Robert's tendency to read himself as the referent of bodily representations depends on the gendered mediation of women around him. In this case, Alicia gives him the note, and while he initially speaks to her about it, his address to 'you' suggests that by the end he speaks only to himself. While I will discuss this mediation in greater detail below, here it is important to set up the female intercessor between bodies and their interiors on the one hand, and Robert's knowledge on the other. The presence of a female body between the representation and the interpretation duplicates the logic of interiority: the physical female body is meant to be a permeable membrane between its interiority and Robert. The body is not meant to impede the reading of interiority, but rather, to assist Robert when he penetrates the material exterior to know the interior.

Unfinished Portraits

Double mediation is particularly crucial when Robert views Lady Audley's infamous portrait. One of the 'secrets' in *Lady Audley's Secret* is the secret identity of Lady Audley. In an effort to uncover her true interiority, Robert (and the reader) continually endeavours to unfold the illusionary layers of representation that Lady Audley spins in front of her. Of all the representations of Lady Audley's body, her portrait seems the most promising mediator between her innocent body and her more sinister social machinations. But, as this section will demonstrate, the portrait instead sets up the central conceit of the novel: that bodies slide out from beneath the easy equivalence between representation and interior.

Lady Audley begins as an enigma whose exterior surface tells nothing of her interior. Robert's initial meeting with his aunt is cut short by her own contrivance, and he is left with 'an imperfect notion of her face' (Braddon 1861b: 147). When Alicia offers to take him into Lady Audley's private room to view her portrait, he leaps at the opportunity, for the external representation of Lady Audley will provide him with deeper knowledge of her interior. The room is locked, and only Lady Audley has the key. But after prompting, Alicia quite suddenly recalls a secret passage that leads into Lady Audley's quarters. The men lower themselves into a tunnel in which they must 'craw[l] upon their hands and knees', unbolt a trap door, and climb up into the chamber. Critics often note the sexual overtones in this escapade, but I most prefer Elizabeth Langland's phrasing: 'Lady Audley's private spaces are curiously vulnerable to penetration' (Langland 2000: 9).[2] Alicia provides the men with the passageway and directions, but does not come with them; she instead offers access to Lady Audley's interior room, which in turn promises the portrait, which depicts Lady Audley's physical body, which ultimately conveys her interiority. The chain of representations is long and winding, but at each step, the men can use a female body to unlock the next layer of signification.

But representation is precisely the game Lady Audley and *Lady Audley's Secret* play. The representational conventions of the mid-century novel demand that a woman should mediate between men and interiority, and so Lady Audley weaves as tangled a web of representation as she can. Tamara Wagner writes that Lady Audley 'is called by five names throughout the course of the novel' – Helen Maldon, Helen Talboys, Lucy Graham, Lucy Audley and Madame Taylor, and I would add 'Lady Audley' as a sixth – 'none of which provides actual interiority for this character' (Wagner 2009: 240). For a character the narrator describes as 'ever alive to the importance of outward effect', interiority is a kind of contradiction; to ask which of her many names points to the real woman is to fall into the trap Lady Audley sets up. In this jumble of representations, the novel offers something of a snare for Robert and the reader as well. Robert spends much of the text learning to read bodies through their representations. But the further he goes, the more entangled he becomes, so that representations and mediation so deeply obscure interiority that it might as well not exist.

The portrait itself seems to offer a conduit to Lady Audley's interior. Up until the portrait, every description of Lady Audley's physical body emphasises her childlike appearance:

> [Lady Audley's] childishness had a charm which few could resist. The innocence and candour of an infant beamed in Lady Audley's fair face, and shone out of her large and liquid blue eyes. The rosy lips, the delicate nose, the profusion of fair ringlets, all contributed to preserve to her beauty the character of extreme youth and freshness . . . she looked like a child tricked out for a masquerade, was as girlish as if she had but just left the nursery. All her amusements were childish. (Braddon 1861a: 122)

Much has been said about her physical body and its childish tendencies. I am interested in the way that the painting's external detail 'exaggerates' her physicality in ways that bring out interior traits. It appears, at first light, that the portrait in fact works as a representation of her interior, for it gives the lie to the innocent appearance of her exterior. The painter's techniques alter her physical features so that they become sinister. The Pre-Raphaelite tendencies of the painter emphasise 'every attribute of that delicate face as to give a lurid lightness to the blonde complexion, and a strange, sinister light to the deep blue eyes', and 'giv[e] to that pretty pouting mouth [a] hard and almost wicked look' (Braddon 1861b: 148–9). Over the course of the novel, the reader and Robert learn that this vision of Lady Audley as 'a beautiful fiend' is, of course, perhaps more accurate than a depiction of her as an innocent child. The representation gives a more accurate portrait of Lady Audley's interior than does her physical body.

The sense that the representation seems more accurate troubles the claim that one can read a body. The portrait challenges the stable relationship between the material and the interior, and undermines the idea that Robert can tell what kind of woman she might be. Where just a few pages before, he believed he could know Lady Audley by her handwriting, the portrait suggests that interiors are perhaps more elusive. Critics tend to fall for this snare as well. In 'Idle Vampires and Decadent Maidens', Heather Braun argues that Lady Audley exists 'contained within her own portrait, a pre-Raphaelite-style painting that remains far more dynamic and threatening than Lady Audley herself' (Braun 2009: 240). When one unpacks the portrait scene, it is tempting to relegate Lady Audley herself to the margins while highlighting the portrait itself.[3] The representation takes primacy over the material body, in large part because it seems to convey something truer, something more important than the façade her body portrays.

But the portrait tangles the relationship between representation and interiority as well. Even if one completely interprets the representation of the body in the painting, some of that body remains always illegible. In the narrator's words, the portrait is 'so like and yet so unlike' Lady Audley (Braddon 1861b: 149). Both like and unlike, the portrait offers a familiar exterior with a hidden, sinister interiority that the men cannot read. When Alicia leads Robert and his friend George Talboys to see the portrait, she notes that it remains 'unfinished', a perpetual work-in-progress (147). The portrait's unfinished state resists reading. A finished portrait might offer insight into the interior of the body represented; the exterior image would encode some key to interpreting – and thereby mastering – Lady Audley. But because this portrait is unfinished, it only reminds its viewers that it cannot yet represent the unseen interior.

The portrait's illegible network of representation ultimately circumvents the male gazes that desire to read and interpret Lady Audley's body. The pacing of the men's viewing experience defuses the affective power of any culminating moment: nearly 1,000 words pass between Robert's excited 'Her portrait! . . . I would give anything to see it!' and his declaration 'now, for the portrait' (Braddon 1861b: 147–8).

Another 125 words delay the unveiling of the portrait as Robert waves George away for a private viewing – and then Robert's actual viewing happens in between lines. George

> fell back, and leaning his forehead against the window-panes, looked out at the night.
> When he turned round he saw that Robert had arranged the easel very conveniently, and that he had seated himself on a chair before it for the purpose of contemplating the painting at his leisure.
> He rose as George turned round.
> 'Now, then, for your turn, Talboys,' he said. (148)

Lacking any chronological measurement and devoid of any description, Robert's encounter with the portrait remains unwritten. Only when George sits to look for a specified 'quarter of an hour' does the narrator describe the portrait (149). In one sense, Robert's viewing could not be more masculine: the reader cannot watch Robert watch, because such meta-voyeurism would expose his feigned authority. On the other hand, this vague not-looking emphasises the textual portrait's immateriality over its materiality: to look at it becomes to step out of time and text, for the power it holds over Robert eludes description.

The portrait constitutes the philosophical quandary of the text: is it possible, reader, to tell the feelings of bodies simply through their representations? The representation of Lady Audley in the portrait confronts Robert Audley and George Talboys with a ponderous dichotomy: her body is aggressively, assertively physical – but also illegible. She is present, but concealed. The narrator offers readers a lens with which to take in the picture, one in which the copious details of the portrait 'combin[e] to render the first effect of the painting by no means an agreeable one' (149). No mere ironic accident, the narrative describes the portrait with a degree of detail that attempts to evoke through language the sensation of looking at the portrait in the flesh. Lyn Pykett observes that the narrator 'both satirises Pre-Raphaelitism and appropriates its sensuous and sensual gaze' (Pykett 1992: 92). I suggest, however, that while potential readers may attempt to harness a sensual gaze, the portrait's sensuality falls apart because of its ambiguity. Her portrait is physical, but that physicality does not map out the interior beneath it; her identity is uncertain, both like and unlike. Illegible and fluid, the text becomes 'an elusive representation that signifies both visual presence and absence', as Lynette Felber puts it (Felber 2007: 473). Lady Audley's painted bodily presence seduces with detail, but its unfamiliar exterior and veiled interior deny the use of the portrait to read her sensations.

Unfinished Observations

Even as the portrait undercuts Robert's desire to read bodies through representation, it also challenges him to try harder to do so. This is something of a snare, for Lady Audley's interiority appears to present a puzzle that the other characters can understand only through external representations – but in the end, her interiority cannot in fact be decoded by representation. In her assessment of the portrait, Alicia says, 'We have never seen my lady look as she does in that picture; but I think she could look so' (Braddon 1861b: 149). Her analysis suggests a correlation between representation and interiority, in that the portrait can tell them something about Lady Audley which her physical body cannot. But it also demonstrates the disjuncture between physical bodies and representations of those bodies, for Lady Audley's body has not appeared as she does in the picture. Robert, unaware of this distinction between representation and physical bodies, takes Alicia's reading of the portrait as an exhortation to hone his ability to read representations.

As a rule, Robert fails to read bodies' expressions of their interiority. When Alicia makes her observation about Lady Audley's portrait, he rejects it outright with the command 'Don't be German', by which he seems to mean to rely on abstraction (Braddon 1861b: 149). Surprisingly, he goes on to insist on the separation between representation and interiority: 'The picture is – the picture; and my lady is – my lady. I'm not metaphysical: don't unsettle me' (149). But he is certainly unsettled, for 'he repeated this several times with an air of terror that was perfectly sincere' (149). On the surface, Robert is unsettled because he is in love with Lady Audley's childlike innocence, which Alicia's reading of the portrait challenges; he assumes she is a vessel he can fill with his own predetermined meaning. Analogously, when Alicia turns out to be an actual authority on reading, this further unsettles Robert because she exposes his ineptitude for empathy. He is 'not metaphysical', but he is not particularly physical, either.

Robert's failure to acknowledge materiality culminates in his treatment of his friend George Talboys after he and George view Lady Audley's portrait. When George sees the portrait, he immediately recognises or at least suspects that Lucy Graham, Lady Audley, is actually his ex-wife, Helen Talboys, née Maldon. Though the reader does not know George's suspicions at this point in the narrative, his physical actions signal distress.

Robert, however, seems completely unaware of his friend's consternation, and performs a series of catastrophically poor readings of George's suffering. George sits 'before [the portrait] for about a quarter of an hour without uttering a word – only staring blankly at the painted canvas' in shock (Braddon 1861b: 149). Robert misreads George's body here, with the repetition that marks erroneous interpretations: 'You've caught a cold from standing in that damp tapestried room. Mark my words, George Talboys, you've caught a cold; you're as hoarse as a raven' (149). George's hoarse voice, which the reader will later (if not immediately) infer is a result of his horror, becomes a mere cold in Robert's eyes. And this is indicative of Robert's core problem with others' feelings: he believes he already knows them. After he sees the portrait, George becomes 'passive' and 'very quiet' (149); however, the narrative, which is focalised through Robert's thoughts, insists that George is 'scarcely more quiet than usual' (149). During the storm that immediately follows the viewing of the portrait, Robert finally understands that George is afraid, and marks the sentiment by physical attributes, for George is 'white and haggard, with . . . great hollow eyes staring out at the sky as if they were fixed on a ghost' – but he misreads the sentiment as fear of the storm (Braddon 1861c: 177). He goes so far as to read George's response to the accusation of fear, declaring, 'you are not only afraid of the lightning, but you are savage with yourself for being afraid, and with me for telling you of your fear' (177). Even after George threatens him, and then goes for a crazed walk-about in the storm, Robert assures himself, 'He [George] was irritated at my noticing his terror at the lightning' (177). To summarise: George sees a portrait that suggests Lady Audley is in fact his wife, whom he presumed dead; he becomes quiet, and then almost catatonic; when he awakes, he paces in a frenzy, and his consternation even drives him to wander aimlessly in the storm. Robert reads all of this as an indication that George is sleepy and does not like lightning – because he had already decided he knows George's body even better than George does.

Robert's reading of bodies mirrors his reading of texts. In both cases, he is not alive to text, but rather, treats them as foregone conclusions. During the entire exchange with George regarding the storm, Robert 'lay on a sofa in the sitting-room, ostensibly reading the five-days'-old Chelmsford paper' (177). He ignores George in favour of old news, which he may or may not in fact actually read. The newspaper connotes a journalistic mode of reading like Boz's, but Robert fails to practise journalistic detachment; he observes lazily and then inserts his own self-serving interpretations of George's physical body. While he has the potential to observe – he does note George's colour, for example – his attachment to his own conclusions forecloses on bodies' expressions. Robert treats bodies like he treats his five-day-old newspaper: he reads them only ostensibly.

Unfinished Novels

Braddon's novel is first and foremost concerned with how law and science insist on the legibility of female bodies, and how that mechanism of power relegates female bodies to the role of self-annihilating mediators. For this argument, I return to Catherine Golden's 'angels', who read books only to be interrupted by men so that they can offer men the ability to read other bodies. Where Ruskin assigns feminine emotion the role of guiding macrosocial and domestic morality, in novels' representations of feminine reading, changes often initially occur at the microsocial level. In other words, when it comes to reading bodies, book-objects and women's bodies are interchangeable.

This equivalence between book-objects and female bodies validates the legal use of science to read and measure bodies. To make stable arguments about how emotion and materiality function, the law must hypostasise feeling and bodies. The self-renouncing woman makes bodies productive and, more importantly, safe. Texts and emotional knowledge may be initially obscured from male characters – but the self-renouncing woman imparts her intuitive knowledge to men, and makes legible texts, bodies and feelings. In short, she turns herself into a metaphor so that she might turn other bodies into metaphors.

Robert Audley seems to know the trope of the Dickensian angel and expects that Alicia Audley and/or George's sister, Clara Talboys, will serve as his angel and teach him his reading lesson. But, as part of Braddon's broader critique of Robert's pseudo-science, these women instead prove themselves superior readers and reject the injunction that they self-renunciate.

If Robert understands anything about bodies, it is that he should be allowed to mould them to his whim. He is convinced that Clara will be his self-renouncing angel, and when he receives a letter from her, he unites his textual reading practices with his bodily practices. Without even opening her letter, Robert suspects that 'it's a long letter', for Clara is 'the kind of woman who would write a long letter' – again, repeating to himself claims that ultimately turn out to be incorrect (Braddon 1862b: 2.113). In this initial declaration, Robert asserts that there is a 'kind of woman' who writes in a particular way, a type of body that corresponds to a type of writing. Clara's gender determines the content of the letter as well, for as a woman, her writing must exist for the sake of men. Robert suspects that it will be 'a letter that will urge me on, drive me forward, wrench me out of myself, I've no doubt' (113). In this moment, Robert conflates writing and writer, text and body, for he knows how to read this letter precisely because he knows how to read the 'kind of woman', like Clara, who would write it.

As Clara's gender prescribes the kind of writing she produces, so too Robert's gender prescribes the way he should read this writing. In a performance for only himself and perhaps the reader, he affects distaste for reading such letters and observes that Clara's desire to lift him up 'can't be helped' (113). He then acts out his discourse with his body as 'he t[ears] open the envelope with a sigh of resignation' (113). As with his 'it's a long letter' preamble, his sigh is a monologue, a shared moment between Robert and the reader alone. In this context, the sigh polices both Robert and the reader, for it assures them both that Robert knows his proper gender performance. As if to say 'You, reader, also know the kind of woman who would write such a letter', the sigh invites the reader to confirm Robert's masculinity and to confirm his or her own sense of proper reading. Reading as Robert understands it is a medium for the performance of properly gendered embodiment: men read with authoritative knowledge, and women read and write to cultivate proper sensations in men.

In these hyper-focalised moments, Robert voices his internal thoughts and feelings, and articulates the thoughts and feelings of the women around him as though he has access to this knowledge. And yet, the novel deconstructs Robert's claims about reading and knowledge. Even as he frames Clara's letter as a moment where a self-renouncing angel will lift him up, he misreads both the letter and the body that wrote it. After all this build-up, the letter can only disappoint, and indeed: 'It contained nothing but George's two letters, and a few words written on the flap: – "I send the letters; please preserve and return them. – C.T."' (113). Robert fundamentally misreads Clara and the way that her 'kind of woman' writes. The monologues fall apart under the actual content of Clara's text, which undercuts his gendered performance reading and writing.

Rather than self-renounce, Clara demonstrates her own superior reading abilities. Robert rightly says to himself that a proper reading angel would craft a letter to sustain him emotionally and to break him from his ennui, but Clara encloses two letters that include 'a description [of Lady Audley] in which every feature was minutely catalogued' – a demonstration of empiricism that Robert apparently lacks (114). Robert imagines Clara as merely moral support in every sense of the word 'moral', but she instead proves herself a more committed investigator than he, for these descriptions ultimately identify and indict Lady Audley. One could read this as a fulfilment of the reading angel, for Clara does serve Robert's purpose. But there are two key differences. Clara does not give herself up for Robert; in fact, she acts out of a desire to avenge her brother. And she does not provide emotional support; she instead provides the empirical knowledge that Robert lacks.

And so, Robert turns to Alicia instead – but here, the text deconstructs not only the self-renouncing angel, but the nature of conclusions as well. When Robert tries to get her attention while she is reading, 'Miss Audley shrug[s] her shoulders, but d[oes] not condescend to lift her eyes from her book' (Braddon 1862b: 2.141). Perturbed, Robert asks:

> 'What are you reading, there, Alicia?' . . .
> '*Changes and Chances*.'
> 'A novel?'
> 'Yes.'
> 'Who is it by?'
> 'The author of *Follies and Faults*,' answered Alicia, still pursuing her study of the romance upon her lap.[4]
> 'Is it interesting?'
> Miss Audley pursed up her mouth, and shrugged her shoulders.
> 'Not particularly,' she said. (142–3)

And she returns to reading. She refuses to act as a domestic angel, ready to have her reading interrupted for the sake of a man; she places the book down on her own time (145).

When Alicia reads again in the third volume, however, she finds that mere thoughts of Robert interrupt her reading. As she waits for Robert to arrive – he has been waylaid by Lady Audley's attempt to murder him via arson – she 'read[s] page after page' of a novel 'without knowing what she ha[s] been reading' (Braddon 1862b: 3.61). It is as though here, in the third volume, Alicia cannot resist her role as a reading angel, and must succumb to Robert's interruption to her reading; the balance of power must be restored. But there are some key differences: rather than set the book down, Alicia 'fl[ings] aside the volumes half-a-dozen times to go to the window and watch for that visitor whom she had so confidently expected' (61). Flinging-aside transforms Alicia into an interrupted angel-reader, the woman who gives up her reading in order to provide emotional guidance and domestic support for the male protagonist.

Where once Robert found Alicia vexing, as the novel approaches its closing gestures, he finally domesticates her.

And yet, the novel and Alicia retain self-referential resistance to such conclusions. In his endeavours to calm Alicia, Robert implores, 'a conclusion isn't a five-barred gate; and you needn't give your judgement its head, as you give your mare, Atalanta, hers, when you're flying across country at the heels of an unfortunate fox' (Braddon 1862b: 1.307). This exhortation resonates doubly. One valence ties the 'conclusion' as a textual form to a 'five-barred gate' which Alicia seeks to hurdle through her 'impetuous' (Robert's word) judgement. Robert suggests that Alicia's judgement should demur to the conclusion, should not attempt to jump it. The second suggests that Alicia's judgement should generally defer conclusions as psychological phenomena, for her feminine judgement should avoid coming to a conclusion about a subject. To Robert's claims, Alicia 'g[ives] her head a little scornful toss' – evoking Atalanta, her mare, who in turn evokes the Greek myth of Atalanta, the huntress who refuses to marry – and replies, 'It's as good an answer as I shall ever get from you, Bob' (307). In the first volume of the novel, at least, Alicia rejects Robert's insistence on conclusions both textual and psychological. She insists on her capacity to jump conclusions and jump to conclusions – in other words, to elude Robert's attempts to tie her to domesticity, and to draw her own inferences.

In fact, the novel itself rejects the very idea of conclusions. *Lady Audley's Secret* was never meant to be read in its entirety. Much like *Great Expectations*, *Lady Audley's Secret* first appeared as the headlining story of a weekly periodical. On 6 July 1861, the novel began the journal *Robin Goodfellow*, a new periodical published by Charles MacKay. The journal lasted all of three months, terminating on 28 September with chapters seventeen and eighteen of *Lady Audley's Secret*. At that point in the narrative, Lady Audley had murdered George Talboys, and Robert Audley had begun to suspect her identity – but that was all. The narrative ended until *The Sixpenny Magazine* began to serialise it again from the start in February of 1862. The ephemerality of the journal in which *Lady Audley's Secret* appeared provided Braddon with an opportunity particular to serial form: the opportunity not to finish the unpublished parts of her novel. In a letter to her mentor, Edward Bulwer-Lytton, she confesses, 'I didn't mean to finish "Lady A."' (Braddon 1974b: 12).

Braddon harboured distaste – or, at least, performed distaste – for the literary market. In her letter to Bulwer-Lytton, she describes herself as 'demoralised' by the 'behind the scenes' of literature. She confesses, 'I have learnt to look at everything in a mercantile sense, & to write solely for the circulating library reader' (Braddon 1974c: 14). The 'mercantile sense' and the tastes of the 'circulating library reader' corrupt her art, and compel her to write only for popular desires:

> I fear I shall never write a genial novel. The minute I abandon melodrama, & strong, coarse painting in blacks & whites, I seem quite lost & at sea. Perhaps this is because I have written nothing but serials, which force one into overstrained action in the desire to sustain the interest. (13)

Serial publication seems not only to come from readers' changed physiology, but also to have changed Braddon's own writerly physiology. She blames 'the curse of serial writing & hand to mouth composition', which requires her to write 'against time' or with inevitable deadlines, and 'with a view to the interests of [her] publishers' (Braddon 1974a: 10). In a later letter, she writes of the frenetic pace serial writing demands: 'I wrote the third & some part of the second vol of "Lady A." in less than a fortnight, & had the printer at me all the time' (Braddon 1974b: 12). She struggles with this adjustment, for she at once 'want[s] to be artistic and to please [Bulwer-Lytton]', but also 'want[s] to be sensational, & to please Mudie's subscribers' (Braddon 1974c: 14). Braddon felt that this tension showed in her novels; she writes that she found *Lady Audley's Secret* 'artificial' (Braddon 1974a: 10). The opposition should now be familiar; she is confronted with the need to make money from her publications, but fears that she will reduce fiction to mere commodity. Again, she must alter her art for the demands of the market.

But the market is only partly to blame for this artificiality. *Lady Audley's Secret* is acutely aware of social pressures that seek to regulate the possible trajectories of its narrative and characters.[5] A review of Braddon's *The Lady's Mile* from the July 1866 *Christian Remembrancer* laments:

> up to this time the success of a book – which means its sale – depends on some outward illogical attention to the decencies of society; a requirement which must exceedingly bore and embarrass any writer who cares for philosophical correctness and the dependence of effects on causes. ('Youth' 1866: 186)

The reviewer observes the tension between the economics of the 'sale' and the preservation of 'philosophical correctness'. In order to publish a successful book, the *Remembrancer* reviewer bemoans, an author must cater 'illogical[ly]' to the demands of society, and as a result her book will not reflect the intellectual integrity of the work, but rather reproduce the desires of her audience. In '"Other People's Prudery"', Ellen Miller Casey reads Mary Elizabeth Braddon's *Vixen* as a prime example of how the external imposition of social expectations forced novelists (especially female novelists) to shape their novels to serve the public's fancy. Casey 'wonders to what extent Braddon was bored and embarrassed by *Vixen*, a novel which succumbed to the pressure of other people's prudery and which is therefore less interesting as a finished work of art' than for its resonance with the historical milieu that produced it (Casey 1984: 81).

If reading digs down past surfaces, attention to social mores stops novels' transgressive potential in its tracks and redirects it toward an acceptable conclusion. The *Remembrancer* critic observes that 'in any novel which hopes to find a place on the drawing-room table, there must be a pull-up somewhere if things seem to be going too far' – an abortion of indecency ('Youth' 1866: 185). Here, in *Lady Audley's Secret* and *Vixen*, the interruption manifests as 'some coincidence preventing the last scandal, and arresting the headlong progress of events' (185). Interruption makes *Vixen* 'less interesting as a finished work of art' according to Casey, because its conclusion accepts the social and generic imposition of solutions to problems and proper marriages. Sally Mitchell agrees when she bemoans that 'the interesting moral issues [women's lack of chastity raises] are seldom followed to their conclusion' (S. Mitchell 1981: 97). 'Outward illogical attention' to social mores translates directly to sales and success, but also imposes a false conclusion on the novel.

Alicia joins in this refutation of false conclusions. When she flings aside her reading in the third volume, she seems to suggest that Robert succeeds in his endeavour to tame her, except for the self-referentiality of the text she reads. As she waits for Robert, 'Alicia shut[s] herself in her own apartment to read *the third volume of a novel*' (Braddon 1862b: 3.53, emphasis added). Specificity matters; one could imagine a counterfactual text which narrates simply that Alicia shuts herself away 'to read a novel'. It is important that she reads the final volume, though, for the third volume of any novel renders judgement and restores balance – and she rejects it outright. 'Heaven help the novelist whose fiction Miss Audley had been perusing', the narrator declaims, 'if he had no better critics than that young lady' (60–1). The dramatic cry, 'Heaven help', establishes Alicia as a critic, even as it makes pretence to dismiss her criticisms. When read self-referentially, Alicia's critical rejection of the third volume takes on new, subversive resonances. When she 'read[s] page after page without knowing what she ha[s] been reading', she silences the content of the third volume; when she flings it aside, she casts away the concluding gesture. She rejects the validity of a novel's third volume as the arbiter of justice. *Lady Audley's Secret* refuses to admit the conclusion and its redistribution of power that transforms Alicia into an angel. In fact, the novel rejects conclusions altogether. When Alicia rejects the third volume of the novel she reads, this self-reference rejects the conclusion of *Lady Audley's Secret*.

In the serial from September 1861 and February 1862, Lady Audley pulls off George Talboys's murder, retains her secret identity, and ultimately thwarts Robert Audley. *Lady Audley's Secret* contains within its form and content a desire to remain incomplete – to allow Lady Audley to escape the prying eyes of the men who investigate her, and to remain illegible. The third volume of the novel, the conclusion, provides a complex site to think about bodies as texts with conclusions. Without the third volume, the novel is the story of a woman who feigns both madness and upper-class decorum, who hides her identity, murders her nemesis, and fools the bumbling lawyer who wants to diagnose her and make her confess. The third volume undercuts all of this: Robert unveils her ostensibly true identity, uses a doctor to diagnose her madness, and condemns her to an asylum. With the third volume, the novel posits order and balance. Without the third volume, the novel offers a cacophony of violence and disruptive surfaces.

Unfinished Investigations

More importantly for the theoretical argument about Associationist knowledge of bodies and ethics, the unfinished sensation novel resists conclusions about bodies. These conclusions intersect different domains of knowledge, so that, in *Lady Audley's Secret*, to know about law is to know about feeling: to read a legal case to a jury is to read the body before the jury, and vice versa. The remainder of this chapter explores how the generic conclusion, epitomised in the third volume of a sensational triple-decker novel, intersects with legal conclusions that rely on scientific evidence, typified throughout *Lady Audley's Secret* by Robert Audley's private investigation of Lady Audley. These deconstructed conclusions come together to destabilise the conclusions one can draw from reading representations of bodies. Legal conclusions, scientific conclusions and social conclusions all mistake knowledge of representation for empiricism, and overlook the complexity of living bodies.

Robert Audley begins the novel terrified by the possibility that Lady Audley's interior may not be legible to him. He then decides that he needs a reading angel to help him – but both Alicia and Clara refuse. Finally, he finds his own associative mode of reading: circumstantial evidence. Robert finds circumstantial evidence useful because it allows him to mimic Associationism, but to nevertheless impose his own, premade conclusions. Circumstantial evidence, according to Robert, is 'that wonderful fabric which is built out of straws collected at every point of the compass, and which is yet strong enough to hang a man' (Braddon 1862b: 1.243–4). The narrator refers to this collection as 'the fatal chain of circumstantial evidence', a phrase which Robert picks up and repeats for the rest of the novel. The phrase evokes at once literal chains (as with *Great Expectations*), metaphoric criminality and association. As he presents it, circumstantial evidence seems entirely associative – a collection of objects that inspire impressions not necessarily logical, but that feel as though they have weight.

Circumstantial evidence is fundamentally associative, but Robert's version of association depends on knowledge rather than acknowledgement, on abstraction rather than empathy and materiality. When Robert first introduces circumstantial evidence, he feels as though it needs qualification: he admits 'I have never practised as a barrister' (243). Only a few days later, however, he boasts to Alicia, 'I am a barrister, Miss Alicia, and able to draw a conclusion by induction' (251). But Robert's theory of circumstantial evidence borders on the absurd. Circumstantial evidence becomes synonymous with deductive evidence, and allows him to accomplish feats like deducing that Sir Harry planned to make an offer of marriage to Alicia:

> first, because he came down the stairs with his hair parted on the wrong side, and his face as pale as the table-cloth; secondly, because he couldn't eat any breakfast, and let his coffee go the wrong way; and thirdly, because he asked for an interview with you before he left the Court. (252)

In Robert's understanding of what has just transpired, he observes Sir Harry's body, feels Sir Harry's feelings, and can therefore draw conclusions about Sir Harry's interiority. Even though the mode of thinking may be associative, it is not scientific. Robert's techniques parody the pattern of ethical reading, but to transform these associations into evidence only serves his own interests. It is not that Robert is wrong about Sir Harry; it is that his logic and 'evidence' is ridiculous. The farce threatens the validity of his circumstantial evidence, for the impressions that lead Robert to his conclusion about

Sir Harry differ little from those that lead him to question Lady Audley: purely circumstantial, purely associative.

The novel's critique of this flattened Associationism includes an epistemological interrogation of circumstantial evidence itself – of its use of narrative and of Associationism. Victorian understandings of circumstantial evidence still depended largely upon Edmund Burke's definition, formulated during the 1787 impeachment of Warren Hastings, the Governor-General of India (Welsh 1990: 607). In this sense, circumstantial evidence provides proof of a claim through narrative and history, rather than through empirical proof. Alexander Welsh sees Burke's paradigm as 'the great triumph of circumstantial evidence over direct testimony': if one can tell a story and associate disparate elements, one 'can turn even false testimony to account', so long as the story has emotional resonance (622). Welsh draws attention to Serjeant Hayward's opening statement in the trial of Mary Blandy, in which he declares:

> Experience has taught us, that in many cases a single fact may be supported by false testimony; but where it is attended by a *train of circumstances* that cannot be invented ... such a fact will always be made out to the satisfaction of a jury by the concurring assistance of circumstantial evidence. (616)

Juries must find circumstantial evidence convincing, Hayward goes on, because 'circumstances that tally one with another are above human contrivance' (616). Such a train of circumstances deploys a logic of its own, one that depends on the presumption or the impression that so many associations together must carry significant weight – enough to hang, as Robert might put it.[6] Most importantly, the associations must feel right, and if the feeling is correct, then the evidence is sufficient.

Hayward's version of circumstantial evidence, which validates associations as judicial evidence so long as they feel correct, paradoxically invests knowledge with the certainty of empiricism, though it is here only based on feeling. Through the logic of impressions, as Jeremy Bentham suggests, 'every chain of causality is a chain of evidence' (Bentham 1827: 3). In William Wills's 1838 *Essay on the Rationale of Circumstantial Evidence*, the link between association and circumstantial evidence becomes explicit:

> So rapid are our intellectual processes, that it is frequently difficult, even impossible, to trace the connection between an act of the judgement,

and the train of reasoning of which it is the result; and the one appears to succeed the other instantaneously by a kind of necessity . . . This fact obtains most commonly in respect of matters which have been frequently the objects of mental association. (Wills 1838: 24–5)

Mental associations seem to follow one another 'by a kind of necessity', so that the *appearance* of necessity proves acceptable grounds for the detective to think of the connections as truly necessary. Evidence becomes association, and association becomes plausible evidence. Material objects such as handwriting in a book or a label provide 'divers psychological facts', and the connections between these facts constitute a logic of their own: a logic of association.[7]

Narrative and storytelling form the basis of circumstantial evidence. W. M. Best's 1844 *Treatise on Presumptions of Law and Fact*, an entire treatise on circumstantial evidence, distinguishes between two primary faculties of mind: knowledge and judgement. Regarding law, in which 'actual knowledge or certainty is unattainable', Best writes that one must rely on judgement – the 'foundation' of which is 'probability' (Best 1844: 26–7). Within this logic of probability, truth or falsehood depends in part on 'the intrinsic probability of [a speaker's] story' (3). Intrinsic probability yields knowledge of interior psychology if the aggregated representations feel probable. This turns all kinds of objects into gateways to the interior – including handwriting, which is so crucial to *Lady Audley's Secret*. According to Best, in 'On the Proof of Handwriting', 'having seen the party write but once, and even then but his signature, or even only his surname, is sufficient to render the evidence admissible' (218). Judgement surmises that an individual's handwriting in all probability does not much alter from one iteration to the next, and that an observer has a high probability of recognising the handwriting – particularly if, as Robert observes of Lady Audley's hand, the handwriting bears distinctive characteristics. In other words, writing can tell one about the kind of woman who wrote it and can map out the interior of the body behind the text.

The discovery of probability and circumstance gives Robert access to a kind of knowledge that *feels* empirical but depends entirely on representation. Where before, Robert only read 'ostensibly', one of George's letters instigates a breakthrough; in a paragraph all to itself, the narrative declares:

Robert Audley read the letter three times before he laid it down. (Braddon 1862b: 1.114)

Now, Robert believes that he has learned to read. He sees the importance of observation, and its capacity to draw connections between bodies and objects. His simplified, associative reading leads Robert to find Lady Audley's body behind Helen Maldon's handwriting. When he comes upon George Talboys's library, the last book is an annual of 1845, containing 'a bright ring of golden hair' and three inscriptions. The first, dated 1845, marks the book as 'a reward for habits of order, and for obedience to the authorities of Camford-house Seminary', to Elizabeth Ann Bince. The second, in Bince's handwriting, 'present[s] the book as a mark of undying affection and esteem ... to her beloved friend Helen Maldon'. The final inscription, from September 1853, is 'in the hand of Helen Maldon, who gave the annual to George Talboys' – and Helen Maldon's handwriting gives her away (Braddon 1862b: 2.10). Robert declares this handwriting 'circumstantial evidence', on the grounds that it 'resembles that of Helen Talboys so closely, and that the most dexterous expert could perceive no distinction between the two', for it is a 'very uncommon' hand, 'presenting marked peculiarities' (2.235). With this turn to circumstantial evidence, the lazy barrister begins to take on the role of detective – a role he plays through what he believes is rigorous, scientific and judicially valid Associationism. When he reads Helen Talboys's inscription, Robert recognises Lucy Graham's distinctive handwriting, and from that recognition, he derives the connection between Lady Audley's various identities and bodies. However, to bring these bodies together, he must conflate bodies and texts: both are legible in the same way, and reading one enables him to read the other.

As for the strength of the evidence of handwriting, Best writes, 'the weakness of it is matter of comment for the jury', but his previous arguments suggest that if the weak evidence tells a good story, the story will win out (Best 1844: 218). When he begins to move toward indicting Lady Audley, Robert acknowledges that the labels he reads may be 'no evidence for a jury', but that it should be 'enough to convince [Sir Michael] that he has married a designing and infamous woman' (Braddon 1862b: 2.172). According to Best and Hayward, a jury may in fact find Robert's evidence sufficient for the self-same reason that Robert believes he will convince Sir Michael of Lady Audley's guilt: Robert's associations tell a convincing story and convey powerful impressions.

But circumstantial evidence mistakes representations of bodies for material bodies. While it sounds associative, the logic behind

Robert's claims ignores the complexity of materiality. Robert's use of circumstantial evidence mistakes naïve mechanism for a formula to yield knowledge of interiors. Emphasis on knowledge turns feeling into a tool of self-regard. The purpose of literary authority based in feeling must therefore aim for acknowledgement – for faithfulness to the complexity of the material surface.

In fact, when Robert confounds his compelling story for actuality, he replicates the very madness of which he accuses Lady Audley. Circumstantial evidence stakes its claim on indirect relationships between otherwise disparate objects. Alexander Bain, in his 1887 article 'On "Association" – Controversies' in *Mind*, posits:

> The flow of representation in dreaming and madness offers the best field of observation for the study of associations as such. In the ascending flood of ideas of the insane, we can sometimes follow step by step the process whereby logical thinking gradually undergoes dissolution by the increasing dominance of association. (Bain 1887: 175)

In addressing this 'Controversy' within Associationism, Bain defines associative thinking separately from logical thinking. One who associates freely, who enters into 'the ascending flood of ideas' and who then acts purely on association does not act logically. He goes on to caution that 'the attempt to derive logical thinking from association is open to suspicion' (175). According to Bain, pure association – the freeform leaps from one link of the chain to the next – signals madness or dreaming.

The novel, too, draws attention to the relationship between Robert's circumstantial evidence, his allegation of Lady Audley's madness, and the judicially inadmissible evidence of dreams. For all the evidence Robert claims to gather, his first major breakthrough comes from the realm of dreams. After his initial frenzied search for George Talboys shortly following the storm, Robert falls into a restless sleep. He finds himself 'tormented all the time by disagreeable dreams', which are 'painful, not from any horror in themselves, but from a vague and wearying sense of their confusion and absurdity' (Braddon 1862b: 1.241). That these dreams are filled with 'confusion' and 'absurdity' is important, for they will later transmute from surreal delusions into proof about reality. In his dreams, Robert attempts to decode a telegraph he received in the installation/chapter previous. He 'gaze[s] at the headstone George had ordered for the grave of his dead wife', and then goes to the headstone to find that the stonemason has removed its inscription for 'a reason that Robert would some day learn' (241). At this point in the text, these dreams at best indicate a sort of residue from Robert's worries about George's disappearance. But hindsight clarifies the prophetic nature of this dream: the headstone and telegraph are texts Robert later uses to unveil Lady Audley's secrets and force her to confess her interior – and, of course, Helen Talboys is not actually dead.

Though Braddon removed the following section from later printings, in the novel's original complete serialisation in *The Sixpenny Magazine,* the following omitted portion of the dream solidifies the accusation that naïve mechanism is akin to madness.[8] Robert's dreams provide him with the conclusion that he must then prove – rather than the inductive order of logic, in which the evidence provides the conclusion. He finds himself at the grave of Helen Talboys, which opens, and

> while he waited, with the cold horror lifting up his hair, to see the dead woman arise and stand before him with her still, charnel-house drapery clinging about her frigid limbs, his uncle's wife tripped gaily out of the open grave, dressed in the crimson velvet robes in which the artist had painted her. (Braddon 1862a: 65)

At a basic level, this dream overflows with bodies that generate impressions. His imagination of Helen Talboys evokes the specific 'charnel-house drapery' and 'frigid limbs'; Lucy Graham's body strikingly replaces Helen's, and her clothing contrasts with the drapery to invoke an associative chain that leads Robert back to the portrait. The levels of fictionality further the associative elements: it is all a dream, but he only imagines (in his dream) Helen Talboys, where he actually sees Lucy – and then imagines again when he recalls the portrait. The dream darts across different forms of materiality from representation to imagination to bodies. Each of these bodies connects to a material object: the telegraph takes Robert's thoughts to George and the grave, to Helen's charnel-house drapery, to Lady Audley's crimson velvet robes, to the portrait that, according to Alicia's contention, depicts Lady Audley's interior. Within the dream 'the places he had last been in, and the people with whom he had last been concerned, were dimly interwoven' into what can best be described as an associative chain (Braddon 1862b: 1.241). And these associations map out the remainder of the text: Lady Audley is Helen Talboys, and is exactly as dangerous as her portrait depicts her. The dream provides all the evidence to indict Lady Audley, but the proof of her madness is madness.

Unfinished Convictions

Though Robert's story carries the weight of circumstantial evidence, Lady Audley turns his logic back against him. Circumstantial evidence depends on probability and the degree to which the story it tells is convincing. This recourse to narrative and probability is common to Victorian critiques of the novel; nearly all nineteenth-century novel reviews at some point address the text's believability based on the probability of its events. The sensation novel occupies a liminal position on this scale, Winifred Hughes argues, 'somewhere between the possible and the improbable, ideally at their intersection' (Hughes 2014: 16). While Robert's association may present insufficient evidence for a lived-world jury, sensation fiction is comfortable with the improbability of his story. Robert understands this at an implicit level, for as he begins to play detective in earnest, he tells himself, 'I haven't read Alexandre Dumas and Wilkie Collins for nothing' (Braddon 1862b: 3.190). Robert imagines himself the hero of a sensation novel: 'I'm up to their tricks,' he tells himself, 'sneaking in at doors behind a fellow's back, and flattening their white faces against window panes, and making themselves all eyes in the twilight' (190). Probability here depends less on a comparison with the lived world, and instead understands the genre of the novel as a kind of reality in itself – an ontology of feeling gone awry. Within the sensation novel, Robert becomes the master of circumstantial evidence: he can tell the story, his story is probable, and most importantly, his story comes from associative evidence. And yet, to become the hero of a sensation novel, Robert embraces a flawed version of associative logic that confounds representation for reality, and manifests most purely in madness. At its core, the novel suggests that whether one uses hermeneutics, science or feeling, if one strives for knowledge, one sacrifices empathy.

Lady Audley's illegibility reveals Robert's flattened Associationism for the ruse it is. While he claims a totalising, logical knowledge of all bodies, she exposes the contradictions within the epistemology of a paradigm that claims to be at once scientific and all-knowing. Fluid identity allows her to slide away from Robert's defining gaze, and to obscure her interiority despite his claims that he can read bodies like texts. When Robert presents his evidence to her, Lady Audley replies that 'a resemblance between the handwriting of two women is no very uncommon circumstance now-a-days' (Braddon 1862b: 3.235). When he persists, she appears to succumb to his evidence of two labels, one that calls her 'Miss Graham' and the other

'Mrs. George Talboys' (238). Robert thinks to himself, 'She knows now that she is lost' and goes on to 'wonder if the judges of the land feel as [he does] now' (239). His self-regard reaches its apex, and he sets himself up as more than a barrister: he is a literary scholar, a scientist and a judge all in one.

And then, she turns the tables: 'I do not choose to do anything but laugh at your ridiculous folly. I tell you that you are mad!' (242). His associative, circumstantial evidence that she bears multiple names undoes itself, in part because his reading requires a self-renouncing woman. Lady Audley is happy to allow her body to become a representation rather than materiality. Self-renunciation would demand that 'Lucy Graham' give up being 'Lucy Graham', and she is most willing to oblige. Like the unfinished portrait, multiple names and multiple identities slide into nothingness; they become mere surfaces that Lady Audley readily discards. Robert's evidence makes him the master detective in a sensation novel – a role that conflicts with his desire to be the cold, calculating, luminous detective and scientist. Unlike the Dickensian angel who interrupts her reading for the man, Lady Audley in fact interrupts Robert's reading. For a while, Lady Audley's body even replaces the bodies in the French novels Robert loves to read, so that

> the yellow papered fictions on the shelves above his head seemed stale and profitless – he opened a volume of Balzac, but his uncle's wife's golden curls danced and trembled in a glittering haze, alike upon the metaphysical diablerie of the *Peau de Chagrin*, and the hideous social horrors of *Cousine Bette*. (Braddon 1862b: 2.5; see also Braddon 1862b: 2.111)

Because of his tendency to conflate representation and physicality, he succumbs to the web of representations Lady Audley weaves around him.

From a hermeneutic perspective, the question of madness either *is* the question or obscures the ostensibly more important questions of the novel. D. A. Miller presents the foundational version of the argument that madness is the real core of the text when he suggests that Lady Audley's 'secret' 'is not . . . that Lady Audley is a madwoman but rather that, *whether she is one or not*, she must be treated as such' – though he concludes more definitively that the novel 'portrays the woman's carceral condition as her fundamental and final truth' (D. A. Miller 1986: 121). Elizabeth Langland reads the physical architecture of the Audley Court as a confining structure designed to constrain and surveille women in the domestic space – an asylum before the novel's closing asylum (Langland 2002: 69–70).[9] On the other hand, scholars like Jill Matus argue that madness is a way to evade the deeper issues embedded in mid-century society: she writes that 'the final focus on madness serves to displace the economic and class issues already raised in the novel and to deflect their uncomfortable implications', because madness 'allows historically specific issues of class and power to be represented instead as timeless and universal matters of female biology' (Matus 1993: 334). No matter which way one leans, the conviction of madness forecloses on possibilities of resistance: either resistance against the surveillance state, against gendered diagnoses, or against larger structures of oppression.

Associationism helps us see that Lady Audley's conviction brings together twin discourses rooted in twisted versions of materialist science. Self-renunciation demands that women's bodies be mere representations that connect materiality; circumstantial evidence conflates representation and materiality. In both cases, the ultimate goal is to make interiority legible, to read and ultimately regulate feelings. Lady Audley herself deconstructs both self-renunciation and circumstantial evidence through her *écrit en abyme*, her capacity to recursively write herself into nothingness. Every time she appears to self-renounce, or Robert appears to uncover the body behind the representation, there is yet another representation. But this is hardly wilful, hardly voluntary; it is a kind of self-mutilation, a choice to pull apart the surfaces of her body to escape being read.

Coda: Unfinished Conclusions

Because it steps in before conclusions – and indeed, without conclusions – surface reading lays out the political and ethical importance of distorted sheets of time, of skin and of sensation in initial encounters. Here, it helps to think about pain: Alicia's pain, Clara's pain, George's pain – even Robert's pain, if I must – and most importantly for my argument, Lady Audley's pain. Rather than seek to know her pain, surface reading sits with it, acknowledges it; rather than seek to interpret and uncover meaning beneath her actions, surface reading looks to the phenomenological experience of struggle. Yes, Lady Audley's machinations subvert the imposition of patriarchal authority. Yes, she challenges law and science, and the ostensible rationality that would have her self-renounce or imprison her. But she also suffers. Even when it affords resistance, self-annihilation still annihilates. We should be suspicious of patriarchy, of heteronormativity, of cisnormativity and the institutions that enforce them – but if we privilege the hermeneutics of suspicion to the exclusion of surfaces, we risk hurrying past and overlooking pain.

This hermeneutics of pain exerts a powerful affective gravity. We want to find some kind of productive, positive outcome in the chaos of pain. We want to snatch moments of resistance out of a text overflowing with compulsory self-annihilation. But surface reading allows us – encourages us – to sit with the pain and let it exist. As I suggested above, Lady Audley's *mise en abyme* still places her into an abyss. And while there is value in finding value in the abyss, we should not smother her pain in an endeavour to feel like it helps. Any conflict over authority, the novel suggests, will inflict casualties – and those casualties are likely to be bodies in the margins.

It is essentially an accepted fact that Victorian liberalism created institutions of biopower and disciplinary control. These exertions of power are an easy target for Foucauldian analysis. Bedlam imprisons women whose affects threaten male power; the dense structures of imperial governance capture the bodies and lives of compulsory subjects; the medical industrial complex lets the wealthy guide the ostensibly free hand of the market to decide who lives and who dies (and how).

But there is something salvageable in the origins of these institutions. Some liberalism – maybe most liberalism – depends on knowledge and fixing, on controlling and shaping bodies. But in the bleak face of the failures of empathy that I have traced, there remains an underlying optimism that we can care, and that caring can in fact matter. Reading, these novelists have suggested, can be a place to reject knowledge, and even to reject a kind of false acknowledgement that only seeks authority. When read well – with feeling, for feeling, about feeling – novels can cultivate not authority, but an ethics of care.

When flattened science and law fail in *Lady Audley's Secret*, materiality remains. Lady Audley's pain persists, and reminds us that bodies matter. And even, ironically, as I reject conclusions, I point to the conclusion of this book, where Walter Besant's liberalism offers a defence of Victorian optimism. If we embrace the complexity of feeling, if we acknowledge and sit with surfaces, Besant wants to believe, then maybe these failures are just steps on the bridge to empathetic connection.

Notes

1. Jennifer Hedgecock makes a similar claim when she argues that the novel 'is not trying to enforce patriarchal boundaries that oppress women, but to express some disquiet about them', and that 'the image of a dangerous woman really does threaten the bourgeois family by literally shaming the family home' (Hedgecock 2008: 127). Elaine Showalter's *A Literature of Their Own* provides the most prominent argument in favour of this agency, and celebrates Lady Audley's exercise of power through violence (Showalter 2009). In their introduction to *Beyond Sensation*, Marlene Tromp, Pamela Gilbert and Aeron Haynie identify the disconnect between these subversive moments and the normativising conclusion when they observe that 'although many of Braddon's novels may seem to capitulate to normative Victorian standards of morality', *Lady Audley's Secret* ultimately 'call[s] into question notions of gendered identity' (Tromp, Gilbert and Haynie 2000: xvii).
2. See also Lynette Felber's 'The Literary Portrait as Centerfold' (2007) and Lyn Pykett's *The 'Improper' Feminine* (1992).
3. See also Saverio Tomaiuolo's chapter 'So Like and Yet So Unlike' in *In Lady Audley's Shadow* (2010) for more on Realism and Lady Audley's Pre-Raphaelite portrait, and another example of the primacy of the representation.
4. Neither of these novels is real.
5. D. A. Miller observes half in jest that the 'morality' of sensation fiction lies in its 'ultimately fulfilled wish to abolish itself: to abandon the grotesque aberrations of character and situation that have typified its representation, which now coincides with the norm of the Victorian household' (D. A. Miller 1988: 165–6).
6. Hayward uses 'train' and 'chain' interchangeably. The narrator of *Lady Audley's Secret* frequently refers to Robert's growing body of associations against Lady Audley as a 'chain of evidence' (Braddon 1862b: 1.103).
7. For a Darwinian reading of circumstantial evidence in *Lady Audley's Secret*, see Saverio Tomaiuolo's *In Lady Audley's Shadow* (2010: 89–90).
8. Natalie Houston's notes on the text in the 2003 Broadview edition of *Lady Audley's Secret* brought this change to my attention (Houston 2003: 34).
9. See also Chiara Briganti's exploration of the relationship between names, architecture and reading in the novel in 'Gothic Maidens and Sensation Women' (1991). Heather Braun observes that Braddon's 'femmes fatales are typically left to wither away in convents and insane asylums, their momentary allure overshadowed by the sensation novel's consuming interests in modern science and modes of surveillance' (Braun 2009: 236).

Chapter 6

Caring Bodies: The Reformer, Sartorial Exchange and the Work of the Novel in Walter Besant's *Children of Gibeon*

In November 1871, Mary Elizabeth Braddon published an up-and-coming thinker, Walter Besant, in her magazine *Belgravia*. Besant's essay, 'The Value of Fiction', inquires 'what is likely to be the real gain from reading or writing works of fiction' (Besant 1871: 48). He answers in accordance with an ethics of care: 'the chief gain is, that it is good at times to get our minds away from ourselves' (48). If a fictional text accurately depicts others' lives, it enables readers to 'share in sorrows and joy alien to [their] own experiences' (48–9). To step outside one's self and to share in others' experiences, even second-hand, should be enough to inspire one to social action. The strength of fiction is that it enables one to sympathise with individuals one would otherwise never encounter:

> Ladies who read *Belgravia* do not often penetrate into the slums of the East-end . . . It is not, however, bad for ladies to know that such things exist. A knowledge of evil *quà* evil is not to be desired; but a knowledge of these forms of evil which can be remedied . . . is surely a good thing; *and this the novel gives us.* (49)

Besant celebrates representations of suffering and sorrow that have roots in lived experience. If a novelist can sit among the bodies and materiality they describe, they can to some degree bring those bodies to life.

This is a lesson that Besant himself learned in his own career as a novelist. Empathy drives Besant's model of social reform, catalysed by intimate, physical experience. The novel that this chapter explores, *Children of Gibeon*, is the spiritual successor of Besant's first social reform novel, *All Sorts and Conditions of Men*. In fact, their plots are so similar, their politics so mirrored, that one might read *Children* as a second draft of *All Sorts and Conditions*. Why the rewrite? Besant himself says that *Children* 'touch[es] a note of deeper resonance', and is 'the most truthful of anything that I have ever written' (Besant 1902: 247). The key difference between the composition of the two novels, Besant writes, is that before he wrote *Children*, he immersed himself in the East End: 'I knew every street in Hoxton . . . I had been about among the people day after day and week after week' (248). Saturated with images and memories from his time among the workers, including a room with three girls 'stitching away for bare life', Besant says: 'All these things and people I saw over and over again till my heart was sore and my brain was weary with the contemplation of so much misery. And then I sat down to write' (248). This intimate knowledge of the people and places provided Besant with the means to sympathise with their experiences, for his model of empathy depends on proximity: 'First I drew what I saw; then my sympathy went out towards my models; the next step was to write for them, to work for them, to speak for them' (260–1). Here, social action is a trajectory: from proximity, to seeing 'things and people . . . over and over again', to empathy, and finally to advocacy and action.

Besant wrote these novels a full twenty years after the other texts I have explored. Toward the *fin de siècle*, past the heyday of sensation fiction, while there is less direct engagement with Associationists proper, the language of Associationism is thoroughly integrated into fiction. More importantly, the epistemology of Associationism and sensation fiction still dominates: if a writer uses material taken from the annals of the world, then the knowledge passed on may manage to awaken something more than merely second-hand. But the only way to achieve that empathy – the only way to avoid the pitfalls of the other novels I have explored – is to attend to materiality, to bodies, to surfaces, and to acknowledge rather than know. Besant's liberalism is Associationism in action; his reformist fiction is sensation fiction made explicitly political. And this demonstrates (I hope) the value of surface reading as a mode of inquiry, for it offers a route to address the material conditions of lived experience both at a systematic level and at the level of individuals and their feelings.

To make this claim, I focus on how physical objects mediate between bodies in *Children of Gibeon*. The closer an object gets to the surface – the more it serves as a material connector between surfaces, rather than a symbol, representation, metaphor – the more it brings bodies together. One of the core preoccupations of *Children of Gibeon* is the degree to which the affective gravity of objects moulds social relations. The central plot of *Children of Gibeon* follows Valentine and Violet Eldridge, a pair of wealthy heiresses. One of the girls is in fact adopted from a working-class family, and upon their coming of age, their true identities will be revealed. Valentine, convinced she is the working-girl (she is not), goes to live with her 'siblings' in the East End. She stays with her sister Melenda and two other girls, Lotty and Lizzie, who work as seamstresses. Here, in the East End, Valentine seeks to connect with her sisters through the objects around them. Initially, she relies on these objects as fetishes that metaphorise the affects and bodies around her. But her politics evolve as she begins to move away from mere representation. Instead, she learns that while she needs to see the dirty rags her sisters wear, she must ultimately look beyond them through an ethics of personal care that acknowledges workers rather than claims to know them. She must attend to surfaces to learn that social conditions are first and foremost material.

Knowledge

Throughout his fiction, Besant uses women's scientific education as a measurement for the development of ethics in British society writ large. The narrator aborts his extended study of the physiological and physiognomic difference between Valentine and Violet by saying that 'a prolonged residence at Newnham would be necessary in order to carry on this delightful investigation to its legitimate end' (Besant 1886: 1.43). The specificity of the statement gestures to a figure more readily available to Besant's 1880s novel than to the 1860s sensation novel: the woman of science. Newnham College, an exclusively female college of Cambridge University founded in 1871, rather quickly established a reputation as a paragon of women's scientific education.[1] At Newnham, 'zealous young ladies daily stud[ied] the physiology of both plants and animals in most practical methods . . . under the care of two experienced demonstrators of their own sex' ('Natural Science' 1884: 10).[2] The idea that the narrator cannot complete his reading of Valentine and Violet without time at Newnham might on the one hand simply mean that Newnham is a good place to study the faces of women. But the broader context of Newnham in Besant's work suggests something deeper: that this kind of physiological and psychological knowledge is the domain of the female scientist and requires a special knowledge exclusive to the educated woman. In short, Newnham connects women, emotion and science in a nexus with the ability to read bodies and feelings, so that socially impactful science requires the feminine element of empathy.

Besant's distinction between academic knowledge and emotional acknowledgement reflects his emphasis on sensation as a primary means of argumentation and social reform. In *All Sorts and Conditions*, Besant's other wealthy-socialite-turned-reformer Angela Messenger uses her wealth and Newnham expertise to bring change to the East End. Valentine and Violet, however, very specifically 'knew no political economy' – a direct gesture to Angela. Valentine's education is merely an education 'at home', rather than at Newnham or another college. At the opening of *All Sorts and Conditions*, Angela recognises the lack of emotional acknowledgement in her own education – a crisis that causes her initial break with her past life and her turn to social reform. Shortly after 'passing a really brilliant examination' in political economy, Angela delivers a speech in which 'she went out of her way to pour contempt upon Political Economy' (Besant 1882: 1.8). She declares that political economy is 'a so-called science', and 'not a science at all', but instead 'a collection of theories impossible of proof'. It fails as a science not because of a lack of rigour, however; political economy fails instead because 'it treat[s] of men and women as skittles . . . [and] had been put together for the most part by doctrinaires who lived apart, and knew nothing about men and less about women' (8). For Angela and for Besant, science without sympathy is no science at all.

While *All Sorts and Conditions* and *Children of Gibeon* share many characteristics – from their hidden-identity plot to their lovers out to change the world, or at least the East End – their politics in fact differ subtly but importantly. Angela Messenger reforms with money. She several times acknowledges that her Palace of Delight, where the working class can enculturate themselves, 'has been tried by men, but . . . has never succeeded, because they wanted the capital to start it with', but as one of the wealthiest women in London, Angela most certainly does have the money (217). More importantly, she insists that the goal of the Palace is 'the introduction of a love of what we call culture', and that the people will introduce themselves to that love (283). As we will see with Jack, the man of Arnoldian culture, *Children* rejects the idea that culture is enough to save the working class. In a development that coincidentally mirrors the later (1907) transformation of the 1887 People's Palace – the lived-world manifestation of the Palace of Delight – into part of the University of London, from *All Sorts* to *Children of Gibeon*, Besant's representation of liberalism shifts: *All Sorts* uses mass amounts of capital to fund enculturation, where *Children* instead provides culture through educational texts. Valentine believes she has no money and was not burdened with an academic education. Besant's logic posits that sensational reading surpasses academic training, and that Valentine's emotional acknowledgement surpasses academic knowledge.

A paradigm built on acknowledgement demands a shift in the epistemological grounds on which one encounters other bodies – a shift away from the certainty of representation and toward the ambiguity of surface. Following his interjection regarding a study at Newnham, the narrator declaims:

> one need not here discuss questions on which even novelists, who are the only true philosophers of modern times, and ought to be the only statesmen, might disagree; besides, these girls were neither philosophers nor mathematicians. They were only girls who had been carefully educated at home . . . But they knew no political economy, and they were not brought up to consider themselves bound to consider or to solve any social questions at all. (Besant 1886: 1.43)

The trajectory of this section is complex. The claim that novelists are the only true philosophers might be in earnest, but the addition of the claim that they 'ought to be the only statesmen' reads as possibly ironic, particularly to the twenty-first-century eye. On the momentum of this ambivalence, the narrator dismisses Valentine and Violet as 'only girls' who are neither 'philosophers nor mathematicians'. Instead of philosophy and maths, the two girls 'knew a great many accomplishments and arts, had curiously pretty customs and pleasing manners, and practised, without knowing it, the most charming graces' (43). In the moment of its iteration, the selection that dismisses Valentine's education seems rather straightforward. But Valentine's knowledge is the final irony of the section: though she is educated only at home, and 'not brought up to consider [herself] bound to consider or to solve any social questions at all', Valentine will ultimately create a system of education that solves directly the social questions of the East End. Their knowledge is not academic; it is female, domestic, and most importantly, empathetic.

Metaphor

One of the great ironies of *Children of Gibeon*'s seamstresses is that they spend all day working to produce clothing they themselves probably could not afford.[3] Variance in pricing makes it all but impossible to pin down the price of a dress in 1886, but a bit of estimation demonstrates the alienation between the worker and her product. The girls in *Children of Gibeon* are 'outdoor hands' – seamstresses who work from their own quarters rather than in a shop. Such labourers work piecemeal for the dressmaker, who would interact directly with clientele at the shop.[4] Valentine's sister, Melenda, and her friends make buttonholes, which means they are not milliners, who would perform some of the finer work on clothing. According to F. Mabel Robinson in an 1887 *Fortnightly Review* article, a skilled milliner could make £1 to £3 per week, while 'second-class outdoor hands' like Melenda, Lizzie and Lotty made between 15s and 18s per week in 1887 (Robinson 1887: 52). In *Children of Gibeon*, however, the girls' earnings are at the whim of the Law of Elevenpence Ha'penny, a reference to David Ricardo's argument that wages will stay as close as possible to the lowest cost 'which is necessary to enable the labourers, one with another, to subsist and to perpetuate their race, without either increase or diminution' (Ricardo 1817: 90).[5] Altogether, the three women manage to make 17s.3d per week (Besant 1886: 1.148). Whether this discrepancy between Robinson and Besant lies in a miscalculation or an exaggeration, the point remains that, practically speaking, there is little difference in spending power behind Robinson's estimation (2s per day) and Besant's (17d per day). To put this in perspective: an 1888 article in *The Nineteenth Century* estimated an annual £35.8s.4d cost for a middle-class woman's clothing, or a little more than the annual pay of all three girls after rent (Layard 1888: 243). An advertisement for C. Hayman's clothing store in 1885 lists dresses from 20s to £5; the women who made these dresses would probably have needed anywhere from one to five weeks' salary to purchase them. Valentine encounters a woman who uncannily prices out the cost of the young philanthropist's clothing: her dress is £3.3s, her boots £1.1s, and her gloves 4s.6d (Besant 1886: 2.63). This is particularly upsetting for Valentine because it reminds her that her dress would cost her sisters four weeks' pay. Valentine's consternation offers a crucial insight into the Victorian representation of the seamstress. The seamstress's work is particularly alienating – and particularly upsetting for the middle and upper classes – because she can afford neither the time to sew her own clothing, nor the capital to purchase the clothes she makes.

The alleged need for a second-hand market to clothe labourers translates exploitation into a charitable service provided for workers. Particularly in the late nineteenth century, creative writers and philosophers alike referred to the second-hand market as a need, and an opportunity for the upper classes to fill that need.[6] In an 1880 issue of the *Saturday Review*, one author writes that 'it is certain that many of the respectable lower classes must always dress themselves in cast-off apparel' ('Old Clothesmen' 1880: 170). In the face of this inevitable need, to sell second-hand clothing is to 'render useful service to the poorest class of all, the purchasers of this rejected gear, which is better than no clothing at all' ('The Old Clothes Exchange' 1882: 66). Henry Mayhew repeats this discourse when he relays a story from an old shoemaker, who also understood second-hand markets as a service for the poor:

> such places as Rosemary-lane have their uses this way. But for them a very poor industrious widow, say, with only 2d. or 3d. to spare, couldn't get a pair of shoes for her child; whereas now, for 2d. or 3d., she can get them there. (Mayhew 1861: 221)

It is important to note the language of virtue embedded in this quotation. This is not merely a woman, but an 'industrious widow' – and she does not buy shoes for herself, but 'for her child'. Modifications like these emphasise the charitable service of the second-hand market over the pragmatic exchange of money. The shoemaker goes on to add that 'there's a sort of decency, too, in wearing shoes'. The shoemaker's simple, genuine-sounding reflection is in fact a double-edged sword. On the one hand, it validates the notion that to sell one's old shoes provides decency to a worker in need; on the other, it points out the indecency of a system that reduces a class of people to something less civilised.[7] To think of second-hand markets as virtuous means the upper classes do not simply sell undesirable commodities to recuperate a fraction of the money originally spent – instead, they impart virtue or ameliorate a need.

In these discourses, clothing supplants the bodies it covers, and encodes them with markers of identity such as 'labourer'. Dress epitomises the social condition of these women: they labour in the piecework production of dresses but cannot afford to wear anything but rags. What they wear marks them as labourers, and reduces their bodies to mere markers of labour, to mere machines. The rags are, in a word, metaphoric. An 1877 article in the *London Reader* best summarises this idea, so that the clothes people wear

> become almost as closely identified as their skins . . . The garments so express the character of the person, that by a stretch of fancy one might be tempted to speculate whether the individuality has not itself been so absorbed by the clothes, that in another dress the individuals, to use their own expression, 'would scarcely know themselves'. ('Cast Skins' 1877: 570)

Second-hand clothing is a sort of sloughed-off skin; the cloth all but literally embodies the person who once owned it. The 'cast skins', as the *London Reader* calls them, 'expres[s] the characteristic peculiarities of their wearer', so that they connote or even are the bodies they cover (571). Second-hand boots and shoes invite one to 'speculatively associat[e] them with the people who have stood, or are again about to stand in them', and 'a pair of "second-hand" trousers hanging at the door of a pawnbroker's shop are sometimes more indicative of humanity than an anatomical preparation' (571). In other words, clothing can become a more-real body than a real body. Clothing – put over one's body so it becomes a 'cast skin' that supplements flesh – is so intimately bound up with the individual that others interact with it as though it is part of another body even once it is sold, and perhaps especially once it is sold.

With such an intimate relationship between clothes and their wearers, a gift of clothing exposes the social relations bound up in things. Marilyn Strathern writes in *The Gender of the Gift* that '"Gift economy", as a shorthand reference to systems of production and consumption where consumptive production predominates, implies . . . that things and people assume the social form of persons' (Strathern 1990: 144). To fetishise clothing fetishises the bodies behind the clothing, so that the dressmaker's rags embody the general idea of labour; bodies become, in a word, symbols.

The best example of this erasure of bodies in *Children of Gibeon* is the gift of a handkerchief meant to transform a body into a source of academic value. One of the working-girls, Lizzie, has a paramour, Jack Conyers, who imagines himself a man of 'Art, Culture, and the Higher Criticism' (Besant 1886: 2.145). Jack's desire to be a man of art requires him to have a beautiful, Pre-Raphaelite model. He chooses Lizzie as his model and tells her that he 'desire[s] above all things to get that face and those beautiful eyes into his own studio' (110). This declaration fetishises Lizzie's body piecemeal. She is not a living body; she rather has two useful parts, and they are useful only insofar as Jack can gain social (and potentially pecuniary) capital from them in a painting. To further underscore the way Jack dissociates Lizzie's parts from her body, the narrator tells the reader that Jack believes the painting's 'hands . . . would have to be chosen from another model' (111). Jack rejects her hands because 'making button-holes in thick coarse shirts does really pull the fingers into all sorts of shapes' (112–13). But it is not simply that her hands are unpleasant; they are unpleasant because of the labour they perform. For Jack to gain the social status of an artist, he must obscure the labour that Lizzie embodies.

To accomplish this mystification, Jack turns to clothing. In her rags, Lizzie is a symbol, a general caricature of the working-girl, the physical embodiment of the street. And so, Jack obsesses over her clothing. Despite Lizzie's beauty, 'her ulster still covered a ragged frock and her hat was shabby to the last degree' (110). And so, when he attempts to beautify her, Jack insists that Lizzie 'want[s] nothing but a little better dress to outshine them all [higher class models]', for the new clothing would replace the markers of exploitation (116). He finds her 'a bright-coloured kerchief, one of the cheap things in jute which look so pretty', and

> with a dexterous hand . . . he twisted the kerchief round her neck, and over her shapely head, so as to let the curls of her fringe play about the folds and to set off the singular beauty of her eyes with a frame rich and full of colour. (116)

The addition of the kerchief allegedly brings out Lizzie's beauty, and makes her a worthy symbol, a Pre-Raphaelite model. In a rare moment of insight, however, Lizzie sees through Jack, and 'shudder[s], because it seem[s] to her as if all her beauty l[ies] in the crimson handkerchief' (117). To Jack, this is true: Lizzie remains marked by the shabby dress, and cannot take on the beauty that to him exists independently of her body, outside the reach of her class. This alteration disembodies Lizzie; the gravity of the handkerchief pulls in her body and erases her.

The equivalence between persons and things is reinforced in the interchangeability of cloth skins and the bodies they cover. When Jack gives Lizzie the handkerchief, he in some sense offers to transform her into a higher-class body. But Lizzie cannot exist in her second-hand form; her labourer's body marks the handkerchief as out of place. Nothing about her condition has changed; she is merely, for a moment, covered in something cheap that might obscure her labour. The handkerchief – and, by extension, Lizzie's body itself – becomes a metaphor, a small part that can stand in for the whole.

Symbol and Representation

Knowledge is at the root of this bodily annihilation. Jack transforms Lizzie's body because he needs her to be knowable, to prove that he is a valuable scholar and artist. Lizzie's body disappears into the metaphoric handkerchief so that if Jack can know the handkerchief, he can know and thereby capitalise on Lizzie.

But not only capitalists erase bodies, Besant argues. *Children of Gibeon* critiques knowledge as it manifests through radical socialist Sam Monument, one of Valentine's alleged siblings. Like Jack's handkerchief, socialism is a political system handed down from on high, with the specific intent to aggrandise its proponents.[8] Crucially, socialism as Sam presents it overlooks the suffering of individuals, and instead focuses on systems: the bodies of the workers become their rags. Sam's socialism turns the worker into symbols of systemic issues, people whose bodies do not matter outside of their function in the larger struggle.

Knowledge is central to Besant's critique of socialism, for the socialist's self-regard belies its claims of egalitarianism. In response to Valentine's scepticism about socialism, Sam warns her that 'the working men are the masters of the country, and we are the masters of the working men. They are looking to us already. We are going to be their leaders' (Besant 1886: 1.199). Sam's rhetoric of socialism establishes an equal society with the schoolmaster above that equality; the working man is merely a mechanism to understand the system. A government of schoolmasters will surpass Parliament, because the government knows nothing about 'the working man' – but 'as for us [schoolmasters], we do know him' (200). The resonance of the word 'know' in this context speaks beyond academic knowledge, and even beyond material conditions of existence. Sam claims an intimate, thorough understanding of the working man's existence as such. However, Sam's version of knowledge abstracts the working men's bodies from their material conditions and reduces them to mere labour. And this is socialism's primary foible in Besant's novel: it focuses on systematic change rather than people, and thereby ignores individual suffering.

Socialism reduces labourers' individual bodies to a collective because it resists capitalism as a system. Though the word *system* appears first when Valentine's other brother, Claude, describes Sam's nemesis, he attributes the word to Sam (Besant 1886: 2.49). Valentine implores Claude, 'think of those poor girls working every day and all day long, and for so little! Is it just and right? Who is to blame for it, Claude?' He responds, 'The system, I suppose, is to blame – whatever the system may be' (49). In this early conversation, Claude translates the 'poor girls' – by which Valentine means Lotty, Lizzie and Melenda – into a collective mass oppressed by the collective 'system'. Valentine finds this proposal initially compelling, and adopts socialism as her new creed. She declares that 'if we cannot help her [Melenda] in any other way, we will help her by altering the System, even if we have to call in Sam, and all become Socialists' (56). Though she intends to 'alter' rather than 'overthrow' (Sam's word) the system, Sam's monolithic 'system' proves an attractive target for Valentine's budding concern for the working class because it offers a single project for her to fix.

Besant critiques socialism for its wilful disregard for individual suffering. And indeed, Valentine's time as a socialist crusader is rather short-lived. She finds herself confronted with the impending death of one of the working-girls, Lotty; the seamstress will not live to see the collapse of the old system and the rise of socialism. Valentine begs Sam, 'Never mind the Competitive System: that will take a good many years to destroy' (124). Instead, he should 'try and find some readier way to help those girls. Consider, one of them is dying slowly; we can't save her; we can only make her easier: the other two are wasting their lives in the most terrible poverty' (125). When Sam resists, Valentine responds:

> 'Think, Sam, oh, think . . . of their rags and their misery and try to help them.'
> 'I do think of their rags. Good God! . . . I think of their rags and their misery for weeks together after I have seen Melenda.'
> 'Then I wish, Sam, that you saw her every day.'
> 'If I did I should only hate the system more and more.' (125)

This passage is full of rich moments, but I draw attention to one key element: Sam's insistence on abstraction over the lived experience of the bodies in front of him – embodied by their clothing. When Valentine implores him to 'think . . . of their rags and their misery', his first response is that he does 'think of their rags'. Crucially, he drops 'their misery'; he thinks only of their material conditions as metaphoric evidence of economic wrong. He does not acknowledge that the rags are truly material, and thereby disregards the girls' emotional distress. Because he understands the rags through interpretive depth rather than seeing them as a surface, he affords them a similarly annihilating gravity that pulls affects away from the girls and into knowledge. He analyses systems; he does not empathise with individuals. Valentine's dismissal of Sam carries surprising emotional resonance: 'I ask you for advice, and you offer me the chance of a new System. Go away and rail at Competition, while we look after its victims' (127). Socialism as Sam practises it cannot care for individuals, for it transforms labourers into mere symbols – the general 'labourer' as a victim of a system that does not care for her misery.

Most importantly, because socialism cares only for labour and not for labourers, Besant understands it as a system external to the working people. While Sam understands socialism as a form of knowledge the schoolmasters offer to the working people, Claude recognises the dangerous abstraction of this kind of knowledge. He says:

> I am certain there is no System, or Institution, or code of laws, whatever, which can be imposed upon a people, unless they are ready for it, and desire it for themselves . . . it will be always impossible to make the men of ability, who are the only men to be considered, desire a system in which they themselves shall not be able to [do] good to themselves first' (Besant 1886: 3.186–7)

While socialism remains an external imposition, it will remain a gift in the most exploitative sense of the word. Sam expects authority in the system to come as recompense for his commitment to the war against exchange, and the labourer remains merely a cog in his quest to know the system.

But Sam's socialism demonstrates a crucial paradox in Valentine's quest. Sam sees his sister's rags, but he does not see her misery. Valentine must answer for both: she seeks to improve both the working-girls' material conditions embodied in the rags, and the emotional condition of misery. In fact, the rags offer a material handhold for Valentine to begin to understand the seamstresses' feelings. In other words, Sam is not looking in the wrong place; he is merely short-sighted. This is the paradox of the strange materialism of the rags: Valentine must look first to the rags, for the rags lead her to sympathise with the seamstresses – but she must also look beyond them.

To look beyond the rags, Valentine must learn to humanise her science of reform. As Ezra Jennings offered an emotional science as the antidote to scholarship's self-regard, so too *Children of Gibeon* offers an emotionally educated doctor.[9] The doctor becomes the discursive centre where the political rhetoric of Sam meets the rhetoric of science and its homogenisation of bodies. The scientist turns bodies into mere representations: exteriors that expose interiors and the knowledge they hold within.

When Lotty continues to deteriorate in the second volume of the novel, Valentine speaks with the doctor, who, unbidden, outlines his own political philosophy. The doctor's philosophy lies somewhere between liberalism and socialism. He believes Lotty is a 'case in which man, meeting no power of self-defence, has worked his wicked will, pretending that he is obeying the laws of political economy' (Besant 1886: 2.97). In words similar to Marx's argument that capital turns labourers into 'implement machine[s]', the doctor says that 'he [the capitalist] turns this girl into a machine for doing what she ought not to have done at all' (97). He offers an alternative to Sam's schoolmaster-hero socialism with the possibility that 'the ladies of the country shall unite to form a Protection League for their working sisters', or that 'the working people themselves' would form 'a grand universal League, or Federation, or Brotherhood of Labour' which would 'control wages and work' (98). But, he cautions, the only way it will work is if 'not one prophet but ten thousand all preac[h] the same gospel at the same time' (98–9). This is the key difference between the doctor's politics and Sam's socialism, as the doctor sees it: 'my League will be formed by the people for the people,' he says, but 'the Socialists want to impose their scheme on the people' (100). Here, Valentine learns an important lesson, for at this point in the narrative, she still believes in Sam's socialism. When she replies, 'Why not, if it is good for them?' the doctor answers, 'Because, young lady, you can't improve people by any scheme or law or government at all. They must improve themselves' (100). The doctor offers the idea of a home-grown, socialist utopia brought about by the people rather than an avant-garde. However, he lacks the capacity to implement this change, or to articulate how it might come about.

And this political failure comes from his scientific failure. When he actually treats Lotty before he harangues Valentine, he asks her, 'what do you think of the working girl? You have got three of them to study. There are thousands just exactly like them' (95). Valentine responds, 'I can think of these three only and how to help them.' Her answer exposes the key error in his thinking, as the novel sees it: that each working-girl is exactly like the others. Valentine insists that she can attend only to those individuals whom she knows, whose feelings she has experienced first-hand. By way of answer, though it is in fact no answer, the doctor 't[akes] up Lotty's arm and bare[s] it to the elbow', and proceeds to offer an analysis of her anatomy: 'You see: a strong bone and a good length of limb. Nature designed this arm for a stout strong woman . . . Nature meant this girl to be a really fine specimen . . . Yet, you see, a splendid model ruined' (95–6). Though he intends to use his scientific analysis to discuss how capitalism has ruined such a fine specimen, his argument provides rather less evidence for his claims, and more for his failure as a socially minded reader.

Even when he attempts to speak to the individual, his reductive mechanism sees Lotty as nothing more than a representation, an external body to be manipulated and abused in a startling mimicry of the way capitalism objectifies her. The doctor cannot conceive of a way to bring about social change because he understands the group as a homogeneous whole composed of legible bodies. While this may be necessary for his scientific rhetoric, it impedes his capacity to create or imagine social change. Like Sam's socialism, both the doctor's science and politics require knowledge that ossifies the individual experiences of labouring people into representations that can be known.

Valentine understands that the doctor fails to recognise the individual feelings of his patients; he has detachment, but does not temper it with empathy, and so falls into the fallacy of mechanism akin to Huxley and Cuff. He sees bodies as representations of interiors, mere mediators of knowledge. Valentine learns to oppose the doctor's philosophy of social mechanism and emphasises women's ability to supplement and improve science with the addition of emotion.

Embodiment and Acknowledgement

As with other ethical characters like Biddy and Ezra Jennings, Valentine's intuitive empathy is pre-coded in her body in ways that indicate the problematic pattern of self-renunciation. Her receptivity contrasts distinctly with her (truly working-class) sister, who is anything but receptive. This difference is written on the girls' bodies: Valentine embodies connection in opposition to Violet's repulsion. They both have hair 'of the light brown hue which is so much beloved by the English youth' (Besant 1886: 1.41). But where 'Violet's was full of curls and curves and twists, which caught the light and scattered it about as a little waterfall in a mountain brook breaks and scatters the sunshine', Valentine's hair has 'a wave in it, and in her hair the sunshine lay and rested' (41). Violet reflects and scatters outward, away; Valentine draws in and offers rest. Both the girls have blue eyes, but 'Valentine's were certainly darker than Violet's, and, like the hair, they absorbed the light which Violet's received and reflected' (42). And finally Violet 'paint[s] with no mean skill' – an art of observation and reflection (44). Valentine, on the other hand, is 'a musician and a singer' – one who creates and evokes vibrations and resonance (44). Violet's body resists and maintains its impermeability, while Valentine's body invites and transforms from encounters with the outside. When she goes to live with her sisters in the East End, this receptivity is key to her ability to take on the feelings of the dressmakers, and to become the triumphant advocate for the working class.

But unlike the self-renouncing angels of previous chapters, Valentine does not self-renounce for a man, or annihilate herself for the edification of others. She does not merely sing and resonate in order to disappear; instead, she connects, builds coalitions, and acknowledges the relationship between other bodies' suffering and her own. She touches the surface, and instead of vivisecting herself to help others read, she binds together with it through empathy.

Valentine uses song as her initial medium for connection with the working class. Her singing both incites others to self-reflect and forms emotional connections between bodies without drawing attention to herself. Her singing is a literal impression – a vibration that impacts the senses of those around her. The physicality of her singing transforms those who hear, beginning with herself. Valentine visits the woman she believes is her birth mother, the now-blind Hester Monument. But when Hester describes her daughter Polly to Valentine, Valentine realises that Polly became Violet and not her.

Rather than reveal her true identity, however, Valentine opts to sing Hester a hymn. For Hester, the hymn confirms that Valentine is Polly – but it is not her voice, for Hester observes that 'Valentine's voice is like her ladyship's [Lady Mildred]', her true birth mother. Despite that coincidence, however, Hester declares that Valentine's 'ways are all [her] own – my own little Polly's soft and pretty ways' (Besant 1886: 1.299). Valentine realises that she is *not* Polly, but somehow, even when she sings in her own voice – a voice that immediately reminds Hester of Lady Mildred – she remains Polly. Even the narrator seems confused about her identity, for when the story follows Valentine from the church where she meets Hester back to the working-girls' home, he wonders, 'Was it imagination? or had there already come upon Valentine in one short hour, namely, since the Discovery, a subtle change, so she no longer regarded the people with quite the same sense of relationship?' (301). The narrator insists that Valentine must disengage from Polly's siblings, for 'she was no longer their sister in the narrower sense', and instead can 'only' be a 'universal sister' (301). While the narrator seems suspicious of Valentine's transformation, Valentine's response to her discovery gives the lie to the narrator's persistence; after she returns home, she twice proclaims herself 'Melenda's sister' (306). Her new identity begins the moment she decides to sing for Hester, for her singing shapes and connects her body with others.

And yet, the instabilities of this transformation narrative suggest a broader tension in *Children of Gibeon*'s use of song: while singing appears to connect Valentine to others, and connect others through Valentine, it is in fact only ever an appearance. Not her voice, but her actions make Valentine into Polly.

Besant's novel is in conversation with other reformers who hold song as the ideal mode of emotional communication and the ideal site of social reform. But, while it acknowledges singing's power, the novel maintains that the emotional effects of song are fleeting, and instead posits the more permanent medium of print as the most effective form of emotional communication and social reform. Inspired in part by the call of thinkers like Matthew Arnold, who believed late-nineteenth-century mass culture would benefit from an education in the oft-cited 'sweetness and light', reformers in the 1870s and 1880s coupled music – particularly song – with social reform.[10] In an 1878 article in *The Contemporary Review*, William Stanley Jevons writes that while 'there are many modes by which recreation and culture may be brought within the reach of the multitude . . . it is my present purpose to point out that the most practicable and immediately efficient mode is the cultivation of pure music' (Jevons 1878: 503). The 1880s saw the apotheosis of this movement, with public concerts in the Crystal Palace, and religious movements like the Tonic Sol-fa College, which taught labourers to sight-sing. These movements were both social and religious, for, as Rev. Hugh Reginald Haweis writes in 1884, music 'draws people together; oils the wheels of the social system . . . I am convinced the influence of music over the poor is quite angelic. Teach the people to sing, and you will make them happy' (quoted in McGuire 2009: 3). While Haweis was a minister and Jevons a philosopher, they agree in their hedonist philosophy that happiness is the end goal, and that music is the best way to spread happiness to the unhappy working class.

The happiness music inspired was no mere fleeting pleasure, and was often opposed to the working-class songs of the music hall in language startlingly reminiscent of anti-sensation rhetoric. J. Proudman offers a *Christmas Carol*-esque narrative in which the angel of music takes him through the East End and shows him the uses and abuses of music that take place there. The angel laments that in the music hall 'sweet sounds are seasoned with every sensuality', when in fact 'music was given to be a ministering angel, to lighten care, to dispel gloom, to aid the remembrance of holy truths, to prepare the way for pure feeling' (Proudman 1875: 331, 332). An anonymous writer for the 1881 *Musical Times* concurs, and in his example of music's reformative capacity, the primary challenge he believes reformers face is that 'the taste of the people has been affected by that curse of modern times, the music-hall; and the workmen of Ancoats frequently found the serious and sentimental ballads "slow" compared with [the songs of the music hall]' ('Music for the People' 1881: 457). Singing should not be 'fast', however, these reformers argue. When one listens to music, 'there [should be] no straining of the nerves or muscles, no effort of any kind, but mere passive abandonment of the mind to the train of ideas and emotions suggested by the strains' (Jevons 1878: 504). To listen to music is to embrace impressions and completely give up one's conscious will.

As Jevons's claim indicates, Associationism dominated the scientific conversation about the positive effects of music.[11] In keeping with the tendency to conflate bodies, written texts and other media, Haweis refers to singers' interpretations as 'readings' (Haweis 1870b: 282). John Curwen, the founder of one of the Tonic Sol-fa reform movements, conducted philosophical experiments to determine why a given tone might elicit sadness in one song, and happiness in another. He concludes, 'after many experiments I was at last convinced that the mental effect of tones depends chiefly on the tone relationship which is thrown around them' (Curwen 1882: 58); in other words, music's ties to emotion depend on the association between notes and feelings. But even in these scientific frameworks, acknowledgement slides out from underneath the scientific impulse. As far back as the 1850s, Alexander Bain, at the conclusion of a rather comprehensive section on music and the science of hearing, acknowledges that music causes 'a certain intoxication of excitement . . . in some minds that does not answer the ends of [language] acquisition' (Bain 1855: 429). This philosophy persisted into the 1870s and 1880s, so that an anonymous contributor to *The Musical Times* writes: 'the philosophy of music, as explained by Dr Pole, amounts to the acknowledgement that beyond the dissection of the crude and amorphous materials, science is comparatively impotent in art questions' ('The Philosophy of Music' 1879: 420). Science supports music as a tool of social reform, but it also must confess its own insufficiency to explain the power of music.

And so, predictably, music becomes the realm of the feminine. Haweis explains this in a particularly misogynist passage:

> The woman's temperament is naturally artistic, not in a creative, but in a receptive sense . . . It was rumoured that Madame Grisi had to be taught all her songs, and became great by her wonderful power of appropriating suggestions of pathos and expression which she was incapable of originating herself . . . Most women reflect with astonishing ease. (Haweis 1871: 501)

This ability to 'reflect' and 'rece[ive]' is typical not only of a dominant Victorian understanding of gender roles, but also of a pseudo-scientific understanding of the relationship between bodies and emotions. The self-renouncing woman cannot create music, but her music can act as a conduit through which bodies can connect with one another. John Curwen compares female musical education to male education in a gesture resonant with the tendency to require women teachers: 'Professional habits of thinking are so strong', he writes, 'especially amongst musicians, that I do not know how their trammels could have been sufficiently thrown off by a professional teacher' (Curwen 1876: 11). Instead, the success of the Tonic Sol-fa movement 'required a lady whose sympathies with children would be so strong as to make her thinking lightly of fashion and prejudice, and think *only* of how to teach music in the simplest and plainest way to the children of the poor' (11). This is because the content of music should not be informational or formal, but instead, emotional.[12]

Besant was also invested in movements that sought to create places where the working class could simultaneously amuse and educate themselves. In *All Sorts and Conditions of Men*, Angela funds a Palace of Delight for just such a purpose, including instruments for concerts (Besant 1882: 3.233). Besant seemed, at this point, to agree with Jevons's statement, 'it is greatly to the low state of musical education among the masses of English population that I attribute their helpless state when seeking recreation' (Jevons 1878: 504). By *Children*, though, where these musical reformers hold that women's role as the guardians of intuitive knowledge about emotion makes them better singers, and that song can make the working class happy, Besant questions the effectiveness of song – and most importantly, he questions it for its lack of material tangibility and its demand that the singer self-renounce.

Music's ephemeral sensations were crucial to the arguments of the musical reformers. In Proudman's dream of the angel of music, music momentarily helps the children of a Ragged School 'forget their rags' (Proudman 1875: 331). Jevons argues that music 'holds the mind enchained just so long as there is energy of thought to spare' – but as soon as the music abates, so too does its relaxing elements (Jevons 1878: 504). And when Valentine sings, the effects are profound – but only temporary. After her first few days working with the dressmakers, Valentine declares that she must sing. Her song 'str[ikes] upon all ears' and goes 'straight to the heart by reason of the air' (Besant 1886: 2.33). The narrator's gaze moves to the street, where he describes a doctor and an assistant priest, both of whom the narrator calls 'pragmatic, pedantic, and conceited' (34).

Hearing Valentine's voice, however, inspires a brief moment of self-reflection in the two men:

> 'Oh Lord!' cried the Doctor, who only believed in himself, and therefore generally called upon the Lord.
> 'Dear me!' said the Assistant Priest, who didn't believe in himself at all, and therefore swore by his own name. (35)

These self-reflexive utterances signal a momentary collapse of the isolated stability and arrogance of some of those other characters in the novels I have investigated who rely on their own knowledge and insist on their own superiority: Wendover, Pip, Robert Audley, Betteredge, Cuff. For a few pages, Valentine's song reduces the two men to inarticulate feelings – an act all the more poignant when the priest 'profess[es] to know the secret ways of the Almighty' and the doctor 's[ees] no soft place anywhere in his stupendous intellect' (34). The change does not last long, however; a few pages later, the men return to their pedantic bickering. And there the chapter ends – anticlimactic and deliberately sardonic.

Singing, in short, is only a temporary remedy, and it is temporary because it is immaterial. Valentine's song ultimately unites her with universal sisterhood and with her working-girl sisters only because it emphasises the material reality of the working-class experience. As she nears her home, she passes a man who 'step[s] aside to make room for her and t[akes] off his hat to her' (Besant 1886: 1.304). Later, Valentine learns that the man is Mr Lane, a 'ragged gentleman' who notices her immediately after she sings to Hester – an event he could not have witnessed – and who 'heard [her] singing upstairs' (Besant 1886: 2.67, 68). Toward the end of their first conversation, he asks her to sing again, and the song appears to initiate a complex, reality-shaking connection between Mr Lane and Valentine (76).

In fact, however, Valentine's physical action – that she comes to visit Mr Lane – creates real change in both of them. Immediately after the song, Mr Lane confesses that if Valentine continues to visit, he 'might get to look for [her] coming, and that would interfere with [his] dream' (76). This dream, Mr Lane explains, possesses him at night with visions of a different life he could have lived. He crafts an entire narrative, complete with a career as a scholar 'of such eloquence and learning' that he refuses a Deanery, since 'a Bishopric is the least he will take' (80). Imagining an alternative reality allows Mr Lane to escape poverty, for as he tells Valentine, 'what you call my dream is my reality – my life' (190). He insists that 'no one would live a life such as that', 'a procession of days and hours which are possessed of mocking devils, except when you come to me' (190). When he proclaims to Valentine, 'You are a dream and Ivy Lane is a dream, and Lizzie is a dream, and all the hunger and poverty and misery are part of a dream' (190), Valentine's song threatens to ground Mr Lane in the reality of the East End, to confront him (and the reader) with the material reality of his and the other labourers' conditions.

Mr Lane's dream vibrates throughout the novel, inspiring dreams as it goes – but these dreams, no matter who dreams them and to what end, must all dissolve when they encounter the physical world of the East End. Following Mr Lane and his dream, the novel moves on to a chapter entitled 'Lotty's Foolish Dream', in which Lotty dreams 'that she was in a workshop – lofty, well aired, and beautiful', where all the other girls work, 'laughing and talking happily' (103). At the end of her dream, Mr Lane, 'dressed like a gentleman', begins to play an organ, and 'Valentine st[ands] up to sing' (103). Once again, Valentine's song inspires connection, and connects to a dream – but in this dream, when 'all the girls tried to sing too, [they] could not, because of the tears – tears of joy and happiness – and the memories of the cruel past, which choked them' (103). Here, the novel explicitly addresses the shortcoming of the musical reformer: to sing may make one happy (à la Haweis), but any emotion not rooted in materiality is fleeting and false. Lotty's dream instigates a pair of crises into Valentine's narrative: she can sing, but the reality of the working-girls' conditions keeps them from singing with her. One can dream, but the dream futilely denies reality.

Physical objects, specifically the 'rags' Mr Lane and the working-girls wear, provide the only tenable response to these challenges. 'Sometimes', Mr Lane confesses to Valentine, 'I understand that my dream is only a dream, and the real life is here, among these rags' (193). Reality among the rags becomes the slogan of Valentine's liberal reform. Materiality and Valentine's impulse to connect with others – the impulse that drives her to sing – become the markers of effective reform. Rather than inspire the labourers to happiness through song, Valentine opts to acknowledge the material surfaces that surround her and the workers of the East End. When she returns for the final time to her home with Lady Mildred, Valentine looks back on her experience with the working-girls and decides 'it must have been a dream . . . unless, perhaps, everything is a dream' (Besant 1886: 3.230). But the death of one of her working-girl sisters, Lotty, propels Valentine into the final chapter, 'Valentine Speaks'. She does not sing; instead, to speak, to declare in the constative rather than to sing and resonate, becomes Valentine's new mission. In order to ground herself in the working-girls' world, rather than lose sight of it as a dream, Valentine must give up her songs; she must find reality among the rags.

Reform without Exploitation

But even as she fixates on the rags, Valentine must learn not to use them as a source of knowledge. They are not metaphor; they are not symbol; they must be surfaces that connect bodies. Most importantly, these surfaces cannot be used for knowledge; they must enable acknowledgement. Without acknowledgement, like Sam's socialism, even ostensibly altruistic motives annihilate bodies' materiality. Novelist Dinah Mulock Craik calls this condescending knowledge 'benevolence' in her essay 'Benevolence – or Beneficence?', which appeared in her 1875 *Sermons out of Church*.[13] Craik opposes these two terms to argue against benevolence, which

> consists in mere kind feeling; doing good certainly sometimes, but in a vague and careless way, and more for its own pleasure than for another's benefit; giving, because to give is agreeable, but taking little pains to ascertain what has been the result of the gift. (Craik 1875: 152)

Benevolence, in short, is naïve. The intent may be noble, but such motives are merely virtuous, rather than effective. Benevolence provides a stepping-stone forward for the would-be reformer in that it replaces self-regard and focuses on the individual rather than the system. But, as Valentine's gift of second-hand clothing to her sister Melenda demonstrates, benevolence does not solve the problems it attempts to address. While benevolence in *Children of Gibeon* is superior to the other kinds of fetishisation above, it still fails to acknowledge labourers' bodies as material surfaces. Though idealism itself is not usually a problem for social problem novels, naïve benevolence does not provide material solutions because it is too abstractly motivated. In fact, a blindly idealised gift is even more dangerous than Jack's self-serving charity. Where Jack's gift obviously comes from an ulterior motive, the most problematic gift in the novel is an even more idealised form: a naïve gift between sisters.

Early in the third volume of *Children of Gibeon*, the seamstresses' work angers their employers. And so, when Melenda goes to retrieve payment for past work and accept new work, her employers 'drill' her (Besant 1886: 3.58). She must stand and wait for her money and new work. If she leaves, she will be 'told when [she] come[s] back that the work's come down and been given to another girl' (63). Melenda stands without food or water until the evening, when she returns home physically weakened from her ordeal. On the third day, Valentine finally intervenes – and loses Melenda her job in the process. She announces that this change in social relations necessitates a change of clothes: 'Do you think I am going to have my own sister go about in such shocking rags as these any longer? ... Everything has got to be changed' (93). She dresses Melenda in some of her own clothing, so that on the third day of her drill, Melenda is resurrected, transfigured into a new woman.

Traditionally, gift-giving has been understood as an inherently feminine form of exchange. As it applies to the nineteenth century, the logic is seductive: if capitalism is a masculine, public exchange with inequality and competition built into it, and gift-giving is the opposite of capitalist exchange, then gift-giving must be feminine and therefore 'resis[t] an economy based on the exchange of commodities' (A. Miller 1995: 41). And indeed, as Jill Rappoport argues in *Giving Women*, Victorian women's 'gift exchanges radically reconstructed [their] private relationship and public activism' (Rappoport 2012: 5).[14] As Valentine is Melenda's sister both allegedly by blood and by spirit, it makes sense that she would use a gift economy to subvert the exploitation of the capitalist production that threatens Melenda. But the argument that the gift economy is separate from capitalism nostalgically 'presupposes (individual and collective) misrecognition (*meconnaissance*) of the reality of the objective mechanism of the exchange' – that is, the social shifts and obligations the gift demands (Bourdieu 1977: 5–6). When Valentine gives Melenda new clothes, she evokes imagery of the ideal, sisterly gift between women, but in fact, the novel recognises that this gift is not really about material conditions after all; it is merely another form of abstract knowledge.[15]

Valentine's ostensible assistance comes from a place of knowledge; she believes that she knows what is best for Melenda. On the first day of being drilled, Melenda rejects Valentine's help. When Melenda finally gives in to Valentine's offers of help, she surrenders that independence, particularly the distinctiveness of her body. The distinction between the narrator's physical treatment of the drill and Valentine's analysis of Melenda's body is telling, for where the narrator emphasises the embodied distinctiveness of the seamstress,

Valentine subsumes Melenda's experience into her own sense of embodiment. The narrator writes an anatomical treatise:

> the girl feels first of all grievous pains in her limbs; she shifts her weight from one foot to the other, her feet swell, her back and shoulders ache, her head becomes an aching lump of lead ... after an hour or two, her cheeks have become flushed, her lips tremble, her hands shaking, and her eyes are unnaturally bright. (Besant 1886: 3.69)

Close attention to the physical effects of the drill offers an avenue, however second-hand, into the experience itself. Most importantly, the narrator acknowledges the seamstress as an independent body with distinct sensations; the acute physicality of the description demands that the reader acknowledge the seamstress as a body.

Valentine's actions, however, insist that to move outside her suffering, Melenda must become a body like her own. As she dresses her sister, Valentine elides the differences between them: 'You are not quite so tall as I am, but the frock is short for me ... The frock is a little loose in the waist, but you will fill out very soon now' (93). While she acknowledges their differences in height and girth, the frock itself becomes a cover that will eventually make their bodies similar. Most crucially, she evades Melenda's suffering with a compliment: 'Artists would give anything to paint that beautiful dead gold hair' (93–4). The correlation with Jack's fetishisation of Lizzie deliberately challenges the benevolence of Valentine's actions, for even if she does not seek to paint Melenda herself, Valentine nevertheless obscures her sister's body behind a façade of clothing. Even the clothes themselves emphasise the correlation, for she gives her sister a 'gray dress ... with *a red handkerchief* in front, with a white collar and white cuffs' (94, emphasis added). Like Lotty, it seems as if all Melenda's upward mobility is tied up in the red handkerchief.

Where Jack's charity turned Lizzie into a machine for his own aggrandisement, Valentine's benevolence unwittingly reduces Melenda to a symbol of the raised-up worker, swathed in a series of metaphors, an empty frame devoid of individual value and communal connections. The broader ramifications of Melenda's makeover emphasise the danger of benevolence that gives without thinking of the ramifications. Melenda's employer insists that Valentine 'take her *protégée* elsewhere' for work – and in fact, Melenda never finds work again in the novels (80). Valentine's benevolence in some ways even causes the drilling, for the 'glimpse of the better life' that Valentine offers Lizzie 'made her ... careless in her work' – and for this, Melenda is drilled

(60–1). Moreover, as Valentine re-dresses Melenda, 'no one, unfortunately, noticed Lizzie', who leaves the house out of fear that Valentine will leave her behind. Lizzie flies to Jack, who takes her shopping for the red handkerchief. In short, Valentine's gift indirectly causes Melenda to be drilled, loses the girls their work, and inspires Lizzie to fall into temptation.

All these ills derive from obligation: to change oneself, and ultimately, to shift allegiance to a new community. When Valentine gives Melenda her gift, she obligates her to change herself, and abandon the working community. Valentine intends to establish a new community, a sisterhood that reaches across class boundaries to connect the labourer and the aristocrat. But this dissolution of the working-girls' community underscores the reality that 'within social systems where possession and control of the transfer of goods reside predominantly with a privileged group . . . gifts participate in the reinforcement of the status of that group and the power to control others through binding obligation' (Murphy 2006: 203). So, while Valentine's gift offers a new degree of kinship to Melenda, that offer dissolves Melenda's kinship with other workers. When Melenda walks outside in her new clothes, 'for the first time in her life, she did not like the crowd. She left the street, therefore, and went back to her own room' (Besant 1886: 3.100). Lizzie feels that her family has fallen apart, and so seeks out her exploitative lover. Where Jack's charity demands recompense in the form of social and symbolic capital, Valentine's gesture is admirable in that she asserts a universal sisterhood and invites Melenda to leave off being a labourer and join her as a sister. But as we have seen, the 'invitation' of a gift is often an obligation, in this case one that devalues both Melenda's autonomy and her community. And this is the critique Besant makes of benevolent politics: it does not acknowledge the value of the labourer's current life. Benevolence, like socialism, strives for knowledge, and so addresses labourers as symbols of labour rather than as individuals. Because it seeks to interpret beneath surfaces rather than care for people, it cannot help but replicate the same abstracting mechanisms of the very system it seeks to replace.

The Physicality of Care

Against socialism and benevolence, Besant offers the Sense of Humanity – a politics of individual care that acknowledges and sympathises with the suffering bodies behind the rags. When Valentine works through this process, she explores the genesis of empathy to challenge and rework alternative models of social action that require women's bodies as sacrifices. Initially, Valentine believes socialism is the best mode of social action; she then moves to benevolence; finally, she arrives at embodied, direct sympathy for the working-girls.

Here, again, the paradox of the rags emerges. Physical objects like the working-girls' rags ground Valentine in the reality of the labourers and prevent her from abstracting the labourer into a mere sign of work. But, when the time to reveal Polly's identity comes, her mother claims that 'Valentine is not an artist; she neglects the rags, whether they are picturesque or not, and looks for the man below them' (Besant 1886: 3.234–5). Though she must begin with the rags, Valentine must also move past them. When she 'neglects the rags', Valentine circumvents the exploitative systems that abstract bodies in *Children of Gibeon*: the production of clothing itself; the benevolent offering of second-hand clothing; the exploitative second-hand gifts of the socialists like Sam and social climbers like Jack; women's mandatory self-annihilation. By connecting individuals and their clothes, Valentine learns to acknowledge the bodies behind the rags, to feel for them and listen to their stories rather than to tell them. Empathy does not mean solving problems for others; it means acknowledging their pain and supporting them as they act.

For Besant, to acknowledge the personhood of the labourer is to acknowledge their bodily autonomy in their material conditions, and to allow them to move free of the warping gravity of knowledge. As a person, the labourer does not need an externally imposed political revolution or an unasked-for red handkerchief; instead, she can help herself. Craik writes that, where benevolence does not care about material results, justice 'aims less at helping people than at enabling them to help themselves' (Craik 1875: 153). Shared sorrow, in turn, might enable the reader to transcend the exploitation of charity, socialism or benevolence; instead, through empathy, readers might become like Valentine, and care for the person rather than the rags. As Valentine prepares to leave the East End just before her coming of age, the narrator adds:

> There is a Sense which lies dormant with most of us . . . Let us call it, if you please, the Sense of humanity. It is not philanthropy, nor benevolence, nor sentimentality; it is a thing much fuller and wider than any of these . . . It is a Sense by means of which one is enabled to separate the man from his clothes, whether they are rags or gowns of office. (Besant 1886: 3.161–2)

The recognition of the person is central to the Sense of Humanity; it is a politics of personal care, built on the acknowledgement of the labourer as a person, rather than a marker of labour. When she returns for the final time to her home, Valentine looks back on her experience with the working-girls in language that Besant would later replicate in his autobiography: 'These faces haunt me ... I shall carry home with me a ghostly crowd of faces. How many thousands of faces have I seen here and none of them alike' (193). These faces, and the irreducible differences between them, take the place of rags.

Of course, the notion that liberalism is a politics of individuals is hardly surprising. What is most interesting about Besant's liberalism is not that it turns away from the rags, but that it needs them to begin. There is something of Carpenter's acquired habitude here, the intentional cultivation of a feeling through the proper culture of care. Valentine's deliberateness answers the ethical question of *how* one develops empathy; while her body may have (problematic) predisposition toward empathy, she must learn how best to extend her compassion into the world. William James, in his 1884 'What Is an Emotion?', writes: 'If we wish to conquer undesirable emotional tendencies in ourselves, we must assiduously, and in the first instance cold-bloodedly, go through the *outward motions* of those contrary dispositions we prefer to cultivate' (James 1884: 198). This plodding, methodical conditioning is a material practice that requires material markers. And so, *Children of Gibeon* fixates on how clothing works in these systems precisely for the same reasons it critiques them. Liberalism needs the obligation of charity, because it hopes to give the labourer an opportunity to improve herself; it needs the materialism of socialism, because it seeks to ameliorate working conditions; and it needs the utopian vision of benevolence to motivate empathy. This strange materialism requires the rags in order to reject them. It begins and ends with surfaces.

Notes

1. The College figures prominently in Besant's work as a symbol of women's education: Angela Messenger, social reformer and protagonist of Besant's 1882 *All Sorts and Conditions*, attended Newnham and studied political economy; in his 1883 *All in a Garden Fair*, Newnham symbolises the passage of time that 'converts ... the fresh-girl, into a high wrangler, at the mention of whose name the Senior Moderator

raises his cap, and the undergraduates in the gallery shout' (Besant 1883: 277); later in *Children of Gibeon*, Claude mentions the room of a Newnham student in a rambling associative chain that ties together 'cleverness ... and beauty' (Besant 1886: 1.236).
2. Not only was Newnham a college of science for women, it was a well-respected college that supported those who argued in favour of women's education; one student of the college 'was fortunate enough to gain more marks than any of her male competitors in the first part of the Natural Sciences Tripos', which a writer in *The Times* suggested was 'a fact in itself a sufficient justification for the efforts made to promote women's education' ('Natural Science' 1884: 10).
3. In *The Leisure Hour*, 'Old Clothes and What Becomes of Them' describes the process by which clothes become second-hand, then are translated into other clothes, then into rags, and finally into 'shoddy' and 'mungo' – the bare wool used to make new clothes. The author makes the fascinating claim that 'No man can say that the material of the coat he is wearing has not been already on the back of some greasy beggar' ('Old Clothes' 1865: 174) – emphasising that as much capital is extracted from the commodity as possible before it becomes a commodity again.
4. While 'dressmaking was considered more genteel and respectable than working in a textile factory or mill', the distinction between 'dressmaker' and 'seamstress' is crucial. According to Christine Kortsch, 'dressmakers were portrayed as malicious tyrants who overworked the fragile, corruptible young seamstresses in their employ' (Kortsch 2009: 112). See also Nicola Pullin's chapter in Beth Harris's *Famine and Fashion* (2005) for the way the middle-class dressmaker is obscured in needlewoman narratives.
5. Besant refers to this as the Law of the Lower Limit. The term 'lower limit' seems to have been a common reference to this law at the time, as it appears in texts such as Simon Nelson Patten's 1885 *Premises of Political Economy* to refer to Ricardo's principle (S. Patten 1885: 37).
6. Never mind that, even in the second-hand market, these girls would be hard-pressed to purchase the clothing they make. A short play in an 1886 issue of *The Argosy* priced a discounted gown at £6.6s, or nine weeks' pay for all three girls in *Children of Gibeon*; even a second-hand skirt for each girl at 5s, which one of the characters in *The Argosy* rejects as a waste of 5s, would take an entire week's pay ('Arabella at the Sales' 1886: 208).
7. Beverly Lemire, who argues that the second-hand clothing market 'reflected the demand of the men and women in more straitened circumstances, and which in turn developed to meet the needs of this portion of the population', is just one example of the persistence of this narrative (Lemire 1988: 3).
8. I want to clarify that my critiques in this section are my glossing of how Besant sees 'Sam's socialism', or socialism as the represented character

Sam Monument articulates it in Besant's novel, and not of socialism as a broader political movement.
9. Victorian literary scholars noted this trend toward the doctor-hero. Even as far back as 1860, M. M. writes in his *Fraser's* article 'Novels of the Day': 'Those frivolous warriors [heroes who are military officers] have passed away, and curates have reigned in their stead . . . They were not an amusing race, and but ill-provided with argument; but peace be to their memory, for they are ousted now by the Doctor. At length we have found the perfect hero. The doctor combines the learning of the church and the courage of the United Services, with an amount of universal knowledge peculiar to himself' (M. M. 1860: 207). The doctor is the perfect blend of cold rationale and heartfelt sympathy. This merits further exploration not just as part of scientific and medical discourse, but in terms of class, masculinity and professionalisation.
10. Key among these movements was the teaching of Tonic Sol-fa, a method of sight-singing that formed the core of a social reform movement spearheaded by John Curwen. For more on this movement, see Charles McGuire's *Music and Victorian Philanthropy: The Tonic Sol-Fa Movement* (2009).
11. Many scholars, such as Ben Mosselmans in *William Stanley Jevons and the Cutting Edge of Economics* (2007), seem inclined to portray Jevons as anti-Associationist. While Jevons was adamantly anti-Mill (both John and James), he was opposed primarily to their psychology-heavy approach, and preferred closer recourse to physiology. As I have indicated through Bain, this was typical of Associationism post-1850. Though Jevons was not necessarily a card-carrying Associationist, his understanding of the anatomical and physiological structures of the brain were soundly Associationist.
12. In a comparison of poetry and music, Haweis writes that 'what the poem really means is a certain succession or arrangement of feelings, in which emotion is everything' (Haweis 1870a: 371). Music 'alone is capable of giving to the simplest, the subtlest, and the most complex emotions alike that full and satisfactory expression through sound', he continues, so that 'if we are to have words to songs, let them subordinate sense to the emotion' (375, 378).
13. Besant himself presents the political solution of *Children of Gibeon* in opposition to what he calls 'benevolence', so while it is unclear if he is responding directly to Craik, the word has a similar meaning for both of them.
14. See especially chapter 5, 'Service and Savings in the Slums', which spends a great deal of time on the women of the Salvation Army, whom Besant held in high regard (Besant 1902: 257).
15. Some Victorians seemed acutely aware of the similarities between gift-giving and capitalism. Margueritte Murphy's study explores how 'in *Daniel Deronda*, George Eliot demonstrates the imbrication of gift and

commercial economies in British and Judaic culture in the latter half of the nineteenth century' (Murphy 2006: 203). Ilana Blumberg's analysis of *The Moonstone* suggests Wilkie Collins understood that 'gift-giving can function like robbery as an uninvited, unilateral act whose consequence is a demand or claim' (Blumberg 2016: 165).

Coda: In Defence of Victorian Optimism

This book ends on the streets.

For three weeks in the summer of 2019, the students of HNRS 380: 'London Streets' walked the alleys of Victorian London. They waited beside a young Dickens with his father in Marshalsea Prison. They crowded into the cloying humidity of the attic operating theatre in St Thomas' Hospital and witnessed the frantic amputations in a race against infection. They stood over the cesspool where the 1854 cholera epidemic began, and scoured the streets with John Snow as he wrapped his head around a new theory of disease transmission.

Look at materiality, I told them. Think about the ways that new institutions lunged up from the cultural fabric, bent and warped the channels through which the city's bodies flowed. New feelings, new modes of embodiment became possible, even as those structures altered or cut off old formulations – sometimes for the benefit of the working people, sometimes not. Pay attention to the physical surfaces around you.

I completely missed him.

I would like to think I was concerned with my students' safety, was looking at my phone to find a route to our next destination. But that is probably untrue. More likely, as I've trained myself to do, I skipped over him as part of the scenery. I was too busy interpreting and reading, too busy with exerting knowledge over the surfaces around us.

Open sores. Brittle, skeletal. Homeless.

I completely missed him.

But one of my students did not.

Victorian institutions create problems, to be sure. We shrank before the physical restraints in Bedlam psychiatric hospital. We cringed as the Salvation Army celebrated military metaphors like 'opening fire' to describe their social work. We balked as the hospital transformed patients into statistics and problems to solve.

They also open room to think about surfaces. Bedlam begins conversations about the expression of psychological pain, begins to embrace the infinite multiplicity of human experience. The Salvation Army insists that labourers matter, propels the welfare state to its prominence, protects the marginalised more than laissez-faire ever could. The hospital defeats cholera, extends life-expectancy, heals and helps those in need.

The Victorians had their problems: the Empire, horrific misogyny, paternalistic classism. But no one can say they didn't care.

I have never seen this student as focused as she was in that moment. She parted the clotted streets of Camden Town with precision that would make a Victorian surgeon weep. Straight through the crowd to the coffee shop with premade sandwiches and bottled drinks. She fired off a prescription: Protein. Fruit. Hydration. Rang it up. Back to the streets, back through the crowd.

The liberal protagonists of Besant's novels present an argument that can feel naïve. The city is sprawling, an often indomitable mass too large to get hands or heads around. The system is broken.

But, as Valentine rebukes her brother, 'Go away and rail at Competition, while we look after its victims.'

If we care hard enough about each individual person, the liberals argue, we might not fix the system – but we will fix that person, if only for a while. And if we all care, and all help, maybe the city can fix itself.

Is it naïve? Maybe. Is it optimistic? Perhaps. Beautiful? Absolutely.

We find him. He's trying on a pair of shoes someone had thrown out. I look away. It feels like a violation of his privacy to watch – a violation of a concept completely unavailable to him. He finishes, slumps back down against the lamppost. She gives him the food. We walk away.

On the way to Primrose Hill that evening, we felt Valentine's frustration. After three weeks of watching institutions grow, of thinking about how to leverage power for those in need, all the Foucault felt a little silly in the face of a suffering body. What was the answer? Could we feel the anguish – and what could we do about it? Marx felt too mechanical, Arnold too abstract, Mill too philosophical, Dickens too idealistic. The surface was difficult to spot beneath all the theory.

Surface reading is not subtractive; it is additive. There is incredible power and value in traditional critique – power I have tried to mobilise when appropriate throughout this book. But there is also a risk, a profound risk, that in the rush to unpack and unfold, we bury the surface.

Associationists call for us to attend to surfaces. We should look for bodies, for feelings, for sensations, and do the difficult work of sitting with them and acknowledging without interpreting.

Did we solve the NHS crisis or save global capitalism's countless victims that day? No. Did we help that man find housing, a sustainable source of sustenance? No. But the impulse, Besant might argue, is the foundation that can lead to actual improvement: to see bodies, to keep sight of the surfaces behind theory and institutions.

Bibliography

Ablow, Rachel (2014), 'Harriet Martineau and the Impersonality of Pain', *Victorian Studies*, 56.4, pp. 675–97.
Ablow, Rachel (2017), *Victorian Pain*, Princeton: Princeton University Press.
'Advertisement' (1850), *The Athenaeum*, 17 August, p. 859.
'Advertisement' (1855), *Literary Gazette*, 17 February, pp. 97–8.
'Advertisement for Chapman and Hall *Great Expectations*' (1861), *All the Year Round*, 5.117, p. 408.
'Advertisement for *Great Expectations*' (1860), *All the Year Round*, 4.79, p. 72.
Ahmed, Sara (2010), *The Promise of Happiness*, Durham, NC: Duke University Press.
Allen, Garland E. (2005), 'Mechanism, Vitalism and Organicism in Late Nineteenth and Twentieth-Century Biology: The Importance of Historical Context', *Studies in History and Philosophy of Biological and Biomedical Sciences*, 36, pp. 261–83.
Altick, Richard Daniel (1957), *The English Common Reader: A Social History of the Mass Reading Public, 1800–1900*, Chicago: University of Chicago Press.
Anderson, Amanda (2001), *The Powers of Distance: Cosmopolitanism and the Cultivation of Detachment*, Princeton: Princeton University Press.
Anderson, Amanda, and Joseph Valente (eds) (2002), *Disciplinarity at the Fin de Siècle*, Princeton: Princeton University Press.
'Arabella at the Sales' (1886), *The Argosy*, 42, pp. 205–10.
Armstrong, Isobel (2008), *Victorian Glassworlds: Glass Culture and the Imagination 1830–1880*, Oxford: Oxford University Press.
Armstrong, Nancy (1987), *Desire and Domestic Fiction: A Political History of the Novel*, Oxford: Oxford University Press.
Arnold, Matthew (1864a), 'The Function of Criticism at the Present Time', *The National Review*, pp. 230–51.
Arnold, Matthew (1864b), 'The Literary Influence of Academies', *Cornhill Magazine*, 10, pp. 154–72.

Arnold, Matthew (1869), *Culture and Anarchy: An Essay in Political and Social Criticism*, London: Smith, Elder, & Co.

Arnold, Matthew (1880), 'Introduction', in Thomas Humphry Ward (ed.), *The English Poets, Selections*, London: Macmillan & Company, pp. xvii–xlvii.

Austin, Alfred (1870a), 'Our Novels: The Fast School', *Temple Bar*, 29, pp. 177–94.

Austin, Alfred (1870b), 'Our Novels: The Sensational School', *Temple Bar*, 29, pp. 410–24.

Bain, Alexander (1855), *The Senses and the Intellect*, London: John W. Parker and Son.

Bain, Alexander (1861), *On the Study of Character: Including an Estimate of Phrenology*, London: Parker, Son, and Bourn.

Bain, Alexander (1864), *The Senses and the Intellect*, 2nd edn, London: Longman, Green, Longman, Roberts, and Green.

Bain, Alexander (1868), *The Senses and the Intellect*, 3rd edn, London: Longmans, Green, and Co.

Bain, Alexander (1887), 'On "Association" – Controversies', *Mind*, 12.46, pp. 161–82.

Bain, Alexander (1889), *Logic*, London: D. Appleton and Company.

Beatty, Arthur (1922), *William Wordsworth: His Doctrine and Art*, Madison: University of Wisconsin.

Bentham, Jeremy (1827), *Rationale of Judicial Evidence: Specially Applied to English Practice*, London: Hunt and Clarke.

Bentley, Richard (1693), 'Letter, 18 Feb 1693', *The Newton Project*, <http://www.newtonproject.ox.ac.uk/view/texts/normalized/THEM00257> (last accessed 29 September 2021).

Besant, Walter (1871), 'The Value of Fiction', *Belgravia*, 16, pp. 48–51.

Besant, Walter (1882), *All Sorts and Conditions of Men: An Impossible Story*, 3 vols, London: Chatto & Windus.

Besant, Walter (1883), 'All in a Garden Fair: "Chapter XVI: The Emancipation of Hector"', *Good Words*, 24, pp. 277–94.

Besant, Walter (1886), *Children of Gibeon*, 3 vols, London: Chatto & Windus.

Besant, Walter (1902), *Autobiography of Sir Walter Besant*, London: Hutchinson & Co.

Best, Stephen, and Sharon Marcus (2009), 'Surface Reading: An Introduction', *Representations*, 108.1, pp. 1–21.

Best, William Mawdesley (1844), *A Treatise on Presumptions of Law and Fact, with the Theory and Rules of Presumptive or Circumstantial Proof in Criminal Cases*, London: S. Sweet.

Blumberg, Ilana (2016), 'Collins's Moonstone: The Victorian Novel as Sacrifice, Theft, Gift and Debt', *Studies in the Novel*, 37.2, pp. 162–86.

Bourdieu, Pierre (1977), *Outline of a Theory of Practice*, Cambridge: Cambridge University Press.

Braddon, Mary Elizabeth (1861a), 'Chapter VII: After a Year', *Robin Goodfellow*, 1.5, pp. 121–5.

Braddon, Mary Elizabeth (1861b), 'Chapter VIII: Before the Storm', *Robin Goodfellow*, 1.6, pp. 145–9.

Braddon, Mary Elizabeth (1861c), 'Chapter IX: After the Storm', *Robin Goodfellow*, 1.7, pp. 177–81.

Braddon, Mary Elizabeth (1862a), 'Chapter XIII: Troubled Dreams', *The Sixpenny Magazine*, 3.11, pp. 65–80.

Braddon, Mary Elizabeth (1862b), *Lady Audley's Secret*, 3 vols, London: Tinsley Bros.

Braddon, Mary Elizabeth (1974a), 'Letter No. 1 D/EK C12/119. December 1862', Robert Lee Wolff (ed.), *Harvard Library Bulletin*, 22.1, pp. 10–11.

Braddon, Mary Elizabeth (1974b), 'Letter No. 3 D/EK C12/122. Monday, 13 April 1863', Robert Lee Wolff (ed.), *Harvard Library Bulletin*, 22.1, pp. 12–13.

Braddon, Mary Elizabeth (1974c), 'Letter No. 4 D/EK C12/124. May 1863', Robert Lee Wolff (ed.), *Harvard Library Bulletin*, 22.1, pp. 13–14.

Brand, Dana (1991), *The Spectator and the City in Nineteenth-Century American Literature*, New York: Cambridge University Press.

Brantlinger, Patrick (1982), 'What Is "Sensational" about the "Sensation Novel"?', *Nineteenth-Century Fiction*, 37.1, pp. 1–28.

Brantlinger, Patrick (1988), *Rule of Darkness: British Literature and Imperialism, 1830–1914*, Ithaca: Cornell University Press.

Brantlinger, Patrick (1996), *Fictions of State: Culture and Credit in Britain, 1694–1994*, Ithaca: Cornell University Press.

Brantlinger, Patrick (1998), *The Reading Lesson: The Threat of Mass Literacy in Nineteenth-Century British Fiction*, Bloomington: Indiana University Press.

Braun, Heather L. (2009), 'Idle Vampires and Decadent Maidens: Sensation, the Supernatural, and Mary E. Braddon's Disappointing *Femmes Fatales*', in Tamara S. Wagner (ed.), *Antifeminism and the Victorian Novel: Rereading Nineteenth-Century Women Writers*, Amherst, NY: Cambria Press, pp. 235–54.

Braun, Marta (1984), 'Muybridge's Scientific Fictions', *Studies in Visual Communication*, 10.3, pp. 2–21.

Breslow, Julian (1997), 'The Narrator in Sketches by Boz', *ELH*, 44.1, pp. 127–49.

Briganti, Chiara (1991), 'Gothic Maidens and Sensation Women: Lady Audley's Journey from the Ruined Mansion to the Madhouse', *Victorian Literature and Culture*, 19, pp. 189–211.

Brooks, Cleanth, and Robert Penn Warren (1938), *Understanding Poetry; an Anthology for College Students*, New York: H. Holt and Co.

Brown, Homer O. (1971), 'The Displaced Self in the Novels of Daniel Defoe', *ELH*, 38.4, pp. 562–90.

Buchwald, Jed Z. (1989), *The Rise of the Wave Theory of Light: Optical Theory and Experiment in the Early Nineteenth Century*, Chicago: University of Chicago Press.

Buckle, Stephen (2007), 'Hume's Sceptical Materialism', *Philosophy*, 82, pp. 553–78.

Byrd, Max (1976), '"Reading" in *Great Expectations*', *PMLA*, 19.2, pp. 259–65.

Carlyle, Thomas (1831), *Sartor Resartus: The Life and Opinions of Herr Teufelsdröckh*, London: Chapman and Hall.

Carpenter, William Benjamin [1842] (1853), *Principles of Human Physiology with Their Chief Applications to Psychology, Pathology, Therapeutics, Hygiène, and Forensic Medicine*, 4th edn, London: John Churchill.

Carpenter, William Benjamin (1871), 'The Physiology of the Will', *Contemporary Review*, 17, pp. 192–217.

Carpenter, William Benjamin (1872), 'On the Hereditary Transmission of Acquired Physical Habits', *Contemporary Review*, 21, pp. 295–314.

Carpenter, William Benjamin (1874), 'On the Doctrine of Human Automatism', *Contemporary Review*, 25, pp. 397–416.

Carpenter, William Benjamin [1874] (1876), *Principles of Mental Physiology with Their Applications to the Training and Discipline of the Mind, and the Study of Its Morbid Conditions*, 4th edn, London: H. S. King & Co.

Casey, Ellen Miller (1984), '"Other People's Prudery": Mary Elizabeth Braddon', in Don Richard Cox (ed.), *Sexuality and Victorian Literature*, Knoxville: University of Tennessee Press, pp. 72–82.

'Cast Skins' (1877), *London Reader*, 29.754, pp. 570–1.

Caufield, James Walter (2012), *Overcoming Matthew Arnold: Ethics in Culture and Criticism*, New York: Routledge.

Cavell, Stanley [1958] (2002), *Must We Mean What We Say?*, 2nd edn, Cambridge: Cambridge University Press.

Cavell, Stanley [1987] (2003), *Disowning Knowledge: In Seven Plays of Shakespeare*, 2nd edn, Cambridge: Cambridge University Press.

Clark, J. W. (1866), 'Editor's Preface', in Daniel Defoe, *Robinson Crusoe*, ed. J. W. Clark, London: Macmillan and Company.

Cohen, William A. (1993), 'Manual Conduct in *Great Expectations*', *ELH*, 60.1, pp. 217–59.

Cohen, William A. (2009), *Embodied: Victorian Literature and the Senses*, Minneapolis: University of Minnesota Press.

Cohn, Elisha (2016), *Still Life: Suspended Development in the Victorian Novel*, Oxford: Oxford University Press.
Collini, Stefan (1991), *Public Moralists*, Oxford: Oxford University Press.
Collins, Wilkie (1858), 'The Unknown Public', *Household Words*, 18.439, pp. 217–22.
Collins, Wilkie (1868a), 'The Moonstone: Prologue, Chapters 1–3', *All the Year Round*, 19.454, pp. 73–80.
Collins, Wilkie (1868b), 'The Moonstone: Chapters 4–5', *All the Year Round*, 19.455, pp. 97–103.
Collins, Wilkie (1868c), 'The Moonstone: Chapters 6–7', *All the Year Round*, 19.456, pp. 121–7.
Collins, Wilkie (1868d), 'The Moonstone: Chapters 11–12', *All the Year Round*, 19.460, pp. 217–23.
Collins, Wilkie (1868e), 'The Moonstone: Chapters 13–14', *All the Year Round*, 19.461, pp. 241–6.
Collins, Wilkie (1868f), 'The Moonstone: Second Period; Chapters 3–4', *All the Year Round*, 19.469, pp. 433–9.
Collins, Wilkie (1868g), 'The Moonstone: Second Period; Second Narrative – Chapter 3 and Third Narrative – Chapter 1', *All the Year Round*, 19.474, pp. 553–9.
Collins, Wilkie (1868h), 'The Moonstone: Second Period; Third Narrative – Chapters 2–3', *All the Year Round*, 19.475, pp. 577–83.
Collins, Wilkie (1868i), 'The Moonstone: Second Period; Third Narrative – Chapter 4', *All the Year Round*, 19.476, pp. 601–6.
Collins, Wilkie (1868j), 'The Moonstone: Second Period; Third Narrative – Chapters 5–6', *All the Year Round*, 20.477, pp. 1–8.
Collins, Wilkie (1868k), 'The Moonstone: Second Period; Third Narrative – Chapter 9', *All the Year Round*, 20.480, pp. 73–9.
Collins, Wilkie (1868l), 'The Moonstone: Second Period; Third Narrative – Chapter 10', *All the Year Round*, 20.481, pp. 97–103.
Collins, Wilkie (1868m), 'The Moonstone: Second Period; Fifth Narrative', *All the Year Round*, 20.484, pp. 169–76.
Collins, Wilkie (1868n), 'The Moonstone: Second Period; Sixth Narrative, Seventh Narrative, Eighth Narrative, Epilogue', *All the Year Round*, 20.485, pp. 193–201.
Collins, Wilkie (1868o), *The Moonstone*, vol. 1, London: Tinsley Brothers.
Colombetti, Giovanna (2014), *The Feeling Body*, Cambridge, MA: MIT Press.
Coombs, David Sweeney (2017), 'Does Grandcourt Exist? Description and Fictional Characters', *Victorian Studies*, 59.3, pp. 390–8.
Coombs, David Sweeney (2019), *Reading with the Senses in Victorian Literature and Science*, Charlottesville: University of Virginia Press.

Coplan, Amy, and Peter Goldie (eds) (2014), *Empathy: Philosophical and Psychological Perspectives*, Oxford: Oxford University Press.

Costa, Michael J. (1986), 'Hume's Argument for the Temporal Priority of Cause over Effect', *Analysis*, 46.2, pp. 89–92.

Court, Franklin E. (1992), *Institutionalizing English Literature: The Culture and Politics of Literary Study, 1750–1900*, Stanford: Stanford University Press.

Craig, Edward (2000), 'Hume on Causality: Projectivist *and* Realist?', in Rupert Read and Kenneth A. Richman (eds), *The New Hume Debate*, London: Routledge, pp. 113–21.

Craik, Dinah Mulock (1875), 'Benevolence – or Beneficence?', *Sermons out of Church*, London: Daldy, Isbister, & Co., pp. 139–70.

Curwen, John (1876), 'Music for the People and the Tonic Sol-Fa College', *Tonic Sol-fa Reporter*, pp. 8–14.

Curwen, J. Spencer (1882), *Memorials of John Curwen*, London: J. Curwen and Sons.

Cvetkovich, Ann (1992), *Mixed Feelings: Feminism, Mass Culture, and Victorian Sensationalism*, New Brunswick, NJ: Rutgers University Press.

Daly, Nicholas (2004), *Literature, Technology, and Modernity, 1860–2000*, Cambridge: Cambridge University Press.

Dames, Nicholas (2007), *The Physiology of the Novel: Reading, Neural Science, and the Form of Victorian Fiction*, Oxford: Oxford University Press.

Davis, Colin (2010), *Critical Excess: Overreading in Derrida, Deleuze, Levinas, Žižek and Cavell*, Stanford: Stanford University Press.

Defoe, Daniel (1719), *Robinson Crusoe*, London: W. Taylor.

Defoe, Daniel (1866), *Robinson Crusoe*, ed. J. W. Clark, London: Macmillan and Company.

Deleuze, Gilles, and Félix Guattari [1980] (2009), *A Thousand Plateaus*, trans. Brian Massumi, Minneapolis: University of Minnesota Press.

Deleuze, Gilles, and Claire Parnet [1977] (2007), *Dialogues II*, trans. Hugh Tomlinson and Barbara Habberjam, New York: Columbia University Press.

Dickens, Charles (1837), 'The Hospital Patient', in *Sketches by Boz*, 2nd edn, London: John Noon, pp. 132–42.

Dickens, Charles (1840), *Oliver Twist*, 2nd edn, London: Bentley.

Dickens, Charles (1860a), '*Great Expectations*: Chapters 1–2', *All the Year Round*, 4.84, pp. 169–74.

Dickens, Charles (1860b), '*Great Expectations*: Chapters 3–4', *All the Year Round*, 4.85, pp. 193–8.

Dickens, Charles (1860c), '*Great Expectations*: Chapter 5', *All the Year Round*, 4.86, pp. 217–21.

Dickens, Charles (1860d), 'Great Expectations: Chapters 6–7', All the Year Round, 4.87, pp. 241–5.

Dickens, Charles (1861a), 'Great Expectations: Chapters 16–17', All the Year Round, 4.93, pp. 385–90.

Dickens, Charles (1861b), 'Great Expectations: Chapter 18', All the Year Round, 4.94, pp. 409–14.

Dickens, Charles (1861c), 'Great Expectations: Chapter 22', All the Year Round, 4.97, pp. 481–6.

Dickens, Charles (1861d), 'Great Expectations: Chapters 43–44', All the Year Round, 5.110, pp. 217–21.

Dickens, Charles (1861e), 'Great Expectations: Chapters 51–52', All the Year Round, 5.114, pp. 313–18.

Dickens, Charles (1861f), 'Great Expectations: Chapter 57', All the Year Round, 5.118, pp. 409–13.

Dickens, Charles (1861g), 'Great Expectations: Chapters 58–59', All the Year Round, 5.119, pp. 433–7.

Downs, Jack M. (2015), 'David Masson, Belles Lettres, and a Victorian Theory of the Novel', Victorian Literature and Culture, 43, pp. 1–21.

Doyle, Brian (1989), English and Englishness, New York: Routledge.

Duncan, Ian (1994), 'The Moonstone, the Victorian Novel, and Imperialistic Panic', Modern Language Quarterly, 55.3, pp. 297–319.

Duncan, Ian (2019), Human Forms: The Novel in the Age of Evolution, Princeton: Princeton University Press.

Dutheil, Martine Hennard (1993), 'La Leçon de Lecture de Great Expectations', Études de Lettres, 3, pp. 105–19.

Dutheil, Martine Hennard (1996), 'Great Expectations as Reading Lesson', Dickens Quarterly, 13.3, 164–74.

Dvorak, Wilfred P. (1984), 'Dickens' Ambivalence as a Social Critic in the 1860s: Attitudes to Money in All The Year Round and The Uncommercial Traveller', The Dickensian, 80.2, pp. 89–104.

Eliot, George (1856), 'Silly Novels by Lady Novelists', Westminster Review, 66.130, pp. 442–61.

Eliot, George (1871), Middlemarch: A Study of Provincial Life, Edinburgh: William Blackwood and Sons.

'The Enigma Novel' (1861), The Spectator, 34.1748, p. 1,428.

Epstein, Hugh (2020), Hardy, Conrad and the Senses, Edinburgh: Edinburgh University Press.

Falzi, Sabina (2012), 'Indian Diamonds in Victorian Fiction', in Frauke Reitemeier (ed.), Strangers, Migrants, Exiles: Negotiating Identity in Literature, Göttingen: Universitätsverlag Göttingen, pp. 103–91.

Farina, Jonathan (2012), 'On David Masson's British Novelists and their Styles (1859) and the Establishment of Novels as an Object of

Academic Study', in Dino Franco Felluga (ed.), *Britain, Representation and Nineteenth-Century History*, <https://www.branchcollective.org/?ps_articles=jonathan-farina-on-david-massons-british-novelists-and-their-styles-1859-and-the-establishment-of-novels-as-an-object-of-academic-study> (last accessed 15 October 2021).

Felber, Lynette (2007), 'The Literary Portrait as Centerfold: Fetishism in Mary Elizabeth Braddon's *Lady Audley's Secret*', *Victorian Literature and Culture*, 35.2, pp. 471–88.

Felski, Rita (2015), *The Limits of Critique*, Chicago: University of Chicago Press.

Feltes, N. N. (1986), *Modes of Production of Victorian Novels*, Chicago: University of Chicago Press.

Flint, Kate (1993), *The Woman Reader, 1837–1914*, Oxford: Clarendon Press.

Fraser, Hilary, and Stephanie Green (2003), *Gender and the Victorian Periodical*, Cambridge: Cambridge University Press.

Freegood, Elaine (2006), *The Ideas in Things: Fugitive Meaning in the Victorian Novel*, Chicago: University of Chicago Press.

Gallagher, Catherine (1994), *Nobody's Story: The Vanishing Acts of Women Writers in the Marketplace, 1670–1820*, Berkeley: University of California Press.

Garratt, Peter (2010), *Victorian Empiricism: Self, Knowledge, and Reality in Ruskin, Bain, Lewes, Spencer, and George Eliot*, Madison, NJ: Fairleigh Dickinson University Press.

Gilbert, Pamela K. (2007), *The Citizen's Body: Desire, Health, and the Social in Victorian England*, Columbus: Ohio State University Press.

Gilbert, Pamela K. (2011), *A Companion to Sensation Fiction*, Hoboken, NJ: Wiley.

Gilbert, Sandra M., and Susan Gubar (1979), *The Madwoman in the Attic: The Woman Writer and the Nineteenth-Century Literary Imagination*, New Haven: Yale University Press.

Golden, Catherine (2003), *Images of the Woman Reader in Victorian British and American Fiction*, Gainesville: University Press of Florida.

Gould, Marty (2012), *Nineteenth-Century Theatre and the Imperial Encounter*, New York: Routledge.

Graff, Gerald (1989), *Professing Literature: An Institutional History*, Chicago: University of Chicago Press.

Gregson, Samuel (1854), *Indian Fibres. A Letter to . . . Sir C. Wood, Etc. (Appendix. Extracts from the Transactions of the Society of Arts, Etc.)*, London: Smith, Elder, & Co.

Greiner, Rae (2011), 'Thinking of Me Thinking of You: Sympathy versus Empathy in the Realist Novel', *Victorian Studies*, 53.3, pp. 417–26.

Greiner, Rae (2012), *Sympathetic Realism in Nineteenth-Century British Fiction*, Baltimore: Johns Hopkins University Press.

Hack, Daniel (2005), *The Material Interests of the Victorian Novel*, Charlottesville: University of Virginia Press.

Haddan, Thomas Henry (1855), *The Limited Liability Act, 1855 with Precedents of a Deed of Settlement, for Constituting a Company with Limited Liability under the Act*, London: W. Maxwell.

Hadley, Elaine (2010), *Living Liberalism: Practical Citizenship in Mid-Victorian Britain*, Chicago: University of Chicago Press.

Haldane, John (1898), 'Vitalism', *The Nineteenth Century*, 44, pp. 400–13.

Hales, J. W. (1867), 'The Teaching of English', in Frederic William Farrar (ed.), *Essays on a Liberal Education*, London: Macmillan & Company, pp. 293–312.

Hall, Marshall (1833), 'On the Reflex Function of the Medulla Oblongata and Medulla Spinalis', *Philosophical Transactions of the Royal Society of London*, 123, pp. 635–65.

Harris, Ron (2000), *Industrializing English Law: Entrepreneurship and Business Organization, 1720–1844*, Cambridge: Cambridge University Press.

Hartley, David (1749), *Observations on Man: His Frame, His Duty, and His Expectations, in Two Parts*, London: S. Richardson.

Haugtvedt, Erica (2016), 'The Sympathy of Suspense: Gaskell and Braddon's Slow and Fast Sensation Fiction in Family Magazines', *Victorian Periodicals Review*, 49.1, pp. 149–70.

Haugtvedt, Erica (2017), 'The Victorian Serial Novel and Transfictional Character', *Victorian Studies*, 59.3, pp. 409–18.

Haweis, H. R. (1870a), 'Music and Emotion', *The Contemporary Review*, 15, pp. 363–82.

Haweis, H. R. (1870b), 'Music and Morals: Part II', *The Contemporary Review*, 16, pp. 280–97.

Haweis, H. R. (1871), 'Music and Morals: Part III', *The Contemporary Review*, 17, pp. 491–508.

Hayden, John (1984), 'Wordsworth, Hartley, and the Revisionists', *Studies in Philology*, 81.1, pp. 94–118.

Hearn, Jonathan (2016), 'Once More with Feeling: The Scottish Enlightenment, Sympathy, and Social Welfare', *Ethics and Social Welfare*, 10.3, pp. 211–23.

Hedgecock, Jennifer (2008), *The Femme Fatale in Victorian Literature: The Danger and the Sexual Threat*, Amherst: Cambria Press.

Heidler, Joseph B. (1928), *The History, from 1700 to 1800, of English Criticism of Prose Fiction*, Urbana: University of Illinois Press.

Hoffman, Martin L. (2001), *Empathy and Moral Development: Implications for Caring and Justice*, Cambridge: Cambridge University Press.

Holland, Norman N. (2009), *Literature and the Brain*, Gainesville: The PsyArt Foundation.

Holway, Tatiana M. (1992), 'The Game of Speculation: Economics and Representation', *Dickens Quarterly*, 9.3, pp. 103–14.

Houston, Natalie M. (2003), 'A Note on the Text', in Mary Elizabeth Braddon, *Lady Audley's Secret*, Peterborough, ON: Broadview Press, pp. 32–6.

Huehls, Mitchum (2010), 'Structures of Feeling: Or, How to Do Things (or Not) with Books', *Contemporary Literature*, 51.2, pp. 419–28.

Hughes, Linda K., and Michael Lund (1991), *The Victorian Serial*, Charlottesville: University Press of Virginia.

Hughes, Winifred (2014), *The Maniac in the Cellar: Sensation Novels of the 1860s*, Princeton: Princeton University Press.

Hume, David (1739), *A Treatise of Human Nature*, London: John Noon.

Hume, David [1748] (1777), *Enquiries Concerning the Human Understanding and Concerning the Principles of Morals*, 2nd edn, London: Clarendon Press.

Hunter, J. Paul (1966), *The Reluctant Pilgrim: Defoe's Emblematic Method and Quest for Form in Robinson Crusoe*, Baltimore: Johns Hopkins University Press.

Huxley, T. H. (1874), 'On the Hypothesis that Animals Are Automata, and Its History', *Fortnightly Review*, 16.95, pp. 555–80.

Jaffe, Audrey (2000), *Scenes of Sympathy: Identity and Representation in Victorian Fiction*, Ithaca: Cornell University Press.

Jaffe, Audrey (2010), *The Affective Life of the Average Man: The Victorian Novel and the Stock-Market Graph*, Columbus: Ohio State University Press.

Jaffe, Audrey (2016), *The Victorian Novel Dreams of the Real: Conventions and Ideology*, Oxford: Oxford University Press.

James, William (1884), 'What Is an Emotion?', *Mind*, 9.34, pp. 188–205.

Jarvie, Paul A. (2005), *Ready to Trample on All Human Law: Finance Capitalism in the Fiction of Charles Dickens*, New York: Routledge.

Jevons, W. Stanley (1878), 'Methods of Social Reform', *The Contemporary Review*, 33, pp. 498–513.

Jewsbury, Geraldine (1868), 'The Moonstone (Book Review)', *The Athenaeum*, p. 106.

Jones, Anna Maria (2007), *Problem Novels: Victorian Fiction Theorizes the Sensational Self*, Columbus: Ohio State University Press.

Jones, H. S. (2007), *Intellect and Character in Victorian England: Mark Pattison and the Invention of the Don*, Cambridge: Cambridge University Press.

Katz, Peter (2017), 'Redefining the Republic of Letters: The Literary Public and Mudie's Circulating Library', *Journal of Victorian Culture*, 22.3, pp. 399–417.

Kearns, Michael S. (1986), 'Associationism, the Heart, and the Life of the Mind in Dickens' Novels', *Dickens Studies*, 15, pp. 111–44.

Keen, Suzanne (2007), *Empathy and the Novel*, Oxford: Oxford University Press.
Kidd, David Comer, and Emanuele Castano (2013), 'Reading Literary Fiction Improves Theory of Mind', *Science*, 342.6156, pp. 377–80.
Kim, Benjamin (2013), *Wordsworth, Hemans, and Politics, 1800–1830: Romantic Crises*, Lewisburg, PA: Bucknell University Press.
Klaver, Claudia (1999), 'Natural Values and Unnatural Agents: Little Dorrit and the Mid-Victorian Crisis in Agency', *Dickens Studies Annual*, 28, pp. 13–43.
Kortsch, Christine Bayles (2009), *Dress Culture in Late Victorian Women's Fiction: Literacy, Textiles, and Activism*, New York: Routledge.
Landow, George (1971), *Aesthetic and Critical Theories of John Ruskin*, Princeton: Princeton University Press.
Langland, Elizabeth (2000), 'Enclosure Acts: Framing Women's Bodies in Braddon's *Lady Audley's Secret*', in Marlene Tromp, Pamela K. Gilbert and Aeron Haynie (eds), *Beyond Sensation: Mary Elizabeth Braddon in Context*, Albany: SUNY Press, pp. 3–16.
Langland, Elizabeth (2002), *Tell Tales: Essays on Gender and Narrative Form in Victorian Literature and Culture*, Columbus: Ohio State University Press.
Lanning, Katie (2012), 'Tessellating Texts: Reading *The Moonstone* in *All the Year Round*', *Victorian Periodicals Review*, 45.1, pp. 1–22.
Layard, George Somes (1888), 'How to Live on £700 a Year', *The Nineteenth Century*, 23.132, pp. 239–44.
Laycock, Thomas (1845), 'On the Reflex Function of the Brain', *British and Foreign Medical Journal*, 19, pp. 298–311.
Lemire, Beverly (1988), 'Consumerism in Preindustrial and Early Industrial England: The Trade in Secondhand Clothes', *Journal of British Studies*, 27.1, pp. 1–24.
Levine, Caroline (2003), *The Serious Pleasures of Suspense: Victorian Realism and Narrative Doubt*, Charlottesville: University of Virginia Press.
Levine, George (1992), *Darwin and the Novelists: Patterns of Science in Victorian Fiction*, Chicago: University of Chicago Press.
Levine, George (2002), *Dying to Know: Scientific Epistemology and Narrative in Victorian England*, Chicago: University of Chicago Press.
Levine, Philippa (2006), 'Sexuality and Empire', in Catherine Hall and Sonya O. Rose (eds), *At Home with the Empire: Metropolitan Culture and the Imperial World*, Cambridge: Cambridge University Press, pp. 122–42.
Lewes, G. H. (1877), *The Physical Basis of Mind*, London: Trübner & Co.
Lewes, G. H. (1891), *The Principles of Success in Literature*, London: Walter Scott, Ltd.

'Lewes's *Physical Basis of Mind* (Review)' (1877), *Saturday Review*, 43.9, pp. 706–8.

'Literary Dram-Drinking' (1888), *The Spectator*, 3183, pp. 13–14.

Locke, John [1689] (1849), *An Essay Concerning Human Understanding*, 13th edn, London: William Tegg & Co.

Lovell, Terry (1987), *Consuming Fiction*, New York: Verso.

Lynch, Deidre (1998), *The Economy of Character: Novels, Market Culture, and the Business of Inner Meaning*, Chicago: University of Chicago Press.

MacDonald, Tara (2019), 'Bodily Sympathy, Affect, and Victorian Sensation Fiction', in Stephen Ahern (ed.), *Affect Theory and Literary Critical Practice: A Feel for the Text*, New York: Palgrave Macmillan, pp. 121–38.

McGuire, Charles Edward (2009), *Music and Victorian Philanthropy: The Tonic Sol-Fa Movement*, Cambridge: Cambridge University Press.

McKeon, Michael (1987), *The Origins of the English Novel, 1600–1740*, Baltimore: Johns Hopkins University Press.

Macmichael, J. Holden (1906), *The Story of Charing Cross and Its Immediate Neighbourhood*, London: Chatto & Windus.

Maibom, Heidi L. (ed.) (2014), *Empathy and Morality*, Oxford: Oxford University Press.

Mangham, Andrew (2007), *Violent Women and Sensation Fiction: Crime, Medicine, and Victorian Popular Culture*, New York: Palgrave Macmillan.

Mansel, Henry Longueville (1863), 'Sensation Novels', *Quarterly Review*, 113, pp. 481–514.

Marshall, David (1988), *The Surprising Effects of Sympathy: Marivaux, Diderot, Rousseau, and Mary Shelley*, Chicago: University of Chicago Press.

Martineau, James [1860] (1866), 'Cerebral Psychology: Bain', in *Essays, Philosophical and Theological*, Boston: William V. Spencer, pp. 244–79.

Martineau, James (1885a), *Types of Ethical Theory*, vol. 1, London: Clarendon Press.

Martineau, James (1885b), *Types of Ethical Theory*, vol. 2, London: Clarendon Press.

Masson, David (1851a), 'Literature and the Labour Question', *North British Review*, 14.28, pp. 382–420.

Masson, David (1851b), 'Pendennis and Copperfield: Thackeray and Dickens', *North British Review*, 15.29, pp. 57–89.

Masson, David (1859), *British Novelists and Their Styles; Being a Critical Sketch of the History of British Prose Fiction*, London: Macmillan and Company.

Matus, Jill (1993), 'Disclosure as "Cover-up": The Discourse of Madness in *Lady Audley's Secret*', *University of Toronto Quarterly*, 62.3, pp. 334–55.

Maunder, Andrew, and Grace Moore (eds) [2004] (2016), *Victorian Crime, Madness and Sensation*, London: Routledge.

Mayhew, Henry (1861), *London Labour and the London Poor*, vol. 3, London: Griffin, Bohn, and Company.

Mayor, John (1855), 'Latin-English Lexicography', *The Journal of Classical and Sacred Philology*, 2.6, pp. 271–90.

Mehta, Jaya (1995), 'English Romance; Indian Violence', *Centennial Review*, 39.3, pp. 611–58.

Metzger, Bruce M. (2004), 'Sortes Biblicae', in Bruce M. Metzger and Michael D. Coogan (eds), *The Oxford Companion to the Bible*, Oxford: Oxford University Press, p. 713.

Mill, James [1829] (1869), *Analysis of the Phenomena of the Human Mind*, ed. John Stuart Mill, London: Longman, Green, Reader and Dyer.

Mill, John Stuart (1833), 'What Is Poetry?', *Monthly Repository*.

Mill, John Stuart [1873] (1874), *Autobiography*, New York: Henry Holt and Company.

Miller, Andrew (1995), *Novels Behind Glass: Commodity Culture and Victorian Narrative*, Cambridge: Cambridge University Press.

Miller, Andrew (2008), *The Burdens of Perfection: On Ethics and Reading in Nineteenth-Century British Literature*, Ithaca: Cornell University Press.

Miller, D. A. (1986), '*Cage aux folles*: Sensation and Gender in Wilkie Collins's *The Woman in White*', *Representations*, 14, pp. 107–36.

Miller, D. A. (1988), *The Novel and the Police*, Berkeley: University of California Press.

Millican, Peter (2010), 'Hume's Determinism', *Canadian Journal of Philosophy*, 40.4, pp. 611–42.

Minney, R. J. (1967), *The Two Pillars of Charing Cross: The Story of a Famous Hospital*, London: Cassell.

Mintz, Alan L. (1978), *George Eliot and the Novel of Vocation*, Cambridge, MA: Harvard University Press.

Mitch, David (2004), 'Education and Skill of the British Labour Force', in Roderick Floud and Paul Johnson (eds), *The Cambridge Economic History of Modern Britain: Industrialisation, 1700–1860*, vol. 1, Cambridge: Cambridge University Press, pp. 332–56.

Mitchell, Rebecca N. (2011), *Victorian Lessons in Empathy and Difference*, Columbus: Ohio State University Press.

Mitchell, Sally (1981), *The Fallen Angel: Chastity, Class, and Women's Reading, 1835–1880*, Bowling Green, OH: Bowling Green University Popular Press.

Mivart, St. George (1887), 'Hermann Lotze and the Mechanical Philosophy', *Fortnightly Review*, 42.251, pp. 696–702.

M. M. (1860), 'Novels of the Day: Their Writers and Readers', *Fraser's Magazine for Town and Country, 1830–1869*, 62.368, pp. 205–17.

Mondal, Sharleen (2009), 'Racing Desire and the New Man of the House in Wilkie Collins's *The Moonstone*', *Nineteenth-Century Gender Studies*, 5.1, <http://www.ncgsjournal.com/issue51/mondal.html> (last accessed 15 October 2021).

'The Moonstone (Book Review)' (1868), *Lippincott's Monthly Magazine*, 2, pp. 679–80.

'The Moonstone (Book Review)' (1868), *The Spectator*, 41.2091, pp. 881–2.

Morgan, Benjamin (2017), *The Outward Mind: Materialist Aesthetics in Victorian Science and Literature*, Chicago: Chicago University Press.

Moses, Omri (2014), *Out of Character: Modernism, Vitalism, Psychic Life*, Stanford: Stanford University Press.

Mosselmans, Ben (2007), *William Stanley Jevons and the Cutting Edge of Economics*, London: Routledge.

'Mudie's Library' (1860), *Saturday Review*, 10.262, p. 550.

Müller, F. Max [1866] (1877), *Lectures on the Science of Language*, 9th edn, vol. 2, London: Longmans, Green, and Co.

Murfin, Ross C. (1982), 'The Art of Representation: Collins' *The Moonstone* and Dickens' Example', *ELH*, 49.3, pp. 653–72.

Murphy, Margueritte (2006), 'The Ethic of the Gift in George Eliot's *Daniel Deronda*', *Victorian Literature and Culture*, 34, pp. 189–207.

'Music for the People' (1881), *The Musical Times and Singing Class Circular*, 22.463, pp. 456–9.

'Natural Science at Cambridge University' (1884), *The Times*, 2 December, p. 10.

'The New Sensation Drama' (1861), *The Spectator*, 1743, p. 16.

Newton, Isaac [1693] (1959), *The Correspondence of Isaac Newton*, ed. H. W. Turnbull, New York: Cambridge University Press.

Nuttall, A. D. (2003), *Dead from the Waist Down: Scholars and Scholarship in Literature and the Popular Imagination*, New Haven: Yale University Press.

'The Old Clothes Exchange' (1882), *Illustrated London News*, 66.229, p. 66.

'Old Clothes and What Becomes of Them' (1865), *The Leisure Hour*, 690, pp. 172–4.

'Old Clothesmen' (1880), *Saturday Review*, 50.1293, pp. 170–1.

Oliphant, Margaret (1862), 'Sensation Novels', *Blackwood's Edinburgh Magazine*, 91.559, pp. 564–80.

Olmsted, John Charles (ed.) [1979] (2016), *A Victorian Art of Fiction: Essays on the Novel in British Periodicals*, New York: Routledge.

Palmer, Beth, and Adelene Buckland (2011), *A Return to the Common Reader: Print Culture and the Novel, 1850–1900*, London: Ashgate.

Palmer, David John (1965), *The Rise of English Studies: An Account of the Study of the English Language and Literature from Its Origins to the Making of the Oxford English School*, Oxford: Oxford University Press.

Pater, Walter (1888), *The Renaissance: Studies in Art and Poetry*, London: Macmillan and Company.

Patten, Robert L. (2012), *Charles Dickens and 'Boz': The Birth of the Industrial-Age Author*, Cambridge: Cambridge University Press.

Patten, Simon Nelson (1885), *The Premises of Political Economy: Being a Re-Examination of Certain Fundamental Principles of Economic Science*, Philadelphia: J. B. Lippincott.

Pattison, Mark (1876), 'Philosophy at Oxford', *Mind*, 1, pp. 82–97.

Pattison, Mark (1877), 'Books and Critics', *Fortnightly Review*, 22.131, pp. 659–79.

Paul, Annie Murphy (2013), 'Reading Literature Makes Us Smarter and Nicer', *Time*, 3 June, <https://ideas.time.com/2013/06/03/why-we-should-read-literature> (last accessed 15 October 2021).

Phillips, Richard (1997), *Mapping Men and Empire: A Geography of Adventure*, New York: Psychology Press.

Phillips, Walter C. (1919), *Dickens, Reade, and Collins: Sensation Novelists: A Study in the Conditions and Theories of Novel Writing in Victorian England*, New York: Columbia University Press.

'The Philosophy of Music' (1879), *The Musical Times and Singing Class Circular*, 20.438, pp. 418–23.

Pinch, Adela (1996), *Strange Fits of Passion: Epistemologies of Emotion, Hume to Austen*, Stanford: Stanford University Press.

Pinch, Adela (2010), *Thinking about Other People in Nineteenth-Century British Writing*, Cambridge: Cambridge University Press.

Poovey, Mary (2008), *Genres of the Credit Economy: Mediating Value in Eighteenth- and Nineteenth-Century Britain*, Chicago: University of Chicago Press.

Pratt, John Clark, and Victor A. Neufeldt (1979), *George Eliot's Middlemarch Notebooks: A Transcription*, Berkeley: University of California Press.

Price, Leah (2013), *How to Do Things with Books in Victorian Britain*, Princeton: Princeton University Press.

Proudman, J. (1875), 'Music's Mission', *Tonic Sol-fa Reporter*, pp. 331–3.

Pullin, Nicola (2005), '"A Heavy Bill to Settle with Humanity": The Representation and Invisibility of London's Principal Milliners and Dressmakers', in Beth Harris (ed.), *Famine and Fashion: Needlewomen in the Nineteenth Century*, New York: Routledge, pp. 215–28.

Pykett, Lyn (1992), *The 'Improper' Feminine: The Women's Sensation Novel and the New Woman Writing*, New York: Routledge.

Pykett, Lyn (2011), *The Nineteenth-Century Sensation Novel*, 2nd edn, Northcote: British Council.

Rancière [2006] (2011), *The Politics of Literature*, trans. Julie Rose, Cambridge: Polity Press.

Rappoport, Jill (2012), *Giving Women: Alliance and Exchange in Victorian Culture*, Oxford: Oxford University Press.

Rauch, Alan (2001), *Useful Knowledge: The Victorians, Morality, and the March of Intellect*, Durham, NC: Duke University Press.

Reed, Edward S. (1998), *From Soul to Mind: The Emergence of Psychology, from Erasmus Darwin to William James*, New Haven: Yale University Press.

Reed, John R. (2006), 'The Riches of Redundancy: *Our Mutual Friend*', *Studies in the Novel*, 38.1, pp. 15–35.

Reid, Ian (2004), *Wordsworth and the Formation of English Studies*, London: Ashgate.

'Review: Sketches by "Boz"' (1836), *The Monthly Review*, 1.3, pp. 350–7.

Ricardo, David (1817), *On the Principles of Political Economy, and Taxation*, London: J. Murray.

Richards, I. A. (1924), *Principles of Literary Criticism*, New York: Harcourt, Brace & Company, Inc.

Richardson, Alan (2001), *British Romanticism and the Science of the Mind*, Cambridge: Cambridge University Press.

Roberts, Lewis (2006), 'Trafficking in Literary Authority: Mudie's Select Library and the Commodification of the Victorian Novel', *Victorian Literature and Culture*, 34.1, pp. 1–25.

'Robinson Crusoe. Edited after the Original Editions by J. W. Clark' (1866), *The Spectator*, 1,973, p. 22.

Robinson, F. Mabel (1887), 'Our Working Women and Their Earnings', *Fortnightly Review*, 42.247, pp. 50–63.

Robinson, Marilynne, and President Barack Obama (2015), 'President Obama and Marilynne Robinson: A Conversation—II', *The New York Review of Books*, 19 November, <https://www.nybooks.com/articles/2015/11/19/president-obama-marilynne-robinson-conversation-2> (last accessed 15 October 2021).

Rogers, Frederic (1875), 'Professor Huxley's Hypothesis that Animals Are Automata', *Contemporary Review*, 26, pp. 614–38.

Rose, Jonathan (1992), 'Rereading the English Common Reader: A Preface to a History of Audiences', *Journal of the History of Ideas*, 53.1, pp. 47–70.

Rose, Jonathan (2010), *The Intellectual Life of the British Working Classes*, 2nd edn, New Haven: Yale University Press.

Rudrum, David (2013), *Stanley Cavell and the Claim of Literature*, Baltimore: Johns Hopkins University Press.

Ruskin, John (1865), *Sesame and Lilies*, 2nd edn, London: Smith, Elder, & Co.

Ruskin, John (1888), *Modern Painters*, vol. 1, New York: Wiley and Sons.

Ryan, Vanessa (2012), *Thinking Without Thinking in the Victorian Novel*, Baltimore: Johns Hopkins University Press.

Sayre-McCord, Geoffrey (2013), 'Hume and Smith on Sympathy, Approbation, and Moral Judgment', *Social Philosophy and Policy*, 30.1–2, pp. 208–36.

Scarry, Elaine (1985), *The Body in Pain: The Making and Unmaking of the World*, Oxford: Oxford University Press.

Scarry, Elaine (1999), *Dreaming by the Book*, Princeton: Princeton University Press.

Schaefer, Donovan O. (2015), *Religious Affects: Animality, Evolution, and Power*, Durham, NC: Duke University Press.

Schaefer, Donovan O. (2019), *The Evolution of Affect Theory: The Humanities, the Sciences, and the Study of Power*, Cambridge: Cambridge University Press.

Scheer, Monique (2012), 'Are Emotions a Kind of Practice (and Is That What Makes Them Have a History)? A Bourdieuian Approach to Understanding Emotion', *History and Theory*, 51.2, pp. 193–220.

Schivelbusch, Wolfgang (1986), *The Railway Journey: The Industrialization of Time and Space in the Nineteenth Century*, Berkeley: University of California Press.

Schlicke, Paul (1999), *The Oxford Companion to Charles Dickens: Anniversary Edition*, Oxford: Oxford University Press.

Schroeder, Natalie (1988), 'Feminine Sensationalism, Eroticism, and Self-Assertion: M. E. Braddon and Ouida', *Tulsa Studies in Women's Literature*, 7.1, pp. 87–103.

Scott, Alexander John (1849), *On the Academical Study of a Vernacular Literature*, London: Taylor, Walton, and Maberly.

Sedgwick, Eve Kosofsky (1985), *Between Men: English Literature and Male Homosocial Desire*, New York: Columbia University Press.

Selbin, Jesse Cordes (2016), '"Read with Attention": John Cassell, John Ruskin, and the History of Close Reading', *Victorian Studies*, 58.3, pp. 493–521.

'SENSATION! A Satire' (1864), *Dublin University Magazine*, 63.373, pp. 85–9.

'Sensation Novels' (1863), *Medical Critic and Psychological Journal*, 3, pp. 513–19.

Shouse, Eric (2005), 'Feeling, Emotion, Affect', *M/C Journal*, 8.6.

Showalter, Elaine (2009), *A Literature of Their Own: British Women Novelists, from Brontë to Lessing*, Princeton: Princeton University Press.

'Sketches by Boz' (1836), *The Examiner*, 1465, pp. 132–3.

Smith, Adam (1759), *The Theory of Moral Sentiments*, London: A. Millar.

Smith, T. Southwood (1836), 'Medical Reform', *London and Westminster Review*, 4.1, pp. 58–92.

Solnit, Rebecca (2003), 'The Annihilation of Time and Space', *New England Review*, 24.1, pp. 5–19.

Stewart, Dugald (1792), *Elements of the Philosophy of the Human Mind*, London: A. Strahan and T. Cadell.

Stewart, Dugald (1802), *Elements of the Philosophy of the Human Mind*, 2nd edn, London: A. Strahan and T. Cadell.

Stewart, Garrett (1996), *Dear Reader: The Conscripted Audience in Nineteenth-Century British Fiction*, Baltimore: Johns Hopkins University Press.

Strathern, Marilyn (1990), *The Gender of the Gift: Problems with Women and Problems with Society in Melanesia*, Berkeley: University of California Press.

Stueber, Karsten (2010), *Rediscovering Empathy*, Cambridge, MA: MIT Press.

Sutherland, John (1998), 'Journalism, Scholarship, and the University College London English Department', in Jeremy Treglown and Bridget Bennett (eds), *Grub Street and the Ivory Tower*, London: Clarendon Press, pp. 58–71.

Sutherland, John (2013), *Victorian Novelists and Publishers*, London: Bloomsbury.

Taylor, Jacqueline (2015), *Reflecting Subjects: Passion, Sympathy, and Society in Hume's Philosophy*, Oxford: Oxford University Press.

Taylor, Jenny Bourne (2000), 'Fallacies of Memory in Nineteenth-Century Psychology: Henry Holland, William Carpenter and Frances Power Cobbe', *Victorian Review*, 26.1, pp. 98–118.

Thackeray, William Makepeace (1849), *Vanity Fair*, London: Bradbury and Evans.

Thomas, Ronald R. (1991), 'Minding the Body Politic: The Romance of Science and the Revision of History in Victorian Detective Fiction', *Victorian Literature and Culture*, 19, pp. 233–54.

Tomaiuolo, Saverio (2010), *In Lady Audley's Shadow: Mary Elizabeth Braddon and Victorian Literary Genres*, Edinburgh: Edinburgh University Press.

Tomkins, Silvan S. (1962), *Affect Imagery Consciousness: Volume I: The Positive Affects*, New York: Springer Publishing Company.

Tompkins, J. M. S. (1976), *The Popular Novel in England, 1770–1800*, Westport, CT: Greenwood Press.

Tromp, Marlene, Pamela K. Gilbert and Aeron Haynie (2000), 'Introduction', in Marlene Tromp, Pamela K. Gilbert and Aeron Haynie (eds),

Beyond Sensation: Mary Elizabeth Braddon in Context, Albany: SUNY Press, pp. xv–xxviii.

Vermeule, Blakey (2011), *Why Do We Care about Literary Characters?*, Baltimore: Johns Hopkins University Press.

Waal, Frans de (2009), *The Age of Empathy: Nature's Lessons for a Kinder Society*, New York: Broadway Books.

Wagner, Tamara (2008), 'Speculators at Home in the Victorian Novel: Making Stock-Market Villains and New Paper Fictions', *Victorian Literature and Culture*, 36.1, pp. 21–40.

Wagner, Tamara (2009), *Antifeminism and the Victorian Novel*, Amherst, NY: Cambria Press.

Wagner, Tamara (2010), *Financial Speculation in Victorian Fiction: Plotting Money and the Novel Genre, 1815–1901*, Columbus: Ohio State University Press.

Walsh, Marcus (1997), *Shakespeare, Milton, and Eighteenth-Century Literary Editing: The Beginnings of Interpretative Scholarship*, Cambridge: Cambridge University Press.

Ward, Mrs Humphry (1888), *Robert Elsmere*, Macmillan and Company.

Welsh, Alexander (1990), 'Burke and Bentham on the Narrative Potential of Circumstantial Evidence', *New Literary History*, 21.3, pp. 607–27.

Willey, Vicki Corkran (2006), 'Wilkie Collins's "Secret Dictate": *The Moonstone* as a Response to Imperialist Panic', in Kimberly Harrison and Richard Fantina (eds), *Victorian Sensations: Essays on a Scandalous Genre*, Columbus: Ohio State University Press, pp. 225–33.

Williams, Raymond (1978), *Marxism and Literature*, Oxford: Oxford University Press.

Wills, William (1838), *An Essay on the Rationale of Circumstantial Evidence: Illustrated by Numerous Cases*, London: Longman, Orme, Brown, Green, and Longmans.

Wilson, Catherine (2016), 'Hume and Vital Materialism', *British Journal for the History of Philosophy*, 24.5, pp. 1,002–21.

Wimsatt, W. K., Jr, and M. C. Beardsley (1949), 'The Affective Fallacy', *The Sewanee Review*, 57.1, pp. 31–55.

Winter, Alison (1997), 'The Construction of Orthodoxies and Heterodoxies in the Early Victorian Life Sciences', in Bernard Lightman (ed.), *Victorian Science in Context*, Chicago: University of Chicago Press, pp. 24–50.

Winter, Sarah (2011), *The Pleasures of Memory: Learning to Read with Charles Dickens*, New York: Fordham University Press.

Wordsworth, Charles Favell Forth (1859), *The New Joint Stock Company Law (of 1856, 1857, and 1858) with All the Statutes, and Instructions How to Form a Company: And Herein of the Liabilities of Persons Engaged in So Doing*, London: Shaw and Sons.

Wordsworth, William, and Samuel Taylor Coleridge (1800), *Lyrical Ballads, with Other Poems*, 2 vols, London: Longman.

Wordsworth, William, and Samuel Taylor Coleridge (1802), *Lyrical Ballads: With Pastoral and Other Poems*, 2 vols, London: Longman.

Wright, John P. (2000), 'Hume's Causal Realism: Recovering a Traditional Interpretation', in Rupert Read and Kenneth A. Richman (eds), *The New Hume Debate*, London: Routledge, pp. 88–99.

Wynne, Deborah (2001), *The Sensation Novel and the Victorian Family Magazine*, New York: Palgrave.

'Youth as Depicted in Modern Fiction' (1866), *The Christian Remembrancer; Or, The Churchman's Biblical, Ecclesiastical and Literary Miscellany*, 52, London: John and Charles Mozley, pp. 184–211.

Z (1860), 'Mr. Mudie's Monopoly', *Literary Gazette*, p. 285.

Zunshine, Lisa (2006), *Why We Read Fiction: Theory of Mind and the Novel*, Columbus: Ohio State University Press.

Index

Ablow, Rachel, 39, 149
acknowledging (vs knowing), 30, 70–1, 81, 89, 96, 100, 102, 105, 108, 109–11, 120, 127, 151–2, 161–2, 170, 179, 183, 187–8, 191–2, 193–4, 200, 204, 206, 210, 212–13, 213–15
acquired habitudes of thought, 123–4, 125–7, 131, 138, 145, 149, 151, 215; *see also* habit
affect
  and acknowledgement, 70, 96, 100–1, 108, 153, 192, 200
  and Associationism, 4, 15, 50, 54, 119
  and biology, 5, 30n, 60, 62
  and character, 56, 67, 87, 100–1, 119, 145
  Deleuze vs Tomkins, 5
  and embodiment, 4–5, 30n, 35, 41, 50, 55, 60, 62, 96, 119, 145, 147, 153, 192
  and empathy, 55, 56, 62, 67, 70, 78–80, 108, 120
  and habits, 1, 7, 7n
  and language, 4–5, 35, 41, 44–6, 55, 147
  and literary studies/authority, 3, 4–7, 32–4, 41, 54, 70, 119, 153
  and materiality, 5, 87
  and representation, 4, 67, 87, 119, 153
  and surface, 6–7, 78–80, 89
  see also pain, phenomenology
affective gravity, 63, 89, 145, 188, 192, 198, 200
Ahmed, Sara, 5
All Sorts and Conditions of Men, 191, 193, 207
Anderson, Amanda, 10n, 55, 77
Arnold, Matthew, 7, 11–12, 12n, 42, 205, 215
Armstrong, Isobel, 66–8

Armstrong, Nancy, 153
Associationism
  defined, 2, 40, 97
  and embodiment, 2–3, 4, 28, 30, 34, 35–6, 41, 49–50, 58, 60, 68, 69, 80–1, 101, 102, 119–20, 142, 178
  and empathy, 14–17, 19, 30, 46–7, 49–50, 54–5, 58, 69, 70–2, 78–9, 80–3, 147–9, 179, 191
  and ethics, 3, 15–17, 19, 30, 49–50, 54–5, 58, 60, 72, 77, 101, 102, 108–11, 119–20, 121–2, 147–8, 178, 188, 191, 221
  flattened Associationism, 132, 137, 161–3, 179–80, 182, 185, 187–8
  and language, 2, 4, 5, 19, 28, 32–4, 35–7, 38, 41, 43–6, 49–50, 69, 119, 148, 160
  and liberalism, 14–15, 23–4, 54, 191
  and literary authority, 2–3, 5, 38, 30, 42, 43, 46–7, 49–50, 58, 71, 81–3, 101–2, 119–20
  and materialism/empiricism, 2–3, 14, 15, 17, 27–9, 32–3, 37–40, 43–6, 50, 58, 67–8, 69, 72, 73, 77–81, 87, 117–19, 121–2, 126, 160, 191
  and memory, 62, 73–7, 88–9, 120, 139, 160
  and music, 206
  and physiology/anatomy, 5, 14, 17, 19, 38, 121–2, 127, 150, 160
  and reading, 3, 5, 19, 30, 49–50, 55, 56, 58, 60, 70, 89, 101–2, 124, 151, 160, 206
  and temporality, 73–7, 88–9, 101
  see also chains, circumstantial evidence, dreaming, handwriting, imagination, impressions, memory, reading
Austin, Alfred, 91, 91n, 93, 119
automatism, 120–3, 141–3; *see also* mechanism

Bain, Alexander, 16, 43–7, 87–8, 97–8, 101, 125–6, 141, 160, 162, 183, 206
Beardsley, Monroe, 2
benevolence, 210, 212–13
Bentham, Jeremy, 14, 17, 180
Bentley, Richard, 27–8
Besant, Walter
   on *Children of Gibeon*, 191
   on fiction, 190
   on the East End, 191
Best, Stephen, 5–6, 54, 95
Best, William Mawdesley, 181, 182
bodies *see* embodiment
book as commodity, 135–6
Boz ("The Hospital Patient)
   as both character and narrator, 57, 58–60, 70–1, 74–5, 77
   history of, 55–6, 74, 76
Braddon, Mary Elizabeth
   on publishing, 175–6
   and Walter Besant, 190
Brantlinger, Patrick, 29n, 49n, 134n
Bulwer-Lytton, Edward, 175–6
Burke, Edmund, 180

Carpenter, William Benjamin, 120–4, 126–7, 141, 147–8, 150–1, 215
Casey, Ellen Miller, 177
Cavell, Stanley, 30, 30n, 161
character (ethical), 75, 77, 119–20, 124–7, 146–7
character (fictional)
   and affect, 99, 119
   and embodiment, 2, 7, 20, 31, 47–9, 54–6, 58, 58–60, 99, 118–19, 126, 145
   and empathy, 15, 45, 55–8, 60, 68, 149
   and interiority, 18, 92, 100–1, 108–9, 118–19, 124–5, 163, 167, 170
   and literary value, 2, 47–9, 73, 83, 92, 100–01, 119, 149
   and temporality, 76–7, 86–7
chains (associative), 67, 75, 77, 97–8, 103–4, 106–8, 110–11, 123, 132, 139, 148, 167, 179–80, 183, 184
circumstantial evidence, 179–83, 185
classics, 7, 9, 10, 12, 13, 42
Cohen, William 23, 50, 98n
Cohn, Elisha, 23, 55
Collins, Wilkie
   on character, 119, 124–5
   and popular readers, 7

Colombetti, Giovanna, 30n
coloniality, 129–30, 146, 146n
commodity fetishism, 133, 137
   of books, 132–3
common readers, 7–10, 19, 93–4
   and the academy, 12, 42
   as intellectuals, 9
conclusions, 171, 175, 177–8, 187–8
consciousness, 5, 16, 17, 35, 36–8, 44–6, 68, 73, 76, 78, 80, 83, 117–18, 121–3, 150–1
Coombs, David Sweeney, 15, 16, 29n
critics *see* scholars

Dames, Nicholas, 101
Deleuze, Gilles, 5, 6, 23
detachment *see* disinterestedness
detective, 127, 128, 140–2, 174, 185–6
   as narrator, 140
   see also mystery
Dickens, Charles
   as 'great literature', 19
   on Realism, 47–9
   and *Sketches by Boz*, 55–6, 74
   and serialisation, 100–2, 103
   and speculation, 100–1
Dickensian angel, 110–11, 154–5, 174, 179
disembodiment, 29–30, 30–4, 34n, 55, 101, 105, 128, 136, 138, 139–44, 198
disinterestedness, 17, 46, 47, 55, 77–8, 80, 102, 104, 139–40, 171, 203
Dissenters, 8–9
   and books, 131
dreaming, 183, 209
Duncan, Ian, 29n, 130, 130n
Dutheil, Martine Hennard, 86–7

East End, 191–2
education, 7, 9, 19, 42, 63–4, 93–4, 105, 107, 143–4, 152–3, 192–4, 201, 205, 207
Eliot, George, 138n
embodiment
   and Associationism, 4–5, 28, 30n, 35, 41, 50, 55, 60, 62, 96, 119, 145, 147, 153, 192
   and affect, 4, 23, 30n, 63, 86
   and character, 2, 20, 58–9, 86, 102, 119–20, 127, 145
   and emotion, 3, 14, 44–6, 70, 80, 87, 93, 102, 150, 163, 207
   and empathy, 14, 55, 61–2, 81, 141–2, 149, 151

embodiment (*cont.*)
    and ethics, 20, 50, 54, 90, 108, 185, 188, 203–10, 213–15
    and language, 2, 4, 28, 30, 32–3, 35–6, 47, 71, 86–7, 111, 148, 149, 160
    legibility of, 30, 55, 58, 89, 101, 126, 129, 141–2, 148–9, 151, 153–4, 160, 163, 165, 169, 178, 198–9
    and literary authority, 4, 9, 14, 30–4, 46–7, 70, 82–3, 120, 152, 173
    and materiality, 18–19, 36, 68, 73, 89, 120, 125, 128, 145, 187, 191, 197, 209–10
    and mechanism, 119, 125, 142–3
    and metaphor, 29, 97, 98, 105, 172, 200–1
    and power, 107, 154, 160
    and reading, 3, 20, 47, 86, 101, 102, 108, 143, 160
    and scholarship, 30–4, 34n, 47, 54–5, 136, 138, 139–44, 173, 198
    and sensation fiction, 90–6
    and surface, 5, 28, 29–30, 66–8, 78–81, 83, 154–5, 161–2, 163, 166, 183, 186–7, 191, 199, 200, 209, 210
    and temporality, 76, 87, 89–90, 99, 102
    and writing, 107
emotion
    and acknowledgement, 50, 103, 193–4, 200
    and embodiment, 3, 14, 44–6, 70, 80, 81, 87, 93, 102, 150, 163, 201, 205, 207, 209
    and empathy, 5, 46, 55, 62, 106–7, 145, 147–8, 187–8, 201, 205
    and gender, 146, 152–5, 164, 172, 174–5, 193–4, 204, 207
    and language, 40–1, 44–6, 164, 205–6
    and literary authority, 2, 3, 14, 15, 18, 19, 42, 70, 82–3, 96, 101, 109, 110, 120, 172
    and reading, 54–5, 79, 81, 96, 100, 101, 103, 143, 162, 172
    and science, 1–2, 3, 14, 19, 42–3, 63–4, 132, 188, 193, 201, 203, 207
    signs of, 163
empathy
    and affect, 55, 56, 62, 67, 70, 78–80, 108, 120
    and Associationism, 14–17, 19, 30, 46–7, 49–50, 54–5, 58, 69, 70–2, 78–9, 80–3, 147–9, 179, 191
    for characters, 2, 18, 46, 57, 58, 65, 68–70, 71–2, 82, 187–8, 190
    and embodiment, 14, 55, 61–2, 72, 81, 124, 141–2, 147, 148, 149, 151, 203, 213–15
    and emotion, 5, 46, 62, 187–8
    and ethics, 14–16, 17, 18–19, 30, 55, 58, 81–3, 124, 148, 151, 194, 200, 213–15
    and language, 46, 57, 79, 148–9
    and literary authority, 2, 4, 46, 54, 71, 82
    for living bodies, 2, 46–7, 58, 65, 82, 187–8, 190, 191, 194, 213–15
    opposed vs sympathy, 60–2
    and politics, 14–15, 18–19, 54–5, 58, 188, 190–1, 194, 200, 209, 213–15
    and reading, 18–19, 34, 45–6, 55, 72, 83, 101–2, 104, 132, 148, 149, 151, 164, 190, 204
    and self, 75, 78–81, 104, 147, 150
    and surface, 3, 78–81, 80, 187–8, 191–2, 200, 204, 210, 213–15
empiricism *see* materialism
ethics of care, 14–16, 29–30, 48–9, 57, 80–3, 121–2, 127, 149, 151, 188, 190, 192, 213–15
Epstein, Hugh, 23

feelings *see* emotion
Felski, Rita, 6
formal snares, 102–3, 108–9

gifts, 197, 201, 210–13
Gilbert, Sandra and Susan Gubar, 162
Golden, Catherine, 110–1, 154, 172
Greiner, Rae, 70

habit, 1, 7, 18, 40, 62n, 93, 105, 119–20, 122–4, 124–7, 131, 133, 138, 145, 149–51, 152, 207, 215; *see also* acquired habitudes of thought
Hadley, Elaine, 14
Haldane, John, 117
handwriting, 165, 181–2, 185; *see also* circumstantial evidence
Hartley, David, 29, 38–40, 43, 123
Haweis, Hugh, 205, 206
Hayward, Serjeant, 180
hermeneutics
    history of, 30–1
    of suspicion, 6, 19
    see also interpretation
History of the Book
    copyediting, 165
    publication history, 175–61, 184

homosocial triangle, 154
Hughes, Linda, 99
Hume, David, 36, 62, 75
Huxley, Thomas, 121

imagination, 29, 45–6, 57–9, 60, 61, 62, 65–6, 66–7, 70, 71, 72–3, 80, 82, 86–7, 88–9, 108, 120, 160, 184
impressions
   and associative chains, 132, 148, 179–80, 182
   and emotion, 49, 103
   and empathy, 70–1, 80, 104, 134, 143, 145, 204, 206
   and ethics, 50, 59, 102, 103, 125
   and language, 1, 3, 32, 35, 58, 44, 88
   and materiality, 36, 37, 40, 58, 59, 67, 70, 72, 73, 81, 89, 97–8, 123, 150–1
   and memory, 73, 75–6, 85, 88, 92–8, 102
   and reading, 58, 65, 143
India (in fiction), 130
interiority
   and character, 18, 92, 100–1, 108–9, 118–19, 124–5, 163, 167, 170
   and economics, 100–1
   and gender, 166–8
   interpretation of others', 80–1, 83, 96, 126, 127, 140–2, 147, 161, 163, 165–6, 170, 179, 181, 183, 184–5, 187, 201, 203
   and language, 164
interpretation
   ethics of, 29–30, 55, 80–1, 102, 104, 105–8, 110, 147, 149–50, 185, 187–200, 220–1
   and gender, 160, 163–6
   as knowledge, 2, 4, 5–6, 10, 14, 18–20, 29–30, 30–4, 55, 66, 80–1, 96, 97, 102, 104–5, 108–9, 125, 136, 143, 161, 163–6, 168, 171, 185, 187, 200, 213
   and literary studies, 4, 5–6, 10, 15–16, 18–19, 29–30, 70, 95
   and popular readers, 10, 19, 90, 99, 102
   and surface, 5–6, 29–30, 54–5, 95, 163, 168, 187–8, 200, 213
intuition, 50, 89, 102, 103, 108, 110, 130, 152, 153, 162, 172, 203, 207

Jaffe, Audrey, 47n
Jevons, William Stanely, 205, 207
Jewsbury, Geraldine, 130, 145

journalism
   and observation, 78–9, 171
   and reading, 94–5, 171

Keen, Suzanne, 15
Klaver, Claudia, 100
knowledge
   of bodies, 65, 71, 106–8, 126, 141–2, 148–9, 153–4, 160–2, 163, 165, 169, 178, 185, 187, 198–9
   and emotion, 50, 103, 193–4, 200
   of feelings, 165–6
   of language, 28
   literary, 2–3, 8, 10–11, 48
   and narration, 78–80, 140, 141, 142, 152
   of the other, 72, 78–81, 110, 106–8, 109, 128, 141, 161, 179, 185, 187
   and philosophy, 3, 118, 143–4

labourers, 195–7, 199–200
Langland, Elizabeth, 166, 186–7
language
   and affect, 4–5, 35, 41, 44–6, 55, 147
   and Associationism, 2, 4, 5, 19, 28, 32–4, 35–7, 38, 41, 43–6, 49–50, 69, 119, 148, 160
   and embodiment, 2, 4, 28, 30, 32–3, 35–6, 47, 71, 86–7, 111, 148, 149, 160
   and emotion, 40–1, 44–6, 164, 205–6
   and empathy, 46, 57, 79
   and materiality, 4, 33, 69
   and representation, 4, 33–4, 109
   and signification, 30–4, 35–6, 39, 79
law
   and authority, 140, 178, 185, 187
   and bodies, 178, 185, 187
   lawyer, 161, 179
   see also circumstantial evidence, handwriting
letter-writing, 106–7, 154–5, 172–3, 182–3
Levine, Caroline, 102, 153–4
Lewes, George Henry, 118
liberalism, 193, 202–3, 208
   and Associationism, 14–15, 23–4, 54, 191
   and empathy, 14–15, 18–19, 54–5, 58, 190–1, 188, 194, 200, 209, 213–15
   and literary authority, 12, 190
   see also disinterestedness

literacy, 93
literary authority
  and affect, 3, 4–7, 32–4, 41, 54, 70, 119, 153
  and Associationism, 2–3, 5, 38, 30, 42, 43, 46–7, 49–50, 58, 71, 81–3, 101–2, 119–20
  and capitalism, 92, 94
  and character, 2, 47–9, 73, 83, 92, 100–1, 119, 149
  and embodiment, 4, 9, 14, 30–4, 46–7, 70, 82–3, 120, 152, 173
  and emotion, 2, 3, 14, 15, 18, 19, 42, 70, 82–3, 96, 101, 109, 110, 120, 172
  and empathy, 2, 4, 46, 54, 71, 82
  and gender, 163
  and interpretation, 4, 5–6, 10, 15–16, 18–19, 29–30, 70, 95, 111
  and politics, 12, 190
  and popular readers, 8–10, 42, 72, 92
  and scholars, 11–12, 108
literary studies
  as academic discipline, 1, 2, 7–8, 10–14
  as domain of knowledge, 2, 11–14, 19, 42, 109
literary value *see* literary authority
Locke, John, 35
Lotze, Hermann, 117–18
Lund, Michael, 99
Lynch, Deidre, 101

madness, 184, 186–8
materialism
  and affect, 5, 87
  and Associationism, 2–3, 14, 15, 17, 27–9, 32–3, 37–40, 43–6, 50, 58, 67–8, 69, 72, 73, 77–81, 87, 117–19, 121–2, 126, 160, 191
  and character, 58–9
  and embodiment, 18–19, 36, 68, 73, 89, 119, 120, 125, 128, 142–3, 145, 187, 191, 197, 209–10
  and emotion, 119, 125, 142–3
  and ethics, 14, 16, 58, 133
  and language, 4, 69, 85–6
  and literary studies, 5
  and psychology, 14, 119
  and representation, 169, 192
  and science, 1, 14, 16, 27–8, 36–7, 58, 59, 186–7
  and social reform, 190–1, 208
  see also mechanism
Marcus, Sharon, 5, 54, 95
Martineau, James 16–17
Masson, David, 13, 47

Mayhew, Henry, 196
mechanism, 16, 120–4, 125, 142
  naïve mechanism, 160, 188
  see also flattened Associationism
medicine, 63–4, 132, 149–50
memory, 29, 36, 41, 45–6, 73–4, 75–6, 77, 87–8, 111, 120, 150
  and storytelling, 56, 68–9, 139, 141
metaphor, 27–9, 30–4, 39, 50, 55, 86, 87, 96–9, 102–5, 106–8, 109, 110, 120, 127, 141, 147, 172, 192, 196, 198–9, 200–1, 210, 212
  different from representation, 161, 165
metatextual references, 141, 144, 151, 152
Mill, James, 69, 73, 75–6
Mill, John Stuart, 17, 126
Miller, Andrew, 15
Miller, D. A., 85n, 130n, 141, 176n, 186
Morgan, Benjamin, 5, 18, 23, 162
Moses, Omri, 119
Mudie, Charles, 8–9
Müller, Max, 32–3, 35, 110
music, 203–9
mystery, 103, 166
  and reading, 129, 152
  see also detective
mysticism, 129

narrator
  as detective, 140
  and knowledge, 140, 141, 142, 152
New Criticism, 1–2, 3–4, 27
Newnham College, 192–3
Newton, Isaac, 27–8

observation
  and detectives, 140–2, 182
  and embodiment, 60–1, 62, 72, 79–81, 141, 170, 179–80, 182, 200
  and journalism, 78–9, 171
  and knowledge, 39, 56, 60–1, 62, 68–9, 108, 109, 111, 140–2, 170, 179–80, 181, 200
  and science, 71–2, 73, 77, 79–81
Oliphant, Margaret, 95–6
Oliver Twist, 49
ontology of feeling, 46–7, 87, 108, 185

pain, 1, 46–7, 49, 57–8, 63–4, 67–8, 70–1, 76, 78–81, 122, 147–9, 153, 187–8, 190, 200–1, 212, 214, 219–21
painting
  of Lady Audley, 167–9, 184
  of Lizzie (*Children of Gibeon*), 197

Pattison, Mark, 11
Paul, Annie Murphy, 18
Pendennis, 47
People's Palace, 193
phenomenology, 5, 7, 36–7, 62, 76, 86–7, 121, 122, 125, 149, 187–8
phrenology, 125, 141, 203–4
physiology, 146, 192
  and language, 2, 5, 6, 15, 17, 119
  and materialism, 14, 40, 62, 69, 87–8, 117, 119–20, 120–4, 127, 160
  and reading, 90–4, 101, 150–1, 176, 191
plasticity, 119, 125–6, 150
poetry, 1, 39
political economy, 100–1, 193
Poovey, Mary, 100
popular literature
  and empathy, 19
  and emotion, 91–2
  validity of, 13, 18–19, 72, 82–3, 90–6
popular literature, metaphors for
  fast, 18, 92, 95, 95n
  fatty, 92n
  light (vs heavy), 95, 131
  loud, 92, 95
  shallow, 18
  spicey, 92
popular readers *see* common readers
Price, Leah, 6
probability, 48–9, 181, 185
Proudman, Joseph, 205
pseudo-science *see* scientificity
psychology, 17, 119–22, 127, 149, 181
Pykett, Lyn, 169

queerness, 145–6

Rancière, Jacques, 3
reading
  and Associationism, 3, 5, 19, 30, 49–50, 55, 56, 58, 60, 70, 89, 101–2, 124, 151, 160, 206
  and embodiment, 3, 20, 47, 86, 101, 102, 108, 143, 160
  and emotion, 54–5, 79, 81, 96, 100, 101, 103, 143, 162, 172
  and empathy, 18–19, 34, 45–6, 55, 72, 83, 101–2, 104, 132, 148, 149, 151, 164, 190, 204
  and impressions, 58, 65, 143
  and music, 204
  and temporality, 89–90, 90–6

reading bodies
  legibility of bodies, 30, 55, 58, 89, 101, 127–8, 129, 141–2, 148–9, 151, 153–4, 160, 163, 165, 169, 172, 178, 198–9
  reading in novels, 85–6, 109–10, 129–31, 161, 171, 174, 185, 186
  reading others' bodies, 55, 70, 77, 100–1, 102, 104, 105–8, 127–8, 129, 141, 143, 153, 161–6, 170–1
realism, 7n, 47, 47n, 70
reform *see* liberalism
representation, 4, 50, 72, 161, 165, 167, 192, 203
  different from metaphor, 165
  Lady Audley's portrait, 167–9, 184
  see also interpretation
Ricardo, David, 195
Richards, I. A., 1–2, 3–4, 27
Robinson Crusoe, 133–8
Ruskin, John, 152–3
Ryan, Vanessa, 127n

Scarry, Elaine, 2n, 147n
Schaefer, Donovan O., 4, 5
Schivelbusch, Wolfgang, 93
scholars, 11–12, 30–4, 4n, 47, 54–5, 108, 136–7, 138, 139–44, 173, 198; *see also* disembodiment, interpretation, literary authority
science
  and affect, 5, 30n, 60, 62
  and education, 192–4
  and emotion, 1–2, 3, 14, 19, 42–3, 63–4, 132, 188, 193, 201, 203, 207
  and empathy, 14, 16, 19, 50, 80–1, 188, 193, 202
  and empiricism, 3, 27, 28, 37, 70, 77, 78, 202
  and ethics, 16–17, 50, 188, 202
  and language, 2, 27, 29, 58
  and materiality, 1, 14, 16, 27–8, 36–7, 58, 59, 186–7
  and observation, 71–2, 73, 77, 79–81
  and uniformity, 125–6, 172, 185
  see also Associationism, materialism, physiology, scientificity
scientificity, 161–2, 185
seamstress, 195–7, 211–13
second-hand clothing, 195–6
Sedgwick, Eve Kosofksy, 5, 154
self-abnegation, 16, 55, 77, 81–3, 104–5, 110–1, 120, 147, 149, 150, 151, 153–5, 161, 172, 186–7, 203–4

self-aggrandizement *see* self-regard
self-annihilation *see* self-abnegation
self-regard, 17, 30, 34, 105, 110–11, 137, 139, 144, 151, 185
self-renunciation *see* self-abnegation
serialisation, 89, 95–6, 99–100, 101, 102–4, 109, 162, 175–8
sensation
   feeling, 5, 16, 30, 32, 33, 36, 37–43, 43–5, 49, 50, 65, 68, 68–71, 76–7, 87–8, 88–9, 101–2, 111, 122–4, 143, 149, 153, 155, 161, 164, 173, 197–9, 212
   fiction, 1, 16, 19, 23, 46–9, 65, 78, 85, 80, 90–6, 99–101, 103, 119, 131, 176, 178, 185–6, 191
   others', 57, 60, 72, 79–80, 81–2, 96, 109, 146
Sense of Humanity, 213–15; *see also* empathy
singing, 203–9
social reform *see* liberalism
socialism, 199–203
sortes Biblicae, 133–4, 137–8
speculation
   economic, 99n, 100n, 100–1
   about others, 102–3, 105, 140
Spinoza, Baruch, 41
storytelling, 2, 49–50
   ethics of, 190
   and law, 181, 185
   and memory, 56, 68, 139, 141
surprise, 102–3
suspense, 103
Smith, Adam, 57, 60–2
Stewart, Dugald, 38–40, 68, 73–4, 123n
surfaces
   and affect, 6–7, 78–80, 89
   and bodies, 5, 28, 29–30, 66–8, 78–81, 83, 154–5, 161–2, 163, 166, 183, 186–7, 191, 199, 200, 209, 210
   and empathy, 3, 78–81, 80, 187–8, 191–2, 200, 204, 210, 213–15
   and interpretation, 5–6, 29–30, 54–5, 95, 163, 168, 187–8 200, 213
   and language, 5, 28, 163
   and power, 5–7, 177–8, 186–7, 213
   and representation, 163
   and temporality, 89
symbol, 58, 61, 65, 72–3, 78, 81–3, 198
sympathy, vs empathy, 60–2; *see also* empathy
symptomatic reading *see* hermeneutics

temporality
   and affect, 63, 89
   and Associationism, 73–7, 88–9, 101
   and character, 76–7, 86–7
   and embodiment, 76, 87, 89–90, 99, 102
   and knowledge, 144
   and narration, 144, 169
   and reading, 89–90, 90–6
   and serialisation, 89, 95–6, 99–100, 102–4, 109, 175–8
   and surface, 89
   and writing, 176
Thackeray, William Makepeace, 47
Tomkins, Silvan, 5
Tonic-Sol Fa, 205–7
triple-decker, 177–8

unconscious, 124, 183
unconscious cerebration, 127

vitalism, 117, 128
   of books, 131–4, 137
volition, 17, 45, 120–4

Wagner, Tamara, 167
Walsh, Marcus, 30
will *see* volition
Williams, Raymond, 7n
Wills, William, 180
Wimsatt, William, 2
women's bodies
   infantilisation of, 168, 170, 207
   interchangeability of, 172, 185–6, 197, 202
   legibility of, 154–5, 161, 163, 167–9, 172–3, 188
   objectification of, 197, 202
   sacrifice of, 16, 81, 110–11, 120, 147, 149, 153–5, 161, 172, 186–7, 203–4
Wordsworth, William, 1, 38, 40–3
writing
   and class, 106–7
   ethics of, 194
   and gender, 139, 154–5, 172–3, 194
   and interpretation, 110
   and literary authority, 106–7, 182, 194
   and self-regard, 137–8, 139
   see also History of the Book, handwriting, letter-writing, serialisation

EU representative:
Easy Access System Europe
Mustamäe tee 50, 10621 Tallinn, Estonia
Gpsr.requests@easproject.com